Jeffrey Lee  ca
at Oxford. ffairs
producer an News.
After receiv now
involved in lives
in London. claimed *Dog
Days*; *Butterfly Man* is his second.

Also by Jeffrey Lee

DOG DAYS

and published by Bantam Books

BUTTERFLY MAN

Jeffrey Lee

BANTAM BOOKS

LONDON • TORONTO • SYDNEY • AUCKLAND • JOHANNESBURG

BUTTERFLY MAN
A BANTAM BOOK : 9780553815016

Originally published in Great Britain by Bantam Press,
a division of Transworld Publishers

PRINTING HISTORY
Bantam Press edition published 2006
Bantam edition published 2007

1 3 5 7 9 10 8 6 4 2

Set in 11/13pt Caslon by
Falcon Oast Graphic Art Ltd.

Bantam Books are published by Transworld Publishers,
61–63 Uxbridge Road, London W5 5SA,
a division of The Random House Group Ltd,
in Australia by Random House Australia (Pty) Ltd,
20 Alfred Street, Milsons Point, Sydney, NSW 2061, Australia,
in New Zealand by Random House New Zealand Ltd,
18 Poland Road, Glenfield, Auckland 10, New Zealand
and in South Africa by Random House (Pty) Ltd,
Isle of Houghton, Corner of Boundary Road & Carse O'Gowrie,
Houghton 2198, South Africa.

Printed and bound in Great Britain by
Cox & Wyman Ltd, Reading, Berkshire.

Papers used by Transworld Publishers are natural, recyclable
products made from wood grown in sustainable forests. The
manufacturing processes conform to the environmental
regulations of the country of origin.

For T & T

Madero, Colombian Amazon

On the slopes of the sierra, the stretch of primeval forest lay quiet under the rain and stifling heat. Then, in a silent convulsion, the hummocked green canopy of treetops buckled, rippled and leapt into the air in a confusion of flying branches, earth and rocks. The sound of a massive, booming explosion followed. The wave of sound rattled the tin shanties of the mine workers, rumbled over the sweltering town of Madero, and rolled away down the black Madero River until it faded back into the great deadening silence of the jungle.

The dust cloud subsided to reveal a ravaged hillside of mud, rocks, broken trunks and stumps of trees. Huge yellow bulldozers crawled in, clearing off the topsoil to reveal the emerald-bearing seams for the picks and shovels of the mining gangs.

At the foot of the hills, in the muddy run-off from the mines, Tenoch, the old, one-eyed *guacero*, sighed in exhaustion and went back to work. He and his fellow *guaceros* – freelance emerald hunters – scrabbled in the mine waste for the scraps of emerald that slipped through the processing above. There were hundreds of these men digging and panning the glutinous mixture for a shard of emerald. Barefooted, they tramped the morass of mud and broken pegmatite rock, their gaze glued to the ground for that elusive flash of green.

The lure of emeralds could consume a man. It was almost as if the stones had some mysterious power. Simple beryl crystals coloured by traces of vanadium or chromium, they had fascinated Egyptian pharaohs and Mogul emperors. Sacred to indigenous American peoples like the Inca, the lustrous green gems had driven Spanish conquistadors mad with greed. They had long been associated with ill fortune, but still men lusted after emeralds. The best stones, carat for carat, were worth more than diamonds.

Tenoch himself had not come to make his fortune. He was searching for one stone only. But he had been searching for many years. And he had to eat. That day the slope seemed muddier than ever. The black slurry running off from the mines was mixed with shards of rock and cloying clay washed down by the morning's torrential rains from the deforested hillsides. Apart from some tiny, almost worthless chips, Tenoch had not found a stone for almost a week. He was hungry.

There had been a time when he was the most skilled of all the *guaceros*. He could tread the slopes upright, criss-crossing them swiftly, his one eye sharp as a hawk's two. Now he would take hours to cover his area, bent double, peering at the ground.

And yet, more and more often, he missed the stones that others would find. He sighed again and shook his head. He often felt far from his homeland on the distant shores of the Yucatán. Soon he would have to return to his people – the Maya. He would have to abandon his quest. He was getting too old.

Tenoch paused to remove his grimy felt hat for a moment and wipe the sweat from his face. Then he stopped breathing. He tried to stay calm, failed, and pretended to cough to cover his excitement. In the manner of a true, professional *guacero*, he replaced his hat, pulled it low over his forehead, and betrayed no sign of seeing anything. His heart pounding out of control, he carefully, slowly, angled his way across the slope towards the clump of mud where he had absolutely, definitely, possibly, glimpsed a sparkle of green. He couldn't be sure, though. Another *guacero* had just passed it and the green had disappeared. But perhaps he had just covered it up. No, there it was – clear as day. How could the other man have missed it? Tenoch ambled over as slowly as he dared.

It was always a balancing act when you saw a stone. Move too slowly and someone else might pick up the prize before you claimed it. Move too eagerly and you could trigger a stampede – and in a wrestling match, a stronger, younger man would emerge with the find. But this was huge, Tenoch could see that now. It was enormous. A dull green curved shape – perhaps a whole crystal that had somehow been missed by the miners! It was winking at him, calling him. It looked even big enough to perhaps contain a stone the size he sought, a stone that could fulfil his destiny and that of his people. With alarm, Tenoch saw two *guaceros* converging on it. They were moving methodically across the slope, treading the mud, eyes glued to the ground. One or other of them would see it for sure.

In a panic, Tenoch lost control. He could not hold back. He took a deep breath, gathered up his strength for the struggle he knew would ensue and leapt towards the small patch of green. He landed in mud two feet deep, and felt the cold hardness of the gem in his hands. He clutched it to his body, curled himself into a protective ball and rolled away from grasping hands. Thankfully, none came. Tenoch sat up, covered in mud, crying with joy and excitement. Around him he heard laughter. There was a ring of *guaceros* encircling him and they were all laughing – at him. But why?

In his hands he held an emerald crystal the size of a quetzal's egg. It was huge. He could feel it hard and smooth as glass. He wiped the mud gently from it. Yes, he saw the green appear. And it seemed of a remarkably clear, transparent quality. A hideous doubt crossed Tenoch's mind. He wiped his find again and drew his hand away sharply. Blood was welling up from his fingertips. The *guaceros* around him hooted with laughter.

'Ha, ha, ha! The Mayan is a millionaire – in glassware!'

'A glass eye sees glass better!'

'Enjoy your fortune, old man. Just don't drop it – it may break!'

10

Smooth as glass ... and just as sharp. Tenoch looked at the green shard in his hand and saw the mark of the beer manufacturer. It was the oldest trick in the emerald hunter's book and he had fallen for it. Around him the *guaceros* were crying with laughter, beating their thighs with their hats, taunting him. Overcome with exhaustion and despair, he collapsed forward into the mire.

Tenoch lay face down in the mud and for a while he did not care whether he lived or died. He had been searching for so long. He believed now that he would never find what he sought. He had failed.

Then he felt a strong hand seize him and pull him from the sucking mud. He was turned over onto his back and found himself looking up into a black form, a silhouette against the blazing sun. Shading his eye, Tenoch moved his head until he could make out the face of his rescuer, a rainforest Indian.

'I am Neman,' the man said, in Spanish. He was tall for an Indian, with a pale complexion. His chest and shoulders were broad and powerfully muscled. His left side was deeply scarred. 'I am of the Jemberí. How are you called?'

'I am Tenoch, of the Maya.'

Neman picked Tenoch up and wiped the mud from his face with a hand rough as sandpaper. Then he handed Tenoch a gourd of the thick, fiery *kicha* – the glutinous, saliva-preserved maize alcohol of the Jemberí. He watched Tenoch drink, took a long draught himself, then said, 'We must talk. The Jemberí need your help.'

PART I

THE GREEN EYE

I am a true man from a land of palm trees,
And before I die, I want to set down this song
   of my soul.

My song is of a shining green
And a burning scarlet.

From *Versos Sencillos* by the
revolutionary poet José Martí
Words used in the Cuban song 'Guantanamera'

Xcalan Island, Mexico

It is a commonly quoted idea that the wingbeat of an insect in China can cause a hurricane in the Gulf of Mexico. This does not mean storm warnings should sound in Tampa every time a moth is sighted flitting round a light in Shanghai. Such minuscule turbulence can take centuries to ripple out across space and time before it has that quaintly destined effect that mathematicians call 'Chaos', most of us, 'Fate'.

That jungle encounter between Neman and Tenoch, for instance, was the product of a mingling of tribal destinies set in train almost five hundred years before. And the meeting itself had repercussions, rippling out along the strange fractal pathways of Chaos. Some three months later, two thousand miles north of Madero, these ripples reached Burr Whitman, bodysurfing towards a beach in Yucatán.

Burr's breaker bent with a smooth face, then rose and plunged in a perfect tumbling arc, shooting him onto the sand in a roar of speed and bubbles. He

15

stood up before the next wave broke, and let the blazing sun dry him as he walked naked back up the high dunes. He had been at Xcalan for many weeks, and his body was a deep golden brown, barring the jagged white streaks of a dozen different scars.

The climb was long and the sand was hot. At each step Burr made sure he dug his feet into the cooler sand below the surface. Close to the top of the slope he caught an astringent scent like witch hazel. He looked for the *Heliconius erato* he knew must be nearby and saw the red-and-blue longwing butterfly in its slow, looping flight. The male would have deposited the smell on a female during mating – to discourage subsequent suitors.

In the estuary to his right, now hundreds of feet below, he could see the fins of the bull sharks coming up the river again in numbers. The crocodiles watched lazily from the bank, still sapping heat from the sun. At dusk the crocs would slip into the muddy current and, where the fresh water met the salt, they would defend their territory against the sharks in snapping whirls of foaming water and blood.

As he climbed the dune, Burr tried to ignore the boat outside the reef. With deliberate calm he walked slowly into the forest where it rose in a green mat to the crest of the sand hills. The shade was a cool relief from the sun. Burr's old friend Pachal lay there, watching the boat through binoculars.

'It's them,' Pachal said.

Burr lay down beside the Mayan, the mixture of

sand and leaf litter warm on his stomach. Pachal handed him the binoculars and he brought the visitors into focus, their dark suits absurd on that sweltering day. They were still too far away for him to make out their features clearly.

An imperceptible swell slid towards the beach on the still rising tide, pushing the visitors' ski boat closer to the reef. The boat was a beast, built for shark hunting and fast work inshore. Its engines were massive and its pointed hull was tall and tough enough to launch straight out through a high sea, or power straight in over breaking surf, right up onto the beach. But here at Xcalan it could find no way through to the beach, which was protected by the seemingly unbroken reef half a mile out.

The visitors seemed convinced there was a way through, and they worked the ski boat patiently along the line of white water that marked the reef. They were floating the boat in on the tide, coming dangerously close to the rocks before gunning the engines in reverse to pull the boat away. Then they would idle again, drifting the boat in to check a spot further along the reef. Through the binoculars, Burr could see one of the two men on board leaning over the bow of the boat, searching for a gap in the submerged rocks. He was signalling to a second figure at the wheel, his face hidden under a blue baseball cap.

'I wonder what they're after,' mused Burr.

Pachal looked serious. 'You know. They are after you.'

'They could just be tourists who want to picnic on the beach,' Burr said, doubtfully.

Pachal shook his head. 'No, brother. Isaiah saw these men two days ago. They were trying to drive up from the mainland, but they could not find the path and stopped at the lagoon. Two of them, Isaiah said. Wearing black like these.'

'Why didn't you tell me about them before? When they came first.'

'We did not want to bother you.' Pachal's mouth spread into his broken-toothed grin. 'After all, they could have just been tourists who wanted to picnic on the beach.'

Burr smiled – Xcalan was not a common picnic spot. Lying at the tip of a remote peninsula in the southernmost reaches of Mexico's Yucatán State, it was made even more inaccessible by the river and lagoon. At high tide the brackish water of the lagoon would creep up over the causeway and the peninsula would become an island. But some people made the trip nonetheless. Xcalan was famous for its shark cave, where for some mysterious reason the sharks slept. It was also famous for its dunes, some of the tallest in the world. Hundreds of feet high, the dunes were more like white hills, rising steeply from the beach to meet the rare sand forest – an outlier of the great Petén – growing on their landward slopes. When they were young, Burr and Pachal, lugging their small palm-wood surfboards, whose undersides were coated with slippery beeswax, would climb the hot dunes and toboggan, screaming, down the long, smooth slopes to the sea.

Apart from the Mayan villagers who fished the

18

lagoon and the estuary, most visitors to Xcalan were on official business: they were scientists, military officers and government agents. The few tourists who did come were either invited by Burr, or were extremely hardy backpackers.

'Oil company?' Burr wondered aloud. Mexico was in the midst of a black gold rush. The multinationals had struck crude all the way down the Yucatán coast. The threat of oil drilling offshore hung over Xcalan like a cloud. And soon the very island itself could be bought from under the local Maya.

'Maybe,' said Pachal, 'but I do not think they would come alone.'

Pachal was right. With Burr as leader, Mayan opposition to exploration – including some intimidating interventions by Pachal and his fellow Mayan warriors – had become highly effective. They had managed to delay the prospective sale of Xcalan. And if the oil prospectors dared to come, they did so en masse with a gang of armed guards.

No, whoever the figures in the boat were, it was likely they wanted to talk to Burr. But he was retired. If the visitors found him, that meant trouble had found him once again. It hurt a surprising amount to see that his past could follow him to this place – his home. Burr remembered that was one of the reasons he had avoided having a home for so long. Home meant a place that caused you pain when it was violated. He sighed. What was that quotation? *No man is an island*. When he was around, it appeared not even an island was an island.

In the dappled light of the tree line on the ridge of the dunes, Burr adjusted the focus on the binoculars and saw that the visitors were nearing the entrance to the channel. In this calm sea, if the man in the prow knew what to look for, he would see the signs of slack water and glimpses of sandy sea bed that gave away the narrow, dog-leg passage. It was almost as though someone had told them where to look. Now was the best time to try the passage, too. The channel was only navigable during the half-hour each side of high tide. Burr was surprised to find that part of him wanted them to succeed, to come through the channel and confront him with whatever upheaval they intended to thrust into his calm existence.

But the boat was coming too close to the submerged rocks now, at the wrong angle. Unless the man at the wheel was an expert, they would touch.

'Shall I go down and show them the channel?' asked Pachal casually.

Burr hesitated. Subconsciously he rubbed at the callus in between his right thumb and forefinger. The skin had been hardened over the years by the recoil of thousands of pistol shots.

'The knot always reaches the comb,' Pachal said quietly. 'We can let them go, but if they want you, brother, they'll be back.'

Just then a slightly larger wave lifted the ski boat and dumped it with some force against the reef. The man in the prow was jarred, sprawling, onto the deck. He clung to the rail as he was swamped by the wave bursting on the rocks. Burr could see him in the spray, gesticulating angrily back at the cockpit, where the helmsman waved his arms helplessly. The boat pulled back from the reef and the two figures seemed to confer. Then the taller figure turned back to the wheel, the stern dug deep into the swell and the bow pointed skywards as the big motors gunned the boat back towards the open sea.

With an aching mixture of regret and relief, Burr watched as the boat continued out to sea then swung south in a broad arc, on course for the regional capital of Chetumal, down on the border with Belize. Then he stood up, brushed sand from his body and started to walk along the edge of the forest, back towards the house.

Ethnobotanical Research Centre, Madero

Leila Walcott was pleased she had taken a holiday. She needed a break from the hardships of jungle life. Now she happily dragged her bare feet through the calm Caribbean, its gentle waves rolling up the perfect crescent of Trinidad's Maracas Beach. The palms rustled softly. A light breeze off the water helped to cool her body temperature, which had been raised by the sun and the man in the distance. He was a shadowy figure, but one she was walking across the wet sand to meet. Leila realized that she was naked, but she didn't mind. As he approached, Leila could see the man was naked too. She could see the hard trigonometry of his shoulders and waist, the legs moving loosely in an easy stride and, between them, his penis swinging left and right in an intricate oblique rhythm. She could still not see his face. Suddenly the man knelt down and began knocking something against a rock. She moved closer and over his smooth, broad back she could see him pounding a mussel shell against the wet stone. She realized it was very hot. The heat increased as the knocking grew louder and Leila woke up into her humid room. She was still in Madero, still in the jungle.

It was already fully light. She must have overslept – again. The knocking was coming from the window by her bed. She sat up slowly and pulled back the threadbare curtain. A heavily tattooed Jemberí man stood there, nodding and grinning at her with rotten teeth. Leila smiled back politely. After waiting a moment to make sure Leila was awake, the Jemberí replaced the pointed penis gourd he had been using to tap on the window and walked back to his place in the queue for the morning clinic.

To the weary Leila, it looked like a very long queue indeed.

She dropped the curtain and got up. She cursed the alarm clock that had not gone off, until she saw it in the far corner of the hut where she must have thrown it earlier. She picked up the clock and shook it. It rattled and was no longer ticking.

Pulling a light silk robe around her, she scampered from her hut to the outside shower with its walls of woven palm mats. From the main building, she could hear the British project head, James Makepeace, laughing. At her, probably. Well, at least *I* provide some entertainment, she thought uncharitably. She pulled the cord in the shower and a torrent of clear rainwater poured down on her grateful head. The huge rainwater storage tank was one of the Madero research station's few blessings.

Since she was a girl on the Caribbean island of Trinidad, she had always loved the forests. Trees, she had learned in school, sucked in carbon dioxide and pumped out oxygen. They helped us to breathe. Animals and birds lived in the forest, which was a place of flowers, shade and quiet. The forest was also a place she associated with some of the happiest times of her life. On weekends, her father, a Trinidadian lawyer and politician, would take her up into the jungle-covered hills north of Port of Spain. They would walk the forest trails up across the divide and down to the sea. Leila's English mother disliked the jungle. She would drive round in the car and they would all meet up at the shark-and-bake stall on Maracas Beach. From her mother, Leila had inherited that part of her that still detested Madero's swarming insects, fungal infections, heat and dirt. She was not proud of this aspect of her character and tried to keep it under wraps. But there it always was, niggling away about the state of her hair and the ravages of the harsh tropical climate on her once perfect skin. Yes, she adored the forest, but two years stuck in Madero was wearing for anyone other than a native forest dweller.

In Trinidad they would say the town of Madero was 'behind Gawd back' – so remote not even God could find it. And the research station was even more remote. It lay a few miles outside the town, buried in the jungle of the Madero National Park, a vast portion of the Colombian Amazon protected as the homeland of the Jemberí indigenous people. The project was spread over two forest clearings. In the main compound were the creosoted huts that served as living quarters and the cramped cabin which Leila used for her clinic. The main clearing also contained the long, low research centre building, which held the labs and offices. All the buildings were of wood, smelling permanently of tar, damp and the layers of zinc chloride applied to repel wood-eating insects. The second, smaller clearing held the project's horticultural plot for cultivation of specimens.

Standing at the window of his office in the main building, Makepeace chuckled as he watched Leila's lithe form scurry across the muddy compound. He could never understand how she could be so painstaking in her work and yet so hopeless about timing. Actually he could never really understand much about her, including what she was doing there in the first place. She seemed so vibrant to him, her vitality and fine-featured Trinidadian beauty so out of place in such a melancholy, God-forsaken spot. With her youth and idealism she had the unnerving capacity to make him feel all and more of his fifty years, but young at the same time. For the thousandth time he thanked whatever gods may be for Leila. Without her, well, he didn't know what he would have done. And, of course, she was great fun to tease.

Makepeace leaned out of the window, about to point at his watch.

'I know, I know,' she shouted at him, pre-empting any wisecracks. 'Alarm clock's broken.'

'I was only going to say there's no hurry. You're ahead of schedule this morning – only about forty-five minutes late.'

'Ha, ha,' muttered Leila grumpily. It wasn't as though the clinic was part of her job description. She was a qualified doctor, yes, but she had come to Madero as an ethnobotanist. With a successful, if predictable, medical career developing in Trinidad, her impulsive, romantic mind had wandered to the great discoveries of people like Pasteur and Lister. When she received a lucrative offer from a hospital in the United States, Leila had to make a choice. She decided that she would rather take a chance on saving the world than be certain to save a few individuals as a hospital consultant. So she qualified in ethnobotany and signed up to Makepeace's long-standing Madero Project.

The discipline of ethnobotany was based on the theory that indigenous peoples know of plants with curative properties. Researchers investigate traditional tribal remedies and analyse them for real medicinal value. But as soon as Leila started interviewing the Jemberí about plants, she had begun to treat them as well. If she was talking to a woman with ringworm, it was impossible for her not to apply some antifungal ointment. Seeing an inflamed eye, she would rinse it with Optrex. Indigestion was magically cured with chalk. She cleaned and stitched wounds, lanced boils and administered antibiotics. Her reputation spread and the research centre became a clinic for the 'civilized' Jemberí – that portion of the indigenous tribe that had come out of the forest and settled in the town of Madero. To Makepeace's annoyance, many of these Jemberí built their huts around – and sometimes in – the research centre clearings. It wasn't that he was uncharitable, it was just that the Jemberí had a loose understanding of the concept of ownership. It irked Makepeace when they gaily appropriated such things as his microscope, or his rare variety of *Oncidium* orchid.

Makepeace's grumblings had faded when he realized that photographs of Leila surrounded by smiling Jemberí children were a public relations coup for the project's pharmaceutical sponsors. In a mood like today's – hurried and overheated – it irritated Leila that she was achieving little more than guaranteed funding for Makepeace's un-glamorous botanical survey of one 25-hectare block of forest. For well over a decade now, he had been exhaustively, not to say obsessively, labelling and documenting every accessible root, bole, bud, shoot and sapling. It was enough to drive most normal people mad.

Leila hurried over to the clinic. She normally looked forward to working with her patients but today her oddly unsettled mood did not improve. Annoyingly she already felt hot and sweaty again from rushing around. It was not turning out to be a fun morning.

'Where are you going, Plant Doctor?' said Leila's first patient when she finally began the clinic about an hour late.

'Where are you going, Maria?' replied Leila – the Jemberí had no word for hello.

Maria, a plump, jovial Jemberí woman, smiled and then suddenly her right arm quivered uncontrollably. Her face clouded over and she sat on her hand.

Leila sighed inwardly. Maria was trying to conceal it, but Leila had already noticed she was beginning to show symptoms of the wasting disease. The sickness afflicted many of the Jemberí around the age of thirty. It was unidentified and apparently incurable. Maria's grave-looking ten-year-old, Tupo, stood quietly next to his mother. Unless a cure was found, Maria would soon be gone as well. Tupo would be an orphan before he was eleven.

Leila gave a smile that she hoped seemed cheerful, and ruffled the boy's hair. 'What can I do for you, Maria?' she asked.

This time it wasn't Maria who sought help. Tupo thrust his arm forward and Leila saw that he had a broken finger. The Jemberí referred to all non-Jemberí as ghosts, and Tupo explained that his finger had been broken by a 'faraghost' – meaning a FARA guerrilla. The rebel had hit him simply 'because he was a human being' – that is, a Jemberí.

Leila gritted her teeth in anger. The FARA had captured Madero and its damn emerald mine almost a year ago and since then she had again and again heard stories of the rebels persecuting, beating, even killing, the Jemberí, who many Colombians, right- or left-wing, seemed to regard as almost subhuman. So alongside her jobs as doctor and ethnobotanist, Leila had also appointed herself human rights crusader. As such, she made repeated complaints about the situation in Madero to the local rebel command, to the government in Bogotá, and to anyone who was prepared to listen – as well as to many who were not.

The more cautious Makepeace tended to discourage her. 'It won't do any good,' he would warn. 'All you'll do is make the wrong people angry – powerful people who can damage us and our work. Nobody cares about the Jemberí, Leila. They have been slaughtering the indigenous peoples in this country for five hundred years. Even where there is law in Colombia, killing an Indian was made a crime only about a century ago, and in most of Colombia there is no law.'

This defeatism frustrated Leila, even though she knew Makepeace might be factually right. As late as 1917, thousands of Indians were being enslaved and massacred along the Putumayo River, not far away. But Leila believed things could change. If Makepeace wanted to be jaded and pessimistic, that was up to him. She sometimes thought that he cared only about protecting his precious project and his fruitless hunt for a Crafoord Prize, the closest an ecologist could get to a Nobel. In contrast, Leila burned with the desire to make a difference – to make things better. 'I'm going to kick up a fuss,' she would promise. 'Just you watch me . . .' But the myriad small incidents like this attack on Tupo were simply not worth investigating, and they were on the increase.

For the last three months or so, Madero had been restless. There was something different in the air. The mines had expanded apace and a trickle of new fortune-seekers had begun seeping into the region, many of them not stopping in the town, but carrying on into the forest, looking for new strikes. Leila had even heard whispers of the legendary El Verde, a lost city full of emeralds. Few of these prospectors were ever seen again. As the emerald rush continued, and in the absence of any government restrictions, loggers, coca farmers and mineral companies were clearing great swathes of the Madero National Park, carelessly killing Jemberí and destroying their unique, irreplaceable habitat. The forest was swept by rumours of clashes in the jungle and worries that the fragile rebel–government cease-fire was going to collapse. Then, a few weeks ago, a team of scientists had disappeared. They had been working at the other scientific research camp near Madero, and had simply vanished into the thick jungle air. Leila was convinced that the government and their shadowy militia allies were behind the unrest. But nobody really knew.

She sighed as she gently straightened Tupo's finger, set and splinted it. The boy held out his other hand, giving her a limp plant. Its tubular, fleshy grey-green stalk was open at one end.

'*Kiragi*,' he said. 'Good life, Plant Doctor.'

'Good life, Tupo. And thank you,' said Leila, smiling kindly. *Kiragi* was one of a number of plants the Jemberí had brought her before. It was a species new to science – in fact, Makepeace and Leila had yet to classify it and give it an official taxonomic name. Initial tests, however, had revealed no positive medical effects. Leila could testify that ingestion of the leaves caused a slight headache. *Kiragi* was, if anything, mildly poisonous.

It was a compensation of her medical work that the Jemberí brought Leila specimens in return for her attentions. But, in two years of research, she had not found one plant with any definite medical benefits. What is more, the Jemberí were extraordinarily unhealthy. If they were so knowledgeable about natural cures, she would wonder on bad days, how come they had a life expectancy of only about forty? They showed no ability to cure even the most common of ailments. She had to admit too that Makepeace was right: they were often thieving and untrustworthy. She had lost count of the times her stethoscopes had gone missing. They sometimes turned up again, but she was still looking for a couple of mobile phones, two shoes (both left foot) and innumerable small items such as moisturizers, facecloths and books – even though not one of the Jemberí could read.

Of course, she reminded herself, the Jemberí of Madero were living in an unnatural state, a blighted, impoverished existence on the fringes of a world they could not understand. Removed from the nomadic rhythms of their forest life, reliant on charity handouts, these 'civilized' Jemberí were listless, confused and prone to illness. They neglected their customs and forgot their tribal knowledge. Many simply surrendered to the mysterious wasting disease.

It was possible that they had forgotten details of

their pharmacopoeia – their collection of medicinal plants – or at least had forgotten how to prepare them for medical use. This was all the more possible because in Indian societies medicine was often the preserve of the tribal shaman, cloaked in secrets and taboos. The Jemberí were adamant, for instance, that *kiragi* had strong curative powers. But whenever Leila requested more precise details, they would become vague and forgetful, rambling on about curses and magic, sometimes using an obscure phrase that tested Leila's Jemberí vocabulary and which she translated as 'storm of gold'.

The coming of the ghosts had been devastating to the Jemberí. Apart from the killings and the destruction of their land, epidemics brought by the invaders regularly swept Jemberí communities. Isolated in the forest for millennia, the Amazonian tribes had no effective antibodies against relatively minor Western diseases such as measles, chicken-pox and mumps. To the Jemberí, even the common cold could be lethal. Entire ethnicities had been wiped out after contact with the white man.

It was said that uncontacted bands of Jemberí still survived deep in the forest. It was whispered that they were headhunters and cannibals. Sometimes one of these 'wild' people would come, blinking, out of the trees to Leila's clinic. These tribespeople were generally suspicious and uncommunicative. Unless they were too ill to move, they would return to the forest immediately after treatment. They never brought plants for Leila. This frustrated her. The hidden clans were said to have powerful healing shamans, but their knowledge was hidden with them.

When Tupo's finger had been splinted and bandaged securely, his mother pressed the sheaf of *kiragi* stalks into Leila's hands again. 'You are good, Plant Doctor – for a ghost. This is good *kiragi*,' she insisted. Leila noticed that the tubular stems did seem stiffer and more bulbous than usual. She looked down the open tube of one of the stems and saw that it contained what appeared to be the cocoon of a butterfly or moth. It wasn't unusual. Quite a lot of her specimens came riddled with insects, often perfectly camouflaged. More than once Leila had reached for a plant only for its leaf or twig to flit away at her touch.

With a smile and a wave Tupo and Maria wandered off to their nearby hut in the forest. Leila thought she could detect a slight spasm in Maria's left leg as she walked. It would not be long now. Once the wasting disease took hold, the decline was generally swift and catastrophic. A patient would be bedridden within weeks, dead within months. Leila felt a deep welling of sadness and frustration, and a sense of emptiness. One day, she told herself determinedly – one day soon – she would find something, something that would make it all worthwhile.

Xcalan, Mexico

'The knot always reaches the comb,' Pachal had said. Burr feared he might have been right. Burr had tried to return to a peaceful existence, but the awareness of the mysterious visitors lurked dully in the background of his thoughts and interrupted his sleep. For the first time in years, glimpses of the tennis match began intruding into his dreams. As a child, Burr had been a talented tennis player, relentlessly driven by his father to become a star. When he was just fifteen, his success had peaked and ended after one memorable match, in which he had made a decision that still haunted him. Burr had lost the match and his father had forbidden him to play again. Burr had moved on instead into the traditional Whitman military career.

He had always lived at someone else's behest, he thought. First his father's, then his superior officers'. Then, after he left the military, he had founded his successful military company, Argonaut Security, and fought at the orders of his employers – big corporations. Xcalan was his chance to live his own life at last – a peaceful life. The life under orders had always been one of violence and turmoil. The island was meant to be an antidote to all that, perhaps in some way an expiation. The period of his life when men died at his hand was meant to be over.

In any case, he could not leave Xcalan, because the very existence of the island was under threat. The rights for oil drilling offshore had been sold some time ago, but now the land itself could be bought out from under the Maya, who had lived there for thousands of years. Apart from the small portion owned by Burr, most of the island belonged to the Mexican state. The Maya held no title deeds and the government had zoned Xcalan for development. Development proposals had to be presented in the regional capital, Chetumal, in just over six weeks. A couple of months after that, all schemes approved in principle would go forward to a sealed auction, in which the highest bidder would win ownership of the island. Without someone like Burr to lead their bid, the Maya would never succeed. Burr told himself, for the thousandth time, that he was glad the boat had not come through.

Trying to forget the visitors, he had turned back to his butterflies. He had been fascinated by the delicate creatures since his first childhood encounter with them in the sunshine of Xcalan. The young Burr was amazed by the winged adults – the imagos – emerging from their silken cocoons, their limp, crushed wings flexing and spreading to reveal their glorious colours. He was entranced by the shimmering rainbow dust that coated his fingers after cupping a bright blue morpho in his hands. Later he would learn how butterfly dust comes from the covering of tiny scales on a butterfly's wings, and how the scales gave butterflies and moths their scientific name, *Lepidoptera* – Greek for 'scaly-winged'.

Ironically, the brutal work of soldiering had encouraged his affinity for these delicate creatures. Many of his Special Forces missions and covert 'wet work' for the CIA had been under the guise of research or studies for scientific journals. Burr's cover was usually as an entomologist. It had proved very plausible: apart from the polar ice caps, wherever you go there are always plenty of insects. And over time Burr's cover story had evolved into true expertise. He metamorphosed into something of an expert lepidopterist. He had written papers for scientific journals and was a contributing editor of *International Geo*. Butterflies still surprised him though. Recently he had learned that the ancient Romans rubbed oak processional caterpillars onto their genitals to increase sexual enjoyment. Burr had been even more surprised when the US Air Force made a request for his latest research on *Heliconius* flight. Apparently, its unpredictable, fluttering nature was deemed ideal for next-generation pilotless spy aircraft.

Two days after the visitors' appearance, Burr sat in his butterfly 'aviary' – an area of forest the size of two tennis courts, enveloped in an almost invisible, fine-mesh net – watching two *Heliconius* caterpillars collide as they munched ponderously through a succulent passion leaf. He had liked to think he could be a butterfly farmer, but, truth was, he felt a restlessness, a rustiness of skills not put to use. Burr remembered how after he stopped playing tennis his right hand missed the racket grip. Now, since the ski boat had appeared, he had noticed his fingers flexing automatically into the trigger grip of an M4. He could feel how his shoulder anticipated the familiar press of the stock, his eye prepared for the squint into the crosshairs. He thought of a return to the field with surprising relish. Maybe he would always be a soldier after all. On the passion leaf in front of him, the larger caterpillar began, slowly, to devour the other, tail first.

Then he heard Pachal calling him.

They were back.

Burr and the quiet Mayan watched through the fringe of palm and *mahahual* leaves as the boat containing two suited figures nudged up to the reef. This time Pachal looked at Burr knowingly. 'Shall I go down and show them the channel?' he asked.

Life hangs on a series of moments. We all learn very early that the breath we exhale can carry a sound or not. We learn that we can mould our larynx, tongue and lips to shape that exhalation into words of our choice. Rarely are we aware of how that tiny puff of air – so small it would not mist a tooth glass – can quickly generate storm-force winds in our lives and those of others.

Later Burr realized, and was to be aware for the rest of his life, that in that instant he could have said no.

'Yes,' he said.

Pachal moved out of the forest and into the harsh sunshine on the open dune, waving his arms. On the boat, the shorter of the two figures waved back.

His heart pounding, Burr walked back towards the house. He had built it himself, from knotted driftwood and red cedar trees blown down by Hurricane Betsy five years before. Solar-powered and built entirely of natural materials, the building was self-sustaining, ecologically impeccable and designed to blend with its surroundings. Palm trees grew from it. The very dunes submerged the walls at either end, the sand reaching halfway up the roof.

It was a labour of love rather than expertise. In the Special Forces he had built log cabins, igloos, desert-survival shelters and snipers' hides, but before Xcalan his most complex civilian project was the treehouse he had built as a kid. It had perched high in one of the old Spanish-moss-laden oaks that lined the splendid drive of the Whitman plantation house in Alabama. Burr's father, a strict traditionalist, declared that his son's efforts spoiled the sweeping approach to the antebellum mansion and had the treehouse torn down.

There was more than a little of that treehouse in Burr's Xcalan building. It was an organic creation, dictated by the lie of the land and the patterns of the forest as much as by Burr's imagination. He loved it, though sometimes he felt something was missing. Pachal would insist it was missing a woman. Burr disagreed with that. A woman or two had come and gone from the place; it made no difference to him. For Burr the house was his place, his alone. As Xcalan was his – his island.

Now he walked through the silent, empty spaces of the house to his bedroom, which opened directly into the forest. In the cupboard he saw the dusty trainers left by the last woman who had spent some time at the house, two years before. He reminded himself again to throw them away.

He wondered if he was making a mistake, allowing the visitors onto the beach.

This was not a change of plan, Burr told himself. He had made no decision yet. He did not even know what the visitors wanted. He was just going to hear what they had to say. And he would certainly do nothing that would put Xcalan at risk.

He had first come to the island aged three and it meant more to him than anywhere else on earth. In a scandal that shocked the strait-laced world of Alabama aristocracy, his mother had left his father. With her she took Burr, her youngest child. Eventually, she had drifted onto the hippy trail and down through Mexico to the Yucatán. His earliest, vague memories were of this place – broad-nosed Mayan faces smiling down at him, butterflies, palm fronds, and a brightly coloured bird with a long, green tail. He lived on the island for years and it became his home.

After his mother died, the eight-year-old Burr returned to live with his father and he did not see Xcalan for many years. Not long after leaving the military to start Argonaut Security, he took some employees on a jungle warfare course. They went down to Belize, the former British colony on Mexico's southern border, not far from Xcalan. Burr found himself being instructed by none other than Pachal. For years the Mayan hunter had been training the SAS, Britain's elite Special Air Service, in the forests of the Petén. The two friends had recognized each other immediately, and Pachal invited him back to his childhood home. Soon afterwards, Burr bought the one private plot on the island and began to work on his house. When he left off active duty at Argonaut, he retired to Xcalan.

Burr pulled on jeans and a loose linen shirt, then moved out to the deck at the front of the house. He saw that Pachal and the visitors had pulled the ski boat up onto the sand. Three sets of footprints led up the dune and out of sight behind the trees. The footprints of one of the tracks were surprisingly close together.

Burr made his way to the north side of the house, where his office looked along the line of the dunes to the estuary. It was his favourite room in the house. Long and spacious, it had solid walls of closely fitted palm logs and a floor of cool Yucatán slate. Broad fans hung from the dune-curved wooden ceiling, held up by bowed mahogany beams like the ribbing of an inverted ship's hull. Along the outer wall, column-like trunks of living palm trees grew as part of the structure. To the landward side of the room, tall glass doors opened into the forest and the butterfly aviary. The room also contained a row of glass hatching and observation cases filled with wriggling pupae and silken cocoons. The furniture consisted of a desk and chair by the window, along with some seats and a daybed of local mahogany set around a coffee table of twisted shape, carved from driftwood he had found on the beach – a massive log of African yellowwood.

The sound of raised voices bickering in Spanish came to him a good minute before Pachal stepped into the office to announce the visitors. The Mayan wore a completely bland expression, which instantly told Burr he was not keen on their new guests. After showing them in, he left the room.

'I'm Elizabeth,' said the first visitor, stepping forward confidently. '*Buenos días*, Señor Whitman.'

Burr had not made out her gender through the binoculars, but he had guessed one of the boat party was a woman from the short paces leading up the dune. Now he took in the delicate, feminine cast of her features and the curves of her body beneath the suit jacket. Latina, he thought, from her accent and light olive skin – perhaps Venezuelan. She removed her Florida Marlins baseball cap and shook out a head of long, bottle-blonde hair. Burr realized that she was not unattractive, especially not to someone who had hardly seen a woman since a visit to the market in Chetumal three months before. Now she was looking at Burr with keen, intelligent eyes.

She extended a firm hand and, gesturing perfunctorily at her companion, added: 'And this is Lester.' Her voice was low, her words measured. 'You're a hard man to reach, Señor Whitman.'

'*Encantado*,' said Burr politely. 'You can call me Burr. I'm hard to reach for a reason. I don't want to be reached. I guess my *trusted partner*, Dan, didn't make that clear.'

'It's an unusual name, *Burr*' – she pronounced it in a Spanish way, like 'poor' – 'but nice.' Elizabeth smiled impishly. 'To be honest, we were told you would not welcome visitors, but you have no phone, no email. What choice did we have? I hope you will listen to our proposition.'

Burr inclined his head politely, but said nothing. He moved over to the table and poured out long glasses of fresh lime juice. There was a job on offer, he had been right about that, but he still did not know what kind. The visitors were giving him no clues. Elizabeth, with her striking looks and polite approach, was an unusual messenger of fate. Lester appeared to be a more predictable type, but Burr had not yet heard him speak.

Lester was watching Burr and Elizabeth suspiciously, his eyes flickering from one to the other like a spectator at a tennis match. 'Yes. It took us almost two days to get here,' he said. 'I mean, this place really is the *pichado* ass-end of nowhere, right?' Like Elizabeth, he was Latin American, a sallow-skinned, muscular man with a pugnacious stare. He was a couple of inches shorter than his colleague. He had taken off his sweat- and sea-soaked jacket to reveal a short-sleeved white shirt with dark blotches of sweat on the chest and under the armpits. His right arm was covered by a dark-blue tattoo of a large crab, carapace and legs wrapped round his biceps, the stalk eyes on his elbow, the jagged pincers reaching down to clasp either side of his wrist. He too had removed a Marlins baseball cap to mop his heavily perspiring forehead. His round face had small, bland, almost childlike features. His eyes were flat and expressionless, with a dull emptiness that Burr recognized from somewhere he could not place.

'You really called Burr?' Lester asked sourly. 'Like those prickly little plant balls that stick to your clothes?'

'That's right,' answered Burr patiently. He handed the cool glasses of lime juice to his guests.

Lester drank thirstily and wiped his mouth with the back of his tattooed hand. 'That one of those Indian names? You know, like a burr was the first thing your father noticed after you were born?'

'No,' said Burr, 'it's not.' He placed Lester's accent somewhere between Medellin and Miami. He still couldn't place Lester's empty look, though he knew he didn't like it. 'OK, what's the story?' he asked.

'We like it here,' said Lester, with a smirk. 'Your Indian servant tells us the lagoon is great for snorkelling.'

'Pachal's Mayan. And he's not my servant.'

Lester looked up sharply; the expression in his pig eyes said he was trying to work out if he should take offence. Then he shrugged. 'OK,' he said, before sauntering with deliberate casualness to Burr's rows of butterfly cases.

'Sorry about Lester,' said Elizabeth, shooting her colleague a withering glance. 'He has learned bad

43

habits in Miami. Anyway, he is from Valle del Cauca, where many men are *maleducado*.'

So, a Colombian, then. That figured. It was a country so riddled by murder and civil war that it had even given the world a new science – violentology. There was a barely subdued thuggery about Lester and Burr wouldn't trust him an inch. He wasn't quite sure about Elizabeth either. There was something hard underneath her feminine exterior, though he did feel – as a man who had lived a celibate, solitary life for a while – that her exterior was pretty attractive. Maybe he wouldn't want to give her cupboard space, but he wouldn't have minded seeing her clothes strewn about his bedroom. He wondered if she thought the same thing about him.

'We have a job for you,' Elizabeth said.

'That's all handled by my partner in Miami.'

'Yes, but you don't understand. We don't just want Argonaut.' Elizabeth looked at Burr with meaning. 'We want you.' In a subconscious and surprisingly sensual movement, Elizabeth's delicate, pointed tongue peeked out from between small white teeth, leaving a glistening touch of moisture on the curve of her upper lip.

Burr watched the moisture evaporate. 'Thing is, I really am retired. I'm afraid you've wasted your journey. I'm no longer involved with the day-to-day business of the company. Everything goes through Daniel in Miami. And by the way, just what did you give him to tell you how to find me?'

Elizabeth smiled confidently. '*Nada*. We did not

44

give Mr Gold anything. We were told how to find you for the same reason I believe you'll take the job.' She paused, waiting for Burr to ask for the reason.

'Don't do that,' Burr said to Lester, who was absently tapping a butterfly-hatching case full of cocoons with a long fingernail: 'it disturbs them.'

Elizabeth scowled again at her companion. He tapped a few more times, then stopped. 'The reason,' she went on, 'is six million dollars.'

Burr had to admit it was a compelling reason. 'OK,' he replied slowly, 'so why me?'

Elizabeth smiled. 'They say you're the best jungle-warfare man around.'

'Says who?'

'Your company brochure.'

'Fair point.' Burr chuckled. 'Daniel always exaggerates. So, it's a jungle operation?'

'Yes, in Colombia. We work for a company called GemCorp. Almost a year ago, the GemCorp emerald mine in Madero was taken over by FARA rebels – the Fuerzas Armadas Revolucionarias de Amazonas. We came to Argonaut to help us get the mine back.'

'Hold it right there,' said Burr. 'I already refused this job. Daniel asked me about it three months ago. When I said no, he told me he was going to send another team.'

'Yes. After you refused the job, Daniel led the mission himself.'

'Fine, so why do you need me? Daniel's there. He can handle anything just as well as I could.'

45

Elizabeth cleared her throat. 'That's the trouble. Daniel and his team were there. Now they're not. Daniel's disappeared.'

Burr was stunned by the news. He remembered the last time he had seen Dan, tousled red hair flopping as he begged Burr to take the Colombia job. He had not minimized the risks. Dan was highly superstitious and when he consulted the cards about the mission his reading had not been auspicious. 'I've seen the hanged man a few times,' he had said. 'But also the ten of discs – that could mean riches. There's obviously a big upside, but it may be tricky.'

And Daniel was not just Burr's partner in Argonaut Security, he was Burr's friend. They had been through the Citadel Military College together. Burr had subsequently joined the Infantry and Rangers, while Daniel had gone into the Marines and Marine Recon. Years later they had served together in the Special Forces. The two friends had then resigned their commissions and set up Argonaut. Burr was constantly irked by Dan's insistence on Marine ways of doing things, but his partner had always been an able soldier, if impetuous and – despite his experience – strangely naïve. Burr had always looked out for him. Dan had not told him he was going to lead the Madero job himself – Burr would never have let him go. His partner had not been in combat for years, and Burr had just felt there was something wrong with the job. But Daniel was never one to turn down a challenge. As long as Burr had known him, he had been on the edge, looking for the margin, the scam. Daniel had honed his skills in the unorthodox world of the Special Forces, and in the private sector he had found his element. He was Argonaut's deal-maker, the pushy one, the one who took risks. It looked as though this time he had taken one too many.

Daniel's disappearance was also a blow because Burr had been relying on a share of the GemCorp contract to fund the purchase of Xcalan. To convince Burr that Argonaut should accept the contract, Daniel had promised him a cut of around two million dollars. That was enough capital for Burr to borrow the rest of the eight million dollars that he would bid in the sealed auction.

'When did they disappear?' he asked.

'Three weeks ago,' answered Elizabeth.

'All right, I'll think about it. Let you know tomorrow.'

'*Estas loco?*' complained Lester. 'You'll think about it? That's all you can say, after we come halfway across the goddamn world, all the way from Bogotá to Miami, then to this God-forsaken place – twice! That's just goddamn rude.'

'Aw, gee, sorry. That was very impolite of me,' agreed Burr. He repeated, 'I'll think about it,' paused for effect, then added, with the exaggerated etiquette and accent of a Southern gentleman in *Gone with the Wind*, 'and permit me to say thank you evuh so much for taking the trouble to come all this way.'

Elizabeth stifled a laugh, and to Burr's satisfaction the bullet-headed Lester glowered at him.

'Seriously, though, Burr,' said Elizabeth, 'we would appreciate an answer now. Bear in mind that, if you refuse, we will cancel the contract and Argonaut will have to repay the million dollars GemCorp has already advanced. We have done some research and it appears that Argonaut has zero cash in the bank. Your partner spent the advance on hiring and outfitting his expedition. As you can imagine, GemCorp is reluctant to advance any more, since your first team messed up so bad. But I get the feeling that might change if you take the job.'

'I understand, but let's not jump to conclusions about who messed up,' said Burr calmly. 'And I don't make snap decisions unless I have to. If Daniel has been gone for three weeks, another few hours will make no difference. If you want an answer right now, then the answer's no.'

'Well, that's just fin—' began Lester.

'*Callate*, Lester,' interrupted Elizabeth.

Lester glared at her belligerently. '*Bueno*. Take your time, Señor Burr,' he said. 'And let us know by phone tomorrow.'

Burr smiled. 'I can let you know in person. See, it doesn't make any difference whether I tell you now or tomorrow, Lester. You're not going anywhere today. You'll have to be my guests for the night. You've missed your tide.'

Lester grumbled, but Elizabeth seemed quite happy to stay. She complimented Burr on the house as he showed them to guest-rooms looking out into the forest. They would not normally have been on

48

his guest list – well, Lester certainly wouldn't. Burr wasn't quite as opposed to having Elizabeth around for a brief visit. Was it just his imagination or had she been a little suggestive? She struck him as the sort of woman who was quite prepared to use flirtation to get her way – and quite used to it working. When he left them, Burr heard them bickering like an old married couple.

He walked out into the butterfly house to think. He picked a sprig of orange and white lantana and held it up beneath a sleeping cluster of zebra long-wings – *Heliconius charitonius*. He remembered Daniel sitting there. 'Great to see the 'flies doing so well, Burrito,' he had said. 'You know, they're really good feng shui. I think they bring new beginnings and recovery from illness.' Burr wondered if he would ever see Daniel again. If his friend had been gone three weeks in that jungle, it was possible he was not coming back.

Burr brushed past a passion vine and a bright red-and-yellow caterpillar fell onto his shoulder and down onto the sand. Gently he put the caterpillar back onto its leaf, where it went back to munching steadily. Awoken by the heady scent of lantana nectar, the zebras fluttered down to feed. Burr's hand was covered in their black-and-white-striped wings.

He remembered Daniel had been a little nervous when he had last visited Xcalan. He had almost begged Burr to take the GemCorp job. 'Why?' Burr had asked. 'Because it's good feng shui? Because the tarot cards tell you that? You're meant to be the businessman: why don't you do one of those things that real businesses do? Outsource. Subcontract.'

Daniel had sighed. 'Actually, the tarot suggests that you should take this job, but that's beside the point.' He had babbled some business speak about subcontracting not being viable. It would reduce Argonaut's gross operating margin and CRM. Apparently Burr was a 'USP' or something and he helped 'span the business value chain'. Daniel had also done the business on GemCorp with the contract. Burr remembered the sly, covetous look in his eye as he rubbed his thumb and index finger together.

Burr had refused. The money was attractive, but the truth was, what with Argonaut's growth and the Miami high-life, Daniel had grown fat and greedy. Burr didn't know much about luxury labels, but he knew Daniel's clothes had been expensive. His shoes and belt were crocodile, his wristwatch studded with diamonds. Money was Dan's credo now. Fleetingly, Burr had wondered whether Daniel might even put money before friendship. He had quickly dismissed this thought as shameful and absurd, but he did feel that there was an unusual vehemence, almost desperation, behind Dan's pleas. If it wasn't greed, Burr did not know what it was.

Now it appeared he would have to take the job. But did he trust GemCorp? He watched a *Heliconius melpomene*, a 'postman' butterfly, flutter past in a series of slow loops and whirls. A beautiful red-and-black longwing, the postman was deadly poisonous.

Like every *Heliconius* its flesh was infused with cyanide, metabolized from the passion vines it ate as a caterpillar.

He wondered about his guests and their motives. Elizabeth had the brains as well as the looks. Burr could see that she had a good reason to make the mission work. She had hired Argonaut in the first place and seemed bright enough to know that if the GemCorp management had to cancel Argonaut's contract and start again with a whole new security company, she was going to look pretty bad. Lester appeared to be the muscle, pure and simple, with an edginess to him that Burr did not trust. He was obviously crazy about Elizabeth, though. As long as she could manage Lester, Burr reckoned he could just about work with the man.

Burr paused just inside the enveloping net of the butterfly house and looked down the back of the dunes through the lush trees of the sand forest. He could catch glimpses of Xcalan's lagoon, dotted with pelicans and scarlet ibis. The tiny mesh of the net gave the view an almost impressionistic, slightly out-of-focus feel. He realized the survival of the place was on a knife edge. He might have no choice but to take the mission. He figured that if he led a new team himself, saving on a team leader's salary, and imposed Daniel-like levels of cost-cutting, he might still clear close to the two million dollars needed to purchase Xcalan. Burr and the Mayans had developed a good bid, based on the development of the island for limited eco-tourism. He was confident that the regional council would approve it for inclusion in the auction. For that, he estimated that a bid of eight million dollars should be enough to win. If he realized the maximum from the GemCorp job, they might just about be able to scrape together the rest. The question was, who would present the development plan and manage the process if Burr wasn't there? He might just be able to complete the Madero mission in time to present to the council. Still, it all seemed very risky. And that was even without knowing what had happened to Daniel.

He went to Elizabeth's room and knocked on the door. After a moment she let him in with a drowsy, quizzical look. The shutters were closed and she had obviously been resting. The bed was rumpled and the room was muggy, cooled only by a slowly rotating ceiling fan.

'Tell me more about what happened to Daniel,' he said.

She yawned and stretched. 'He split his team. Half stayed at our base camp in the mountains, to train our militia – the Bond. The other half went down to gather intelligence in Madero. The men down in Madero were posing as scientists from Argonaut Ecology. I guess it's your usual cover story.'

'One of them,' confirmed Burr. 'So what went wrong?'

Elizabeth shrugged. 'We really don't know. Of course, Lester and I weren't actually at the base the whole time. We spend most of our time in the capital. One day all the signs were normal, with

Daniel in daily contact. The next day, he and his men were gone. Just like that.'

'Rebels?' asked Burr.

'No evidence.' She sat at the mirrored dressing table and began to brush her long hair with deliberate, sweeping strokes.

Burr stood watching her. The falling sun sent slats of dust-reddened light through the shutters. 'Well, I suppose we'd have had a ransom demand by now if the rebels had kidnapped them.'

'I guess so. I can't really tell you what happened in Madero. GemCorp operatives are not welcome down there these days. Your communications team in Miami probably knows just as much as we do. Daniel reported to them regularly.' She paused and looked straight at Burr in the mirror. 'I know you must be worried about Daniel. But I'll be honest: we don't want you looking too hard for him. The jungle is a vast waste . . . you might never find him. And our priority – and Argonaut's contract – is to recover the mine. Of course it is important to know what happened to Daniel – even if just to make sure it doesn't happen again.'

'Maybe this mission is tougher than it looks,' mused Burr. 'It's not going to be easy to get good people to go in now that Daniel's disappeared.'

Elizabeth nodded agreement. 'Especially not at short notice. That's another reason why you have to do it, Burr. We've asked around and there are people out there who will do it, but only if you're in charge. People like Ricardo.'

He guessed they had already asked Ricardo and

been turned down. Burr certainly would not want to embark on a job like this without his old friend, though he wasn't so sure Ricardo was taking on any jobs these days. His right-hand man on dozens of active-service operations, Ricardo Martinez had not been on a combat mission for a long while.

Elizabeth turned back to Burr from the mirror. 'Will you come?' she asked. 'It is only Colombia. I believe you know it well.'

'That's precisely the problem,' he answered. Daniel's disappearance was just the sort of thing that happened in Colombia. Burr had worked there officially and unofficially many times. Colombia had long boasted the world's highest per capita murder rate. Whole swathes of the country were in total chaos. In the inaccessible reaches of the Andes mountains and the Amazon forests, drug gangs and policemen fought one war, while the army, Marxist rebels, and right-wing paramilitaries like the Bond fought out another. The wars raged across the same turf with confused local alliances and feuds. This was the maelstrom in which Daniel and his men had disappeared. Did Burr really want to dive into it again? For GemCorp? He looked at Elizabeth, who was appraising him with an artful expression. Burr hadn't always been proud of private soldiering, but at least Argonaut tried to work only for the good guys. They had turned down many lucrative but unsavoury commissions, including *coups d'état* and repeated pleas to form the praetorian guard of a genocidal African dictator. Daniel had been disgruntled at some of these moral decisions, but he always got over it.

'Come out on the terrace for supper, in a few minutes,' Burr said. 'We'll talk some more.'

'Thanks,' replied Elizabeth demurely, with a knowing smile.

Burr served his guests a light dinner of fresh flying fish out on the decked terrace above the beach. Elizabeth drank some white wine and was pleasant enough company. A couple of times Burr wondered whether her foot brushed his on purpose under the table. Lester drank a lot, but stayed sulky and quiet. After dinner, Burr was alone in his office when Pachal appeared, dressed in a simple white tunic. 'Can you come down with me to the ticket house, Capitan?' he asked.

Burr accompanied the Mayan without asking why. He was well used to this people's cryptic meetings. In silence they walked down the tree-covered landward side of the dunes to the old city in the forest. Before the Spaniards came, almost five hundred years before, Xcalan had been one of the greatest Mayan cities. In 1532 it was sacked by the conquistador Don Rodrigo de Ayala y Vivar and fell steadily into ruin. Recently, in a tourist development phase, the regional council in Chetumal had excavated temples from the sand and even set up a ticket booth. But the island was too far south from the epicentre of Yucatán tourism at Cancún. The ticket-sellers had returned to fishing, and the few hardy tourists who came found the site empty and dilapidated. Sand had sifted over the ruins and was building up in drifts along the seaward side of the temples. Soon they would be hidden again under the shifting dunes.

In a forested fold of the sand hills, behind a dense stand of thorn bush, they came upon a young Mayan dressed in white like Pachal. He nodded a greeting, dropped to his knees and lifted a mat of thorn and branches to reveal a large hole in the sand floor of the forest. A rope ladder was attached to one side. Pachal and Burr climbed down into the darkness. At the bottom of the ladder, the hole was pitch-black. Pachal turned and led Burr with a whisper into a passage that curved downwards through the earth. In the inky darkness, Burr could feel that the sand walls had given way to solid rock and there were hard stone steps under their feet. Then ahead there was a faint light, which grew stronger as they approached, and he blinked in surprise as they turned a corner into a glittering cavern.

It was one of the secret cenotes of the Maya.

Burr knew about these underground caverns that run like a web beneath the Yucatán peninsula. They were created sixty million years ago by the impact of a giant meteor. This was the massive collision that threw up a blanket of dust across the globe – a catastrophe that led to the extinction of the dinosaurs. Over the ages, water, seeping down through the limestone rock, had filled many of the cenotes to form underground streams and crystal-clear lakes. For millennia in the riverless Yucatán, these caverns had been the Maya's source of fresh water. Some branched out into hidden tunnels with streams of fresh water that stretched far out under the sea bed. Cenotes were sacred to the Maya, who saw them as gates to the underworld, places of worship and sacrifice.

Burr had known Xcalan since childhood, but he had never heard of this cenote or anything like it. It was an awesome place. Amid giant, pointed stalactites, sparkling mineral deposits streaked the ceiling like scatterings of stars. Torchlight lit the walls, revealing intricately chiselled hieroglyphics and carvings of the Mayan corn gods. Reflected flames shimmered on the clear pool that stretched across the cavern. Along one wall, calcified skeletons of adults and children reminded Burr that human sacrifice was an integral part of the old Mayan rites. Ancient skulls and bones lay clearly visible beneath the surface of the pure 'virgin' water of the pool.

And at the foot of the steps, in front of the pool, a great carving of Itzamna, the Celestial Serpent, rose like a dragon from the stone floor. Its scales were formed of jade, prized for its green hue – the colour of the life-giving corn before it ripens and so sacred to the Maya. The serpent's barbed tongue was plated with hammered gold. Its baleful eye was ivory white, but with a gaping hole at its centre. Around the statue were gathered the Mayan *chacs*, the elders, all wearing simple white shifts.

One of them came forward. Burr recognized Isaiah, the old fisherman who worked the lagoon. 'Come,' Isaiah said. 'We must talk of the fate of Xcalan.'

Burr nodded assent and followed him down to the sandy space in front of the statue of Itzamna. For a while they said nothing. They simply sat round a small fire, eating corn on the cob and drinking *balche* – fermented honey – from large plastic beakers. The fire was built up, the light of the flames flickering on the heavenly serpent. Some of the Maya began to chant slowly and plaintively in a rolling rhythm. It was then that Isaiah began to talk.

'Pachal tells us you think perhaps to travel south to the jungle of the great river.'

'I am thinking about this,' Burr replied. 'It could earn money that would help save Xcalan. And a friend of mine has gone missing. It is possible I can find him, or what happened to him.'

Isaiah continued solemnly. 'We do not believe that money will save Xcalan, Capitan Burr. Money is of the modern world, and using it will help bring your modern world and that will be the end for us. We know of the oil fields, where the sea sprouts the metal drilling trees and the water is slippery with colours like an evil rainbow. And where there is no oil, the concrete comes. We know of Playa del Carmen and of Cancún, where the land has been covered in concrete. Many Americans and some people called Germans come and lie there on the sand. The forest is gone. The fish are gone. The heart of things there is gone.'

Isaiah fell silent and Pachal continued. 'Burr, we know you have done a lot for us, but we no longer believe that meetings or protests will work. Nor do we believe we can buy the island. The big companies are too powerful for us. We do not have the money or the influence to fight them.' The old Mayan leaned forward and clasped Burr's forearm. 'To save Xcalan, Capitan Burr, to save our world, all the prophecies agree: the stone must be replaced.' He looked up at the gaping pupil of the monumental snake. 'We seek a green eye for the Serpent God.'

Burr gazed at the blank eye of the statue. The empty socket was a black shadow in the firelit glow of the serpent. A chanting Mayan threw a handful of *copal* incense onto the flames and billows of perfumed smoke swirled up around the figure. Isaiah pointed at some painted carvings in the rock at the base of the statue. Through the heady clouds of incense, Burr could see a depiction of the serpent's head, complete with a green, globed eye, its pupil a blazing yellow gash.

The *chac* went on. 'Some Maya have looked all their lives for a stone to fill that hole. The green eye of Itzamna was stolen from us by the Spanish many centuries ago. It was taken back to the land whence it came. There are Maya looking for it even now in the jungles of the south. Do you remember Tenoch?'

Burr remembered him, a quiet and earnest Mayan with one eye. He had opened coconuts for Burr and Pachal when they were kids. Tenoch had carved Burr his first surfboard out of a fallen branch from the great balsa tree by the estuary.

'Tenoch is there,' said Isaiah drowsily. 'He has been searching for many years. We have recently received a message from him. He believes he is close to finding a stone...' The *chac*'s head drooped. Burr wondered if the chanting and the heavy atmosphere had lulled the old man to sleep. Then after a while Isaiah spoke again with a deep sigh. 'The Maya of Xcalan have declined, yes, but that is the way of the world. Now we face extinction. If the oilmen take this place, we will vanish. But I tell you this: fighting will not achieve our aim, whether you fight the oilmen here, or somebody else in the forests of the south. The only way we will be saved is through peace and the green eye. If you go to save, if you go in peace to search – for your friend or for the green eye – then you should go south. If you go in anger, with arms, the signs say that you should not go.'

Burr wondered if the 'green eye' referred to an emerald. He knew little about emeralds, except that Colombia would be the right place to look for them – it was the source of the world's finest stones. He also had the feeling that an emerald big enough to fill the statue's eye socket would be impossibly rare, and that to buy such a jewel would probably cost as much as buying Xcalan. Anyway, Burr steadfastly did not believe in prophecies and magic, or even fate.

'Isaiah,' he said, 'you cannot rely on a prophecy about green eyes. A piece of stone can't save you. You must continue fighting for this place. You must protest and campaign. I will fight in Colombia and earn what we need to continue our fight here.'

The Mayan nodded. 'But even if we do keep the

land safe, they will come and drill in the ocean. And the fish will hide, or die.'

'Do you really believe that the stone can save you from that? That's just magic. Magic isn't real, Isaiah, even for the Maya.'

The *chacs* conferred among themselves, then Isaiah turned back to Burr. 'Tonight, if you agree, you will drink *ayahuasca*. With this, men can see to the heart of things.'

'It's also what the *chacs* used to give the sacrificial victims,' said Pachal with a mischievous smile. He passed Isaiah a jug of *balche*. The Mayan elder tore strips from the pithy inside of a piece of bark, put them in his mouth and chewed them. After a few minutes he spat them into the potion. He frothed the honey mixture up, muttered some words over it and handed it to Burr.

'You may be right about magic, brother,' Pachal said quietly. 'But you should not ignore the prophecies. The green eye itself might not save us, but it could give us the strength to save ourselves.'

Burr nodded and drank deeply, trying not to betray any distaste for the glutinous concoction. The *balche* had an odd, bitter tang to it, salty, with the slight fizz of fermenting orange juice. For a while he felt no effect. He and Pachal took their leave of the *chacs* and went up out of the cenote and onto the beach. The night was black, with a fine web of stars. Burr, beginning to feel drowsy, lay down on the sand. He noticed his mouth was dry and he tried to swallow, but couldn't. He had no saliva. The moon pulsed in the sky and he blinked and felt his eyelids rasp over parched eyeballs. The stars revolved in the heavens. He tried to pee, but his bladder had dried up too. A wind blew from the sea and set off a thudding in his ears. He felt desiccated, wrung out, then stretched, disoriented and somehow translated. He was staring close up at a shining green eye. It filled his vision, then suddenly the green was a smooth, fast surface, the wind was a breeze on a tennis court and the thudding was Burr bouncing the ball, about to serve. He was dreaming about the match – living it clear as day. And he was fifteen again; he was that boy with a match point in the final at the National Collegiate Championships. Burr was aware that winning this point could mean a career at the very top of the senior game. He was even more aware of his father watching, hawklike, up in the stands. Burr's opponent was a boy two years older, a clean-cut Latin American who had lurked back on the baseline and slammed cultured ground strokes with agonizing patience. He was crouched low now, in the dream, swaying, ready for the serve.

Half-aware in his dream state, Burr wondered whether the match would end differently this time, but it all seemed to be unfolding just as it had years ago. His serve should have been an ace, going in fast and deep, skidding off the smooth green hard court. Behind the serve, the dream-Burr moved in towards the net. Incredibly, and just as he had in real life, Burr's opponent returned the serve with a desperate lunge. Burr had to dive across to reach the ball and despatch it with a brilliant cross-court volley.

Scrambling back to the middle of the court, Burr watched in amazement as his opponent got to the ball again, curled the head of his racket around it and whipped it high into the air. Burr knew instantly that the ball was too high to reach, and he turned to race it to the back of the court. But the shot was too good. The dream slowed and Burr felt that terrifying helplessness all over again as the ball looped tantalizingly over his head in slow motion, just beyond his lunging racket. The spin pulled it down fast, right onto the baseline and away – a perfect topspin lob. Burr's match point was gone.

Then there was the confusion. For some reason, the linesman called 'Out!' Burr turned to serve again before he realized. The crowd was applauding and shouting. The umpire was calling: 'Game, set and match – Whitman.' His opponent appeared speechless with shock. In his dream, Burr glanced up at the players' box and saw his father looking down at him with a strange expression. For a moment in the dream, as in life, he hesitates, and Burrell Whitman is National Collegiate Champion. Then he makes his choice and walks over the perfect green of the court to the umpire's chair and says clearly, 'The ball was in, ump.' The umpire looks at him as though he is mad. 'It's the truth,' says Burr simply. 'That's just the way it is.' He does not dream on to his eventual defeat. The crowd and the court begin to swirl. And in the dream Burr falls down onto the green cement and he is seeing the green close up – the green eye again ... no, green *eyes* this time, two of them – the eyes of a person.

Then, suddenly, Burr was awake. 'That's just the way it is,' he was saying. The moon had set and Pachal was watching him in the starlight. Burr was fizzing with energy and adrenalin. He had not remembered the tennis match so clearly for years. Why it absorbed his subconscious now, he did not know. The dream had filled him with doubts and questions, but he had made his decision.

'You will go south,' Pachal said.

Burr nodded.

'The dream told you that?'

'I don't know. It was just a dream. Something that happened long ago.'

Pachal helped Burr to his feet. 'Maybe you are right, maybe it was just a dream. But with belief, men can make dreams real. Things happen for a reason.'

Burr went back up to the darkened house. Passing the open door to Elizabeth's room, he heard a faint noise and glimpsed a flicker of silver. He looked through the open door. Elizabeth was moving across the room to the bed on long, slender legs. Her body was smooth and curved in the moonlight; the soles of her bare feet showed white as she walked. She wore nothing but her baseball cap.

'Aren't you going to come in?' he heard her ask in a low voice.

'What about Lester?' he murmured.

'Well, I guess he'd kill at least one of us – if he knew.'

'You know, Elizabeth, you don't have to do this. I'm going to take the job anyway.'

'Good,' she replied silkily. 'I'd do it even if you said no.' She moved across to him and kissed him on the lips, her warm body pressed against his, her tongue fluttering.

Burr kissed back for a moment, then gently pulled away. A floorboard creaked from Lester's room. 'Unfortunately,' Burr said, quietly, 'I don't think it's a good idea to go to bed with clients.' Another creak sounded from next door.

'Maybe you're right,' agreed Elizabeth with a forced smile. 'Let's leave it for now.'

Burr turned and left. Elizabeth ran her finger along her lip and put it in her mouth, tasting him again, a slight tang of salt and honey. It was probably right to be wary of Lester. In any case, client or not, she would have Burr sometime, if she still wanted him. She was confident of that.

Madero, Colombian Amazon

The liberator of Colombia, Simón Bolívar, said: 'He who serves the revolution ploughs the sea.' Javier Diaz, leader of the FARA rebels in the southern Amazon zone of Colombia, sometimes well understood the great hero's complaint. Not today, however. Standing outside his headquarters in the old Madero mission station as the sun came up, he was content with his situation.

The mission stood in a commanding hilltop position overlooking Madero. To the north, between the hill and the Madero River, stood the old town, with its crumbling colonial mansions and decaying boulevards occupied by hawkers and indigents. To the west was a mass of shanties, already sprouting up the Mission Hill and sending rusting corrugated-iron tendrils deep into the forest. Huge bare patches showed where trees had been cut for building and for firewood. To the south were the mines and a landscape barren as the moon. Tunnels were blasted into the earth and machines belched smoke into the air. Trucks rumbled over the muddy wasteland. Streams of black slurry ran down the hills from heaps of waste rock. This was the source of Madero's – and currently FARA's – wealth. For almost one year Diaz had run the emerald mines and he now had piles of uncut emeralds worth millions of dollars at its disposal.

To the east, however, from the foot of the Mission Hill, the virgin forest rolled endlessly across the sierras into the morning haze, a smooth, unbroken quilt of a million green shades. It was this view that Javier Diaz was admiring. Not so much the forest – he had seen far too much of that in ten years of guerrilla warfare – but the figure of the charming Dr Leila Walcott in the foreground.

'Good morning, Doctor,' he called jovially.

'Good morning, Comandante,' she said, smiling. 'You look as handsome as ever.'

Diaz's pressed combat fatigues, which fitted snugly round his short, paunchy body, were pristine. His beret was red, matching his perfectly tied bandanna. He smoothed his moustache, tilted his beret just so, in imitation of Che Guevara, and beamed back at her. The rising sun behind Leila clearly outlined her shape through her white cotton shirt. *Que rica!* he thought: what a beauty! As a Creole, Leila would not normally have been to Diaz's taste – he preferred his women white – but in her case he would be more than prepared to make an exception.

'Dr Walcott,' he called, to prolong the view, 'did you know that another group of scientists will be joining us in Madero soon?'

'I had heard a rumour. Who are they?'

'A group of zoologists. It appears that they were not put off by the fate of their predecessors.'

'You have no more news about their disappearance, I suppose?'

Diaz laughed. 'You think we might have had something to do with that. Well, who knows?'

Leila gave a forced smile and hurried on to the barracks building on the hilltop, where a number of rebel patients were waiting. All medical staff had long fled the town, so two mornings a week Leila held a clinic for the rebels. It was part-payment for allowing the research station to remain open. The FARA cases were mostly malarial and venereal. The current cease-fire with the government meant that gunshot wounds were less common. The rebel mine guards also brought in emerald miners. The guerrillas would watch as Leila treated pick-axe injuries to limbs, hands with fingers lost to explosives, and head injuries from falling rocks.

This morning they brought in a patient who was shaking violently and running with sweat. Initially Leila thought he was gripped by fever. Examining him, she realized he was sweating just as much from pain and fear. He had obviously been smuggling emeralds from the mine by hiding them under his teeth. Now the gum had become infected. In the yellow-green pus, Leila could see the greener glint of an emerald, trapped by the swelling. The man was terrified of discovery.

When the FARA captured Madero, the change in master had meant no change in regime for the mine workers. The GemCorp management had fled, but most of the security personnel stayed. There were still strict searches to prevent theft. Every worker had to strip on leaving the mine and walk through an X-ray machine. In a cabin by the gates, random workers were selected for invasive searches by the chortling, rubber-gloved 'Mr Sticky Fingers'. Anyone caught smuggling an emerald would be brutally punished. With GemCorp in charge, the usual penalty was a severe beating. Under the rebels, the penalty had been simplified: any-body caught smuggling an emerald would be shot on the spot.

'You have an abscess on your gum,' Leila said to the man, for the guards' benefit. 'I'm afraid it needs to be lanced.'

Leila made sure the man's mouth was obscured, then she tweezered out a rough, dark-green emerald the size of a pea and slipped it into the man's hand. He gasped and tried to smile at her, weeping with relief and gratitude. Leila felt depressed. She was not an expert, but she had learned enough to know that this man was risking his life for a poor-quality, opaque emerald chip of about two carats. In Madero, the going rate for such a stone was perhaps three dollars.

Thunder cracked and rain began to pour down as Leila drove back into the research centre com-pound. She could make out the grey figures of some sick Jemberí shambling aimlessly about in the downpour like souls in limbo. What a day, she thought, what an awful place this is. Recently she had been nagged by feelings of sadness and frustration. Now these returned and Leila felt a deep pang of doubt. Sometimes, lying awake in the darkness of that remote, suffocating place, the insidious worries would creep up on her. In the small hours they would whisper that it was all folly, that the jungle held no miracle cures, that it had been a mistake to leave her blossoming medical career for this fruitless quest. With these thoughts came even deeper feelings, sensations that cramped the pit of her stomach and seemed, on occasion, like loneliness. Usually, Leila could brush these aside. After all, there was always another promising plant compound to isolate and analyse. And how could she be lonely? She mingled with plenty of people every day, people who liked and needed her. Diaz, the local rebel commander, was in love with her, for God's sake. A new group of scientists would soon be in residence at the other research station. And of course she had James Makepeace. Today, however, her uneasiness lingered.

Leila took a deep breath, then jumped out of the car and dashed through the rain to the field laboratory. Inside, she picked up some of the plant specimens she had been given over the last few days, and she noticed something new. Some of the *kiragi* stalks little Tupo had given her – the ones with cocoons inside them – carried the beginnings of small buds. It was the first time she had seen anything like a *kiragi* bud or flower. Suddenly excited, she began to work. As rain drummed on the windows of the sweltering field lab she removed one of the budding stalks to keep and press as part of the *kiragi* voucher specimen. She put some aside for chemical analysis and some into a pot of water on the window ledge. Then, ignoring the relentless downpour soaking her to the skin, she walked along the short path through the forest to the research project's second clearing. There she planted the rest of the *kiragi* in the muddy puddle of the station's attempt at plant cultivation. Makepeace would scoff at her, but she just had a hunch about *kiragi*. And if the latest batch thrived, they might have enough to solve the mystery of the plant.

Leila's depression had evaporated. Maybe the day would turn out to be a good one after all.

Miami, Florida

From the outside, the headquarters of Argonaut Security was a drab, single-storey block at the end of a concrete pier that enclosed one of the many upscale pleasure-boat marinas along the shore of Miami Beach. Below the surface, however, the Argonaut offices occupied the interior of the pier's massive hollow drum, stretching down through the water and well into the sea bed below. Walking inside for the first time in months, Burr did a double-take. The interior had been completely – and, it appeared, expensively – redecorated. Any clutter had disappeared, leaving a minimalist look. It was sleek and modern, every wall and hallway curving smoothly.

'Daniel said it keeps the chi energy circulating smoothly,' said Janine sheepishly, in response to Burr's bemused expression. In her late twenties, Janine Granger was a former Marine Recon sergeant. Quiet and reliable, she was one of the few permanent Argonaut employees, and would be the comms specialist in Burr's Madero unit.

Burr hardly heard her as he gawped at the subtly lit lobby decorated with eight scarlet and black lacquer vases carrying the interlocking comma symbols of yin and yang. Each vase contained a pure white lotus flower. 'Eights are good luck in feng shui,' explained Janine as they took the elevator down to the main operations floor, fifty feet below the water.

They passed into the darkened comms room and surprised Carlo, who jumped up nervously, mumbling, 'Hi, Burr.' The room was filled with a soft electronic hum and was almost cold with the air conditioning required for the banks of communications equipment.

'Hey, Carlo,' Burr greeted him warmly.

A shy man with a mop of black hair that he let fall over his eyes, Carlo Maldini was a civilian employee of Argonaut and a bit of a geek. His closest experience of combat was level seven of the latest Tomb Raider video game, which he had been playing when Burr and Janine came in.

'You can get back to Lara Croft now,' said Burr with a smile, tapping a button to reveal the comely game heroine frozen on the screen in mid-leap. 'I'm surprised you're not jealous of her, Janine.'

Carlo was Janine's boyfriend. He was also Argonaut's accountant and organizational genius. He was responsible for the company's logistics and would be the main point of contact at base during their mission. He was also Burr's choice to help down at Xcalan in case the mission took longer than expected.

Burr thought Carlo was a lucky guy. Janine might not have been the most obviously attractive package – she had a square, muscular frame and kept her hair shaved military-short – but she was sweet and clearly loved him deeply.

Argonaut Security was an ideal place for people like Janine to use skills they had learned in the army. It was one of the new breed of Private Military Companies that replaced the old-school mercenary freebooters in the decades following the Cold War. Lucrative global businesses, these PMCs supplied security, training and sometimes even private armies to corporations and governments worldwide. Argonaut had the added advantage of being one of the elite companies to enjoy the privileged 'X-access' relationship with the US Military and the Central Intelligence Agency.

Competitors without X-access enviously called it 'Ex-access', because current soldiers and spies handed out the contracts to their ex-soldier and ex-spy friends. And that was how ex-Special Forces captains Daniel Gold and Burrell Whitman had got their first assignments. X-access contacts could also be useful in other ways, such as allowing use of covert communication channels with rebel groups.

'Have you contacted the FARA?' Burr asked.

'Done,' replied Janine. 'We used the same contacts as we did before Daniel left.'

'Under the cover of Argonaut Ecology,' Carlo confirmed. 'They're expecting a new group of scientists in Madero in a week or so.'

'Good,' said Burr. He nodded his satisfaction and wandered out of the comms room.

Janine and Carlo looked at each other anxiously and a moment later they heard a loud exclamation. Janine winced, then went through into the brightly lit briefing area to find Burr looking around in astonishment.

'How could you let him do this?' he asked. The rest of the ops floor had been redecorated like the lobby above. Daniel had even installed a large, round window giving onto a rather murky undersea view. Burr shook his head in disbelief. 'It looks as though we've gone and spent all the GemCorp contract money on the decor.'

Janine wrung her hands unhappily. 'I knew you would hate it, but what could we do? We didn't know how to reach you. And you know how un-stoppable Dan is...' A yellowfin grouper nudged slowly by outside the round window. 'You see, the Chinese word for fish is "yu" – same as the word for success...' Janine's voice tailed off lamely.

'What's wrong with a fish bowl? And where are all the manuals and maps? Where is all my stuff?'

Janine turned to a line of fitted lacquer cabinets and pressed the corner of a door. The catch sprang open to reveal neatly arranged bookshelves. 'Daniel said you mustn't have books pointing towards you on open shelves. It's bad feng shui. Their spines are like knives.'

'Am I the only person in this organization who's not in the grip of some medieval superstition? If it's not magic green eyes, then it's Chinese mumbo-jumbo!'

Burr had always been exasperated by Daniel and his fads. Before feng shui it was I Ching. Before that it was Druidism; before that, tarot ... or was it crystals? Now it was upsetting to see Dan's imprint on things and not have the hyperactive Dan himself, jumping around, talking about his latest business idea, tarot reading or feng shui guru. Burr felt guilty. He was taking out his tension on Janine.

She was looking at him with a worried expression. 'We are going to find him, aren't we?' she asked. 'Daniel, I mean.'

'We're going to try, Janine.' Burr's expression softened. 'But first there's the little matter of an emerald mine we have to return to its owners. Let's not waste time. Show me that map of Madero.' He took a deep breath and smiled broadly. 'It's good to be back.'

Janine gave a relieved grin. 'Good to have you back, Captain.'

Driving with the top down along the coast road towards the Argonaut HQ, Lester looked glumly out of the rented Porsche at the glamorous south Florida sea front. The looming meeting with Burr made him feel anxious and morose. He didn't like being plain Lester. He preferred it back in Colombia, where he was known as *El Cangrejo*, 'the Crab', and his name was feared. 'I keep telling you,' he complained to Liz, 'we don't need these *paila* mercenaries. My *milicianos* have had plenty of training from Daniel. We've got pretty good information on Madero. I reckon we can take these rebels ourselves. I could run the operation.'

'Sure you could,' said Elizabeth soothingly from the driver's seat. 'And I know that your men are competent. But Minister Ayala and the GemCorp management insist on professional assistance. And these Argonauts are professionals. You have to admit they are good. And Burr is better than Daniel, for sure.'

Lester sighed. Professionally, he agreed with her, and *professionally* there was no doubt he looked forward to working with Burr. Liz was sure that Burr was the best man for the job and he trusted her judgement on all things – well, except for the fact that she had divorced him, but he was working on reversing that.

No, professionally it would be fine. And the next few weeks would certainly involve a lot of violence, something at which Lester excelled and which he always found therapeutic. It enabled him to work out his inner demons. He knew that he had many demons, one in particular of which was burning him up at the moment. This also had to do with Burr, but on a personal level. Because, *personally* speaking, Lester had not hit it off with Burr at all.

What worried Lester was that he reckoned Elizabeth had developed some kind of thing with Burr. He was pretty sure he had seen it that day on that beach – the way she said hello to him, going all girly and coy while he did the whole romantic castaway thing. Dropout, more like, living in a house built of fucking driftwood. Then there was the way she brushed her hair back from her face with her fingers when she was talking to him. Lester had seen a documentary about body language once. It was like animals did – grooming, it was called, or preening, maybe. He gritted his teeth. Liz had been like an animal preening for a mate, like a *fufurufa* in heat – right in front of her ex-husband. It would have made anyone mad. What's more, Lester was damn sure Burr had been naked walking back up the dunes at Xcalan and Liz had kept the binoculars on him for a long time while Lester was getting soaked up the front of that damn ski boat.

And as for the night they spent in that weird wooden beachhouse of his . . . He had tried to stay awake to make sure nothing further happened between Burr and Liz. He had fallen asleep, though, so he would never be sure.

'You were flirting with him,' he had grumbled to Liz the next morning. 'He was in your room last night.'

'Well, he said yes to the job, didn't he?' She had yawned, like it was all right to lead a guy on. 'There's nothing wrong with using what you got.'

Just depends how far she wanted to take it, thought Lester. She denied she had done anything with Burr, of course, like she had denied all her affairs through their six years of marriage. He knew she had been lying on at least two occasions, because he had extracted the truth personally from the men in question before they died.

'Not my type,' she had said about Burr. But could

she leave it at that? Hell she could. She made damn sure to add wistfully, 'Though he does have a very good body . . .'

And so Lester stared vacantly out at the spectacular parade of high-rises and hotels. If only he wasn't still so damn attracted to her, he thought. He sneaked a peek at her as she sat beside him in the Porsche, wind fluttering her hair, pretty profile – a real looker and with a little something extra thrown in. He had known it the moment he had first seen her. Those breasts, pert and just big enough to satisfy any man, even a breast man like Lester. Maybe they had even grown since the divorce – she had put on a little weight, he had to admit. Still she had a firm butt and those lo-o-o-ng legs. He ran his eyes down them all the way to where her slim, tanned feet pressed the pedals in white, high-heeled shoes. Damn! Liz was sexy as hell, but more than that she was intelligent. When he had first picked her up she was serving tables in South Beach. He had been lying low outside Colombia after some unfortunate excesses when he was just an ordinary *miliciano* – a foot soldier in the Bond *autodefensa* – 'self-defence' militia. He was running odd quasi-legal jobs for some people who sympathized with the problems the self-defence groups had in protecting Colombian society from the Marxist guerrilla scourge. Soon he had introduced Liz to some big-time players, men like William Walls who appreciated a woman who knew how to play hardball. Lester had risen through the ranks to command the Bond. At the same time, with

Lester as her muscle, Elizabeth had made a series of meteoric career moves herself. Now she was running pretty much the whole unofficial side of GemCorp's operations in Colombia. Plus she had that whole *femme fatale* thing going on and that was physically, not just emotionally. She may have looked delicate, but make an unwanted move and a man risked fatal injury. Lester imagined for the thousandth time that blissful moment when Liz agreed to take him back. He would need firm assurances of safety before making any advances.

'You could still cancel the contract,' Lester suggested hopefully.

'You don't cancel contracts on a man like Burr,' said Elizabeth. 'Not unless you cancel him at the same time. Anyway, Lester *querido*, even led by a Napoleon like you, without professional help the Bond militia will never take Madero against rebels in entrenched positions. You know that perfectly well. No, we need Burr.'

Lester made a sulky face. 'You don't need me. You don't think I can do it.'

'Of course I need you, Les,' she cooed, patting him on the knee. 'And I know you can do it. You are vital to this operation.'

Lester loved it when she spoke to him like that. He beamed at her and after a moment plucked up the courage to ask nervously, 'So have you thought any more about . . . about you and me?'

Her expression changed instantly. 'Not now, Lester,' she said.

'Then when, Liz?' he complained, clenching his fists.

'Look, *guevon*,' Elizabeth snapped, 'idiot! There is no more you and me.' She took a deep breath and went on calmly, 'This is business, Lester. We're just colleagues now.'

'Friends,' he said sadly.

'What?'

'You could at least have said we're "just friends". But I guess I'm not even that to you now.' Lester looked back out of the window. It's that damn Burr, he said to himself – and he comes along just when things were going well again with Liz.

They sat in silence. He saw the sign to the marina and his heart sank. They would be there in a minute.

'How much more do we tell them about Daniel?' he asked.

'We avoid the subject whenever possible and keep them focused on the mission. Sure, we answer their questions. But what they don't ask, we don't volunteer. If they find out what happened to Daniel, we'll just have to see where that leads.'

In the Argonaut briefing room, Janine and Carlo joined the planning session. Lester watched for signs of something going on between Elizabeth and Burr, but it all appeared thoroughly professional. She began by outlining the background on Madero and the initial plan Daniel had developed for GemCorp.

Burr's immediate observation was that the plan

had fundamental flaws. 'For a start, Daniel did not have enough manpower,' he pointed out.

'Well, let's fix that this time,' said Elizabeth. 'But remember, we wouldn't be here if you had taken the job in the first place.'

'And I *liked* Daniel,' Lester added. 'I figure he was doing a good job. Well, until he disappeared.'

'Exactly,' commented Elizabeth, icily: 'disappeared. Leaving us a half-trained bunch of militia imbeciles.'

Lester smarted at the insult to his *milicianos* but kept silent.

'How did Daniel assign his team?' Burr asked.

Elizabeth leaned over the map next to Burr, her low-cut neckline revealing to him the smooth brown skin of his chest and most of her breasts. 'Daniel and half the men stayed at our base to train the militia. The base is in Arroyo Blanco, in the Andes foothills, about two days' journey from Madero. Here.' She pointed at the map. 'The rest of the team went down to Madero – here – as an advance party. As you know, they were posing as scientists from Argonaut Ecology.'

'So what exactly happened?' asked Carlo.

'One day Daniel took himself and the training detail down to Madero to join the advance unit. We had radio contact for a couple of days as usual. Then nothing.'

Burr looked surprised. 'Both units were in Madero at the same time? You said the plan was to keep the training squad up in the mountains with the militia.'

'*Sí*. Daniel would travel back and forth, visiting the Madero team, then returning to the militia in Arroyo. For some reason, he suddenly changed his mind. We don't know why.'

'Any idea why, Lester?' asked Burr.

Lester opened his mouth to answer.

'No, he has no idea,' said Elizabeth firmly.

Lester shut his mouth with a snap.

'And what about you two?' Burr looked at his new employers. 'Will you be working with us at the base in Arroyo Blanco?'

Elizabeth's pointed tongue poked out again in her little subconscious mannerism. 'We will be there if you need us, but most of the time we will be in Bogotá. After all, we somehow have to keep a gem business running through this mess.' She smiled sweetly. 'Of course, if you ever want to visit us in Bogotá you would be very welcome. We'll put you up at the Fiesta Americana Hotel.' She put her hand on Burr's arm. 'So just let me know if there's ever anything you need.'

Lester clenched his fists by his sides and went red enough to explode. Burr could see the crab tattoo on the Colombian's arm pulsating as the muscles tightened. It was too much for Burr to resist. He winked and squeezed Elizabeth's hand in return. 'Shucks, thanks, Liz,' he said with a smile. 'I'll be sure an' call. We can make a night of it.'

Lester was seething. He had changed his mind about this mercenary. Professionally, he now figured that it was Daniel who had all the moves and did all Argonaut's work. And personally, well, it wasn't that he just didn't get on with Burr. Oh no. Now he officially hated the smart-ass *picha*.

Overnight, news came to Elizabeth that the FARA rebels were planning to sell off a large consignment of emeralds from Madero. GemCorp had no intention of letting the rebels flood the market – certainly not with their own emeralds – and so were offering to buy the jewels. Lester and Elizabeth were urgently needed in Colombia to set up the exchange.

This new development meant that the Argonaut mission was brought forward. The first assignment for Burr's new team would be to run security for the transaction. They now had just three days to assemble a unit, equip it and get deep into the Colombian Andes.

Burr wasted no time. After an early start, he left Carlo and Janine to continue the now urgent recruitment effort and drove south from the Argonaut headquarters to a small marina on Key Biscayne for some R&R.

One of the Rs in 'R&R' was Ricardo. Ex-Rangers Sergeant Ricardo Martinez might not have worked for a while, but Burr knew that the Cuban-American, his right-hand man on so many sensitive missions, was the best small-force planner and instructor of foreign troops that he had ever met.

Arriving at the small harbour, Burr felt a little nervous. He knew Ricardo would be pleased to see him. Ricardo's wife, Rosa – the other R in R&R – was another matter.

It was Rosa who met him on the quayside. 'Hello, Burrell,' she said. Her greeting and perfunctory kiss on the cheek were cool at best. 'I thought you were safely tucked away in Yucatán. I can guess why you're here.'

'Hello, Rosa,' said Burr, warily – the 'Burrell' was a bad sign. 'It's great to see you too.'

Perhaps a year or two older than Burr, Rosa Martinez was an attractive woman, a dark-skinned Cubana with curly hair and a forceful personality. Now she smiled at him sourly. 'If you are here to get him on another job, you can forget about it. He's retired. And if you are involved in any of that dirty work, I forbid you to tell him about it, however much he asks – you know he'll join up just for love of you. In fact, if you even mention anything about your filthy profession on this boat, I'll be throwing you straight off, even if we're halfway to Cuba.' Her tone left Burr in no doubt that she meant it.

Rosa turned away and before Burr could reply he was pounced on by two squealing, dark-haired urchins. One hugged his waist, the other pulled at his arm. '*Burro! Burro!*' they shouted, giggling happily. 'Donkey! Donkey!' Even for children, Burr's name seemed to lend itself irresistibly to punning in multiple languages. 'Come on!' they squealed. 'Let's go fishing, Uncle Burro.'

Laughing, Burr picked Ricardito up in one arm, Paula in the other, and walked across the gangway onto Ricardo's sleek motor cruiser, *Guajira*. He put the children down on the deck and turned to see their father coming out of the cabin.

'*Hola!* Burr,' exclaimed Ricardo happily, grasping his old friend in a bear hug. 'Good to see you, *compadre.*' He cast a nervous look at his wife, who was watching them suspiciously. 'Let's get going,' he said to Burr. 'Why don't you cast off forward?'

The Atlantic stretched flat to the eastern horizon in a dead calm. Burr watched his friend as they motored steadily out to where the water turned dark aquamarine, then cobalt. The Cuban's moustache was greying and there were streaks of white around his temples. When the land was out of sight, Ricardo switched off the engine and they fished the clear water for marlin and sailfish while Ricardito and Paula played on the deck, chubby in their bright yellow inflatable vests. Burr caught a couple of tuna, and Ricardo hooked a tarpon, which escaped. He helped his son pull out a small bonefish, and dried his tears when they threw it back. Rosa hovered nearby, but as the languid day stretched on with the beers and the sun and the friends' talk she gradually relaxed. In the afternoon, she took the children into the cabin to sleep.

Ricardo had managed to keep his curiosity in check almost all day, but as soon as he and Burr found themselves alone on the deck he gave in. He pulled a couple of beers from the cooler and handed one to Burr. Then he checked none of his family was in earshot before whispering, 'So what's this about another Argonaut job? I hear Paul and Nicola are recruited already.'

Burr felt guilty about Rosa, but he answered

anyway. 'Yep. Looks like David and Ahmad, too. And of course me.'

Ricardo looked at him quizzically. 'I thought you were out for good. Daniel asked me to do a job a few months ago, but without you as CO I said no.'

'Yes, I know I'm meant to be out of it. But this is different – it's the job Daniel offered you before.'

'GemCorp?'

'Yes – a small-force operation with local militia. But be clear, I'm not trying to lure you out of retirement. I just wondered . . .'

Ricardo chuckled. 'So Rosa has made my retirement official, eh? With no leaving present or pension plan, I see.' He leant on the rail and looked out over the featureless surface of the sea. 'Now tell me more. Daniel gave me no details. I know GemCorp, though – they're a serious operation, part of some much bigger conglomerate, I seem to remember. Anyway I heard they had problems in Colombia – lost a mine to the rebels. Are the FARA guerrillas still commies, by the way?'

'Still claim to be. Strictly, I think they might be Maoist these days. Anyway they're playing capitalism with GemCorp's emeralds. The mine is in a place called Madero. Now GemCorp's hired their own private army – some kind of right-wing militia called the Bond. Daniel went in a team to train the militia and get the mine back.'

'Why can't the Colombian military go in?'

'Madero is in the trucial zone. To encourage the rebels to negotiate, the government declared a cease-fire and demilitarized half of the Colombian

Amazon. They say the rebels have got an area big as Switzerland. The Colombian armed forces can't be seen to mount offensive ops there.'

For a moment they were both silent. The boat rocked faintly on a gentle swell. Like the sea around, the sky above was colourless and empty. Burr could feel his friend already planning the mission.

'This militia got helicopters?' Ricardo enquired.

'Yes. Decent stuff, apparently – newish Black Hawks as well as old Hueys. The US gives military aid to the Colombian army, who then pass it on to their anti-communist militia buddies.'

'So, a few weeks to train up the militia and then an aerial assault. With a few professionals among the attackers, the rebels are going to run. Pretty straightforward, no?'

'Apparently not. That's what Daniel was planning, but it's gone wrong. Daniel and his team are missing. We've . . . I mean, *I've* got to sort out the mess – and maybe find Daniel while I'm at it.'

'Daniel's missing?' Ricardo looked grave. 'Not a good place to get lost. What about the rest of his team?'

'All of them.'

Ricardo shook his head. 'See what happens when you plan things without me . . .' he said wryly. There was a noise from inside the cabin and Ricardo looked guiltily over his shoulder. He cleared his throat. 'Time to head home, I guess,' he said more loudly than was necessary.

They climbed the ladder up to the bridge. Ricardo took the wheel and started the motors. The props churned up a small wash as the engines throbbed into life and the boat began to move slowly across the sea.

Ricardo was quiet for a moment, then asked casually, 'What is GemCorp paying, by the way? It must be a lot to get you working again.'

'A lot,' said Burr eagerly. He knew Ricardo was almost in. 'I could make sure you cleared two hundred thousand dollars, easy. I'm thinking six weeks' work. One condition: we can't pay in advance.'

Ricardo gave a low whistle. 'Two hundred grand, eh? Not bad.' Then he was silent for a moment. Burr could see his mind working, already mapping out the angles. 'I guess my old cover story might prove useful, though it's a long time since I worked with stones, and emeralds were never my speciality.'

Burr nodded – Ricardo had used the cover of a geologist before, and he knew something about gemstones.

Ricardo was thinking out loud now. 'Madero, huh? FARA rebels. Cuban-supplied, I guess. Remote location, deep jungle?' Burr nodded as the Cuban carried on. 'One squad to train the militia, one forward recon squad. You'll need specialists. All told, a team of eight or nine maybe, plus pilots.'

A loud sob interrupted him, and Rosa's head appeared at the top of the ladder. 'I knew it,' she said, looking at Burr with venom.

'I'm sorry, Rosa,' said Burr guiltily; 'he brought it up.' Burr pointed at Ricardo and stepped hastily away from the line of fire.

'It's not really your fault, Burr. It's him.' Rosa climbed up onto the bridge, eyes flashing with anger. 'It's *your* fault, Ricardo. You miss it. I can feel it sometimes even when we are most happy. Sometimes I see the look in your eyes and I know you are thinking of being somewhere far away, with a gun in your hand. Are you not satisfied with what you have?' She stepped forward and stood next to her husband at the wheel. He said nothing, staring straight ahead into the sunset.

She continued berating him. 'Reconnaissance, training, jungles ... you are too old for this dirty work. "Security work", you call it. "Guns for hire" is what it is. Mercenary work, dirty work, danger- ous ...' Rosa's shouts trailed off into silent crying. Then she went on softly, tears streaking her face. 'Ricardo, *mi amor*, listen to me. Why do you want to risk your life? We have more than enough money. When you came from Cuba you floated to America on a raft made of empty oil drums. Now look at this boat you have. You have children who love you, Ricardo. You have a wife who loves you. Are you not satisfied?'

Ricardo turned to his wife with a tender look. 'Of course I am satisfied, *querida*. What more could I want?' He cupped her face lovingly, then began, softly, to sing to her, '*Ay ay ay ay amor, eres la Rosa que me da calor* ...' It was the lilting bachata love song called 'Bachata Rosa'. From the beginning of their love, Ricardo had always sung it at the right time. Despite herself, Rosa smiled through her tears. Her husband smiled back and sang louder, serenading her. '*Eres el sueño de mi soledad, un letargo de azul, un eclipse de mar, pero . . . ay ay ay amor . . .*'

Perhaps awoken by Ricardo's singing, or their mother's shouting, two tousled heads appeared up the ladder. The sleepy kids were gathered into their parents' arms.

Burr felt a little awkward, out of place. Seeing his friend like this, the settled husband and father in the bosom of his family, Burr had to agree with Rosa. The mission would suffer, but he would be happy if Ricardo did not come. He clapped his friend on the back. 'Rosa's right,' he said. 'You'd be crazy to take on another op. Don't even think about it.'

Ricardo turned the boat back towards Miami. 'Well, maybe you're right,' he said with a wistful smile. 'There are more important things in life.'

They were quiet for a while, then Ricardo began to sing again, quietly, almost humming. This time it was the haunting Cuban melody 'Guantanamera'. Burr gripped the rail and looked away, filled with conflicting emotions. 'Guantanamera' was what his friend always sang when going into battle.

And as he sang, the *Guajira* sailed slowly westwards, back towards the land and the sunset, moving steadily across a hard, flat sea the colour of gunmetal. The falling sun lit the faces of Ricardo and his family with a warm glow and streaked the sea with flaming red.

Burr returned to the Argonaut HQ, where he rejoined Carlo and Janine. He briefed Carlo on the

Xcalan situation, then they worked the phones and the Internet into the small hours, trying to piece together the team at short notice. After a brief break for sleep, they were back in the operations room when the first new Argonauts arrived. As far as Burr was concerned they were both top-tier recruits. Nicola James had driven up from her home in the Keys. She was a spirited helicopter pilot who had flown over one hundred combat and medevac missions for Special Forces.

Burr was especially pleased at the second recruit – Paul Hill was an expert at war, which was lucky for him, as he was no good at peace. He was a veteran mercenary who had worked African civil wars with men who remembered the freebooting days of Mad Mike Hoare and Bob Denard. After his last Argonaut job, Paul had taken his pay packet straight to Vegas, where he was on first-name terms with far too many croupiers and call girls. Still, his bankroll stretched to the very night he got the call from Burr about Madero. He had checked out immediately and came in on the red-eye to Miami. Paul must have been around fifty by now and after six weeks in a penthouse suite at the Bellagio he was distinctly overweight. He swore that he would be back in shape quickly, though, and as former head of a Delta Force Close Quarter Combat – 'CQC' – team, he was vital to Burr as a proven squad leader and medic.

With Paul's arrival, Burr began planning in earnest and by the time the third new recruit, Ricardo, walked in he found the previously uncluttered Argonaut operations room covered by maps and satellite images of Madero. The others greeted him effusively, but Burr felt a painful mixture of pleasure and regret. 'Are you sure, Ricardo?' he asked, knowing the answer. Once his friend made a decision, he would stick with it to the end. Burr hated to imagine what Rosa thought of him now. He hoped he would be able to look her in the eye again.

Ricardo hung up his jacket with a grin. 'Just for you, *amigo* – and for Daniel. But this really is the last one.'

'Good to see you, Ricardo,' said Paul. 'Now, can you explain to Burr that we need some sort of heavy support for this job – like a 40 mm cannon. Our miserly boss is still trying to keep costs down.' Paul shook his head in amazement. 'I mean, the amount GemCorp's paying, we shouldn't skimp on kit, right?'

'Right,' agreed Ricardo. 'But I'm sorry, Paul. I'm also against the forty-mil. It's too long-barrelled and too heavy for the jungle. Too much trouble all round. We'll take a Barrett .50 calibre for targeting thin-skinned vehicles and machinery.'

'See!' Burr smirked at Paul. Then he turned to Ricardo. 'What about uniforms?'

'As a Ranger it hurts to say it, but we go with Marine Recon pixellated. The latest issue is the best camouflage around.'

'And what about weapons teams? Indirect fire? Not necessary, I guess?'

'Generally you're right,' said Ricardo. 'Using

mortars in thick forest can be tricky. We're talking about double-, sometimes triple-layered canopies down there. Firing a mortar up through that is dangerous, unless you're in a prepared position with a clear fire path. But it's still worth taking a small mortar capacity. If we have to assault Madero, a sixty-mil will come in handy. A few blasts will be a morale booster for our local allies and will scare the opposition rigid.'

Paul looked at Burr smugly. 'Told you so,' he said.

'We'll need Colt M4s,' continued Ricardo, 'rather than M16s.'

The M4 was a cut-down carbine version of the military staple M16 and was preferred by Special Forces, especially in constricted environments and CQC.

'Even though it's jungle, we'll still need long guns too, of course,' said Ricardo. 'Medium machinegun – MG240, I guess. And a specialist sniper.'

'Are you sure?' asked Paul. 'They're not always much use in thick jungle.'

Ricardo shook his head. 'We need somebody to handle the Barrett, and who's a trained SNOB.'

'How about Anthony?' suggested Nicola.

'Anthony Robinson?' Paul responded. 'I'm not sure. The guy's a freak of nature, plus he's an alcoholic.'

'True enough,' agreed Burr. 'But I hear Anthony's on the wagon and he's also the best Sniper/Observer I've ever known.'

'Or heard of,' added Ricardo. 'But you know my

reservations about Anthony, Burr. He enjoys it too much. It's not right.'

'Maybe, but we need someone who can handle the Barrett. Also we have to recon this assault as well as possible. For that, one trained SNOB is minimum. And listen, when it comes to pulling the trigger on a target, it can help to have someone who enjoys it.'

Ricardo nodded. They all knew that one of the biggest problems with sniping is a variant of Hostage Identification Syndrome, otherwise known as Stockholm Syndrome. A sniper may observe his target through the scope for a long time. He watches the doomed man going to the toilet, bathing, laughing, doing ordinary, personal things. He sees his target's humanity and forms a bizarre, one-way intimacy with him. And when the time comes for the sniper to pull the trigger, he can't. Men like Anthony Robinson were selected because they never had this problem. Anthony also had a great advantage in jungle fighting – he was colour-blind. A colour-blind man in the squad gave a different perspective on things. He was also less likely to be distracted by camouflage. This ability was even more important in the semi-darkness of the rain-forest floor or using night sights, where colours were less important to vision than shapes and contrasts of light and dark.

A short while later they had settled on the composition of the team. Argonaut would send Ricardo and a seven-man combat unit, plus Burr as commander and a two-man flight team. Along with

Nicola, Burr was qualified to fly a chopper if required, but for this op he decided to take a second dedicated pilot, Craig Thynne. Craig had not flown for Argonaut before, but he was a former Air Cavalry pilot and highly recommended by Elizabeth.

All told, the planned complement was almost double the size of Daniel's unit, though they would use essentially the same plan. After acclimatization and some minor operations in-theatre, the Argonauts would split into two squads. For about two weeks, Ricardo and one squad would train GemCorp's militia force at their mountain base in Arroyo Blanco. Meanwhile the recon squad under Burr would use a cover of scientific research to work in Madero. They would infiltrate the rebel defences, set up an observation post to gather intelligence, and provide detailed information for the final assault. The squads would join up again for the assault operation itself.

Carlo's approach to the FARA through X-access contacts had already secured clearance for Burr's recon team from the local rebel commander, Javier Diaz. The FARA was currently encouraging civilian visitors to Madero, partly because they, the rebel forces, had been accused by the Colombian government of complicity in the disappearance of Daniel and his 'scientific research' team. Diaz had denied involvement, but the scandal had not reflected well on the rebels and they were keen to show that scientists could work untroubled in FARA's territory.

'So, we're all set,' said Burr.

All the others jumped quickly towards the table and knocked on wood. 'Well, you never know,' Janine pleaded in response to Burr's sceptical expression.

Ricardo chuckled. 'We shouldn't tempt fate, Burr. After all, "No battle plan survives first contact with the enemy".'

'Still on the Bullyisms?' said Burr, smiling. 'This is just a small-force engagement. We're not planning the invasion of Iraq, you know.'

Ricardo always liked to quote the military wisdom drummed into him by the grizzled Staff Sergeant Bullford at Fort Benning Ranger School a long time ago. When Burr passed through Fort Benning some years after Ricardo, Bullford was still there and had belaboured Burr's class with the same old aphorisms.

'You may scoff, Capitan,' said Ricardo gravely, 'but you know old Bully was always right. He saved your skin more than once, though you'd never admit it.'

Burr smiled acknowledgement. In fact he thought Ricardo was righter than he knew. A lot could, and almost certainly would, go wrong in a mission like this. What's more, some aspects of the mission were still making Burr uneasy. He did not wholly trust Elizabeth and Lester, and nobody knew who was responsible for Daniel's disappearance. No battle plan survived first contact with the enemy, true, but with this plan it was worse. This time, Burr wasn't really sure who the enemy was.

Two days later, Carlo saw Burr off at Miami-Dade airport with a hastily assembled team of Argonauts. Carlo was confident that his logistics were perfect and that, following Burr's wishes, costs were pared to the bone. When Daniel had left, his team had travelled with brand-new equipment in a chartered De Havilland Dash-7. Burr and his unit were travelling economy class on a scheduled flight and picking up second-hand gear in Colombia.

Carlo was pleased that the GemCorp contract had been rescued, because he knew the company needed the cash flow. Daniel was good at cutting deals, but he was a spendthrift and had wasted huge amounts on his feng shui redecoration. Carlo was also thanking his lucky stars because he needed the cash flow for his own, embarrassing, personal reasons. Now, while the Argonauts were in transit, he was looking forward to a brief period of calm. He watched their flight take off for Bogotá then headed for the office. He would play some computer games – Carlo played online, seriously, and for money – and try to forget that Janine was going into danger. The fact that Daniel had disappeared made him even more worried for her. But he would never have let Janine go with Daniel. Burr was different. He would keep them out of trouble.

Arriving back at the Argonaut office, Carlo found trouble waiting for him at the end of the pier. It came in the form of a white Rolls-Royce. Rather, the trouble stood beside it. He was a small, burly man with a deeply tanned face and an arrogant look.

He was wearing a white suit, cowboy boots and a broad-brimmed Stetson.

'Mr Maldini, right?' He had an aggressive, no-nonsense air about him which put Carlo on his guard.

'I'm Carlo Maldini,' he replied warily, scanning for the backup. Guys like this never came alone.

Carlo heard a sound behind him and saw two heavies step out from behind the Argonaut building.

'No need to be alarmed,' said the uninvited guest. 'I'm here to ask for your help. My name is William Walls.'

'O . . . K,' said Carlo, carefully. He had heard of William Walls. He was known as a tough, go-get-'em Texas oilman of the old style. And one who had made a few billion dollars here and there. Walls Oil had pioneered new oilfields across the globe. Carlo looked at the ground and his hair flopped across his eyes. 'Uh, nice to meet you, I guess. But none of our management is here. Perhaps you should come back later.'

'Well, I'm here now, ain't I?' said Walls, meaningfully.

Carlo nodded and ushered him into the building and down to the operations room with its undersea view. He offered his guest a drink.

'Bourbon,' said Walls, who waited until he had the drink, then asked, 'Do you know much about my business, Mr Maldini?'

'Not really. I know Walls Oil has oilfields all over the world. Is there something I, or Argonaut, can do for you?'

The oilman lit a large Cuban cigar. Carlo cringed at what Daniel would have thought of the pungent smoke interfering with the office's carefully modulated aromatherapy scent levels. He coughed pointedly.

Walls ignored him. 'You know, Argonaut and my company have a lot in common,' he said. 'Like Argonaut, I made my money where others are too scared to go. I'll produce and sell oil anywhere. Pariah countries and wars are my speciality – Cuba, Angola, Iraq, Colombia. Top risk, top return. No rules and no competition. You know what I mean.'

'Uh-huh,' muttered Carlo, unsure where this was heading. 'Uh, I really think you should be talking to one of our directors . . .'

Walls continued to ignore him, puffing on his cigar. The ash at the end lengthened and Carlo watched a cloud of small flakes float down and settle on the ice-white stone floor.

'So how's the Madero job going?' the Texan enquired suddenly.

'What job?' replied Carlo innocently.

'Don't worry, Mr Maldini. I know all about it. Has Burr Whitman gone this time?'

'Yes.' Carlo wondered how he knew all this.

'I see. Good. And soon he'll be going down to Madero – out of contact?'

Carlo answered impatiently now. 'Going to Madero, yes. Out of contact? Well, we have sat phones and radios. But what's this got to do with anything?'

Walls smiled and dragged deeply on his Cohiba.

There was now a good two inches of ash clinging to the end of the cigar. The oil mogul smiled slowly. 'Mr Maldini, I have a proposition for you. A little bird tells me you might soon be going down to Mexico to try and buy some land. I just want you to do something simple for me while you're there.'

'You mean Xcalan? The development plan is not due to be presented for six weeks. And why should I do anything for you?'

'As for the timing, I have it on very good authority that the process has been brought forward. Why should you help me? Well, there's some money, for a start.'

'Argonaut pays me just fine, thanks.'

'Do they now? I'm sure your girlfriend appreciates your salary, but I see she still has to go and risk her life to earn her keep. You're planning to marry her, I figure. Does she know everything about you, Carlito?'

'What are you talking about?' blurted Carlo, flustered now.

'I mean we're all hiding something. Does she know you lose money betting online? Does she know you use Argonaut income to pay your gambling debts, Carlito?'

Carlo squirmed. Sometimes, when he was making purchases for Argonaut, he used some of the cash to redeem urgent personal debts, most of them built up by his online betting losses. He had even spent some of the GemCorp advance this way. Of course Carlo always intended to pay the business back when GemCorp paid the balance of the fees. 'How do you know?' he asked resignedly.

Walls smiled broadly and tapped the ash from his cigar onto the floor. 'Well, Carlito, I make it my business to know all about my employees. One of Walls Oil remote subsidiaries – one of my hobbies, you might say – is a mining and gem-dealing business. This little concern is called GemCorp.'

With a sinking feeling, it dawned on Carlo why GemCorp had been so keen to hire Burr.

'You may not like me, Carlito, but for sure you'll do what I say.' Walls smiled without warmth and slowly ground his cigar out on Daniel's white lacquer briefing table. 'You see, I'm your biggest client.'

Ethnobotanical Research Centre, Madero

Working at night in the damp heat of the field lab, Leila paused to make a cup of coffee and listened to the silence of the forest. The room was dark, lit only by the small pool of light around her work station. She could feel the unimaginable weight of the vast jungle – the Amazonian jungle, which covered a quarter of the continent. Surely among its millions of species was one that could help somebody? She knew that around their tiny clearing the rainforest reached four thousand miles from the Andes to the Atlantic. The Madero River, whose black waters came off the mountains, flowed past the research station and down to the Rio Negro, which flowed into the Amazon, the mightiest river on the planet, containing one fifth of all the fresh water on earth. The Amazon basin was a phenomenal ecosystem: two and a half million square miles containing untold treasures of plants and animals, with extraordinary and unique adaptations. It was a naturalist's – and a pharmacist's – dream. Or so the theory went.

Many rainforest plants had yielded useful

chemicals – the anti-malarial drug quinine came from the bark of an Amazonian tree; the curare vine produced a poison that helped thin the blood – but although numerous plants had promising compounds few others had yet shown any positive medical benefit. Leila looked out at the blackness of the canopy. So much of the jungle life took place up there. It was a different world. She knew the Jemberí went up there. Maybe some of their secrets were up there too. There's still hope, she thought – if we can keep the forest safe.

Leila went back to preparing voucher specimens, painstakingly laying the plants between sheets of newspaper, then clamping them into the heated drying press. Usually the repetitive, familiar process would take her mind off any worries, but tonight her thoughts turned again to Tupo's mother, Maria. The Jemberí woman was already noticeably sicker with the wasting disease and Leila could see that she was close to surrendering to the encroaching illness. Typically, when they believed they were fatally ill, the Jemberí simply lay down and waited to die. Maria might do this at any moment. Then she could be dead within days. Tupo could sense something was wrong and had become tearful and withdrawn. Leila was determined that Tupo should not become an orphan, but her inability to help was tormenting her.

She worked fiercely at the voucher specimens late into the night. Eventually, she heard the subtle shift of the night sounds that always indicated the dawn: the chirruping of frogs and crickets giving way to the cawing of birds and the rasping calls of monkeys. A rich, pungent scent like tuberose filled the room. She wondered which of the plants it came from. Looking around, she noticed the first faint hints of greyness softening the darkness outside. The light grew rapidly and Leila decided it was time to get some sleep. She stood up and stretched, yawning. As she did so, she glimpsed a movement out of the corner of her eye. Curious, she moved towards it. It seemed to come from near the *kiragi* plant. The thick scent grew stronger and she saw that the *kiragi* had flowered during the night – bright red and yellow flowers with that heavy perfume. Then she saw some yellow butterflies, a palm's width across, fluttering outside the window-pane next to the *kiragi*. And flapping against the inside of the window was another. Leila wondered where it had come from. She opened the window just as the first rays of sun broke over the camp. The butterflies turned and flew away.

Amazon jungle, west of Madero

The density of the undergrowth told Tenoch he was
close to the road. In the *selva* of the Amazon it
was just like the Petén forests of his Mayan homeland – wherever there was a road, or some other
break in the trees, the growth below would thicken
with the increased flow of life-giving sunlight.
Tenoch pushed his way carefully to the edge of the
thicket and looked out at the road, enjoying the play
of the dappled sun on his face. He had left the road
to avoid the last guerrilla checkpoint, and this was
now some miles behind. Through the thin curtain
of leaves he could see the dirt track lying empty,
stretching in a brown ribbon west towards the
Andes and east back towards Madero. There was no
sound of a vehicle.

The old Mayan had mixed feelings about this
latest journey. On the one hand, he was pleased that
this expedition looked like being another success.
Time had passed so quickly. Was it already three
months since the Jemberí, Neman, had met him
outside the mines? Since then he had been

travelling back and forth almost without pause between Bogotá and Madero. So far his purpose had gone undetected. On previous trips he had been stopped both by rebels and by militiamen working for GemCorp, but no one had discovered the precious cargoes he carried.

He was also pleased to be earning a good return for his suppliers – the Jemberí. He was worried, though, that the dollars he was bringing back were not being put to good use. He also worried that the unusual nature of the merchandise might itself be causing problems. It had certainly caused a stir among jewellers in Bogotá. Recently there had been an influx of explorers and emerald hunters into the forest, and troubling rumours of unrest and upheaval. Tenoch hoped his activities were not somehow responsible. His doubts would not deflect him from his work, though. He had made an undertaking and would stick to it. Just a few more trips and then he believed that the Jemberí could help him find what he sought.

He waited for a while; then, turning carefully to scan with his one eye, he looked again up and down the road. It remained silent and empty in both directions. He was sure that away in the distance he could see banks of cloud shrouding the Andes. Up there was the town of Arroyo Blanco, where he would get the bus for Bogotá. He could sell his goods in Arroyo, but GemCorp and the dangerous Bond *autodefensas* were there. He preferred to continue to the capital. There he could strike a better deal. He moved out onto the road and set off on the long, dusty hike towards the mountains.

He had not walked one hundred yards before he heard a rustling in the undergrowth, a sound far too clumsy for a forest animal. Tenoch's throat was suddenly dry.

'*Oye, guacero!*' called a voice from behind him.

Tenoch came to a sudden stop, his heart pounding. He turned round slowly to see a short, plump figure emerge from the trees. It was Comandante Javier Diaz, leader of the FARA guerrillas. Behind him appeared a group of armed men wearing red bandannas. Only now did Tenoch notice the line of vehicles concealed in the jungle. He was bewildered. What was such a large detachment of guerrillas doing outside the cease-fire zone? Tenoch remembered he had heard about a big emerald sale – perhaps they were here for that. Still, he had the awful feeling they had been waiting for him.

The old Mayan glanced up the road towards the suddenly very distant mountains. He could not run on the open road. They would shoot him down. He might have been able to duck into the forest, but the guerrillas were much fitter and younger. And he had seen Diaz's *subcomandante*, Cinco, in the rebel group. People said that Cinco, a dark *mestizo* with Jemberí blood, could track a raindrop in the Madero River. They also said that when he caught his prey he killed it for pleasure. Lurking behind Diaz, Tenoch noticed, was another rebel *subcomandante*, Cuchillo, and a bony figure he knew all too well: the mine security guard, Mr Sticky Fingers. Tenoch was suddenly very frightened. He prepared for the humiliation that was to come and prayed to Itzamna that they would not find his cargo. 'S-Señor Diaz,' he stuttered. '*Buenos días.*'

'*Buenos días*, Maya,' said Diaz in a smooth voice. 'This is a long way from the mines for a *guacero*.' He stroked his well-groomed moustache thoughtfully. 'So what are you stealing?' He looked at Tenoch with eyes like a fer-de-lance. 'What are you stealing, Maya?' he repeated, oozing barely controlled patience. 'We have heard troubling rumours. These rumours say that certain contraband has been appearing in Bogotá. These goods have not passed through our hands and the people have not benefited from them. Perhaps if you showed us what you are stealing, the revolution may be lenient with you.'

'I-I am not stealing anything, Señor Diaz,' stuttered Tenoch. 'I do not steal.'

'Search him,' ordered Diaz.

The rebel leader watched his men strip the Mayan and go through his clothes. They ripped open the seams of his threadbare shirt and pants. They pulled the elastic from the waistband of his underpants. They cut open his cheap plastic shoes and broke off their worn soles. They found nothing. Mr Sticky Fingers grinned and snapped his surgical gloves on. A guerrilla slammed Tenoch between the shoulder-blades with a rifle butt, knocking the Mayan to his knees. Mr Sticky Fingers moved forward with the look of a man who revels in his work. The rebels held Tenoch down and he groaned in shame and agony as the mine guard expertly performed his internal examination.

'*Nada, mi General*,' reported Mr Sticky Fingers, peeling off his gloves. 'Nothing. Shall we keep the Mayan in the cells a few days? If he's swallowed anything, it will come out eventually.'

Diaz squinted quizzically at Tenoch, who was now standing naked on the road, in the grip of two guerrillas. 'No, *compañero*,' he said, a shrewd smile spreading across his face. 'That won't be necessary.'

Diaz stepped forward and smacked Tenoch, hard, on the back of the head. The old man's glass eye popped out of its socket and fell onto the dirt road. The white glass was simply a thin shell. In the now unprotected hollow of Tenoch's eye were squeezed two clear emeralds the size of sugar cubes.

'Hah!' exclaimed Diaz. He jabbed his stubby fingers into the dry eye socket. Tenoch jerked his head back, screwing up his eye, but Diaz persisted, roughly working his fingertips in behind the stones and gouging them out. He played with them in his palm for a moment. Then something odd seemed to strike him. He held the stones up to the light. His eyes widened, then narrowed in suspicion. 'Where did you get these?' he demanded coldly.

Tenoch's head fell forward in despair. Naked and afraid, he said nothing.

Diaz turned to Cuchillo. 'Cuchy, I am going back to Madero. You stay in the forest until nightfall, then go on to the mountains. You meet the buyers from GemCorp tomorrow. Make sure you get at least two hundred thousand dollars US for the consignment. Those paper tigers can afford it. Otherwise, *compañero*, don't bother coming back.' Diaz slipped

110

one of Tenoch's stones to the *subcomandante*. 'And, Cuchy,' he murmured, 'I would be interested to know what they say about this particular stone. And what price they put on it. Anything over fifty thousand, sell it.'

'Very well,' said Cuchillo. He gestured to his men, who moved back to their waiting vehicles.

Diaz's own SUV and another drove out onto the track. Diaz's bodyguards pulled Tenoch on board.

'General, let me work on the *guacero*,' murmured Cinco. 'He will tell me everything.'

Diaz smiled grimly. 'Not now, *compañero*. We will take him back to Madero. Then you can have him. He will tell us where he got these stones, or the people of Madero will have to see justice done.'

PART II

THE SMALL EYES

These, in the day when heaven was falling,
The hour when earth's foundations fled,
Followed their mercenary calling
And took their wages and are dead.

From 'Epitaph on an Army of Mercenaries',
Last Poems
A. E. Housman

Andes mountains, Colombia

There is often a mist on the damp grasslands of the *paramo*, the high, chill plains of the Andes mountains. Through this thin mist, in a stony valley dotted with tufts of bunch grass and sedge, Burr watched the small, grey-green butterfly flutter round the rebel girl's red bandanna. He hoped to God he would not have to kill her.

Burr doubted the girl guerrilla knew that the butterfly was *Catasticta tricolor tomasi*, a rare pierine species endemic to the *paramo*. Burr doubted too that she knew the ancient Greek word for butterfly was *psyche*, or 'soul', but now it occurred to him that for the next few minutes the girl's soul and those of her comrades had a hold on terrestrial existence just as fragile as this delicate creature.

And all because of a few greenish pebbles.

GemCorp and FARA might have been bitter enemies, but market forces meant that they could deal with each other if necessary. However galling it was to GemCorp, if they wanted to corner the emerald market they were obliged to buy the stones the rebels extracted from GemCorp's own mine. In the months since the FARA captured Madero, the rebels had smuggled out the stones in small quantities, hoarding the rest. Now the rebel officer called Cuchillo – 'knife' – had brought out the first major consignment. The Argonaut contract included providing security for such deals. So, on their first day in Colombia, here they were.

Even in the chill sunshine of the Andes, the stones didn't look anything special – a pile of rough, dull green pebbles on the white handkerchief. But they were special enough. They were raw crystals of beryl with traces of chromium giving their distinctive green tint. This made them one of the earth's rarest and most precious materials – emerald.

Between Burr and Cuchillo, Ricardo sat at the unfolded camp table, smiling and humming to himself. Elizabeth would usually have analysed the goods, but Lester had insisted the Argonauts should run the entire operation. Ricardo's knowledge was judged enough to make a rough appraisal and in any case they were only authorized to offer a derisory amount in payment. Ricardo sifted quickly through the pile, ignoring the smallest emeralds. He held the larger stones between his thumb and forefinger and rolled each one swiftly past his jeweller's loupe before weighing them on tiny digital scales, recording the readout and sorting them into different piles.

'What do you think?' asked Cuchillo. He was getting impatient. He preferred dealing in narcotics, which he understood much better. He did not feel comfortable about the FARA's business venture into the world of emeralds. None of the rebels, including Comandante Diaz, knew much about these mysterious stones. Cuchillo felt they exercised an unhealthy influence. There was something cursed about them. Still, for the moment they brought in good money, so he would follow the comandante's orders – up to a point. The truth was that Cuchillo was becoming sorely tempted to exceed his brief.

He scanned the waving grass and reeds along the valley sides, finger on the trigger of his AK-47 assault rifle. They were at the edge of the demilitarized trucial zone here. The Colombian military ran helicopter patrols over these mountains – search-and-destroy missions aimed at *narco-traficantes* and unwary rebels. Today, in the open, he had twenty heavily armed fighters in four vehicles, including one pick-up mounted with a priceless .50-calibre heavy machine-gun. The vehicles had no cover on these treeless slopes and he could feel his soldiers' uneasiness.

Burr could feel it too. Even in this cold, the rebels' faces were dripping with perspiration. He saw the *tricolor* fluttering even closer to the young girl now, probably attracted by the salty tang of her sweat. She waved the butterfly away in nervous irritation.

Cuchillo was glad of his superior force – the GemCorp team was only four – and it had given him an idea. Waiting in the damp mist while the capitalists examined the merchandise, he came to believe he could take the money and still keep the stones. It was an opportunity not to be missed. Comandante Diaz would honour him as a hero of the revolution.

Down the valley, two figures could be seen sitting in the SUV they said contained the money. The guerrilla on the .50 could probably take them out from here. Of the two men in front of the rebel officer, the gemmologist looked harmless enough, with greying hair and a dark complexion. He wore spectacles and appeared to carry no weapon.

The second man, seemingly the bodyguard, was different. He was tall and lean, his hair a dark blond, his eyes concealed behind dark glasses. He had a scarf pulled up over his mouth like the guerrillas and his hands were hidden deep in the pockets of his coat against the biting wind. On his hip he openly wore a holstered automatic pistol. Idiot, thought Cuchillo. He will never get a chance to draw it.

'So what you think, Yankee?' Cuchillo demanded again.

Ricardo took his time, carefully looking at each emerald. '*En realidad, soy Cubano-Americano,*' he replied, without looking up. Then he said in English, 'I'm Cuban-American, but Yankee's fine.' He put down the eye glass. In front of him on the table were four shimmering piles of stones. 'As for the merchandise,' he said, 'not bad. A few hundred carats of clean green mêlée; a similar amount of stones half a carat to a carat; about four hundred carats of stones between one and two carats.' Ricardo knotted a handkerchief round the final pile.

'And about fifty stones of more than two carats. Some of them quite pure – the green is a bit light – but clear with few blemishes. Reasonable quality.' He paused, holding up one more stone. 'And then there is this.' Ricardo looked perplexed. 'I am really not sure how to judge this. It appears to be a very fine gemstone indeed. It is different from the others. Where did you get it?'

Cuchillo saw it was the large emerald Diaz had taken from Tenoch and given to him. He snatched it away and put it in his pocket. 'The price!' he snapped.

'All told, we will pay one hundred thousand US.'

'And the last stone? I say that is alone one hundred thousand!'

Ricardo shrugged. 'It's rare, sure. Set in a diamond and twenty-four-carat gold pendant by Tiffany it could be worth twice that. But, we're not on Fifth Avenue.'

This irritated Cuchillo, but then he remembered that he was not planning to sell the stones anyway. And now he had justification for his double-cross. Predictably, the capitalists were trying to cheat him. Their greed would be their downfall yet again. Soon he would have the pleasure of killing this humming gemmologist and his strangely unsettling companion.

'We are changing the deal,' he said, lowering his AK-47 to point directly at Ricardo. Behind their commander, his companions did the same. 'You will give us the money, but we will keep the stones. Tell your friends in the car to bring up the *plata*.'

The rebels were surprised at what Ricardo did next.

He began to sing.

In the thin-aired silence of the mountains, Ricardo began to hum the lilting melody 'Guantanamera'.

For a short while, nobody moved. Then the second American slowly removed his dark glasses, revealing piercing blue eyes.

Burr rubbed his glasses deliberately on the corner of his coat. He looked Cuchillo directly in the eye. 'Change your mind,' he said carefully. 'GemCorp will pay you two hundred thousand dollars for the stones, no questions asked. We all walk away.'

The guerrilla officer hesitated. Two hundred thousand would fulfil his orders. No, he thought, he had made his decision. And anyway, how could they bargain? It was going to be so easy to take everything. 'Just bring us the money,' he said, shaking his head in disbelief. The Cuban *Yanqui* was actually singing! The Americans were often said to be cowards, but they were not. They were just imbeciles.

Burr shrugged. He replaced his dark glasses and said, 'I'm afraid we can't do that.'

Cuchillo shouted to the gunner on the .50-calibre. The man nodded, swung his long-barrelled weapon round and opened fire at the SUV. Instinctively, for just a millisecond, the eyes of the guerrillas were drawn to the vehicle. In that fraction of an instant, things happened suddenly and with extreme violence.

Simultaneous with, or perhaps immediately pre-ceded by, a large, red hole in his forehead, a surprised look appeared on Cuchillo's face. This was followed by the sharp crack of a rifle. Before Cuchillo's body hit the ground, a gaping tear appeared in Burr's coat, ripped open by the bullets from the machine pistol beneath it. While that burst was killing three fighters, the gunman next to Cuchillo was knocked down by a second shot from the unseen rifle. At the same time, the vehicle with the .50-calibre exploded, a hidden machinegun raked the bandits and Ricardo the harmless-looking gemmologist shot the two rebels to his left with a stream of fire from a compact sub-machinegun.

Within seconds, all but two of the guerrillas were hit. The remaining two threw away their weapons and had begun to raise their hands when a final burst of fire cut them down. The echoes of the shots were still dying over the bare mountains as Burr pulled up the microphone hidden in his collar. 'Burr all clear,' he said mechanically. 'Argonaut status and regroup on me.'

'Ricardo clear, Captain,' said Ricardo, picking himself up off the damp grass. He looked at Burr, then back at the carnage, and swore to himself again that this would be his very last operation. Then along with Burr he set to triaging Cuchillo and his men for treatable wounded. 'Anthony clear,' a voice crackled in their hidden earpieces, then 'Janine clear' and the others, one by one. From what appeared to be open, empty slopes, seven figures appeared. They wore combat dress camouflaged like scarecrows with *paramo* moss and grasses.

As they began to pick their way down across the scree towards the valley floor, the small *Catasticta* landed tentatively on the guerrilla girl's red bandanna, now stained darker red with blood. The butterfly unfurled its proboscis and began prodding the crimson bloom for nutrients.

The GemCorp SUV bumped up the valley over scattered boulders and hummocks of bunch grass, and jolted to a halt by Cuchillo's body. Lester jumped out, his feet sinking into the spongy turf. He looked around with sour satisfaction at the slaughter. Elizabeth got out more slowly and took a nervous breath of the mixed odours – burning vehicle, gunfire and fresh blood.

She turned to Ricardo, still kneeling by the body of a young rebel he had failed to save. 'Hey, Ricardo,' she said, as casually as she could. 'Hey, Burr. Nice work – except you let the machinegunner open up on us. Are you trying to get rid of me?'

'Yeah, that was sloppy,' added Lester. He had felt the deal would go bad and had been pleased to see his prediction come true. But he had banked on at least one Argonaut casualty. He and Liz were also disappointed that Javier Diaz had not been leading the rebel sales team as promised. It would have been great to have taken him out. Still, this wasn't a bad haul, he thought, looking at the mangled bodies. 'You just took 'em down, eh?' he said to Burr. 'You're not such a nice guy after all.'

Burr looked at him blankly. 'Their choice. They had a chance to take the deal. We made them a decent offer.'

'Yes, two hundred thousand!' Lester snorted loudly. 'I clearly heard Ricardo offer them one hundred thousand dollars. Then you offered two! Just remember that here in Colombia we don't like giving money to Communist *terroristas*. And, by the way, nor do your X-access friends in the CIA.'

Burr turned to Elizabeth. 'How much did GemCorp budget for this deal? Four hundred thousand? Five?'

'Even two hundred thousand was a bargain for you,' Ricardo broke in. 'My guess is this is a million dollars' worth of stones. Face it, if GemCorp wants to vacuum up every emerald on the planet, sometimes you're going to have to pay.' He handed Elizabeth the knotted handkerchiefs. 'Some mêlée chips and small stones,' he said, 'and, in here, about two hundred and fifty carats of larger stones – mostly medium inclusions and impurities. It's all normal Madero quality: average colour, tending towards a lighter sea-green. Nothing special. Well, except that Cuchillo had a stone I didn't know how to value. He took it back.'

Lester bent down by Cuchillo's corpse and began to rifle his pockets. Elizabeth untied the handkerchiefs to reveal the emeralds. 'Mmmmmm,' she said, weighing the handkerchiefs in her hand. She righted Ricardo's camp stool and table and sat down. '*Qué bien!*' she exclaimed as she pulled out her own 10× loupe eyeglass and began to examine the stones. Lester finished with Cuchillo's body, then moved round the scene of the massacre, bending for a few moments over each guerrilla in turn. He appeared to be collecting their bandannas.

Burr said nothing more until the whole team was within earshot. Paul Hill ran up to Burr first. 'Wounded?' he enquired simply. Burr pointed at the rebels who had survived the firefight and Paul hurried across to treat them. The rest of the Argonauts gathered round Burr expectantly. The wind eddied for a moment and black smoke from the burning vehicle swept over them.

'Well,' Burr began eventually, 'anybody got anything to say?'

'Damn good job,' said Pike, a short, unkempt man. 'Anthony took out their main dude with a beauty. Right on the button.'

Nobody seconded his enthusiasm. Burr turned towards him, stony-faced. 'Anybody got anything to say to Pike?'

'I have,' said David Cohen, as Burr knew he would. David was a slightly-built bald man, wiry and hyperactive. Despite being laden with spare machinegun barrels and belts of ammunition, he seemed to be jittering in almost perpetual motion. 'Why did you shoot them, Pike?'

'Shoot who?' replied Pike, lighting a cigarette.

'You know exactly who,' said Ahmad Masri, the stolid, bulky Palestinian. He was carrying the M240 medium machinegun.

'Yes,' added Janine. 'Those last two were trying to surrender.'

Beside Janine, the big Swede, Sven Peterson, nodded in agreement. He looked white with shock.

'They were?' said Pike. 'Oh heck, that's a shame. It was misty. Through the scope I thought they were going for grenades – to blow themselves up – and Burr into the bargain. I, ah . . . I had to drop them.'

Burr shook his head in disgust and turned away. Anthony Robinson, a lanky black man with a Barrett sniper rifle, just spat into the dirt.

'OK,' said Ricardo. 'Listen up! Pike, one of the men you shot is still alive. You go get bloody helping Paul with him and the other casualties. Sven, you and Ahmad bring the bodies together over here. David, you take photos and search them for intel. Janine, call in Nicola for extraction, then check the vehicles. Anthony, you move up the slope and keep your eyes open.'

Burr walked a little way off through the reeds and long grass. The team had functioned efficiently, responding to the circumstance in the textbook Special Forces manner, with speed, surprise and extreme violence. But Burr felt numbed. And it got worse. Paul walked up beside Burr. 'They're all dead,' Paul said grimly. He was wheezing slightly, out of breath in the oxygen-poor air.

'Check again,' said Burr. 'At least two were still breathing. Wounds didn't look fatal.'

'Well, they're not breathing any more.'

'I see.' Burr looked over at Lester, who was talking in an animated fashion to Elizabeth, and wondered exactly what he had done to the guerrillas as he collected his handful of bloodstained trophies. Perhaps he had made sure to twist the bandannas around the rebels' necks, just in case.

Burr thought of something Anthony had said. It was just moments after Lester had greeted the Argonauts on arrival in Colombia. Throughout the trip down from Miami, Anthony had hardly uttered a word. Then, as soon as he had shaken hands with Lester and the crab tattoo, he had sauntered over to Burr. The taciturn sniper had stood silent for a moment before sucking his teeth to indicate concern.

Burr had raised his eyebrows questioningly.

'That Lester is a stone killer, Cap'n,' Anthony had said in his deep Georgia drawl. 'You trust him, we're all crab meat.'

Burr had then recalled where he had seen Lester's eyes before. They were the eyes of a man he had captured years back in Iraq. A psychopath and assassin.

'Burr?' Paul said.

Burr came out of his reverie to hear the dual rotors of the Argonaut's transport approaching over the ridge. The Chinook helicopter clattered overhead. In the wash from the rotors the mist fled and the long *paramo* grass was blown flat. The hair and clothes of the dead guerrillas flapped in the gale, then settled as the chopper flared and sank slowly to the ground. Burr and Paul moved over to join the team piling layers of stones over the bodies of Cuchillo and his men. Soon there would simply be another cairn among the rocks and sedge.

Just before they began to cover the pile, Lester shouted: 'Wait!' He picked up Janine's M4 and called out to David, who was carrying the digital camera. 'Hey, take a couple of me.'

Behind them, Pike began to blow up the rebel vehicles one by one. With a backdrop of the white-capped Andes and flaming trucks, Lester pulled on a black hood, with holes cut for his eyes and mouth, and rolled up his right sleeve to reveal the crab tattoo. Then he put on a white scarf with the black emblem '07' and climbed up onto the mound of corpses. Rifle in one hand, blood-stained bandannas in the other, his wide, white grin filling the mouth hole of his mask, El Cangrejo struck a triumphant pose.

A few minutes into the flight through the mountain passes, Nicola let Craig take the controls again. On the trip down from Bogotá she had observed him carefully from the pilot's seat. Overall, she was impressed. He was clearly a sound pilot and he handled the bulky twin-engined MH-47 Chinook with precision and confidence, weaving the unwieldy craft smoothly through the deep chasms between the peaks. He was also nice, maybe even good-looking – if you liked them short, brown-haired and clean-cut. Craig looked over at her and she smiled her approval, feeling only a tiny bit phoney. There was an indefinable something about her co-pilot that Nicola didn't like, an aspect she felt rather than saw. It wasn't just that his eyes were too close together or something. She hadn't told Burr about her doubts, though – it wouldn't have been fair – and she wouldn't say anything unless she could come up with a concrete concern. Right now, the flight was in good hands. The cockpit was heated and she could relax. Nicola never moved without her comfort blanket, the latest iPod portable stereo. She plugged it via her modified iTrip into the internal comms system and, with some easy listening coming through the headphones, settled back to enjoy the stupendous view.

Back in the draughty, rattling passenger cabin of the Chinook, Burr was thinking about the mission, and about his Argonauts. The unit had been thrown together hastily and had an uneven mixture of personnel, but the brief events of the day suggested that they were an effective fighting unit. Burr still had some lingering concerns about three or four of them.

One of those was Anthony. Like Burr he was from the deep south of the USA – from Georgia, though from the other end of the social spectrum. Anthony was from a black family of sharecroppers, descendants of slaves brought by southern cotton dynasties like the Whitmans from a small island emporium in the Bight of Benin. Silent as ever, he was sitting at the rear of the cabin, on the end of the bench that ran along the side of the fuselage. Oblivious to the racket, and the quivering airframe, he appeared to be fast asleep. Anthony might be the best SNOB Delta Force had ever produced, but as Paul had pointed out he had long been a recovering alcoholic. And now it appeared he had fallen off the wagon in a serious way. Burr had noticed Anthony's hand quivering in the interview. Ricardo said it was delirium tremens and recommended dropping him then and there. Argonaut's policy in-theatre was the 'toucan' rule: no more than two cans of beer a day. 'Anthony will think that means jerry cans,' Paul had warned.

Anthony admitted that he had started having a drink now and then, but insisted, in his taciturn way, that he could stay off the juice, and that his work was not affected. Burr had asked him to prove it, so they had gone down to a rifle range. Burr hadn't been surprised to see Anthony pick up a Barrett he had never handled before and put five rounds rapid through the bull's-eye at 800 yards. After the shot that killed Cuchillo, even Paul decided to forget his doubts.

Burr had never doubted Paul. He had acted in his usual exemplary manner on the *paramo*. The extra pounds he had gained in Vegas had already started to slough off him. Also, however bushed he was, Paul always managed to have breath for his harmonica; and, whatever the kit load, he found room for it in his webbing.

What with Ricardo singing his Latin ballads, Paul on the mouth organ and the literally thousands of songs on Nicola's pet iPod, Burr was pleased that the unit always had music of one kind or another. In fact music had brought the first moment when Burr realized they might just be getting a team together. Fuelling up at Bogotá before the flight down to the *paramo*, the Argonauts had been waiting nervously around the Chinook. Typically, it was Ricardo who had known how to ease the tension. He had talked to Paul, then winked at Burr. Paul started on the harmonica, followed first by Ricardo's voice and then a few moments later the Argonauts – even Anthony – were joining them in singing 'Guantanamera'. Nicola, always an early adopter of new gadgets, brought out the latest mini digital video and filmed the scene. Everybody was smiling, arms around one another. It would have augured well – if Burr had believed in auguries.

There were still the three men Burr hadn't worked with before. The second pilot, Craig Thynne, was a veteran, an ex-Air Cav fly boy who came recommended by GemCorp. He seemed quiet and competent. Nicola had given the thumbs-up to his flying skills, and that was enough for Burr.

The mortar specialist was a big, fresh-faced Swede named Sven Peterson. In theory he was another Tier 1 recruit, claiming to be from his country's Special Forces, specifically a *Fallskärms-jägare*, an Airborne Ranger. In a way Burr supposed was typically Swedish, Sven appeared oblivious to the freezing air. His massive bodybuilder's frame was stretched out in a deep sleep just across the cabin from Burr, who could hear his snoring even over the clatter of the rotors. The Swede was young for mercenary work and Burr had not been keen to accept him at first. He did not appear to be the brightest Special Forces soldier Burr had ever known, but he was obedient, conscientious, and his English was good. 'Will, courage, endurance', he had proudly told Burr, was the Airborne Rangers' motto, and Burr was prepared to give him the benefit of the doubt.

But those doubts were still there. Burr was not convinced Sven had performed very well in the fire-fight on the *paramo* – in fact, it was not clear whether he had even fired his weapon. Still, Burr had a feeling he would deliver in the clutch. The big Swede was also formidably strong, hefting the 60-mm mortar as if it were a toy.

Craig and Sven might have been acceptable, but Burr was on the verge of dumping the third first-time Argonaut, Billy Pike. Even before Pike had gunned down the two surrendering rebels, Burr had been deeply unconvinced about their explosives specialist. A sour-looking former Marine with a greying, scruffy beard, Pike had not endeared himself to his new commander by sniggering when Burr had introduced himself on a sultry Miami day.

'Did you say "brrr"?' he had quipped. 'What, you're cold on a day like this?'

Pike was physically unattractive and he was also very short. This lack of stature was clearly a trial for him – just one of many blights that appeared to weigh on him bitterly. It had taken David Cohen precisely ten minutes to publicly point out what everyone had immediately noticed for themselves – that Pike's boots were built up inside secretly to make him look taller. He was mortified, but he met with little sympathy. He was just one of those people who rubbed you up the wrong way. And on top of it all, he smelt bad – a mixture of stale cigarettes and acrid body odour. In any enclosed space, Burr had quickly learned to sit as far away from him as possible. The others followed suit and, inevitably, Pike would find himself sitting next to the other rookie, Sven, who had no choice, or Anthony, who did not appear to care.

Unfortunately, Pike was the only explosives operator Carlo could find at short notice. On the *paramo* he had impressed with his shooting, if nothing else, and although Pike's smoking was a somewhat risky vice for an explosives man, Burr had to admit he seemed to be obsessed with his job. He always appeared to carry an array of improvised detonators and bomb devices. 'You never know when you might want a few fireworks,' he would say. It was just enough to convince Burr to sign him up.

All in all, there were the makings of an effective outfit. Janine could lead a squad if necessary, and with Paul, David, Ahmad and, of course, Ricardo, there was plenty of experience.

There in the cold, quivering cabin, looking at his men, Burr suddenly felt the crushing weight of his responsibility. They had put their trust in him and their lives in his hands. They were going into the unknown, to fight for people they did not care about, perhaps to kill an enemy they did not hate. It was easier in the army. There it was for country and duty, and in any case you were all just following orders. Here everybody had weighed up the risk and the reward. And he knew that many of his team would follow nobody else on a mission like this.

Many of them were here only because they trusted him.

Burr looked at Ricardo halfway down the cabin. His hair was thinning and his face looked deeply lined. He had put on reading glasses and was going over his militia training plan for the hundredth time. Burr smiled. His friend was by nature a worrier, and he had become obsessive in his old age. He was still the best man to run a unit, though, better than any commissioned officer Burr had known, including himself. He thought back to Ricardo at the final briefing in the underwater Argonaut operations room. As usual, after a brief introduction, Burr had allowed Ricardo to do most of the talking. Behind Ricardo was the unusual backdrop of a hefty grouper idly nosing up against the glass. 'Very "yu",' Carlo had commented.

'All right, everybody,' Ricardo had said. 'I'm Sergeant Ricardo Martinez. Now, Captain Whitman – Burr – may be in command of this outfit, but remember: I'm in charge. Most of you have served with us before in a private capacity, so you know the score. Some of you haven't, so listen good. As Argonauts we have no marks of rank or other insignia. We will have name tags on our uniforms. That's all. There will be no saluting, whether under-cover in civilian dress, or in combat. In fact there will be no army drill at all, with two exceptions: one – in theatre, you will obey orders without question; two – you will at all times maintain equipment in top working order.

'There are three other points to observe. One –

you will not break the laws of any country you are in – here or in theatre.'

'Except killing people, of course,' muttered someone – David, inevitably.

Ricardo didn't miss a beat. 'As a matter of fact we have top-level clearance for that, Cohen, but thanks for your contribution anyway.'

'Two – we do not discuss the mission with anybody. Three – read your contracts. They lay out all the conditions in detail. Breach any of these rules or the other terms in the small print and your contract will be terminated immediately. You lose any rights to insurance or payment and you will be on the first plane home. Worse, you break any of these rules, you or one of your colleagues relying on you will probably end up dead.' He handed out the contracts to the team. 'Sign and hand them in to Carlo at the back before you leave this room. You don't sign, you don't come. And remember, you can change your mind now, no problem. We're not offering a pleasure cruise. You want to bang Colombian *chicas*, it's better to go down to South Beach. You want to drink Club Colombia and watch the sunset, I advise you to take a cab down to the Bar Medellin in Coral Gables and get a lounger. You want to experience the rainforest, take the Florida turnpike north to the Epcot Center. This is not a corporate security breeze. This is not a UN peace-keeping detail. This is a combat mission. And there *will be* casualties.'

He paused for a long moment, looking at each man in turn. 'You all know your jobs. You are experts in your profession. We do things right, the casualties are more likely to be with the bad guys and we will all be back on Miami Beach in a few weeks.'

Now they were hurtling through valleys of ice and stone, over a landscape blank and desolate as the moon. The high-altitude air was freezing in the shadow of the Andes. The warmth of Miami was a world away and Burr knew, as they all did, that some of them might never see the Beach again.

The Chinook sped through the mountains, sixty-foot rotors straining in the thin air, gaining purchase as they descended over a glacier, down through the fog towards the town of Arroyo Blanco. The mighty cordillera of the Andes now towered behind them to the west, the snow-capped peaks still golden in the sun. The town was huddled on the edge of the *paramo*, perched on cliffs that dropped to the forest. And there below was the Argonauts' first glimpse of *la selva* – the great Amazon jungle, a bright green carpet that stretched away to the eastern horizon.

Arroyo Blanco, Andes mountains

The airfield at Arroyo Blanco was a mown strip on the *paramo* with a threadbare windsock and one ramshackle hut. A group of Bond militiamen were waiting there for the Argonauts. After giving Lester a desultory salute, the Bond made no move to help the Argonauts unload, but stood around, eyeing them suspiciously. A mean-looking bunch of ruffians, the paramilitaries wore a chaotic medley of civilian clothes and Colombian army-issue fatigues, often criss-crossed with bandoliers of ammo. The only uniform item appeared to be the white bandanna marked, like Lester's, with the black '07'.

'If this is our side,' Ricardo murmured to Burr, 'I'd hate to meet the bad guys.'

'Please, Lester, what does the number mean?' Sven enquired in his heavily accented singsong English.

'That is why they call us the Bond,' Lester explained proudly. 'Zero-seven.'

Sven looked at him blankly.

'You know – *zero-siete*, zero-seven, licence to kill.'

'Charming allies to have,' remarked Janine.

'I do not understand,' said Sven.

'Strictly shouldn't it be oh-seven?' asked Nicola.

'It is oh-oh-seven, for Chrissakes,' Elizabeth said. 'You know – James Bond.'

Lester nodded proudly. 'That's right. And remember, these boys may not look pretty, but they deserve the name. Many of us have lost family members to the FARA. We are licensed to kill and that's what we do. We kill communists.'

The GemCorp compound was on the windswept *paramo* near Arroyo Blanco, set amid straggling coffee plantations. The Argonauts bunked down in a vacant barracks looking out over the seemingly endless forest. The next morning they set to work with the militia. Nicola and Craig began working with the helicopters and their crews. All four choppers – two Bell UH-1 Hueys and two much newer UH-60 Black Hawks – seemed to be in working order and were heavily armed with recent US-made weaponry, including rockets and awesome Gatling guns, capable of firing four thousand rounds per minute.

'Good to see that the US tax dollar is showing a trickle-down effect,' commented Ricardo.

Burr suspected Ricardo was right and that the armaments had come from the Colombian military courtesy of the United States' Plan Colombia – the programme of support against rebels and drug traffickers. Luckily for private military companies, the Plan Colombia provided billions of tax dollars in financial and military aid, while at the same time restricting the number of official US military personnel who could be committed in Colombia. This led to a strong demand for unofficial personnel – like Argonaut. So, in effect, US taxpayers were underwriting mercenary operations in a neat public–private partnership.

From the relative warmth of the base's main building, Burr and Lester watched the initial training session get underway. On the dusty parade ground, Paul started by removing the weapons from the truculent infantry and trying out some basic drill. In the chill air of the early morning, some two hundred *milicianos* had turned up dishevelled, late and grouchy. Their drill was a complete shambles.

'See what I mean,' Elizabeth said pointedly.

'They're not always that bad,' muttered a red-faced Lester. 'They've just gone soft again since Daniel went.'

With considerable amusement, Burr watched Paul and Ricardo bellowing at the militiamen in the misty cold and savoured his hot cup of the local coffee, fresh from the tree. Some people rated the high-grown Colombian arabica as the best in the world. For Burr it was one of the few compensations for working in the country. Unfortunately, coffee had been largely supplanted as a cash crop by the far more lucrative coca. Burr didn't have the same liking for cocaine – though chewing coca could be useful on a Special Forces mission, providing great amounts of stamina. 'This is what Daniel did for you?' Burr shook his head sadly at the rabble.

'I would back my boys against those rebels,'

declared Lester defiantly. 'This parade-ground stuff is garbage. These guys know how to fight in the forest. The rebels hear them coming, they shit themselves.'

'Point is,' said Burr, 'not to let people hear you coming.'

'*Qué vergüenza!* They are a disgrace,' said Ricardo, coming in out of the cold and gratefully wrapping his hands round a cup of coffee. 'Undisciplined rabble. So far I would not back them against a team of Boy Scouts.'

'Ah, *si*? What about those guys?' Lester pointed at a unit that came jogging round the corner. There were about fifty men moving in good time, all in identical combat uniforms, sporting brand-new weapons. 'My Jaguars,' said Lester, proudly. 'With Daniel we turned them into elite commandos.'

Ricardo peered sceptically at the Jaguar platoon through the grimy window. It did look as though he might have something to work with after all. He turned to Lester with a thoroughly unimpressed expression. 'They're late,' he said.

That night Elizabeth invited Burr to her cabin. 'How about we take up where we left off at your place?' she asked, moving close and running her hand down the front of his combat fatigues.

'I don't think this is a good idea,' Burr said. 'It's tricky . . . especially as Lester is so obsessed with you.'

'Don't worry,' she whispered, pressing herself against him. 'Lester's bedded down with his militia thugs. He won't know a thing.'

In the chill mountain air, Burr felt the heat of her flesh through his shirt. He took her arms and pushed her gently but firmly away. 'I'm sorry, Elizabeth, but, as I told you, I'm not sure I should be doing this with a client.'

Her eyes narrowed and she pulled away with a light laugh. 'Well, don't worry,' she retorted breezily: 'I'm not sure I should be doing it with the help.'

'Listen, it's not that I don't want . . .'

'Don't be silly,' she said. 'Not another word. It's fine. Forget it.'

Burr cursed to himself as he left her room. This was a complication he could have done without. He wanted her, but he felt a coldness behind her warm words and body, a ruthlessness that made him draw back. Truth was, after what he had seen on the *paramo* he could not bring himself to touch her. He was pretty sure that Lester had killed the surviving guerrillas in cold blood. And he was equally sure that Lester had been doing what Elizabeth told him.

As he walked out of her cabin, deep in thought, Burr did not see Lester watching with a malevolent look from across the parade ground.

To Burr's relief, the complication of Elizabeth and Lester departed for Bogotá early the next morning. The Argonauts settled in for a couple of days' training in Arroyo Blanco before the forward recon team split off and left for Madero. Four Argonauts would then remain at the Arroyo base: Nicola and Craig to

140

continue with the Bond helicopter crews, Ricardo and Paul to train the militia infantry.

Things went smoothly until the night when Burr was approached by a highly agitated Ricardo, who was tapping his wristwatch. Burr looked at his own watch. The time was ten past ten. The nightly curfew for the Argonauts was ten p.m.

'Anthony,' Ricardo said, with a told-you-so air, 'and Pike.' He was clearly outraged at the breach of professionalism, which he felt reflected on him personally. He always maintained it was the small things that mattered – keeping your rifle clean, checking your webbing before a mission, and, above all, being punctual.

Burr was more easygoing. 'Stop fussing, Ricardo. This isn't the army. Let's give them a while.'

By midnight, he had changed his mind. 'Where the hell are they?' Burr asked the remaining Argonauts. None of the team wanted to venture the information straight out, but various murmurs suggested that the missing duo might have, possibly, maybe, gone into town. Burr's heart sank. It appeared some of the team were determined to justify his doubts. He calmed Ricardo down, then rustled up a sleepy Bond *miliciano* to give him a ride. They drove across the dark, empty *paramo* into the run-down centre of Arroyo and pulled up outside a building that carried the name El Verde on a rotting sign.

'How do you know they'll be here?' asked Burr.

The driver shrugged wearily. 'Everybody in Arroyo is here for El Verde.'

Just then the door swung open and a drunken Indian staggered out into the night and collapsed onto the roadside. 'Yup,' said Burr, 'this sure looks like the place.'

The El Verde was in a faded mansion from the nineteenth-century Amazon rubber boom when towns like Iquitos and Arroyo fancied themselves as rivals even to Paris and Vienna. Now the building's wooden boards were grimy and rotting, the fine wrought-iron balconies were rusting, but the saloon was the centre of Arroyo social life. Even in the small hours, the bar was still populated: some heavyset *mestizo* whores who had not found partners, a poker-game in the corner and, propped up on the bar counter, a seriously inebriated Pike. Salsa leaked from some crackling speakers and Pike was babbling disjointedly to a group of doubtful-looking barflies, into which the little demolitions man blended disturbingly well. Anthony was sitting on a stool next to him, so drunk he appeared to be moving in slow motion. So much for the toucan rule, thought Burr.

'Hey, Burr,' Pike called over. 'Come and have a drink with us.' He pointed at a particularly shifty-looking individual in shabby clothes. 'Chacal here is a, a . . .'

'A businessman,' said Chacal slyly. He poured Burr a glass of *aguardiente*, the fiery Andean spirit.

'Yes,' Pike went on. 'And he was just telling us about Madero.'

'Hello,' said Burr. 'I'm Burr.'

'Burr? Like *borracho*? You're *borracho*, too? Drunk

142

like your friend.' Burr gave his standard, patient smile as Chacal went on. 'Señor Pike was just about to tell me what you are doing here.'

'Sciensch,' slurred Pike, now noticeably swaying.

'Scientists?' Chacal raised his eyebrows. 'You do not look like scientists.'

Pike winked grotesquely. 'Oh, but we are. We're headed for Madero.'

Chacal looked thoughtful. 'Madero, you say?'

'*Si*, señor,' said Burr, intervening. 'We're on a scientific research project for Argonaut Ecology.'

'*Claro, claro.* Of course. It's just that there were some of you scientists here a while ago. They went down to Madero. One of them was a big man with red hair . . .' Chacal darted a shrewd look at Burr '. . . and I never thought they were scientists.'

'Oh yes?' said Burr. 'What were they?'

Chacal pursed thin lips. 'They were what all men who go to Madero are – fortune hunters.'

'Hey, he's right, you know,' said Pike excitedly. 'It's, like, we make our fortune and it's the rebels' *mis*fortune. Ha, ha, ha, ha!'

'*Ah, si?*' said Chacal, leaning forward eagerly. 'Tell me more.'

Pike drew breath to respond, but Burr stepped in between him and Chacal.

Behind Burr's back, Anthony snapped out of his stupor. Swift as a snake, he clapped a hand over Pike's mouth. 'Are you insane, new boy?' Anthony hissed. 'Talk about the job like that, you could get us all killed. Do that again and I'll kill you myself. Unnerstan'?'

Wide-eyed with shock, a suddenly sober Pike nodded slowly.

'Apologies for my friend Pike,' Burr said to Chacal. 'I guess he's a little drunk. So what kind of business did you say you are in?'

'What kind of research are you in?' enquired Chacal, trying to peer round Burr.

'Butterflies,' said Burr.

'Butterflies, eh? OK, I see.' He looked around theatrically, then leaned towards Burr, saying in a conspiratorial whisper, 'Me, I'm in stones. There are many people trying to smuggle the uncut emeralds out of Madero – even more these days with all the rumours about El Verde. I am a dealer, a *plantero*. I buy the emeralds here and sell for a big profit in Bogotá.' He took a gulp of his *aguardiente*. 'But now you've got El Cangrejo and his filthy Bond *milicianos* working for GemCorp. They make it hard to do business here. They don't want any stones getting out.' He looked meaningfully at Burr and slugged back the rest of his drink with a grimace. 'You don't want GemCorp to catch you with an emerald. No, I'm going back to Bogotá.'

He stood up, wiping his mouth, and handed Burr a soiled, dog-eared business card. 'Now, if you scientists come across any little green "butterflies",' he said with a knowing wink, 'and you think they might be worth something, you come to me. Nobody knows more about the little greens than the great Chacal.'

The emerald dealer left the bar. Burr looked down at his card. It said simply El Chacal, *Hombre de*

Negocios, with the minimal address Calle del Cartucho, Bogotá. Burr smiled. If that was the address, Chacal was definitely a man he could work with. Then he fixed his face into the stern look of an angry Captain Burr and turned to deal with Pike and Anthony.

Government offices, Bogotá, Colombia

Hernando Ayala, Minister without Portfolio in the Government of Colombia, looked out from his office at the grand public buildings of the Plaza Bolívar and north across the sprawling city of Bogotá.

'And so, Minister, we then arranged to meet the communists on the *paramo* . . .' Behind him the GemCorp woman, Elizabeth, was giving her report. The news was quite pleasing. With their American mercenaries, GemCorp had encountered and defeated a rebel group outside the trucial zone, and had recovered a consignment of illegally mined emeralds.

He tried to listen to Elizabeth while shutting out the sounds of her companion, the vulgar Bond militiaman Lester, who was picking his teeth loudly. Despite this latest success, Ayala was regretting, not for the first time, that he had ever started working with these people. He had made many compromises and sacrifices for the sake of his country and his family, but colluding with the Bond was perhaps the most trying.

He was proud of his heritage. His ancestor had been at Gonzolo de Quesada's side when he founded Bogotá back in 1538. Half a millennium later, the minister's home town was a vibrant modern capital where the colonial mansions of the Candelaria mixed with futuristic architecture in the Centro Internacional. The city was dramatically situated against the wall of a high plateau that dwarfed the high-rise hotels and office blocks of the central business district. It was an economic hub and a cosmopolitan city of culture, with art, literature, music and one of the world's greatest treasure troves in the magnificent Museo del Oro.

Of course there were also things he was not proud of. Bogotá was still an extremely violent city, a place where you could be killed by a child assassin for ten dollars. Your body would turn up in the loathsome Calle del Cartucho, or one of the *comunas* – the shanty towns ringing the city – and you would become just another statistic in the spreadsheets of the violentologists.

From the other side of the desk came the sound of Lester belching and smacking his lips. The minister sighed. He had backed many initiatives to reduce the violence and had contributed millions to charities, but the problems were so entrenched. Drug gangs and right-wing death squads were responsible for much of the violence, but to get anything done in Colombia you all too often ended up doing business with the very people you were trying to defeat.

A few months ago, he had agreed with the

American billionaire William Walls on a plan for GemCorp to recapture Madero, without involving the army, and so keep the government–FARA cease-fire intact. But Ayala had not expected GemCorp to enlist the Bond militia for its dirty work. Now the minister was partners with men like Lester, who turned out to be the infamous Cangrejo. Ayala had few scruples when it came to politics, but the Bond was on the very outer edge of acceptability. Working with Cangrejo was bad enough, but his actually coming to his office was another thing. Ayala did not trust him at all. As well as being a *sicario* – a professional killer – he was an uncouth peasant and a thug. He wondered why a businessman like William Walls had to hire such scum. Was there no more honour among thieves?

'All in all, we have dealt the rebels a significant blow,' Elizabeth was saying, wrapping up her report, 'without compromising the cease-fire or involving the Colombian army. I hope the situation is developing to your satisfaction.'

Sitting demurely next to Lester, Elizabeth was more respectful, wary of Minister Ayala's reputation as one of Colombia's wealthiest and most powerful men. He was an impressive figure, a tall, elegant man with a leonine head. Close up, you could feel his charisma flowing from the pure, unquestioned knowledge of his own power. Rumour endowed Ayala with businesses ranging from coca plantations in Bolivia to an investment bank in New York. And it was all true. But his wealth and influence stretched far beyond his own success. His position rested on the inheritance of the Ayala family, one of the oldest colonial dynasties in the Americas.

'It appears so,' said Ayala, turning away from the window and stretching out a hand. 'Let me see.'

Elizabeth passed over a knotted handkerchief bulging with uncut emeralds. Ayala sat behind his desk, spilled out the stones and gave them a cursory look. He pocketed about a third of them and left the rest lying on the leather desktop. 'That is all you recovered?' he asked.

Elizabeth nodded, scraping the stones back together in the handkerchief. Ayala knew that Elizabeth and Lester would have taken their share before showing the emeralds to him.

'And you will be sending those to GemCorp, correct?'

She nodded again.

'Very well,' said the minister shortly. 'What is next?'

'Madero,' Elizabeth answered. 'We expect another week or so for final militia training, then Madero will be retaken. The company we have hired are finally proving very effective.'

'Yes. But be careful not to over-use them. Remember, Yankee mercenaries are not popular in Colombia. And, for your sake, let us hope they do not run off like the previous contingent.'

Elizabeth laughed nervously. The disappearance of Daniel and his team had been a major setback and was still an embarrassment for her.

Ayala let her squirm for a while, then changed

the subject. 'Is there any more information on the rumours of new finds?' he asked.

'Nothing concrete,' she responded with a straight face, 'though there are still stories about special types of emeralds appearing from Madero. We cannot find any proof. We have been trying to restrict entry, but there is still a steady flow of people entering the Madero National Park because of these rumours.'

'You have found nothing at all?'

'Nothing.'

Beside Elizabeth, Lester belched again, giving her a curious look.

Ayala winced in disgust. 'Very well. Now, as for your work on the *paramo* . . . It should be seen as a victory, of course, but this level of rebel casualties will upset many left-wing politicians. Let us make sure that none of your work with the Bond, or with these mercenaries, becomes public until Madero and its mines are recaptured. That will be such a victory that nobody will mind too much about how it was achieved.'

With that, Ayala pressed a hidden bell and a flunkey appeared to hustle Elizabeth and Lester out. Left alone in the heavy silence of his panelled office, Ayala leaned back in his chair and breathed deeply to control his excitement. He was thrilled that Madero would soon be in his hands again. Money was one thing, power another. Retaking Madero would enhance his position in both, but reclaiming that stretch of forest meant much more to him than either. It was the rumours that really intrigued Minister Ayala – the tales of strange new stones emerging from the Madero National Park. He was disappointed that GemCorp still had no hard evidence of the emeralds, but he did not need evidence: he was convinced the stories were true.

On the surface, Hernando Ayala was his calm, urbane self, but for almost three months, since the rumours started, he had been seized by a wild, childish excitement. Ostensibly the minister was a cosmopolitan businessman and politician, a Harvard graduate with a modern outlook. But in at least one area he was as superstitious as the most ignorant backwoods peasant he despised. Hernando Ayala knew that his family was cursed – afflicted with an illness that had no cure. He also knew the prophecies said only one thing could help break that curse – the great emerald of El Verde.

More than five hundred years ago, Ayala's ancestor had ravaged the Yucatán and there he had seized the great stone that had become the Ayala family's birthright. According to the myths, the stone had been mined in a place called El Verde, where emeralds grew on trees, somewhere in the great *selva*. Searching for the green city, Ayala's ancestor had raided south from Bogotá and dis- appeared into the vastness of that jungle.

Now Minister Ayala believed he knew where El Verde lay: in the forests of Madero.

Lester and Elizabeth left the Ministry and began the cross-town drive through busy traffic to their hotel in the Centro Internacional. They were wrapped in their own thoughts.

Elizabeth was thinking of Burr. She had to admit that she really did find him unusually interesting. It still vexed her that he had rejected her advances. Unused to rejection, she hoped that she might soon have the chance to get her own back.

Lester was feeling content about the way they had handled Ayala. The minister was powerful, sure, but he was giving them a free hand to do whatever they wanted. Lester was confused about one thing, though. 'Why didn't you tell him about Cuchillo's emerald?' he asked Elizabeth.

She weaved the car between two of the swarming *busetas*, the overloaded shared taxis of South America's fastest-growing city. 'Why should we tell him? It's our first proof that the stories are true. You realize that? And if there are more of these emeralds out there, I don't want anyone else to know about them.'

'Yes, but everybody's heard of them. The rumours of El Verde started about three months ago. Even Daniel had heard . . .'

'The rumours started five hundred years ago. Everybody's heard about this new source, yes, but they don't know for sure. Most sensible people just think this latest rumour is an outbreak of emerald fever. And Daniel only knew because you told him, you stupid *pirovo*.'

'I thought it would help.'

'You're truly pitiful. Just let me do the thinking, Lester.'

'I would,' he protested, 'if we were a real team again – you know, like before.'

Elizabeth said nothing.

Lester could see her mind was working hard. 'Are you getting a new plan, Liz?'

'Ayala has nothing on us,' said Elizabeth. 'There's nothing to worry about. Nobody else knows we are preparing for an offensive and no one else knows we have hired Americans. Their cover is holding and there were no witnesses up on the *paramo*. The story will never get out. Not even the rebels will ever know what happened to Cuchillo.'

Lester said nothing, but Elizabeth heard him gulp. 'Lester?' she asked in a warning tone.

'Liz,' he said timidly, 'please don't be angry with me.'

'Lester, what the hell have you done?'

'Well,' Lester ventured, 'it is possible that the rebels might know something soon.'

'How, for God's sake?'

'You see, I might have sent something to Diaz.'

'*Picha*, Lester! What have you done?'

Arroyo Blanco to Madero, Amazon jungle

In the fog of an early Andean morning, Burr and the forward recon team drove down through the waving grasslands and acid bogs of the *paramo* towards the rainforest. The recon team wore civilian clothes and travelled in two white armoured Land-Rover Defenders painted with the words 'Argonaut Ecology'. The rugged SUVs were heavily laden with fuel, ropes, wooden planks and scientific paraphernalia. The lead vehicle contained Burr, Pike and David. Following them in the second Land-Rover were Janine, Anthony, Sven and Ahmad.

Despite being a gunnery team, David and Ahmad insisted on travelling in separate vehicles. David had complained bitterly that Ahmad was coming on the recon squad. 'Why do I always get lumbered with this great Arab oaf?' he grumbled. 'Should have blown him away in Gaza when I had the chance.'

David was a New York Jew who had spent much of his life in the Israeli paratroopers. Ahmad was a Palestinian who had spent most of his life in exile.

On the face of it, Ahmad was the least qualified of the team, with little military training, but he had been in combat since his teens playing hit-and-run against the Israeli army from Beirut to the West Bank to the Gaza Strip.

David and Ahmad had fought on opposite sides in a number of Middle East flare-ups. They had waved to each other across front lines and once in Beirut – at least, according to David – Ahmad had deliberately tried to kill him. David would moan about how scared he had been and what a terrible thing it was for a friend to do. Ahmad would retort that David had taken a pot shot at him in Gaza, though he hadn't been scared – David couldn't hit the Temple Wall in Jerusalem if he was standing in front of it.

Burr knew that when it came to the crunch, David and Ahmad together on the M240 were worth a platoon of infantry.

Pike sat in the back seat in stony silence. He had been in a morose sulk ever since the dressing-down Burr had given him for his indiscretion in the bar. The man had few redeeming features as it was. Drawing attention to their mission was a major breach of contract. Following his trigger-happiness on the *paramo*, Pike knew he was just one tiny mistake from being fired. Burr didn't mind Pike's silence in the vehicle – he rarely had anything decent to say anyway.

The temperature and humidity rose steadily as they followed the road down across the *paramo*. The ground was carpeted by cushion plants and dotted with the red and orange spikes of bromeliads. Burr saw terrestrial orchids blooming in splashes of crimson and purple in the long grass. Then the road began to switchback down the escarpment, giving way to elfin forest, then lush cloud forest – '*ceja de la selva*', the mountain people called it: 'the eyebrow of the forest'.

There was a narrow deforested area, then the trees reared up, crowding closer on either side. Eventually the metalled road gave out, becoming a narrow dirt track with just a cleared strip of a few metres on each side. Behind the narrow strip of struggling crops and the odd run-down shack of peasant colonists, the tall trees formed an unbroken wall.

Riding next to Burr in the lead Land-Rover, David rummaged in his pack and pulled out what looked like a crumpled pink plastic bag. He opened it up and placed it on his bald head.

The effect was enough even to bring Pike out of his sulk. He guffawed from the back seat. 'Man, what the fuck is that?'

'Shower cap,' said David, as if it were the most obvious thing in the world suddenly to put a pink shower cap on your head.

'OK, but why did you just put it on?'

'Insects,' replied David patiently. 'Everyone knows the forest is full of insects. You may have noticed that I am follically challenged. I do not like insect bites on my head.'

'Oh,' said Pike.

There was a Bond militia checkpoint where the

tarmac ended – a pole across the road and a concrete bunker with a rickety observation tower. The listless troops waved them through. The forest closed in, a wall of secondary growth, the trees fighting for the light. Every few miles there was another checkpoint, but they were increasingly infrequent, undermanned and poorly tended. Many of them were deserted. There was almost no traffic on the rutted forest highway. Now and again they drove off the road to avoid labouring trucks absurdly overloaded with illegal timber, or they squeezed past battered pick-ups piled high with luggage and with passengers clinging on like ants.

An hour after passing the last militia checkpoint, Burr slowed to a crawl in front of the first rebel outpost. The guards levelled their weapons at the vehicles and shouted at the Argonauts to get out.

'They're jumpy,' observed Burr immediately. He wondered if the disappearance of Cuchillo and his men had left the rebels on edge. 'Everybody, stay calm.'

The guerrillas did seem nervous. They frisked the Argonauts roughly, checked on their travel clearance by radio and searched the Land-Rovers closely. Burr was glad that for this first trip they were not bringing weapons – well, except for two pistols floating in cans of fuel.

The guerrillas looked just like the Bond militiamen at Arroyo Blanco. The only real difference in their dress was a bright red bandanna with a yellow star, instead of a white bandanna and black '07'. Burr handed out some packs of Marlboro, which, despite being capitalist Yankee cigarettes, were enthusiastically received. Janine chatted with one of the guards, then came over to Burr with a meaningful look. 'They're nervous because one of their *subcomandantes* went out with a large force a few days ago and hasn't come back.'

Eventually the Argonauts were waved through and they drove on. They spent the night parked on the banks of a broad grey-green river and the next morning took a rickety paddle steamer, operated by a friendly rebel crew, which ferried them across onto the edge of the Madero region. They drove off the ferry and up into the forested highlands of the Sierra de Madero. The terrain became hilly again, the track winding up and down steep valleys with fast-running rivers. The larger rivers had been spanned by concrete bridges, but these had been washed away by floods or demolished by the guerrillas. Some of these bridges had been replaced by rickety wooden structures – sometimes no more than planks or lashed logs stretched above the water – which the Argonauts inched across, one vehicle at a time. Most of the rivers had to be forded. Luckily the water level was relatively low, but Burr still hustled them across, knowing that flash floods were common in the forest. More than once the fords were deep enough for several inches of muddy water to seep in through the Land-Rovers' doors and cover the floor with a film of sludge.

As the topography changed, so did the forest that covered it. The trees grew even higher, soaring to well over a hundred feet, blotting out the sky except for a bright ribbon of light above the track. A drizzle began to fall and was still falling when, late in the afternoon, they reached another checkpoint, which the guards informed them was Madero. A dopey young guerrilla climbed into Burr's vehicle and guided them on a track that seemed to skirt the town. Burr could see the outskirts of Madero through the trees. In the fading light, they slowed and moved aside to let a shabby Toyota Land Cruiser scrape by. As they passed, Burr noticed the driver, a young woman with green eyes and coffee-coloured skin. Beside her in the passenger seat slept a figure with a battered bush hat over his face. The woman's eyes met Burr's and held them for a split second before passing over him and back to the road. Then she was gone.

'Check it out!' Pike exclaimed with a leer. 'Nice-looking broad.' He whistled and turned to watch her vehicle disappear down the road towards the town.

A few minutes later, it was dark under the trees. Night fell quickly and Burr switched on the head-lights. The Argonauts' yawning guerrilla guide called out and pointed to a small track, which ran off into the blackness of the forest. '*Por allá,*' he said. 'That way.'

The track had obviously not been used recently and the headlamp beams showed new growth surging all over it. As the Land-Rovers bumped slowly along in the faint traces of wheel ruts in the narrow path, they ploughed through great rope-like cobwebs spun across the track. Thrusting shrubs bent under the fenders and scraped along the undersides of the vehicles. The great, glinting green bodies of the *Nephila* spiders scuttled away from their broken webs and the burning eyes of forest animals shone in the lights. The rain stopped.

The Argonauts knew they had arrived when suddenly the forest on either side jumped back out of the beams and the night sky appeared again overhead. They drove on into the overgrown clearing until the lights picked out two dilapidated buildings. They turned off the engines, and suddenly they were in silence. Burr got out into the forest night. The forest dripped around him. It was cooler after the rain and full of the thick smell of drenched earth.

Janine peered into the run-down buildings – a couple of two-room huts with cinder-block walls and roofs of corrugated tin. 'This is it?' she enquired.

The guide shrugged. 'This was where the last group of *Yanqui* scientists stayed.'

'Do you know what happened to them?' asked Burr, picturing Daniel in a place like this. He would have hated it. He was partial to his creature comforts.

'Maybe they went into *la selva*,' the rebel said, waving vaguely towards the encircling forest.

'And?' prompted Janine.

'*Quién sabe?* They went into *la selva*,' he repeated, with a sickly grin. He crossed himself, muttering something about '*indios y tigres*' – 'Indians and jaguars' – then he scurried off into the dark with scared eyes, finger on the trigger of his rifle.

'Oh, that's just great,' grumbled David. 'In the

middle of nowhere with Ahmad, and surrounded by man-eaters.' He swung his flashlight along the black wall of trees. The eyes of unknown creatures glowed back at him, reflected in the beam. 'Soon as I can, I'm exchanging with Paul. Give me the mountains any day.'

'What a shit-hole,' said Pike, peering into one of the buildings through a smashed window. The place had been wrecked. Daniel and his team had been missing for a month. It looked as if the camp had been abandoned for years.

'I don't think we should sleep in the buildings,' advised Janine after a quick inspection by flashlight. 'They're filthy and infested with insects.'

'Let's rig shelters tonight, then,' said Burr. 'We'll start cleaning the place up tomorrow. And remember: we're scientists.'

Burr detailed Sven to take the first watch, then pitched his tent in the eaves of the forest and slung his hammock inside. The others did the same. Within the tent, the air was still and hot. Burr quickly found he could not sleep. He had a nervous feeling of being watched. Restless, he climbed from his hammock.

'Hey, hey, Captain.' Burr was startled by the lilting Swedish greeting whispered out of the darkness. Sven's bulk loomed out of the shadows. 'I guess you can't sleep? I am sure it is just nerves, sir. I am the same. It is always like this with a new job.'

'Thanks, Sven,' murmured Burr kindly. 'But, no ranks, remember? You get some sleep. I'll take over the watch now.'

'Thank you, sir. Good night, sir.'

In the complete darkness Burr could not see or hear the movement, but he somehow felt it. 'No saluting, Sven. You never know who might be watching.'

'Yes, sir!' whispered the Swede. 'I mean, Burr,' he added sheepishly.

Burr wandered round the clearing, looking out into the darkness of the night forest. Maybe Sven's right, he thought. It's only nerves. But his feeling was more than just the usual adrenalin. Despite himself, he felt he was down here in the depths of the jungle for something more than just an operation. His thoughts drifted back to that night with the Maya of Xcalan – the night of his dream – and he felt excited and perhaps even a little afraid. Daniel was out there somewhere – dead or alive – but, more than that, he sensed that somewhere out in the unseen, solid blackness that was the forest something lay in wait for him. Perhaps the green eye? Perhaps his destiny? But, of course, Burr reminded himself, he didn't believe in magic, or in fate.

A grumbling, yawning David took over the watch exactly on time, and Burr climbed back into his hammock. He still had that uneasy feeling of being watched, and again he found it hard to sleep. The jungle night was warm and thick. Soft rain pattered onto the tents of the Argonauts. From somewhere in the treetops above drifted a strong scent of vanilla. Before Burr slept, an image swam unbidden into his mind, a passing image of a profile and a girl with green eyes.

* * *

Early the next morning, the territorial dawn booms of howler monkeys blended with the sound of the Argonauts hard at work. Led by Janine, who could not abide disorder, the team began to scour and fumigate the two buildings and started the battle to reclaim the clearing from resurgent nature. Termites had infested one of the buildings. Large, aggressive 'crying-eye' wasps had built a nest in the other. Fast-growing shrubs and trees had sprung up and creepers of purple-flowering morning glory had wormed their way over everything. Soon the heat was atrocious. With no wind and one hundred per cent humidity, sweat does not evaporate. It ran in sticky rivulets down the Argonauts' bodies. It soaked their clothes and forced them to strip down to their shorts.

Meanwhile, clearing the undergrowth disturbed thousands of insects. Beetles, butterflies, wasps, flies and indeterminate bugs rose in a cloud. Ants swarmed on the ground, up legs and all over bodies, some tiny, fierce *iuturi* even penetrating underneath David's shower cap. Chiggers – tiny red arachnids with an infuriating bite – attacked without mercy, and scratching them off just left their minuscule, itching mouthparts buried in the skin.

The humidity was extraordinary. 'Look at this!' exclaimed Janine, who was busy unpacking the food. Pausing for a moment, she held up a spoonful of salt. It dissolved in front of their eyes in the thick, damp air.

It was still early when huge clouds suddenly

covered the sky, releasing a torrential rainstorm. The Argonauts rushed for shelter in the buildings and watched the track become a muddy stream and most of the clearing a steaming quagmire. Thankfully the rain lowered the temperature a notch and beat down the insect plague.

Idle for a while, Burr took stock of the evidence Daniel's team had left. It was meagre. There were no supplies at the base, and the hammocks and camping gear were gone. So was the communications equipment. This all suggested they might have left on a long patrol. But then again, everything could have been stolen. There did not seem to be any evidence of a fight at the camp – no blood, no shell casings, no bullet marks in trees or buildings.

According to Elizabeth, Daniel's advance team had begun surveillance of the mines and had sent out some reconnaissance patrols. The last radio contact had indicated that a routine patrol was being mounted. Then, nothing. Burr was sceptical about Daniel's final radio contact. Daniel would surely not have committed his entire team to routine patrol. He would always have left at least one team member back at the camp. Either the entire unit had left, in which case it was not a routine patrol – and Daniel had been lying about his plans – or whatever happened to the patrol also affected any men left at the campsite. As yet, Burr had no sense of which was more likely. He looked out at the forest through the driving rain. The answer was out there somewhere. Burr was planning to send out his own routine patrols into the forest to check rebel defences around Madero. They could look out for clues to Daniel's whereabouts, but he doubted the forest would yield much.

When the rain stopped, Burr decided to take the work from the sodden clearing up into the treetops. The forest around Madero appeared to have two distinct layers, one about fifty feet above the ground, and the main canopy at about one hundred and twenty feet. Here and there great lone trees – emergents – rose thirty feet above the rest like islands in a green sea. Inside the forest, reaching the treetops would have meant a difficult climb. The tall trees had high, smooth boles with no low boughs. Also the branches of the trees in the lower canopy got in the way, and, unlike in Tarzan movies, the massive, looping vines – the lianas – which hung everywhere would not make climbing easier, or allow you to swing gaily from tree to tree. The knotted vines, some thick as a man's thigh, hung in forbidding curtains. Many were covered with spines and vicious barbs. Around the edge of the clearing, extra sunlight meant the growth was even thicker, but a few large branches protruded over the camp.

To form the pillars of the canopy system, Burr chose some tall kapok trees on the Madero side of the clearing. Their smooth grey trunks, supported by jutting, fifteen-foot-high buttress roots, were draped in vines. But, sixty feet up, their lowest branches stretched out over the clearing, so there was no obstruction to reaching the upper storeys quickly.

Using a sling, Sven flung a weighted line up and over one of these branches. The line was attached to strong ropes, which Sven then heaved over the branch, and fastened. The operation was repeated with a safety rope, then David and Anthony climbed up to the branch, ratcheting themselves swiftly up the rope with jumar hand-ascenders and footloops.

Once into the branches they climbed higher into the tree, then rigged up a motorized winch system. They moved carefully through the branches, marking out the best positions to rig the walkways and platforms. The location for the central rope walkway was fixed a few feet below the top of the main canopy, a dizzying hundred and twenty feet above the forest floor. Standing on the main rope of the walkway, holding onto the guide ropes on either side, a man would be able to peer over the treetops with an unobstructed view over the forest to Madero.

The Argonauts began to string the ropes for the walkway. They also started to construct small, more stable wooden platforms at points along the walkway. Anthony made sure these gave a clear view of the guerrilla emplacements. With his 10× Steiner binoculars, he could see the faces of the guards 500 metres away. With the team's M49 20× telescope, he should have been able to read the brand name on their cigarettes. As sniper/observer, Anthony would be mapping out most of the rebel defences and patterns of guard duty. He was vital to this part of the plan – if he could hold it together.

'Just one thing, Cap'n,' said Anthony. 'Check this

out.' He handed Burr the scope and pointed towards the bottom of the hill in the centre of town. 'At the foot of the hill. See the sandbags? There's a checkpoint.'

Burr moved the scope round and tried to focus on the checkpoint. The quivering waves of heat haze, mingled with the swarms of flies, mosquitoes and other insects, created a weaving layer so thick it was like looking through murky water.

'Never seen nuthin' like it,' said Anthony.

'Bullet will still go through,' said Burr. 'You can adjust for any effects on trajectory.'

'That's true enough,' said Anthony. 'Just thought you should see, is all.'

By evening the main walkway was well under way and it was possible to negotiate gingerly about fifty yards of swaying rope bridge. Three flimsy platforms were also taking shape. Burr mapped out a second walkway some seventy feet below. It ran through the trees at the level of the lower canopy and hung above the access track to command the approach to the clearing. The walkways would be reached by a pulley lift system attached to a small motor. As back-up the Argonauts hung long rope ladders down the tree trunks. Janine also ran wires up to the canopy – it was the best place for un-obstructed communications. She got a clear triple-satellite fix on the Global Positioning System and decent, if temperamental, connections on the sat phone. She hid the radio antenna in the upper reaches of one of the towering kapok trees, where the signal was clearest.

Once Janine had powered up the sat phone from solar panels placed on the roof of one of the cabins, Burr made first radio contact with Ricardo and Carlo.

'Licence to kill?' scoffed Ricardo, when Burr raised him in Arroyo. 'These Bond idiots couldn't get a driver's licence.'

'Sure, Ricardo,' soothed Burr, listening patiently to his friend's complaints that the militiamen were unresponsive, lazy and ill-trained. Burr knew that Ricardo was just lowering his expectations to make sure Burr was pleasantly surprised when the Bond suddenly turned into an effective, disciplined outfit.

The report to Argonaut HQ was not quite as routine. It appeared Carlo was going to have to go down to Yucatán ahead of schedule. 'I need to be down in Chetumal to present your plans for Xcalan. The regional council has brought the process forward to this week.'

'Any idea why?' asked Burr.

'Er, no,' said Carlo. He sounded unusually nervous.

'Don't worry,' Burr reassured him. He was surprised at the drastic change of date, but confident that Carlo could carry it off. In any case it looked as if he had no choice.

'At least the final sealed auction won't be taking place until after you return,' said Carlo. 'I'll try to keep your plan in the running until then.'

While making the calls, Burr was surprised to see that the sat-phone battery was lower than expected. He made a mental note to ask Janine about it.

Burr himself had little to report to his colleagues beyond the Madero squad's initial progress in clearing and setting up the Observation Post, or OP. He did not bother reporting that there was something troubling him. It was nothing concrete, just that lingering, nagging sense of being watched. There were plenty of eyes in the jungle, but this was more than monkeys or jaguars. He could see nothing untoward from the canopy or on the ground. A few suspicious guerrillas had turned up during the day to check out what they were doing, but that wasn't it. And Burr wasn't the only one to feel something. The knowledge that Daniel's team had disappeared from the camp was keeping every Argonaut fully alert.

By late afternoon the feeling became too strong for Burr to ignore. He stopped working and moved quietly out of the camp. Keeping a few yards inside the forest, he began to circle the perimeter of the clearing. The sounds of the Argonauts at work were instantly muffled. He pushed slowly through the dense growth of ferns and shrubs around the camp. The jungle floor was silent and dark. Suddenly, Burr knew for certain that something or someone was there. He pulled out his Ka-bar knife and tensed for action. In the silence his trousers rasped against an unseen twig and in the same instant a slight sound to his left made him swing round in a crouch, knife at the ready.

Burr saw an Indian turning to face him at the same time. The man was about five foot ten and very muscular, with wide shoulders and a powerful frame. His complexion seemed quite pale and his brown hair fell below his waist. A series of short scars lined the broad muscle on the left side of his chest. There was a bird-of-paradise feather in his hair. Otherwise he wore nothing but a thong about his hips, which secured his vertical penis sheath, and a quiver of arrows. The Indian was raising a huge bow. A bamboo arrow the length of a man was nocked to the half-drawn bowstring. In the dim light Burr saw no fear in his eyes and he recognized the steady look and bearing of a man accustomed to killing. Perhaps the Indian recognized the same in Burr. For a moment they stared at each other. The Indian nodded slowly to Burr. Then he was gone.

Burr realized that he had been holding his breath. He exhaled, sheathed his knife and walked back into the camp. It appeared the Argonauts might have more than the guerrillas to worry about.

'We have company,' he told the team later, over dinner round the fire. 'Indians. I saw one watching us from the forest over there.' He pointed out beyond the tents.

'I wouldn't worry about them,' David said. 'Bows and arrows, man. Anyway, what could they want from us?'

Pike wasn't so blasé. 'Want? Indians? Just our heads, dude. In Arroyo they told me all about these guys. They're headhunters round here, you know. Fucking savages will kill you in your sleep, they said – cut off your head, shrink it real small.'

'Some of us could maybe do with a little head-shrinking,' David said.

'Yeah,' grumbled Pike, 'you'll really laugh when they shrivel your head and hang it up for decoration.'

Anthony did not seem worried. 'Just let 'em try,' he said.

Pike ignored him. 'So what's the line if we see them poking round here again, Burr? Do we do 'em?'

'We're not "doing" anyone,' said Burr – 'not unless and until we have to. These Indians have done us no harm.'

By nightfall, after persistent light rain, most varieties of insect disappeared, only to be replaced by a single-species swarm of mosquitoes. Bats flitted through the air and saturnid moths fluttered around the gaslights. Not far away, the mine entrance was blazing in the glare of massive arc-lights. From the canopy, the Argonaut on watch could see bright spotlights sweeping the rest of the mine and its surroundings, a deterrent to thieves – and to any night-time assault. The only other patch of electric light came from the hill in the centre of Madero, which held the old mission station, now the rebel HQ.

Burr set a rota of two-hour watches. The Argonaut on duty was to carry one of the pistols they had smuggled down. During the day, at least one of the team – normally Anthony – would be in the canopy, observing Madero and recording guerrilla movements. Another Argonaut, patrolling on the ground and the lower walkway, would watch the road and the clearing. The others would be working in the camp or out intelligence-gathering around the town. Their cover for forest patrolling would be to take butterfly nets and collect specimens while noting down defences and possible lines of attack.

The second day dawned with Burr on watch up in the canopy. The morning was damp, misty and cool enough to find him shivering in his T-shirt. In that early-morning half-light, Burr saw something in the distance he had never seen before. It appeared to him to be a gathering of flying insects, possibly butterflies. It left him breathless with its beauty and intrigued as to its purpose. The glimpse he caught of it through the mist and cloud was frustratingly brief. Burr told himself to take binoculars and camera with him the next time he was on dawn watch. Right now he had no time to reflect. Anthony was taking his place on watch, and there was a full day's labour ahead.

The morning continued grey and wet. The Argonauts gave up sheltering from the downpour – everything was soaked anyway – and worked on in the warm rain, dressed in as little as possible. Burr set up some simple research paraphernalia to back up their cover story. With Janine's help, he hung up a number of lights in glass jars with funnels. Attracted by the light, moths would crawl in and many would then be trapped, unable to find the way out through the narrow nozzle. The night before, Burr thought he had spotted a rare type of brown and pink *Rothschildia* moth and he hoped to trap a specimen.

Sven, winching up some planks for the walkway slats, looked confused. 'Captain, please remind me. If someone should ask, what are we researching?'

'Just saying "canopy research" is often enough. It means you could be researching anything you like – from parrot nests to howler-monkey courtship rituals. If anybody wants something more specific, best thing is to get me. Second best is to say we're working on biodiversity.'

'What does biodiversity actually mean?' asked Janine, approaching along the still precarious rope bridge.

'It can mean anything you want it to mean,' said Burr: 'that's the beauty of it. At the simplest level, we can just count the number of species we find.' He had already photographed two butterflies he thought might be new to science.

'And when you have counted the animals, what good do the numbers do?' asked Sven.

'Well, I'm not sure. Ecologists say the more species the better – diversity is good – and that's why we should save the rainforest.'

'I really don't know what all the fuss is about,' said Janine ruefully, slapping down another mosquito. 'There are plenty of species we could do without – like this one.' She showed the large splat of the blood-swollen creature on her hand. 'Let's face it, this place sucks.'

The forest may have been hot, sopping wet and insect-infested, but Burr couldn't agree. He felt at home. Working in the canopy you were more exposed to the elements. When the clouds lifted, there was no shade from the burning sun, but you were cooled by breezes that never reached the forest floor. And it was beautiful. The canopy was a myriad shades of green, splashed here and there with the purple of a stand of jacaranda, or the velvet red of a *Combretum*.

Alongside Burr in the canopy, Anthony was also in his element. Hidden in the dripping leaves, he began his own smooth, systematic observations. He noted the number of guerrillas he could see on guard, their positions and patrols, and the pattern of watch changes. He also watched the rebels' behaviour, assessing levels of training and discipline. He recorded whether their alertness increased or decreased at certain times. Did they keep watch at meal times? Were they hung-over in the mornings? Did they only look alert when an officer was approaching?

Using his educated eye and a laser range-finder, he began to put together a range card, calculating atmospheric conditions, elevations and distances to each potential target. Having time like this was a luxury for Anthony – a luxury that would extend his effective range out to 1,500 metres. He could work out exactly how far off he could be when aiming to hit each guard on the first checkpoint in different conditions. He was also able to calculate the extra elevation the heat and humid air would require. If he was to snipe from here during the assault on Madero, it would be a turkey shoot.

'Company!' Janine's call came from the walkway

above the access track. The Argonauts, who all happened to be involved in unimpeachably un-military activities, simply continued with them as a white Land Cruiser bumped up the rutted track into the clearing. Peering down at the distant ground through the gaps between the walkway planks, Burr could see two people emerge from the vehicle. He saw a semi-naked figure with a pink head moving forward to greet them. Burr was glad it was David and not Sven. David could fool anybody.

A few moments later, Burr heard his name being called up through the leaves. He went over to the winch and strapped himself in for the descent back to the clearing. As he got lower he could see that the two visitors were a man and a woman. It was the girl who had driven past them when they arrived in Madero. Next to her was the man with the battered bush hat, which was currently hanging down his back. He was leaning on a weathered umbrella. Burr saw now that he was substantially older than she was. To his surprise, Burr found himself hoping the man was just her colleague.

On the ground, David was thinking about how he looked in his pink cap, skinny and diminutive, next to Sven's body-builder frame – the dopey Swede had also hurried over to greet the visitors. That irked David, as did the fact that the glowing sweat on Sven's bare torso made him look like a sculpted model, while his own sweat just looked, well, sweaty. There was a reason why David was so acutely aware of the physical contrast, one that David understood very well. It was the same reason why the great ape was staring at the woman called Leila with a goofy grin. The reason was that the woman was very attractive. She had high cheekbones above a bow-shaped mouth. Her skin was the smooth, light brown of a perfect suntan.

Her fine, sculpted features were hard to place – some African blood maybe; some Latin too, perhaps, or Indian. And then, as she turned her head, David thought: maybe Chinese. She was shading her eyes, squinting up at Burr coming down from the canopy with an intrigued expression. Her eyes were a bright, shining green.

Watching Burr descending through the trees, Leila saw a man with dark blond hair and a lean, slightly weathered look. He seemed to shimmer as he descended through patches of sunlight breaking through the canopy.

'I guess you're Professor Whitman,' said Leila after Burr released himself from the harness. 'I'm Leila Walcott.'

'I'm Burr.' Burr guessed it was David who had awarded him the professorship. He hoped his promoter had got the university right, or, better still, hadn't mentioned it.

Leila turned to Makepeace. 'This is my colleague, Professor James Makepeace.' She spoke with a faint Caribbean accent, Burr thought. He couldn't guess which island, though.

The two men shook hands. 'Burr, eh?' Makepeace looked at Burr warily and winked at Leila. 'Watch out, my dear girl, he may be difficult to shake off.'

Burr smiled patiently as ever.

'Sorry,' Makepeace said. 'I suspect I am not the first to make such a stupid joke. Can I offer you a beer? As we're your neighbours, we thought we'd bring you a house-cooling present.'

'Thanks,' said Burr, taking a bottle of Club Colombia from Makepeace's cooler bag. The beer was indeed blessedly cold. David and Sven also took bottles, then with parting beams at Leila they made their excuses and returned to cleaning one of the huts. Burr fetched some folding camp stools and they sat down together in a shady spot at the edge of the clearing. Burr felt keenly how important it was to make a good impression on his neighbours. The Argonauts' cover had survived initial perusal by the rebels. Acceptance by well-known local scientists would add another layer of protective camouflage.

It was not going to be easy to fool Makepeace, though. He was eyeing Burr keenly. 'So you're a professor at . . . ?' he asked.

'University of North Carolina,' said Burr. 'Chapel Hill.'

'Oh yes,' said Makepeace. 'And how is Professor Walker?'

Burr had been prepared for that. Without missing a beat, he gently pointed out that the faculty had been shattered when poor Professor Walker died of Green Monkey Disease in the Congo only last year.

'Oh, how awful,' said Makepeace.

Leila was looking at him oddly. It was clear that he had known all about poor Professor Walker.

Makepeace ignored her and continued to study Burr intently. 'So tell us what you are doing in Madero,' he said, still with an unmistakable note of doubt in his voice. 'Everyone in Madero is looking for something. Question is, is it animal, vegetable or mineral?'

'Definitely animal,' said Burr. 'We're studying biodiversity of the canopy fauna.'

'Brave of you to come here at all. This does happen to be a war zone, you know. Not many scientists fancy working in Madero these days. Especially not after what happened to the last lot.'

'We know it's a dangerous place. And, yes, the disappearance of our predecessors is very worrying,' agreed Burr, 'and mysterious. We've been trying to find out what happened, without much luck so far.'

'Not surprising,' said Makepeace, relaxing a little. 'Nobody knows. We thought they had just left without saying goodbye – they were always a bit of a rude bunch. Kept themselves to themselves.' He obviously did not have a very high opinion of Daniel's outfit.

'We couldn't even say for sure what day they disappeared,' said Leila. 'At first we thought they might just have gone on one of their research trips.'

'Research trips?' asked Burr.

'Yes. They would all go out for days on end, deep into the forest. We guessed we'd see them around when they got back, but we didn't. So one day we drove over for a visit and the place had been deserted for a while. Looked like it had been ransacked, too.' She looked around. 'Actually, they never kept it very tidy anyway. Glad to see you are clearing it up.'

'Yes, we found the camp in a real mess,' said Burr, thoughtfully. He was intrigued by the research trips. Daniel's brief had only been to check the defences around Madero and scout the approaches to the town. There should have been no need for long patrols, deep into the bush. They certainly did not sound like patrols Burr would have regarded as routine.

'Well,' Leila went on, 'it became obvious a few weeks later that they really had simply disappeared.'

'What about armed groups?' asked Burr. 'We wondered whether rogue rebels or maybe a drug gang took them hostage.'

'Who knows?' said Makepeace. 'Frankly, I was never sure just exactly what they were doing there anyway. They seemed to me to be a very un-scientific bunch. That chap with the red hair . . .' He turned to Leila.

'Daniel,' she filled in.

'. . . Yes, Daniel. He knew about as much zoology as a fifth-grade student. Anyway, tell us seriously, what brings you to Madero? You'd have to be crazy to want to set foot here.'

'Well, you're here,' Burr pointed out, 'so I guess we're just as crazy as you are.'

'Fair point,' said Makepeace, with a chuckle. 'Anyway, I guess we'll be safer than you are on the ground. As you can see, we're working in the treetops – canopy research. We've cleared

179

everything with the rebels and the government. And of course – as I'm sure you're finding – the war is an opportunity. Because of the fighting, not much work has been done in the Madero region, especially in my field.'

'What's that?' asked Leila.

'Lepidoptera,' said Burr.

'Is that so?' asked Makepeace, casually. 'Do you know, I saw a beautiful *Urania fulgens* moth the other night.'

'Are you sure you weren't mistaken?' replied Burr smoothly. '*Urania* is a diurnal moth, so it would be very unusual to see one at night. Anyway, don't get me started on lepidoptera. I'm afraid I would bore you terribly. Tell me what *you're* doing.'

Makepeace acknowledged with a nod that Burr had passed his simple test. 'We're saving the world,' he said sardonically.

'Ethnobotany,' said Leila; 'and despite what James says,' she gave her colleague a reproving glare, 'some of us do believe it really could make a difference.'

Makepeace mocked Leila gently. 'She's young and idealistic. Some might say naïve. Still believes that there are miracle cures lurking in some rare orchid.'

'Well, there might be!' said Leila, with a hurt look. 'You never know. It's just not easy. But a quarter of all our medicines come from plants. At least two thousand rainforest plants have already been found that contain alkaloids that might help fight everything from HIV to cancer.

180

And we've got some very promising leads.'

As Leila talked about a vine called *jomo*, which apparently contained some interesting chemicals, and some of their other discoveries, Burr was charmed. He was impressed by her enthusiasm and by her green eyes, which sparkled as she talked with passion about the beauty and worth of the forest and its people.

Burr asked Makepeace for his view of the situation and got a much bleaker view.

'Unfortunately, all factions are equally bad. The civil war here is a fight for resources, you see. The Military–Industrial Complex wants Madero and its forest, and everything underneath it too. They want to chop the trees down for their hardwood timber. Once the trees have gone, drug barons will grow coca in the cleared areas. Multinationals will blast the ground for emeralds and drill it for oil.'

As part of the 'Military' half of Military–Industrial, Burr had sometimes wished the Complex could be as well organized and mutually profitable as Makepeace made it sound. Even diluted, though, the situation appeared to be especially bleak for the local Indians.

'Unfortunately,' Makepeace went on, after taking a glug of beer, 'the only people GemCorp and the rebels can't buy out are the indigenous people – the Jemberí. It's unfortunate for the Jemberí. You see, the government set aside Madero as a protected National Park especially for the Indians. If there were no Jemberí, there would be no National Park, and so no barrier to complete exploitation and destruction of the forest. The Jemberí won't give up the forest. And they can't be bought. No, the only way to get rid of the Jemberí is to kill them.'

'Wouldn't evicting the rebels restore protection for the Indians?' asked Burr. His knowledge of the Maya and their fragile ecosystem made him uneasy about damaging the interests of another indigenous group.

'Actually, Diaz and the FARA try to protect the Park,' answered Leila. 'They try to stop the big corporations from destroying the forest.'

Makepeace waved a hand dismissively. 'Guerrilla, shmerilla. They don't give a damn about the forest. They are fighting for emeralds. After a while, the corporations and the government will buy the FARA off. The rebels are already expanding the mines. And they've been allowing oil and mineral companies to resume seismic transects through the forest. Of course the real, inestimable value in the forest is not in emeralds or oil, but in the flora and fauna.'

'That's right,' said Leila eagerly. Then an idea seemed to occur to her. 'Of course, as you know, we are looking for medicinal plants. Well, the fact is that the real miracle plants may be up in the canopy . . .' Leila was openly fishing for an invitation. 'We have to rely on the Indians to bring us epiphytes from high up. Otherwise we can only cut things down from about twenty feet up, with extended clippers. If only we could get up there . . .' her voice trailed off and she looked longingly up into the treetops.

'Yes?' said Burr.

'Well,' said Makepeace. 'There must be hundreds of species up there, many of them new to science. They say most of the forest's life is up there. After all, it's where all the light is – only one per cent of sunlight gets through to the forest floor.'

Burr muttered something about the walkways not yet being ready, and changed the subject, talking about his work on *Heliconius* butterflies.

Leila seemed prepared to listen, but Makepeace was a bit put out, and clearly remained unconvinced of the team's scientific credentials. After a short while he suggested, 'Why don't we ask your colleagues to join us?'

'Well, they're busy,' said Burr evasively.

Makepeace looked round to see Ahmad wandering in from the jungle with a butterfly net. Before Burr could prevent him, Makepeace beckoned Ahmad over and offered him a beer, which he politely refused, explaining that he was a Palestinian and a Muslim. After a moment's small talk, Makepeace asked, 'So are you also into Lepidoptera? What's your speciality? The urticating *Heliconius* caterpillars are interesting here in Madero, don't you think?'

Ahmad gulped nervously and retreated to a strongly accented pidgin English. 'I am sure they urticate very good, but I am not really specializing. I am working as research assistant. I label. I collect.' He waved his prop – the butterfly net – vigorously.

Makepeace nodded and smiled as Ahmad retreated in confusion.

Makepeace and Leila left a few minutes later. They extended an open invitation for the Argonauts to visit their research station any time. With a bright smile and a flutter of her eyelashes, Leila also made sure to remind Burr that if there was any chance for her to get up into the canopy . . .

'Perhaps in a couple of days,' he replied, 'when we've sorted this place out.'

Behind the wheel, Leila was quiet as they drove away from the clearing.

'All right, what is it?' asked Makepeace after a few minutes of bumping through the jungle.

'You were very rude,' Leila said. 'You made it really uncomfortable, being so untrusting. Testing them like that was insulting.'

'I would watch out for him, if I were you,' said Makepeace. He seemed deadly serious.

Leila was surprised. 'What do you mean?'

'Just that he doesn't look like any scientist I have ever known.'

'Oh, come on. What else would he be doing here?'

'I'm not sure. But I never trusted that last lot of pseudo-researchers and, so far, I'm not so keen on this lot either. And that Burr is a smooth talker. I'm not sure I should let you up into the trees alone with him.'

'Oh, what nonsense. He's probably more into six legs than two.' Leila was being a little disingenuous. Secretly, she was pleased if Makepeace believed Burr's interest in her had not just been academic. She had found his manner calm and intriguing. And she liked the way he spoke, in that restrained but rolling Southern drawl. 'Anyway,' she smiled, 'if you want him to let us up into their canopy system, we might be glad of all the influence we can get.'

Makepeace nodded. The prospect of finally getting up into the canopy was tantalizing. It occurred to him that it might provide some vital skeins of knowledge in the tapestry of Madero's ecology – enough perhaps finally to put him in the running for a Crafoord.

'And let me tell you,' Leila continued, 'he seems to know a lot about *Heliconiidae*.'

'Yes, that may be true, but I am not sure that friend of his was much of an entomologist. He didn't seem to understand what "urticating" meant and he seemed to think that *Heliconius* caterpillars have urticating hairs. But they don't need stinging hairs. They ward off predators with their bright colours, which clearly declare them to be poisonous.'

'Well, he is Palestinian; maybe it's a language problem. Anyway, say you're right, who do you think they are, then?'

Makepeace looked at her kindly. 'I admit that I have absolutely no idea what they may be up to. Just be careful, my dear. I feel I am *in loco parentis* with you, Leila. I just do not want you to get hurt.'

Leila had to admit that Burr did not look like a typical scientist. But the difference made him, well, interesting. Also, genuine or not, he did know his butterflies and she liked that in a man. 'You don't have to worry about me,' she said to Makepeace. 'You should know I can look after myself.' She did not say that Burr had troubled her by suddenly, out of the blue, offering her some kind of solution. The thing was, she hadn't even been aware she had a problem.

Burr watched the botanists' SUV bump down the track. Through the rear window he could see just Leila's dark hair showing above her seat back. Burr realized with pleasure that she had not said anything cute about his name.

After Leila and Makepeace left, Burr despatched Pike and Sven on a return trip to Arroyo to meet the Chinook delivering a load of supplies. They could have avoided this journey by bringing more gear with them initially, but Burr wanted the guards on the road, both rebel and militia, to get used to scientists going back and forth. The guards would soon give up searching the vehicles, allowing the Argonauts to bring in bulkier ordnance without detection.

Burr's next duty was to pay a courtesy call on the local rebel commander. The order had been delivered the day before by a pert young guerrilla girl called Juanita, who had haughtily ignored a wink and lascivious stare from Pike. Juanita wore a flower in her hair and her red bandanna tied like a choker round her neck. The verbal summons was accompanied by a formal note on a slightly damp card, signed with a flourish, Generalissimo Javier Castro Diaz, Comandante, Fuerzas Armadas Revolucionarias de Amazonas.

'Come on, Janine,' Burr shouted up at the trees,

and Janine clambered down the rope ladder from the lower walkway. 'Well, thought I'd better take the most respectable of you,' Burr said in response to reproachful looks from the rest of the team.

'Sexist!' complained Ahmad. 'Why not take me?' He and David were doing some more heavy work in the windless suntrap of the campsite. Wearing nothing but a pair of very tight shorts, Ahmad was sweating heavily. His bulky body was covered in insect bites.

David laughed. 'These rebels aren't that dumb. You think they gonna believe that an A-rab can be a scientist? Two seconds with that ethno-whatanist and you almost blew our cover. No way, man. If you want to convince them that we're all world-famous insectologists, take me. All the greatest scientists are Jews – just look at Einstein.'

'Do you think Einstein walked around wearing only a shower hat?' retorted Ahmad. 'If Burr takes you, they will not think we are scientists. They will think we are lunatics.'

'Just keep working, you two,' said Janine. Burr shook his head ruefully.

Janine and Burr drove down the narrow track that led towards Madero town and the rebel HQ on Mission Hill. Burr, in the passenger seat, took photographs with his digital camera and noted down troop numbers and equipment. At the edge of town was a guerrilla checkpoint, manned by six bored guards with rusty bolt-action rifles. Unlike the guards on the road, they seemed unaffected by

Cuchillo's absence. Little more than kids, they smiled and posed for Burr's camera.

At the bottom of the Mission Hill, there was another checkpoint. This post was guarded by five tough-looking men with brand-new AK-47s. Burr noticed flak jackets piled up against the sandbags. It was far too hot to wear body armour. A camouflaged pick-up truck mounting a 12.7 mm DShK, 'Dushka', heavy machinegun was parked by the road. In the open back of the truck, Burr could see, was a pile of rocket-propelled grenades. Just behind were two dugouts with a large mortar in each.

'Did you see that?' asked Burr, through the gritted teeth of a fake grin.

'Yup. Looks like a couple of 81-mils,' said Janine, waving at the unsmiling guards.

Janine and Burr drove up to the hilltop plateau, where more guards met them and led them across the bare central area to a covered terrace overlooking the town.

From their canopy OP, the Argonauts had seen four buildings on the Mission Hill, plus a sandbagged gun emplacement with a 20 mm cannon. Now Burr could add three more structures on the obscured side of the dusty hilltop: the visible buildings were a wash-house, a kitchen and mess, a clinic with a red cross clearly marked on its roof, a couple of long, low barracks and the old mission chapel, which Burr could quite clearly see was now the rebel command post. Guards were posted outside it and a radio mast was fastened to the bell tower. Between the buildings, also out of sight from the

Argonaut camp, was one more large-calibre weapon – another Dushka – on an anti-aircraft mounting in a sandbagged machinegun nest.

On the terrace, in the shade of a trellis of passion vines, Javier Diaz was taking his breakfast, looking out over the forest and the mines. Although over-weight, he appeared sleek and cool, his hair greased back, his bandanna and combat fatigues perfectly pressed. Burr was reminded of an ocelot, or a plump weasel. His entourage stood around nervously. Their comandante's temper was fickle.

'Good morning, Comandante,' said Burr.

'General,' Diaz corrected him without looking up, his mouth full of food.

'General, apologies. My name is Burr Whitman from Argonaut Ecology. This is my colleague, Janine Granger.'

'Burr. Like a telephone – burrrrrr! burrrrrr! Ha, ha, ha, ha!'

Diaz's men laughed uneasily along with their commander.

Burr smiled politely. 'That's right, just like a tele-phone. Allow me to say how grateful we are for your permission to work here. Our research could be of immense benefit in the future.'

Diaz still didn't look up from his food. 'Che, the hero of the revolution, said . . .' Diaz cleared his throat and changed to a more declamatory tone. '. . . He said: "*La Revolución* supports the scientific venture for the good of mankind. But we know that the enemies of the people are cunning."' Still chewing, Diaz then returned to his normal voice. 'You are sure you are scientists?'

'We try,' said Burr truthfully.

A stocky man with Amazonian Indian features came over. He wore the red FARA bandanna and a bird-of-paradise feather in his hair. He leaned close to Diaz to whisper briefly in his ear. Diaz listened and nodded. '*Gracias*, Cinco,' he said. Then the *mestizo* handed something to Diaz. Burr thought it looked very much like his notebook, which he had left in the Land-Rover.

'It's not very hospitable to spy on your guests,' said Burr.

Diaz stopped eating and licked his fingers clean with a series of smacking sounds. Then he put on his red beret and turned round to look at his visitors properly for the first time. 'And to spy on your hosts does not make you a good guest,' he said. 'Cinco tells me that your people are spying from nests in the trees and that you were writing things down and taking photographs while you drove here. That is strictly forbidden.'

'Yes, we have been working in the trees, but we have not been spying. As you know from our previous communications with the FARA, we are investigating biodiversity in the forest, especially focusing on life in the canopy. As far as the notes and pictures go, yes, I apologize – I did not know it was forbidden. We note down our observations: it is data. We are scientists and we have no interest in anything else.'

'Then, you will not mind me having a look at what you've written in this book.'

'As long as you don't intend to publish the research and claim it as your own,' Burr joked.

Diaz smiled. 'I like you, Señor Burr. At least, I think I like you.' He looked at Burr thoughtfully, then opened the notebook. Burr felt Janine tense beside him as Diaz looked closely at Burr's columns of names and figures. They appeared to be lists of species and numbers found. He flicked through to the current day's date, and saw:

Madero town outskirts – forest/built environment
6 × Dismorphids – Batesian mimics of *Heliconius*
2 × Ichneumon wasps
Madero Mission Hill – low altitude/built
    environment unshaded. Distance to forest
    800–900 metres
5 × *Heliconius*
Coleoptera – *Golofa roprogrens*
Coleoptera – 2 × *Brachinus crepitans* – approx
    80 mm

'What does this mean? What is "Batesian"?'

'Well,' Burr explained, 'Bates was a naturalist who spent many years in the Amazon. He discovered that some harmless species have evolved to look like dangerous ones, to scare off predators. These dismorphid butterflies are harmless creatures that mimic poisonous *Heliconius* butterflies. *Heliconius* are poisonous to predators because they feed on poisonous vines, vines with cyanide-type compounds like this one.' Burr pointed at the large, magenta passion flowers drooping down from the creeper above Diaz's head. 'This Batesian mimicry occurs with many animals – frogs, for instance.'

'And you can tell the difference?'

'If you have a trained eye.'

'Hmmm.' Diaz raised an eyebrow. 'And this? What is *Golofa*?'

'*Golofa*? A very big beetle, with a large single horn – rhinoceros beetle, you might call it.' Burr did not explain that '*roprogrens*' was his own invention – an abbreviation for rocket-propelled grenades.

'And this *Bra-Brachinus*?'

'That is a type of beetle also known as the bombardier beetle. It shoots poisonous liquid at its enemies. It grows to about—'

'*Si, si,*' said Diaz irritably, 'about eighty milli-metres.' He seemed bored already. Cinco whispered in his ear again and he looked at Burr sharply. 'Oh, yes. Show me your photographs!' he ordered suddenly, holding out his hand for Burr's digital camera.

Burr handed over the camera and Diaz scrolled through the images. There were a few of the Argonauts working at the research centre and some more of different butterflies and orchids. Luckily David had erased the images of Cuchillo and his men. Then Diaz saw a shot of a guerrilla check-point, the men posing with their weapons. Diaz looked up at Cinco. The *mestizo* guide's face moved into a grim smile. His eyes, fixed on Burr, did not move.

There was a sudden silence. The tropical heat lay dull and heavy on the hill. From the mine came the distant hum of an engine. In the forest, a parrot cawed. Burr realized he was sweating heavily.

'Explain this,' Diaz said quietly to Burr, his voice full of menace.

Burr stepped forward and took the camera. 'Ah yes,' he said as casually as he could. 'Simple.' Burr re-centred the picture away from the stupidly grinning guerrillas and zoomed in. 'This is what I was after,' he said, 'but I'm afraid your men were goofing around and insisted on being in the shot.' He handed the camera back to Diaz. The image now on the screen was a small cloud of cream and brown butterflies, hovering over a damp patch on the sand.

'Most people think butterflies eat just nectar, but many butterflies feed on mineral salts and sugars wherever they can find them. One very concentrated source of nutrients for them is animal urine. They normally settle for tapir urine, but they appear to like human as well. I guess you should have a word with your men about their hygiene.'

Diaz gave Cinco a reproachful stare, then handed the camera back to Burr. 'You like butterflies, Mr Scientist Man?'

'I study moths too, but I do have a soft spot for butterflies. They are my speciality.'

'Moths too, huh? Mr Butterfly Man. Hey, we can call you Mr Butterfly. *Señor Mariposa*. Hey, it's like *Señor Maricon* – Mr Gay! And he likes butterflies and flowers. Are you a gay? Ha, ha, ha, ha, ha!'

Diaz and his men burst into laughter again. In relief, Janine and Burr joined them.

'Anyway,' panted Diaz eventually, still giggling and wiping away tears of laughter, 'welcome to Madero, Señor Mariposa. I think I can trust you, and I am never wrong. It is just that I like to meet new-comers. There are far too many here these days. *Planteros* and fortune hunters giving us trouble. Feel free to move about as you like. But please do not photograph my men again. There have been some unpleasant incidents recently and they can get nervous. Even I can get nervous. Currently a platoon of my men is missing, you see. If Cuchy does not come back, I might get very nervous indeed. In the meantime, follow our rules and you will be safe. You are under our protection. Of course, you will have to be careful of the forest. We cannot protect you everywhere. The last group of researchers, I suspect, became too careless.'

'What happened to them, General?' asked Burr. 'Some people have suggested that you took them hostage.'

'No, no, Señor Mariposa. Remember, Che said: "The true guerrilla does not take hostages except as a last resort." As you know, we have a no-kidnap policy in place as part of our cease-fire with the government forces. And if we were forced to take hostages again . . .' he looked carefully at Burr and Janine as if he were appraising their worth '. . . rest assured there would have been a ransom demand by now. As far as we know, your predecessors simply vanished. Believe me, we would like to know what happened. It is a little embarrassing for us.'

After the Argonauts left, Diaz and his lieutenant

watched the Land-Rover bump back down the Mission Hill.

'The tracks are deep,' said Cinco. 'We must watch them.'

'If it is armoured, so much the better. We may need another armoured vehicle sometime. I think they are harmless. If they worry you, *compañero*, keep an eye on them. I have a bad feeling about Cuchillo. If Cuchy does not come back, or if these scientists cause any trouble, our no-hostage policy could always change . . .'

Back at the Argonaut base, Burr went straight up to Anthony in the canopy.

'Well?' Burr asked, noticing the hint of a familiar smell that he couldn't quite identify.

'Uh-huh.' Anthony nodded. 'Saw you pretty much all the way. Up on the hill was best – above most of those goddamn bugs. And the heat waves aren't as thick. Through the scope I could see the moustache on the weasel face of that guy you were talking to.'

'Diaz.'

'Yup. Saw the twirly moustache on Señor Diaz's weasel face.'

'Range about one thousand?'

'About twelve hunnerd yards to the chapel; another fifty to where the weasel was sittin'. About thirteen hunnerd to the twenty-mil cannon.'

Burr looked at the sniper questioningly.

'Yeah, it's a long shot, Cap'n, but I could make it. The Barrett would do just fine. No wind would be nice.' He bounced slightly on the walkway, which wobbled alarmingly. 'And for sure I'm gonna need something more stable 'n this for a fire platform.' He looked further up into the sturdy branches of the colossal emergent that supported the central apex of the walkway. 'Way on up there, I guess.'

Burr agreed. The plan he and Ricardo were concocting called for a sniper to be there when the main assault took place. He would be shooting from the OP, taking out vital targets. With the Barrett he would neutralize the gun crews on the guerrillas' heavy weaponry and kill guerrilla officers. Sven would also be in the Argonaut camp, firing the mortar at rebel strongpoints. Finally, Pike would be left to act as back-up and to detonate the explosive charges he would be placing around Madero over the next few days.

Burr sniffed the air – the faint yet incongruous smell was still troubling him. Then he realized what it was. 'Oh no,' he said. As if there weren't enough problems on this mission. This was the last thing they needed. Burr rummaged in the leaves behind Anthony and pulled out a quarter bottle of Jack Daniels, almost empty. Burr had warned him in Arroyo Blanco and he had promised not to drink again. Now the sniper looked Burr balefully in the eye.

'Hold out your hands,' Burr said.

Anthony did. They quivered noticeably. 'I'm fine, Cap'n,' he said, without complete conviction. 'Just fine.'

Burr kept the bottle. 'We're relying on you, Anthony,' was all he said.

Anthony set to building a more stable OP hide, high up in the massive kapok tree. About twenty feet above the main canopy system, it was a true sniper's nest. He disappeared up into it like a child re-entering the womb.

On the ground, Janine had continued her obsessive drive to make the camp spick and span. The team had finally repaired the rainwater barrel, so showers were now available. 'And thank the Lord for that,' commented David, holding his nose and looking at Ahmad. 'The smell was becoming unbearable.'

Janine's diligent cleaning had also unearthed a damp book from the detritus of Daniel's team. It was a basic guide to emeralds. Burr went through it. The pages were wet and stuck together. Many had been partly devoured by insects. Someone had made notes in the margin. The writing was faint and almost illegible, but Burr realized with a chill that it looked like Daniel's. So his partner had been interested in the emeralds. A photograph on one page had been ringed and the caption underlined. It looked like a golden figurine in a glass case. The caption was almost illegible, but Burr could make out that the statue was in the Museo del Oro in Bogotá.

Burr did not know what to do about it. He put the book aside and prepared for the standing daily contacts with Argonaut HQ and the training team in Arroyo Blanco. Again he noticed that the battery on the sat phone was much weaker than expected. This time he did call Janine over.

'Looks fine,' she said, after checking the power cell. 'Maybe someone's phoning their girlfriend.'

'Oh yes?' said Burr.

'OK, well, I have made a couple of quick calls to Carlo,' she admitted, 'but I made sure to top up the battery again from the solar panels.'

Speaking from the Bond militia camp, Ricardo confirmed that training had begun in earnest. 'These *milicianos* are beginning to respond,' he admitted grudgingly. 'Apparently Daniel did actually drum some basic instruction into them. It's just that they've forgotten it.'

'And I'm sure you are giving them some very gentle reminders,' said Burr, chuckling. 'What about the Jaguar platoon of Lester's?'

'Amazingly, those boys do have some aerial-assault skills. Paul is working with them to be the point element of the Madero assault.'

There was still plenty of ground to cover, but Ricardo now estimated it would be no more than a week or two before the Bond would be ready to take the offensive.

Burr then spoke to Carlo, who had just returned from his flying visit to Yucatán.

Carlo was trying to sound upbeat, but Burr thought he detected an odd catch in his voice. 'Are you all right?' asked Burr. 'You sound a bit strange.'

Carlo gave a laugh that sounded fake even bounced up and down from a satellite. 'I'm fine,

Burr. Just a bit worried about Janine and you guys. Please be careful.'

'Are you sure? Did the council like the development plan?'

'It, it went very well, Burr. Just relax. They said they would let us know next week which projects will qualify to submit sealed bids. What about your end?'

Burr sighed and reassured him that everything was progressing smoothly and that of course Janine had everything 'just so'. Their cover was tight and they had already gathered good intelligence. Burr had to admit that they still had no clear picture of what happened to Daniel. He did not mention the book on emeralds, or the Indian he had seen.

'Well, stay alert,' said Carlo. 'The Daniel thing is worrying. It's an unknown, and I don't like those. Anyway, whatever happened to Daniel, we can't afford it to happen to you.'

After the call, Burr wondered why Carlo sounded so odd. He was stressed maybe, but that wasn't quite the word. No, it was almost as though Carlo sounded ashamed.

The next day, Burr went on an all-day patrol, on foot, with David. When he returned, he was confronted with the full fruition of Janine's efforts at spring-cleaning. Pike and Sven had returned with more equipment and had been immediately put to work.

'Oh, no,' said Burr. He was surveying the crisp line of perfectly spaced, brightly whitewashed rocks running around the perimeter. Janine had even collected some of the shards of pegmatite and quartz that littered the forest floor and used them to neatly line the last few yards of the access track like airport runway markers. Janine had added other little touches everywhere, from the blinding coat of white paint on the buildings to the cut flowers on the windowsills. Neat signs on the huts labelled them as 'Storeroom' and 'Office'.

Burr suspected they should dirty the place up a little, and certainly do away with the regimented perimeter markers, but Janine was so proud he could not bring himself to say anything. She had even managed to inveigle the team into doing a morning clean-up. He racked his brains for a way to get them to do a dirty-up instead.

'So?' asked Janine. 'What do you think?'

'It's great,' said Burr lamely. 'It looks . . . just great.'

Janine's plain face broke into a radiant smile. Before Burr could upset her by suggesting his changes, there was the sound of a vehicle drawing up.

'Oh, no,' said Burr again as he saw Leila and Makepeace approaching.

'It's amazing,' said Leila, looking round the spruced-up clearing. 'You've done a great job – and so quickly.' She smiled at a paint-splashed Ahmad and Pike, who broke off from their whitewashing detail to grin back at her lustily.

'Hmm, yes, impressive. A platoon of Royal Engineers couldn't have done better,' mused

Makepeace, looking at the neatly arrayed stones, the line of tents and the perfect order in the storeroom.

'We were thinking . . .'

'Yes?' said Burr warily.

'. . . of your offer to let us up into the canopy.'

Burr prevaricated. Part of him was very pleased to see Leila and very much wanted to show her the glories of the canopy, especially in the early morning: he would welcome another opinion on the unusual phenomenon he had glimpsed in the distance – the mass display of insects he had seen through the morning mist.

More prudent brain messages, however, told him it might not be a good idea to have Leila hanging around on a regular basis.

'Look, Leila,' he tried, 'I didn't offer and I'm not sure it's a good idea. The canopy system's not really designed for another two people.'

'Oh, don't worry about me,' said Makepeace. 'It'll be just one more person. I'm terrified of heights. She's not afraid of anything. Leila, what do you think?' There was no answer. 'Leila!'

'Where did you get that?' asked Leila, almost whispering. She was talking to Ahmad, pointing to a tubular grey stem with a wilting red and yellow flower on the window ledge of the hut behind him.

'What, this? Up high,' said Ahmad, pointing at the canopy. 'Janine said we should make the camp brighter. I was in the trees at dawn and the flowers looked so beautiful . . .' Not sure why Leila was so interested, Ahmad began to wonder if he had done something wrong. 'Is it endangered? Should I not have picked it?' Like a guilty child he pointed at Pike. 'Pike is an orchid expert, so I brought it down for him.'

'Do you know what it is?' Leila asked Pike excitedly.

Pike looked daggers at Ahmad. 'Er, um, no. Well, I haven't really had time to examine it properly.'

'Well, that's not surprising – because I can tell you, you won't identify it. It's not an orchid really. It's a new species – the Jemberí call it *kiragi*.'

'How, uh, interesting,' said Pike feebly.

'Of course, we have been working on the species for some time and we have already sent voucher specimens to the herbariums in Bogotá and Oxford universities.' Leila was quick to put down her professional markers – she didn't want any doubt about who had discovered *kiragi*.

'Oh, yes.' Pike had no idea what a voucher specimen was. 'Of course.'

'But I'd love to see it up in its element . . .' Leila said to Burr, hinting heavily. She picked up the *kiragi* plant and addressed Ahmad. 'You say you found this at dawn. I think that may be the only time the *kiragi* flowers. Well, I'll be here at five o'clock tomorrow morning.'

'But—' said Burr.

'No buts,' said Leila. 'This could be a critical breakthrough for us.' She took a deep breath. 'OK, fair's fair. Whatever our findings, you can write them up for scientific journals. And if you're worried about a credit or a cut of the profit in any products, don't be. We'll make sure everybody gets a fair share.'

'Oh . . .' said Burr. 'But that's not—'

Makepeace patted Burr on the back. 'Good decision, old chap,' he said loudly. Then he added quietly, as Leila strode back to the car, 'Though, to be frank, you didn't have much choice anyway. One more thing. Give yourself an extra half-hour's sleep tomorrow morning. There's no way she'll be on time.'

Burr did not heed Makepeace's advice. He was out of his tent, shaved and dressed, by five the next morning – years of military punctuality were impossible to shake. Janine was on watch in the canopy and the other Argonauts were sleeping. By five-fifteen he was getting impatient. Leila was late. At about five-twenty the muffled rumble of an engine carried to him through the forest. Then he saw the glow of headlights on the bottom of the canopy. Leila's Toyota bumped into the clearing just after five-thirty. The dawn chorus was well under way, with frogs, birds and insects singing. The reverberating booms of a distant tribe of howler monkeys sounded faintly.

'You're late, ma'am,' said Burr icily.

'Sorry, Sergeant-General,' said Leila, yawning. 'You'll survive.' The Trinidadian brogue came through more strongly in her sleepy tones. 'Didn't know you worked on army time. Anyways, you're lucky I'm here at all. Sleep-driving through the forest is not to be recommended.'

Burr said nothing, just clipped her, maybe a little too firmly, into the lifting harness. Leila liked the feel of him pulling the belts taut around her. He had to stand very close to fasten the straps and test the buckles, and despite, or maybe because of, her semi-somnolent state Leila thought very un-scientific thoughts.

'A bit tighter,' she said with a smile, bringing his arms around her once again.

'Just relax,' he said, 'and try not to turn too much: you could tangle the ropes.'

Then he pressed the button on the power box and the winch whined quietly into life, pulling Leila slowly upwards. Down in the clearing there had been the faintest hint of morning half-light. Under the trees it was still black and Leila savoured the slow journey, rising through the different storeys of the forest, a succession of layered sounds and scents.

Leila squealed as the winch stopped and two unseen hands grasped her and pulled her over onto the walkway.

'Don't worry,' said the dark shape. 'It's me, Janine. And I'm leaving. Just hold on to the ropes and you'll be fine. Burr will be up in a second.' Janine clipped Leila's safety rope to the walkway guide rope, strapped on the lift harness and lowered herself out of sight.

Leila was left alone in the canopy. It was cooler than at ground level, with a soft breeze ruffling the leaves. In the almost-darkness among the highest branches, she could hear the quiet cooing of birds and smell strange scents that never reached the ground. She felt the soft breath of moth wings fluttering against her face.

The pulleys beside her stopped, then after a pause started to whirr again. Burr appeared next to her, a dark mass in the shadows, and unhitched himself from the harness.

'It's wonderful,' said Leila. For some reason she was whispering.

'It gets better. Come here.'

Burr guided her out through a curtain of leaves to where the walkway gave a view over the canopy.

Leila gasped. It was like seeing a different planet. The sky above was tinted bright yellow, the tallest trees jutting golden above the rolling, hummocked green landscape of the forest. Around and above the trees, huge coils of mist rose in massive waves, swirling on the faint breeze. Half a mile away, Leila could see, the Mission Hill at Madero rose like an island in a roiling white sea.

It was the transpiration, the breathing of the forest, she was witnessing. Leila had seen the morning mists, but never from the canopy. Up here it looked like the whole world sighing. In fact the forest was breathing out the warm, moist air trapped among the trees at night. Billions of gallons of water vapour. The prevailing winds would sweep the vapour westwards across the forest, where it would condense and fall as rain, be absorbed, exhaled and swept westwards again, until it hit the impermeable mountain wall of the Andes, where it would finally fall again, and run back down to the forest in a myriad streams and rivers. It was a beautiful, startling sight, tinged with sadness for Leila as she thought of the Amazonian forest shrinking, its heart ripped out by miners and loggers, its edges hacked down by cattle ranchers. One day, perhaps, all this – the trees, the mist – all of it would be gone, leaving a sterile desert.

'And here's something I really want you to see,' said Burr, turning Leila to look away from the town. As the sun leapt over the sierras it picked out flashes of glinting fire. In the distance, over the hills, thousands of golden flecks were rising up on the mist like a shower of glittering confetti.

'What is it?' whispered Leila, in awe.

'Some kind of insect – butterflies, I think. I suspect it's a new species.'

'It's like an Impressionist painting,' Leila murmured, enraptured by the golden points of light flitting and swooping among the treetops. 'What are they doing? It's like . . . it's like they're dancing.'

Burr handed her some binoculars. 'Feeding, perhaps, or maybe it's a mating display. I'm not sure. I don't think this phenomenon has been recorded before.'

'Well, unless you were up here you'd never see it. You'd never know it was happening.'

'Yes, and it's also very short-lived.'

As Burr spoke, a swirl of bats shot through the air, feeding on the insects. Then the sun rose and the bats disappeared, to be replaced by swallows. These sailed above the trees, feeding on the last of the golden mist, which disappeared with the full light of the sun. The whole spectacle had lasted less than five minutes.

'You have to document this,' said Leila.

'Yes, but I'm not sure how. Today was the best view I've had of the display. I haven't seen it happen close to the camp, and no butterfly of that coloration has been caught in our traps. Whatever species they are, they don't seem to gather near the town, or near open ground. It may be that they don't like clearings.'

'Perhaps,' said Leila. 'Though I did once see golden butterflies around our field lab. Come to think of it, that was also at dawn. They may have been the same species.'

'What were they doing?' asked Burr eagerly.

'They seemed to be attracted by the *kiragi* flower.'

Leila and Burr pondered on the possible links while the mist burned off and the insects disappeared, presumably to daytime hiding places in the trees. Looking down in the daylight, Leila could see the ground more than a hundred feet below. She felt the dizzying, toppling sensation of vertigo and held on tightly to the rope.

With the coming of the light, Anthony appeared in the canopy and disappeared up to his observation post without a word.

'Friendly, isn't he?' commented Leila.

'Don't worry about Anthony,' said Burr. 'He's never talkative. Secretive about his work.'

'Doesn't want anyone else to publish his research?'

'That's for sure.'

'I know the type,' said Leila.

She then began scouring the canopy for specimens. The sight of the gilded morning display gave her added enthusiasm and in the canopy Leila found she was happy. She loved it there, surrounded by so much of the life you only heard, smelt or glimpsed from the ground. It was like escaping from the bonds of earth, she thought. For a while she could forget the hard, violent reality of the rainforest and lose herself in the dream. Musky orchids she had smelt, but never seen, clung on to the branches, part of the rich epiphyte gardens that grew in this parallel world, closer to the all-precious sunlight. A troop of spider monkeys swung by, oblivious to Leila. Toucans, tanagers and the rare hoatzin glided through the shadows below. Other birds and insects she couldn't name flew, jumped and crawled all round her.

While Leila worked on the plants, she was aware of Burr going about his own research with methodical efficiency. He took observations over the canopy, writing down everything in his field notebook. He came over to her frequently, naming a butterfly, or pointing out pupae that she thought were twigs or an insect that looked just like a blob of moss. Leila liked the way he talked in that smooth, unhurried Southern voice. He seemed at ease – at home – in the forest and there was something calm and certain about him that Leila liked. Now and again she was pleased to catch him stealing a glance at her and after a while she asked him coyly, 'So, are you observing me or the wildlife?'

'Well, you are part of the canopy fauna.'

'How are you recording me, then?'

'As a species new to science. Mammal, I think. I've yet to work out the genus.'

She laughed a thrilling, gurgling laugh and Burr laughed with her.

Burr interspersed observations of rebel movements in Madero with the work of a lepidopterist, emptying his trap of night fliers, noting and photographing species. Some of this was worthwhile research, some of it for Leila's benefit, such as when he opened some rotting passion fruits and laid them on a tree branch.

'To attract butterflies,' said Burr.

'I thought they were nectar feeders,' said Leila.

'Not true,' said Burr. 'They'll go for anything with mineral salts and sugars – some species eat pollen, others eat faeces or urine and some will even pierce skin and suck blood.'

Soon, two iridescent blue morphos appeared. Fat-bodied, broad-winged butterflies, big as saucers, they were designed for swift flight. The sunlight glittered and refracted off the top of their cavorting wings, the bright blue shimmering and changing like the rainbow in a film of petrol. '*Morpho pleiades*,' said Burr. 'They're looking for sugars. A lot of brightly coloured butterflies are advertising poison. These morphos aren't poisonous, but when they perch – as you can see now – they're camouflaged.' The butterflies settled on the fruit and folded up their wings to vanish in perfect crypsis. Their underwings were brown and mottled as the tree bark.

'When they open their wings their bright colours can attract predators, but their speed makes up for their visibility. But to fly fast they need stronger fuel than nectar, so they get extra energy from fermenting fruit. The sugars are concentrated and it gives them a boost.'

'Turbocharged,' said Leila.

'Kind of,' said Burr, watching the butterflies prod the food with their front legs. Burr explained to Leila that when butterflies touch food with their feet, they are tasting it. Their taste organs are on their feet.

'And didn't you say some butterflies feed on faeces?' asked Leila.

'Yes, human is a favourite, actually – very mineral-rich.'

'So when they land on dung they're actually tasting . . .'

'Shit?' drawled Burr. 'Yeah, I guess so.' He smiled as he carefully photographed the butterflies.

Watching Burr absorbed in his work, Leila had soon decided that Makepeace's doubts about the Argonaut Ecology team were absurd. Burr was not only an expert on insects, he clearly adored them. She found this softer side distinctly endearing, but in truth it was only part of the charm he had for her. Once she stood up just as a strong gust of wind hit the unstable walkway. It swayed alarmingly and she toppled into Burr. She gasped not from the fall, but because she suddenly felt an acute awareness of his controlled strength. He caught her as if she were no heavier than a bird. His chest was flat and hard as rock.

These different sides to Burr intrigued Leila. More than once she was startled as he plucked something out of the air with sudden, blinding speed. Through his strong, curled fingers, she would see wings fluttering. 'There,' he would say, opening his hand gently, and cradled on his palm would be a flying beetle perhaps, or on one occasion what looked like a huge wasp.

'You'll be stung,' Leila gasped.

'It looks like a type of *Sesiidae*,' he said, as the creature preened its wings for a moment as though pretending nothing had happened. 'It's actually a moth. Resembles a hornet, but it's a harmless mimic.'

And you? Leila wondered. Are you harmless? For some reason, she harboured doubts about him, yet felt entirely comfortable with him at the same time.

'You must come over to our camp as soon as you get the chance,' she said. 'I'd like to show you more of myself – I mean, of my work.'

She blushed and Burr pretended not to notice the Freudian slip.

In the late morning, Burr was back down in the clearing when he heard Leila yell out from above. He winched himself swiftly back up into the canopy to find that a highly irritated Anthony had already been to check on her.

211

'What is it?' Burr asked.

'Oh, it's nuthin'. Nuthin' at all. Woman found some stupid plant is all.' He stalked off down the swaying walkway, then paused and turned back to Burr with a harsh whisper. 'I don't like to say it, Cap'n. And I always respected you. And I ain't one to talk, but only one thing's a bigger distraction 'n whisky – and that's a woman. She's gotta go. Real soon.' He turned his back on Burr and clambered up into his hide.

A chastened Burr moved carefully along to where Leila was working. 'Look!' she bubbled in elation, pointing at a branch overgrown with a dense thicket of epiphytes. Hidden among the hanging garden of vines and bromeliads nestled a dreary plant with a tubular grey stem, thin, rubbery leaves and straggling aerial roots. It looked something like a sad orchid without a flower.

'Wonderful,' said Burr drily. 'You plant people have a good eye for, uh, form.'

Leila gurgled happily. 'No, it doesn't look very beautiful, does it? But it's something very special.'

Burr waited.

'It's *kiragi*. You don't recognize it without the flower. I've never seen a specimen *in situ*.' She was thrilled and Burr smiled in spite of himself. Her excitement was so genuine and infectious.

Ahmad changed shifts with Anthony, who glared balefully at Leila again as he climbed down the rope ladder. Leila smiled at him politely. She was too excited to worry that some bad-tempered research assistant didn't like her. Burr watched Leila frown in concentration while she cut the *kiragi* carefully from its branch, trying to preserve as much as possible of the aerial-root system. She then left happily, eager to show Makepeace her discovery.

Later that day Janine and Ahmad came in from patrol with a discovery of their own. It was a torn piece of pixellated cloth that appeared to come from combat dress. Janine handed it to Burr.

'What do you think?' he asked.

'I think Daniel was Marine Recon and that he and his men wore Marine-issue camouflage.'

'But why would they be in the forest in their combat gear?' asked Ahmad. 'If they had been seen in uniform, it would have blown their cover.'

Why indeed? Burr wondered. It was baffling. First Daniel had changed plan by joining the whole team together in Madero. Then he had reported that he was mounting a routine patrol. Leila said they had often gone on these patrols, or 'research trips' as she'd perceived them. But they would not normally have gone in combat gear. That would have made it very un-routine. They should only have put on the uniforms for the actual assault on the rebels. Burr felt it had something to do with the emerald book. Had Daniel decided to go emerald mining himself?

That lunchtime, the Argonauts sat in the shade by the clearing. There was little feeling of camaraderie. If anything, Anthony seemed even more taciturn than usual, and David even more disgruntled. The team was distracted by lurking headhunters and the unknown fate of their predecessors. To these concerns, Burr could add some private worries. First, the unauthorized use of the sat phone, and, second, he did not think Carlo was keeping him abreast of developments at Xcalan. He trusted Carlo, but the lack of information was a bit odd.

Among all these issues, Burr was still pretty sure he knew what was unsettling the team. 'OK,' he said eventually, 'what's the problem now?'

Janine cleared her throat. Clearly she had again been appointed spokesperson. 'It's Leila, Burr. We're sorry but she could compromise security.'

'I've thought about this,' responded Burr defensively, 'and if we're careful we can turn it to our advantage.' Anticipating the Argonauts' reaction, he had managed to come up with a number of excuses for Leila's presence. 'It's good discipline for us to have her here – it'll force us to maintain our cover, and we should be able to achieve that if Sven would damn well stop saluting,' Sven looked wounded as Burr went on, 'and if you, Janine, manage to stop painting military signs everywhere. In fact, with Leila being a well-known scientist in Madero, having her working here reinforces our cover.'

'With all due respect, Burr,' said Ahmad carefully, 'that sounds to me like your own cover story. It is not odd – she is an attractive woman. But we are relying on your judgement and women can affect that.'

'Yeah,' said David. 'You expect us to believe it's all for the sake of the mission that you spend all that time discussing leaves and bugs with her.'

'Birds and bees, more like,' sniggered Pike.

'That is not polite, Pike,' said Sven.

'Just joking,' said Pike hastily, adding under his breath, 'you big lummox.'

Pike yelped as the Swede cuffed him across the head with a massive hand.

'That's enough, children,' snapped Janine. 'We want to hear what Burr says.'

'I take the point,' Burr said, 'but keeping her away might raise more suspicion and cause more problems than it solves. For the moment, she can stay.'

Anthony shook his head and everybody paused, listening for a rare pearl of wisdom. 'Mmm-hmmm,' he said. 'That dog won't hunt. This means trouble. Women mean trouble.'

That was exactly what Burr had been telling himself during years of being alone, but for some reason he did not see it applying to Leila. He thought of her softness as she had fallen against him on the walkway and her scent like jasmine. Leila was so different from him. She was frank and open, whereas he was covert and closed. She was bright-eyed and optimistic. And she had the most catching, rippling laugh he had ever heard. It brought a smile to his face just thinking of it. Burr stopped smiling. Obviously the team were right. He was not thinking straight. Truth was, Burr thought, he was getting a bit complacent. He had forgotten his earlier doubts and mistrust and allowed himself to get distracted because, apart from there being no leads on Daniel's whereabouts, the mission was going far, far too smoothly.

The change, when it came, was signalled by Anthony. First he noticed an increase in rebel movements. Through his scope the guards appeared jumpy. Now and then they even fired nervous shots. He reported this to Burr, who was not surprised when the messenger girl, Juanita, arrived in the camp again, this time in a pick-up full of guerrillas. The guerrillas searched the camp thoroughly, messing up Janine's well-ordered huts. They found nothing, but, before leaving, Juanita issued another order from Diaz. Burr was commanded to present himself at the mine gates at noon.

'I'm busy,' he said shortly, but Juanita just repeated the instruction, this time accompanied with a loud spit onto the ground. Burr ignored her, but then she perched the butt of her AK-47 suggestively on her hip and pulled back the bolt.

David sidled quietly over. 'Come on, Burr. I'm sure we can spare a few minutes for the generalissimo,' he said.

Burr left just before twelve, with David driving. Five minutes later, after passing three checkpoints, they rounded a corner and the mine suddenly leapt into view. It was a bleak sight after the verdant green of the forest. The denuded hillsides were naked rock and eroded soil, ringed with a double fence covered in coils of razor wire. The lower slopes running down to the Madero River were a morass of thick mud. Burr could see the *guaceros* trampling in it, eyes downcast. Juanita shouted at the checkpoint guards, who waved the Land-Rover through. The road was lined with armed rebels. Burr counted twenty-five *Blaberus*.

'*Blaberus* . . . ?' asked David.

'Cockroaches.'

Approaching the mine precinct, Burr saw workers walking down towards the exit from all over the site. He moved his view down to the flat, dusty area outside the mine gates. A few more cars and trucks than usual were parked close to the mine fence. Men were gathering from outside the mine as well. Burr noticed that even the *guaceros* working the muddy slopes had stopped moving. Despite the blazing midday sun, most of them had removed their hats.

'I don't like the look of this,' said David. He stopped and started to try a three-point turn in the narrow track. But the guerrillas at the next checkpoint shouted and waved them forward. A truck behind them blocked the road anyway, and they were forced on to where more guerrillas waved them to a stop, indicating that they should park. David pulled off the road and they got out.

Burr saw the tubby figure of Diaz with a group of guerrillas. They were standing around a gigantic lone kapok tree in the middle of the bare, dusty area just outside the mine gates. Burr noticed a group of European-looking men and women standing stiffly towards the front of the crowd. Among them he saw Makepeace and Leila, an appalled expression on her face.

As Burr approached, one of Diaz's men slung a rope up over a bare branch. There was a momentary hush as the noose at the end of the rope swung emptily on the heavy air, drawing everybody's eyes.

'I've seen enough,' said David, pulling Burr back towards the car.

But Diaz had spotted them. 'Welcome, Señor Mariposa,' he said grimly. Diaz seemed very different from the man who had met Burr a few days before. He seemed enraged, almost manic. 'Now you can see how we dispense the people's justice.' His men pushed Burr and David round to join the other summoned onlookers.

'*Compañeros*, citizens of Madero,' Diaz shouted, 'a few days ago the hero of the revolution, *compañero* Cuchillo, went on a vital mission for the downtrodden people of Colombia. Now we know what has befallen them. It is sad, sad news.' Diaz paused and sniffed loudly. His moustache quivered and he wiped away a theatrical tear. '*Compañero* Cuchillo and all his men have been cruelly murdered.'

The onlookers gasped. Diaz paused again for effect, then continued angrily. 'It is clear that the enemies of the revolution will stop at nothing. We cannot relax our vigil. We cannot allow the enemies of the people to escape the people's justice.'

'Now I have a really bad feeling about this,' David whispered to Burr.

'Me too,' agreed Burr.

'Thanks for the show, General,' muttered David, 'but I think we'll take a rain-check.'

Burr and David turned to leave, but as they did so a murmur rippled through the crowd. Burr looked back to see Cinco and two other guerrillas pull a man from the back of a parked truck. Burr saw Leila put her hand over her mouth in dismay. The rebels dragged the captive through the dirt by a chain attached to his handcuffs. Then they pulled him to his feet beside the kapok tree and left him standing by the gaping noose, head lowered.

'Did he tell you where he got them, where he had them cut?' Diaz muttered to Cinco.

The *mestizo* lowered his head, ashamed.

'Are you losing your touch?' Diaz hissed at him.

Angrily, Cinco grabbed the captive's long hair. He jerked the condemned man's head back and thrust it into the empty noose.

As the rope tightened round his neck, the prisoner lifted his gaze, but he did not look at Diaz. He looked straight at Burr.

Burr stifled a gasp of horror and surprise. The man had been badly beaten. His body was covered in cuts and bruises, blood from a head wound had congealed on his face, but that was not what startled Burr. The man had one eye. The second was a bloody, empty socket. He was unmistakably Mayan, and Burr knew him.

Burr remembered him from his youth on Xcalan. He was the *chac*, the elder who was searching for the serpent's eye. *He was Tenoch*.

In a counter-intuitive response so ingrained it was automatic, Burr's Special Forces training took over. Rather than panic and frantically claw for options, Burr's mind slowed and emptied. He tried to absorb and harness the flood of adrenalin. Within seconds he controlled his breathing and cut out all extraneous thoughts and impressions in order to focus on the critical. His options were few. David was unarmed. Burr had only his Ka-Bar knife and there were dozens of armed guerrillas around them. Knock the closest man down and take his gun? Too many guns about. He needed more time. Take the leader first, knife to the throat? He would not get within ten feet of Diaz. Try to buy time was the only practicable option.

'What are you going to do to him?' Burr asked Diaz.

'What are we going to do? We will impose the people's justice in this case, as in all cases.'

Keep talking, thought Burr. 'What is his crime, General?' he tried. 'I could pay a fine. You could show mercy.'

Diaz shook his head. 'He will receive the mercy that poor Cuchillo received. I understand your distaste for such ugly scenes. You are a scientist, a man of peace. Unfortunately, as a leader it is my unpleasant duty to do justice on behalf of the people. And the people's justice is not for sale. Clemency for this man would mean the end of the mines. They would all become criminals like this one. You know what this filthy *guacero* did?'

Diaz brought out something from his pocket. It glinted in the sun as he raised his voice and turned to the crowd. Rage at Diaz and at his own impotence welled up in Burr as he realized that the rebel commander was holding Tenoch's glass eye.

'This pitiful *guacero*,' Diaz declaimed, 'was caught a few days ago in the forest. He tried to smuggle emeralds out of Madero. He tried – he dared to try

– to sell the wealth of the revolution to those paper tigers, the capitalists of Bogotá.' Diaz was shouting, making sure his voice carried to the sullen audience of mine workers and to Tenoch's fellow *guaceros* standing sombrely in the mud below.

'You know that emeralds are a gift from our blessed soil. They belong to the poor – to *los pobres de la tierra*. If this thieving *guacero* had sold his stones to us, everything would have been fine. But he thought he could steal stones from the people. He thought he could hide them from the revolution. Well, he was wrong.'

Diaz flung the glass eye into the air. The entire crowd was hushed for a second, their gaze following the eye's silent parabola. Flashing in the sun, it arced above the crowd and plopped softly into the mud amongst the *guaceros*.

'He committed theft – theft from the poor people of Colombia. And there is only one penalty for stealing from the people.' Diaz turned to his lieutenant and nodded. Cinco's massive arms bulged as he pulled on the rope. The noose tightened round Tenoch's neck.

'Diaz, don't kill this man.' Burr's voice was flat. He took a step forward. Instantly he was halted by a thicket of guerrilla rifles pointed at his chest.

'Be careful, *Yanqui*. My men can be trigger-happy.' Diaz laughed, then paused, suddenly suspicious. 'Anyway, what is so special about this man? You know him?'

Burr said nothing.

Diaz pulled out his pistol and jabbed the barrel

roughly into Tenoch's ear. 'Eh, *guacero*! You have seen this man before? You know him?'

Tenoch shook his head. He lifted his eye to the sun in the clear sky and mumbled a few disjointed sentences in his mother tongue. Burr watched him in horror.

'Pray to your fucking useless gods if you like,' snarled Diaz. He nodded again at Cinco, who pulled hard on the rope. It tightened on Tenoch's throat, choking off his words. Another tug and the Mayan was lifted off the ground, his bare feet kicking helplessly.

'No!' Burr shouted. He lunged forward, but David's wiry arms held him back.

'Wait, Burr!' David whispered in Burr's ear, holding him tightly. 'Not now.'

Tenoch spasmed silently in the noose, his one eye open, staring upwards. Diaz laughed and spat on the jerking body. After a while, Tenoch was still, his blank face still looking up at the pitiless sun.

Burr stared at Diaz with hooded eyes. It was a look David recognized. It meant Diaz was a dead man.

Burr and David returned to the Argonaut camp. Burr was ashen-faced and spoke little for the rest of the day. Mechanically, he maintained his cover experiments and took his shift observing guerrilla movements. But his mind was elsewhere. He was thinking back to Xcalan when he was a child. He remembered a younger Tenoch there, laughing and joking with Burr's mother and her hippy friends. Tenoch had always been kind to Burr, opening coconuts and carving small wooden boats for him.

Until he saw Tenoch's head in the noose, Burr had not thought about the Mayan since Isaiah had mentioned him back in Xcalan. Burr had simply not believed that he and Tenoch would meet in the vastness of the jungle. Things like that did not fit with his world view. They just did not happen. But this had happened. And he had failed Tenoch. More than that, Diaz had hanged the Mayan in a rage brought on by Burr's own actions. The killing of Cuchillo had directly led to the Mayan's death.

Burr buried his head in his hands. It seemed that his mission and the Mayan's were interwoven somehow, just as Isaiah had suggested that night in the cenote. What else should he be recalling from that night? He remembered jumbled talk about the eye. He remembered dreaming about the tennis match. He felt there was a clear link, but it was just out of reach. Perhaps Tenoch could have helped him. He had certainly tried before he died. Tenoch's last words had been uttered in his native Mayan tongue. Burr was the only person there who could have understood them, and he knew that Diaz had been wrong about what Tenoch was saying. The Mayan had not been praying to useless gods. He had been speaking directly to Burr.

Burr tried to remember exactly what the Mayan had said. Some of his last cryptic utterances seemed to refer to what the Maya at Xcalan had seen as the hope of Burr's mission – not the money, but the Serpent's Eye. Burr had found it difficult to hear: Tenoch had been talking fast, through a choked larynx and a mouthful of blood, with a split lip and broken teeth. What Burr heard was something like this: 'Go to La Esmeralda . . . hidden . . . the cattle tree. Warriors guard them – the small eyes . . . Trust Neman . . . Through him you can find a stone . . . Swear you will try – swear!'

Tenoch had looked at Burr then, and in that moment Burr had made the second addition to his mission objectives in Madero. Finding an emerald for the Xcalan statue was not part of Burr's original GemCorp assignment, but neither was killing Javier Diaz, and that specific objective was now very definitely part of the plan.

That evening Burr drove out alone towards the town. He turned off the main road, not far before the first checkpoint, onto a track he had noticed the day before. It was crudely signposted 'Esmeralda'.

The track led to an area close to the mines where a tract of forest had recently been hacked down to make way for a slum of tiny shanties. These now huddled together in a sea of mud and trash among the stubborn stumps of great trees.

Burr asked the residents, mostly penniless *guaceros* and their families, about Tenoch the Mayan. He was met with a suspicious silence. Eventually an old man pointed him to a narrow alleyway that sloped down towards the forest. The passage also served as the slum drain. Burr walked between the backs of shanties, his steps sinking shin-deep in the sludge of mud and human filth. He could feel it oozing in over the top of his boots.

Tenoch's hut was at the end of the alley, just inside the eaves of the forest. Its walls were made from cooking-oil tins, cut apart and beaten flat to form flimsy metal panels. It was a forlorn place. The building had been kicked askew; the whole structure now tilted like a parallelogram. The rough wooden door was smashed. Burr switched on his flashlight and peered inside.

Diaz's men had clearly ransacked the place. The crude roof of branches and palm leaves lay strewn about. The entire floor had been dug up. If Tenoch had anything hidden here, it would have been discovered. Burr found nothing of interest. Apart from some meagre cooking utensils and a blanket, Tenoch seemed to have had no possessions at all. Burr went over Tenoch's words for the hundredth time: 'hidden', Tenoch had said, '. . . the cattle tree'.

Burr set off into the forest, moving carefully back and forth until, after about fifty paces, his flashlight picked out the cattle tree – a species of *Acacia*. Perplexed for a moment, he examined the tree. Its bark was smooth and broken only by the strange Beltian bodies – thorned nodules – looking like the wide-spread horns of zebu oxen. The nodules oozed a slow, sweet sap. There seemed to be no holes in the trunk and Tenoch had left no signs upon it. The lowest branch was fifteen feet up, so whatever Burr was looking for was probably not up there.

Burr sat down and leaned against the tree. Almost

immediately he received a sharp sting on the nape of his neck. He jumped up, brushing off his attackers from his shirt and trousers. They were stinging ants, an aggressive species of *Pseudomyrmex*, Burr assumed. He turned his flashlight downwards and saw dozens more standing heraldic over a nest at the base of the acacia.

'Warriors guard them,' Burr murmured to himself. He picked up a fallen branch and smashed at the hard clay of the nest. The ants went into a frenzy. A line of guards streamed out to repel the intruder. Burr broke off a chunk of nest and then another. Hundreds of soldier ants were now frantically attacking the end of the branch and beginning to run up it towards Burr's hands. Burr jabbed at the nest again. The ants were biting at his hands now, sinking their stings and pincers into his fingers like hot needles. He knocked off another large chunk of clay from the nest and saw a flash of white amidst thousands of clustered ants. Grimacing with pain from the ant bites, Burr enlarged the hole once more, then threw the stick away and jammed his hand straight down into the seething mass of ants.

He gasped and swore as he was immediately bitten more times than he could count. His hand felt as if it was on fire. Burr's groping fingertips touched a soft surface. He clutched at it and closed his fist round what felt like a small bag. Then he ripped it out of the nest and ran back from the tree, desperately shaking and brushing off the ants that covered his hands and forearms, dangling determinedly from their pincers, which would not release

226

their grip even when the ants' bodies were knocked away.

Back at the Argonaut camp, alone in his tent, Burr found his swollen hand was clenched round a white handkerchief, wrapped and knotted into a simple bundle. Using his unbitten hand, he untied it carefully. And he gasped.

It wasn't the first time Diaz had forced them to witness his 'people's justice', but the brutal hanging of Tenoch had left Leila and Makepeace shocked and appalled. They had returned, shaken, to their work. Makepeace had taken refuge in his most effective therapy. He went out into 'his' 25-hectare tract of forest. Makepeace had been studying his patch for so long that some of the aluminium tags he had fixed to saplings in the north-western quadrats (subdivisions of 20 m × 20 m) were now out of sight over one hundred feet high, engulfed by their swelling trunks. This time he chose to study an intriguing wetland quadrat in the north-west corner, where he had found some fascinating hybrids of the Victoria water lily. And some variants of *monstera* – a common household plant with deeply indented leaves, often called a Swiss cheese plant. Except here the leaves were ten feet long.

Makepeace was past fifty, and he had realized that this was now his life's work. He had also realized that his tortoise-like progress and obsession for detail were widely mocked in the scientific community – that is, in those obscure corners of the community where people had actually heard of him. Makepeace did not mind. He believed that history would justify his work. He knew that it might be others who made the great scientific breakthroughs. He was satisfied to do the groundwork, though, and you never knew – sometimes Craford Prizes were given to the most surprising recipients. In a sense he saw himself as an explorer, opening up the great hidden treasures of the Amazon for subsequent generations. More plant and animal species lived in the Amazonian jungle than in any other environment. It thrilled Makepeace that in his small forest tract he had identified at least 270 types of tree, significantly more than the 200 species found in the continental United States. At least one-third of the plants he studied were unnamed and unknown to science. Makepeace was convinced that this diversity would help mankind. He was prepared to put up with just about anything, including Diaz's excesses. For him, losing the project would be the ultimate disaster.

Makepeace spent the rest of the day collecting water lilies, returning to the research centre just in time to see a number of rebel vehicles leaving the camp. 'Who was that?' he asked Leila.

She looked pale. 'Just Diaz,' she said with a strained smile. 'How's it going, James?'

'Fine,' said Makepeace. 'I've finished quadrat forty-seven.'

'Ah, the one with the Victoria lilies.' Leila loved the floating lily pads, five feet across, with their massive white flowers.

'That's the one. Now, tell me, what's going on?'

'Can I help you put the voucher specimens together?'

'Come on, Leila, out with it. What was that scumbag Diaz doing here?'

Leila took a deep breath. 'OK. The thing is, I won't be able to help with many new voucher specimens because I am going to go up to Bogotá tomorrow.'

'What? Has this got anything to do with Diaz?'

'I'm taking a message for him to Bogotá.'

'Are you mad? You saw what he did today. And that *guacero* was not the first man he's had killed.'

'I know,' said Leila, 'I know. Don't you think it makes me sick?'

'But you'll still help him.' Makepeace turned away angrily. Sometimes her naïvety was intolerable.

'I told him what he did was wicked,' she cried, pulling Makepeace back by the shoulder. 'But listen, James. I don't believe Diaz is really like that. He's at war. He is forced to be like that. You heard him talking about that missing rebel unit? Well, it turns out Cuchillo has been killed and his whole platoon massacred – in cold blood.'

Makepeace turned back to Leila. 'Who did it?' he asked slowly.

'The Bond militia.'

'How do you know?'

'They sent a photograph to Diaz.'

'The Bond sent the rebels . . . a photograph?'

'Yes,' said Leila. 'Their leader is that killer El Cangrejo. Apparently he sent it to mock Diaz. You

229

want to see what kind of people these Bond guys are? Look.' She pulled a photograph from her shirt pocket.

'Jesus!' Makepeace exclaimed involuntarily.

The backdrop of the image was the Andes. In the foreground, lit by flaming vehicles, was a grinning figure wearing a black hood and the notorious crab tattoo. He was standing proudly on a pile of bodies.

'They also sent this.' Leila held up a bloody bandanna. 'The message said it was Cuchillo's. Diaz wants me to make the story public in Bogotá,' said Leila. 'He says that the Bond is clearly planning to destroy the cease-fire. He also says that Minister Ayala could stop the Bond before this escalates and that media pressure is the way to get to him. There is a left-wing TV station I know who will run the story.'

'You shouldn't be getting mixed up in this.'

'It was time for one of us to make a trip to the lab in Bogotá anyway,' said Leila determinedly. 'Besides, I have a duty. Diaz thinks they sent it to him as a warning.'

'Of what?'

'Of what will happen to the FARA if they carry on selling emeralds from Madero. James, if we can't rein in the Bond, there will be piles of bodies all over this forest.'

'It's not our business, Leila. We're not crusaders. We're scientists. If you want to save lives, save the Indians, find a cure for their wasting disease.'

Leila glared at him fiercely and he felt a deep affection for her. She was so ardent, so idealistic.

230

She wanted to solve every problem. He didn't want to play the old fogey who told her that was impossible, but he had to. 'Don't you realize,' he asked sternly, 'that you could put our entire project in jeopardy?'

'Well, this should at least get me a meeting with Ayala.'

'It should get you a swift bullet from a *sicario*,' said Makepeace. 'For God's sake, Leila, when did you become official FARA spokesperson? There are ways of doing this.'

'Yes,' said Leila defiantly, 'and I plan to use a few more before I'm finished.'

'Don't you dare.'

'What do you mean precisely?'

'What I mean, precisely, is we are not a human rights group. We are scientists, not saviours. So whatever you're planning, don't you bloody well dare!'

'I can't believe that all you care about is your precious project. People are dying out there! You know that if we can't get Ayala to call off his death squads, everything will collapse. You know that they will destroy the forest. You've said so yourself. Anyway, I'm not scared of Ayala.'

'Well, you bloody well should be.' Despite himself, Makepeace couldn't be too angry. He knew nothing could stop Leila in this mood and, to be honest, part of Makepeace admired her and rather enjoyed her this way, her green eyes flashing like that. 'Just make sure you know what you're doing,' he said. 'And if you could at least pass by the lab to get the latest data . . .' Makepeace knew he couldn't dissuade her. He believed she was making a mistake, but he wouldn't stop her.

'I'm going to get through to Ayala,' Leila said defiantly. 'I won't give up, you know.'

Makepeace sighed. 'No, I bet you won't.'

They were both silent for a moment, then Leila said: 'I'm just going to drive over to see Burr. I want to tell him that I liked what he did today. Do you, uh, want to come?'

'No, thanks,' said Makepeace. 'But good idea to go – say the same from me.'

Watching Leila walk over to her car, he mentally drank a toast to the joyous folly of youth and idealism. He also wondered if Leila's trip, and his irritation, had anything to do with her obvious interest in Burr. Makepeace still had doubts about the Argonaut Ecology team, though he had to admit that Burr was a plausible character. He knew his stuff, he was well mannered, and with that Alabama drawl and quiet ways he had a certain air of antebellum Southern gentleman about him. He had been very brave earlier that day at the hanging, there was no doubt about that. Still, Makepeace just couldn't help feeling there was something fishy going on.

He also wondered if he was feeling a bit possessive about Leila. Well, there was maybe a bit of that. He smiled wryly at his reflection in the grimy window. He thought he looked old and wizened. 'Dirty old man,' he scolded himself. Then he bent back to his work.

* * *

Burr's right hand throbbed painfully as he examined the contents of the handkerchief. He now understood some of Tenoch's last words; he thought he knew what Tenoch meant by 'the small eyes', for instance. But beyond that, the discovery puzzled him. What was Tenoch doing with these? Who was the Neman he said Burr should trust?

He had no time to muse on these questions, however. He was just wondering what to do next when the call 'Company!' rang out again across the clearing. There was the sound of an engine and after a few moments he heard voices outside – Ahmad's and a low female voice with faint Caribbean tones.

Burr folded away his find, and an instant later Leila ducked her head into his tent. She was drawn and pale. For the first time Burr noticed the marks that life and the harsh tropical climate had left on her perfect features.

'What you did today,' she said quietly. 'It was brave.'

'It was useless.'

'It was more than anyone else did. It was more than I did.'

Burr was silent. His face was set in a grim expression. Leila was asking for more from him, but he was not able to provide it. Burr felt stupid – it was as though he was taking out his anger on her.

'I just wanted to tell you that,' she said.

'Thank you.'

'And also to let you know that I will be driving up to the mountains tomorrow. I'll be leaving the vehicle in Arroyo and flying on to Bogotá for a few days. If there's any equipment or anything else I can bring back . . .'

'We're all set,' said Burr shortly.

'What happened to you?' she asked, taking his red, pockmarked hand in hers. 'This needs treatment. Bee swarm?'

'Ants,' said Burr, withdrawing his hand, the fist still clenched. 'And I'll be fine.'

Leila stood there awkwardly for a moment. 'Well, all right, then,' she said. 'See you around.'

Burr sat immersed in thought. He noticed the faint, fresh scent of jasmine lingering in the air. The sound of Leila's car door shutting snapped him out of his reverie and he realized that he did not want her to leave like that. He hurried out of the tent. 'Wait!' he called across the camp.

Leila leaned hopefully out of the driver's window. 'What is it?'

Burr walked over and stood beside the door. 'I'm sorry, Leila. I guess after today I'm still not thinking straight. We need to make a trip to Bogotá as well. Perhaps we could travel together, if that's all right.'

Near Madero, Amazon jungle

Time had passed agonizingly slowly for Neman as he had waited for Tenoch to return. It was especially torturous for Neman to wait around Madero, which he thought was the worst place in the whole world. It could have been a good place, set by the broad Madero River, with plenty of good hunting and food trees nearby. But the houses were ghost houses of ugly blocks, with hot metal roofs. And the Jemberí there were sick. Many simply lay down to die despite the help of the plant doctor.

Neman knew there were good things about the ghosts' way of life – tinned food, for instance, and that powder you could add to water that changed it into a fizzy orange drink. Rifles were good too, though not ideal for hunting, because if you missed, the target would be alerted. Neman preferred the blowpipe: miss with a silent dart and the monkeys would not notice. And of course there were the clothes; currently Neman was wearing a tattered pink T-shirt, dirty khaki shorts and fluorescent yellow flip-flops. On the whole, however, Neman preferred the old way of life.

But now this too was being destroyed. He had seen the forest blasted for the green stones, and the very trees taken away. He had seen more and more peasants, colonists from the cities, coming into the forest. And now many more came, looking for El Verde. There seemed to be no way to stop them. He had seen the new men who built nests in the trees and pretended to be like the plant doctor but were obviously warriors. Neman feared for his people. They had survived in their forest for ever.

The ghosts from the country called Colombia had promised them what they called a National Park to protect the Jemberí. But this was not working.

Tenoch had been trying to help them, but that day, watching helplessly from the forest, Neman had seen Tenoch beaten and killed. It was enough.

Neman peeled off his garish flip-flops, his filthy shorts and T-shirt and dropped them on the ground. Sunbeams breaking through the forest cast dancing shadows on the hard planes and angles of his face and chest. His eyes were black.

Naked, Neman searched deep into the jungle, along tracks known only to the Jemberí, looking for a sign. For days he walked aimlessly, trusting his direction to Pacha Mama and the other forest gods. And an unseen hand did seem to guide his steps, for he came upon the shaman of his tribe. He was a true jaguar shaman, one of the last and most powerful of his kind. A wizened and ancient man, he was sitting motionless on the forest floor, contemplating an ant tree.

He showed no surprise at Neman's appearance. 'Look,' he said.

Without a word, Neman sat. They stayed there for hours, not moving. Neman watched the tree. Unlike its neighbours, it was unencumbered by lianas. Neman knew that, unlike other trees in the forest, the ant tree grew slender and weak. It had no thick bark, no thorns, no poison to protect it. It risked being infested, eaten, overgrown, or starved of light. But fire ants live in the ant tree. The ants attack any animal that tries to eat or damage the tree, and they cut back any vine that tries to strangle it, or branch that overshadows it.

In a trance-like state, Neman watched the hypnotic movements of the ants ceaselessly patrolling up and down the trunk in their intricate patterns. He saw them bite back the tendril of a vine that fell against the tree from a taller neighbour. They constantly trimmed back the undergrowth below the tree and investigated any monkey or bird that shook its branches. Neman watched as a spider monkey broke off a twig to scratch itself and almost instantly was chased, squealing, from the tree by the sharp stings of the ants.

Exhausted, Neman fell asleep. When he woke the next morning, the shaman was gone.

Neman watched the ants feeding from the sweet sap released by the tree to recompense them for their protection. Neman thought he understood. The ant tree was the forest and the fire ants were the Jemberí. It was the Jemberí's task to protect the forest, which in turn would nurture them. Neman stood up.

The only answer was the killing spears.

Argonaut forward OP, Madero

'Good morning, sir!'

Sven's barked greeting and snap to attention startled Burr as he savoured his morning coffee in the surprisingly cold morning. Looking down from the canopy in the dawn, the forest had been invisible under a dense blanket of mist, the high sierras hidden by massive thunderclouds, flashing with white sheets of lightning. Below the cloud the jungle was all murk and rain, booming with thunder and riddled with lightning bolts flickering down through the grey. In the wet and wind, the air was sharply chill. Burr heard a vehicle and saw Makepeace and Leila turn into the clearing.

'Sven!' Burr hissed.

'Yes, Captain?' He spluttered, 'I mean, Burr.' He saluted again in confusion.

Burr saw Leila and Makepeace getting out of their SUV. Burr looked down at the ground, trying to get Sven to lower his salute. The Swede just looked more confused. 'At ease, soldier,' said Burr through gritted teeth.

Sven snapped into the prescribed military at-ease position.

'Jesus, Sven, just load up,' said Burr.

'Yes, sir!' said the Swede, finally relaxing and bending to pick up a heavy crate just as Leila and Makepeace walked up.

Leila took Burr's hand. 'Looks a lot better,' she said.

'Swelling went down in the night,' said Burr. 'Is this all you have?' he asked, looking at Leila's small duffel bag.

'There are some specimens in the car,' said Makepeace, 'but it's just Leila coming with you. I'm staying.'

'OK,' said Burr, sensing the tension between them. 'I'll try and look after her.'

'Hello, Sven,' Leila said, and he replied nervously.

Makepeace shook hands with the muscular, shaven-headed Swede, then looked knowingly at Leila as if to say 'I told you so'.

Here we go, Burr said to himself, mentally crossing his fingers.

'So, Sven, I guess you're doing research too. What field are you in?' Makepeace promptly asked.

'Oh, yes, um, my research. Well . . .' said Sven, clearing his throat, then continuing in a rehearsed singsong. 'Yes, well, Professor, I am studying the frequency of fig seeds in the droppings of *Ateles geffreyi* spider monkeys. Specifically seeds of the fig, although I also record incidental data on stones of fruits like annona and papaya.'

'Oh,' said Makepeace, 'I see. That sounds very interesting.'

'Oh yes,' said Sven, warming to his theme. 'You must let me show you my data some time – a few hours should be enough for me to take you through the basic formulae. And of course you must see my specimens. In fact, perhaps you can help me go through some new samples? The smell can be unpleasant, and it gets into your hair, but it will probably start to fade after a couple of weeks. Unfortunately some of the latest samples are quite liquid – the *Ateles geffreyi* have had diarrhoea. But I'm sure we'll manage. How about next week? I think we will all be back.'

'Er, well, I'm afraid I'm busy. But thanks awfully. I'll leave Leila in your tender care. Look after her, Burr.' Makepeace rolled his eyes at Leila and fled.

Burr concealed his amusement. Sven had recited his script perfectly. The Swede jumped into the back seat of the vehicle. 'Nice work, Sven,' Burr murmured and the young man beamed, his open, childish face glowing with pleasure.

After almost twelve hours of constant rain, the track towards the mountains was liquid mud. Leila was quiet and preoccupied as the vehicle crawled and slid along at a slow pace. Sven sat silently in the back and slept most of the way. Beside the road-blocks, guerrillas huddled in lean-tos under the beating rain. At the ferry, the friendly rebel crew greeted Leila with a smile and gratefully accepted a carton of cigarettes from Burr. The sun broke out as the paddle beat them out into the stream and, standing on the top deck of the ferry, Leila and Burr began to talk.

'Listen, Burr, I'm sorry about Makepeace,' Leila said. 'For some reason he thinks that every person in Madero – apart from him – is after something.'

'That's OK,' said Burr uneasily. He had never before found the dissimulation so difficult. It was as if she was calling into question his entire *raison d'être*. She had an annoying ability to get under his skin.

Then Leila asked Burr about himself, and without warning, standing on the sunny deck of a ferry, sliding across a sluggish Amazonian river, Burr found himself talking about his life. The past poured out. He told her about his home on the Isla de Xcalan and how his mother had taken him there. He told her about the high dunes and the sleeping sharks and the house he was building. He told how his mother had died, when he was just eight years old.

'I'm sorry, Burr.' Leila laid a soft hand on his forearm. 'That must have been hard.'

'It was a long time ago,' Burr said. 'After that I returned to live with my father – on the family plantation in Alabama. The Whitmans have grown cotton there for almost three hundred years.'

'Slave owners!' exclaimed Leila, with a wicked grin. 'Well, fancy that. An' here we are together, Massah, with me a Trini Creole and all. An' you trying to much up to me . . .'

'Much up?'

'You know, mamaguy, sweet talk . . .'

242

Burr chuckled. 'I'm just talking,' he said. He told her about his college tennis career, but after that the truth stopped. He left out the military.

'So you gave up tennis for science?' asked Leila.

'Well, sort of. Now tell me about you.'

Leila told Burr about Trinidad. About her house up in Fort George, overlooking Port of Spain, about Carnival, cricket in Queen's Park Oval and horse racing on the Savannah. They were talking intimately, but at the same time each was acutely aware of the barriers they had erected. Both of them were hiding things and they felt uneasy about it. Leila wondered if she should just tell him about her mission for Diaz, but decided against. She felt uncomfortable with that. Her nature was frank and open, and she had never dissembled in her life. But she realized that, for some unknown reason, she did not yet wholly trust Burr.

Outside rebel-held territory, the Bond militiamen were as uninterested as the rebels had been, mostly ignoring the Argonaut vehicle. For Burr, driving with Leila was excellent cover. Everybody on the road knew her as a harmless scientist, and it was unlikely that her car would ever be searched too closely. This would help if, on the way back, the vehicle contained, say, a couple of dismantled Colt M4s and some 1,000 rounds of 5.56 mm ammunition.

It soon began to rain again, and at one Bond checkpoint some bored *milicianos* forced them out into the downpour so that the vehicle could be given a pointless, cursory search. The willing Sven stood by in the rain, making sure nothing was stolen.

Leila and Burr huddled under the outpost's dripping palm-leaf shelter. Leila observed the Bond with contempt. 'See this lot?' she asked Burr. 'You know why they call them the Bond?'

'Tell me.'

'Licence to kill. They're murderers.'

'They don't look that wicked to me,' said Burr, watching a spindly teenager poking vaguely at his luggage. 'Are they as vicious as the rebels?'

'They're death squads. They'll work with anyone for money – multinationals, drug gangs, logging companies, anyone. It's thanks to people like this that the forest is being destroyed. Currently they're working for the mining company, GemCorp. That rebel detachment Diaz was talking about – the one led by Cuchillo – the mercenaries killed them. Massacred them in cold blood.'

Burr was taken aback. How could Leila know? There had been no witnesses up on the *paramo*. Had someone talked? 'You know a lot about this Cuchillo,' Burr said. 'How did you hear about this?'

Again Leila was tempted just to show Burr the photograph and the bandanna. But she pursed her lips. 'I don't want to talk about it. Trust me. These guys . . . well I know James is cynical about them, but the FARA are better than these fascist bastards.' She nodded at the Bond militiamen. 'They don't give a damn about anything or anyone. They even hire mercenaries to do their dirty work.'

'That so?' said Burr carefully. 'What sort of mercenaries?'

Leila flicked a damp lock of hair from her face. 'Oh, there are plenty of real low-lifes in Colombia. Anyone who's into violence seems to end up here eventually. These mercenaries don't call themselves mercenaries. They are "security consultants" or "private military services". They are mostly Americans who have left the army but haven't had enough killing, so they come down to get their fix in Colombia.'

'Wouldn't it be good if the mercenaries could come in and put a stop to people like Diaz, his cruelty?' In his mind's eye, Burr saw the rebel comandante's cold eyes signalling Tenoch's execution.

'I know he's a violent man,' said Leila. 'Sometimes he is cruel. He goes too far. You saw that when he hanged that poor *guacero*. But I guess Diaz would say he is fighting a war. And against great odds.'

Burr was appalled. He looked at Leila, the water dripping onto her through the makeshift roof and running down between her breasts. She looked beautiful and frail. He could not understand how she could even try to justify what Diaz had done.

'Have you ever met one of these mercenaries?' asked Burr quietly.

'I would never speak to one, except maybe to slap his face.'

'Perhaps they just don't know any better.'

Leila looked at him. 'There is always something better than that.'

Bogotá, Colombia

'Not you too?' moaned Lester. Liz had been scolding him ever since he told her about sending Diaz the package. Now this snobbish politician was on his case as well. And just because he had wanted to rub Diaz's nose in it. Lester felt he had the right. He had a grudge to settle with the FARA. Still, Liz had really given him a going-over. He had not known anything like it since they had been married. It had made him think twice about getting back together with her.

'Are you deranged?' an incensed Ayala was shouting at him. He banged on his desk and the sound echoed through the cavernous office in the Palacio Nacional. He looked again with disbelief at the photograph of Lester on the mound of bodies. 'I cannot believe you sent this to Diaz. Do you not realize he could use this in the media to embarrass us? There can be no more mistakes. I want the Madero project expedited. If it can be done quickly, GemCorp will be given full support short of official military intervention.'

'Good,' said Elizabeth. 'Nice and unofficial's the best way.'

Ayala looked at Lester with open contempt. What a terrible mistake Walls had made to hire these two for GemCorp. 'I believe,' said Ayala softly, 'that we should first rein in these paramilitary excesses in Madero. It is one thing to fight rebels; it is another thing to slaughter them wholesale, then gloat over piles of dead bodies. And give away information at the same time.'

'But all you can see is the tattoo,' protested Lester. 'Everyone already knows about the crab tattoo.'

'And what kind of weapon is that?' Ayala pointed to the rifle Lester was holding in the picture.

'Colt M4.'

'Exactly, bearing a PVS-14 night sight. Weaponry your Bond militia does not possess. This is a weapon of American Special Forces. You might as well invite Diaz to a training session.'

Lester squirmed in silence.

Elizabeth cleared her throat. 'We apologize for Lester's stupidity. Believe me, I knew nothing about it. We all need to work together now, so we have a favour to ask.'

'What is that?' asked Ayala.

'Our sources tell me we have an interesting visitor coming to town.'

'Indeed? Who might that be?'

'A certain Mr – formerly Captain – Whitman. Burr Whitman.'

Ayala gave Elizabeth a querying look.

'He is the man leading our mercenary force in Madero.'

'Ah yes, Argonaut Security. He has replaced Daniel. I hope there has not been any problem with this new unit . . .'

'There's no problem,' said Elizabeth hurriedly. 'Just getting used to the change in personnel.'

'Hmm. Anyway, I do not think you have mentioned this new man's name before. Now that you do, it sounds familiar. Burr . . . Burr Whitman . . .' Ayala rolled the name on his tongue thoughtfully a couple of times. 'No, I cannot place it. Why does it worry you, his coming to Bogotá?'

'Because he should be down in Madero and I don't know why he's here. Remember it was when Daniel altered his planned timetable that he disappeared. We don't want anything to go wrong this time.'

'Surely you do not see this mere mercenary as a threat?'

'Of course he's not a threat,' she said. 'We just want to keep tabs on our people. Lester knows that, don't you, Les?'

Lester was irritated. He didn't like this unannounced visit to Bogotá. He still didn't trust the *pichado Yanqui*, especially as he reckoned Liz was still hung up on him. Now he noticed Ayala looking at him with an amused expression, as though Liz wore the trousers. He said, in a more peremptory tone than was probably advisable, 'You must have him followed. Don't worry, we'll take over if any "embarrassing" action is needed.'

Ayala slowly selected a Cohiba from the mahogany humidor on his desk and rolled it thoughtfully between his fingers.

'Well?' said Lester impatiently. 'He will be arriving at the airport soon. We could lose him unless we get someone onto it *pronto*.'

Very deliberately the minister picked up a cigar cutter, sliced the end of his cigar and lit it with the big silver desk lighter emblazoned with the Ayala family crest, a dragon rampant with a fiery green eye.

'Lester,' he said quietly, 'nobody, not even the President of this country, tells me what I must or must not do. Out there in the jungle, you may have plenty of thugs at your disposal, but remember, my friend, this is the city. And Colombia has been the Ayalas' country for five hundred years.'

Lester was annoyed. He thought Ayala was full of crap – he wouldn't last ten minutes on the mean streets of Medellin, or in the Calle del Cartucho. Lester knew these aristocrats were proud and tricky and that he should humour him. But the minister irritated Lester with his old-world airs and graces, aristocratic pretensions and his family tree that went back to the conquistadors and beyond. He just had a way of making him feel like a crude thug. That may have been a fair reflection of Lester's character, but Lester did not like being reminded of it. He suffered enough criticism from Elizabeth.

Lester tried to stay calm, reminding himself what Liz had been telling him. He was the man in command on the front line. Liz had also explained to him that things had gone too far for Ayala to call them off now. Not least, Liz had all the money to pay the Argonaut contract in an account she controlled.

Now Ayala spoke to Elizabeth with contempt. 'Why do you stick with him? It says something about you, the people you choose to work with.'

For Lester, insulting Liz was the final straw. 'Well, I guess that says something about you, then, Ayala,' he said. 'You work with me, don't you?'

Ayala raised his eyebrows. It was a fair point.

'And at least I have my reasons,' said Lester, jumping up in anger. 'You live in luxury in rose gardens above Bogotá. I have never had anything. You think of me as a peasant – well, you're right. Those penniless peasants who live in those *comunas* you can just see from here on the edge of your view – I could have been one of those people. My life was destroyed by those Communists. They burned our farm and killed my family. Don't talk to me about patience, about reason. This is war, Minister, and we are on the same side.'

Ayala puffed on his cigar and sighed inwardly. The whole GemCorp deal was proving a nightmare. Walls had a cheek involving him with scum like this. Lester was a foul, stupid *sicario*, but he made a good point. This was a complicated situation, and it would pay to be patient – for the moment. After all, Ayala still had his other, more personal interests in Madero.

He smiled at Lester and picked up the phone.

* * *

250

Burr dropped Sven in Arroyo Blanco, where he was going to continue some mortar training, and picked up Ricardo for the flight to Bogotá. They got round the Cuban's total lack of scientific knowledge by describing him as Argonaut Ecology's 'logistics manager'.

With Leila present throughout the trip from Arroyo, Ricardo kept a curb on his curiosity. After checking into their rooms in the downtown Fiesta Americana Hotel, the Cuban went and joined Burr in his room.

'So what's going on?' asked Ricardo. 'And what is the story with you and this *chica de Trinidad*? Not only do I feel like a third wheel,' he complained, 'but it could compromise the mission.'

'Don't be ridiculous, Ricardo,' Burr responded guiltily, knowing his friend had a point. 'Forget about the girl – she's just useful cover. OK, we're planning a dinner tomorrow night, but that's not why we're here.'

Ricardo looked sceptical. 'I don't like seeing you distracted,' he said. 'And even as a happily married man I can tell you she is extremely distracting.'

Burr poured two large whiskies from the minibar. 'I didn't want to talk about this, but I have to tell somebody. You're the only person I can really trust.' He took a deep breath, then told the whole story of Tenoch's hanging and of his own link with the Mayan. He also told of his anguish concerning Xcalan and the threat hanging over the place and its people.

'I'm truly sorry about Tenoch, Burr,' said Ricardo

251

compassionately. 'Well, if that's the way the rebels work, at least we seem to be on the side of the good guys. But it seems Carlo has the Xcalan thing covered. And you still need to tell me what we are doing here and what this has to do with the mission.'

Burr hesitated. Then he delved into his pocket. 'This is what Tenoch was smuggling.' He passed Ricardo the handkerchief bundle.

Ricardo opened it and his eyes widened in amazement. He went over to the bedside table and looked at the contents under the light. He was gazing at a collection of emeralds the like of which he had never seen. There were perhaps two dozen clear, pure sea-green stones ranging from the size of a pea to a large sugar cube. Unlike the rough emerald crystals that emerged from the mines, these were expertly faceted and polished jewels. Some were of a perfect emerald cut. Others were shaped in hexagons, with flashes of bright silver deep within them that radiated from an invisible central heart like petals of a flower or the rays of a star. Others were worked into faceted globes or into cabochons, perfectly flat on one side, the other side ground smooth and rounded like a half-moon, each with a streak of yellow fire flashing in the light like the eye of a cat – or snake.

'I don't know much about these,' Ricardo said in a voice that had fallen to a whisper, 'but I can tell you I've only seen anything like this once before. That one stone Cuchillo had. Lester took it from his body.' He looked up at Burr, a worried expression on his face. 'Burr, you need to talk to a real expert – like Elizabeth.'

'I thought so,' said Burr. 'That's why you and I are going out tomorrow morning.'

'To ask Elizabeth?'

'No. GemCorp know nothing about this visit, and I want it to stay that way.'

'Have you told Carlo?' asked Ricardo.

'Not yet. I don't like phoning from the camp. This mission has been worrying me from the start, Ricardo. I just don't know who the enemy is, and I think we may have some in our own outfit.'

Ricardo looked concerned. 'What are you talking about, *amigo*?'

'The sat phone. The battery was running down very quickly. Janine told me the only way that would happen was if it was in use. At first I thought that I might have left it on by mistake. So then I made sure the phone was off and the battery fully charged every day. Sure enough it's still gone down much further than you'd expect, given that I only make a couple of calls a day.'

'So?'

'So last time I used the sat phone, I checked. I hit Last Number Redial.'

'And?'

'It showed a Bogotá number, which I had definitely not called.' Burr wrote the number on a cocktail napkin and handed it to Ricardo.

Ricardo punched the number into the phone by Burr's bed and listened for a moment.

'*Bienvenido a GemCorp Colombia*,' he mimicked in

the slightly metallic singsong of a corporate answering system. 'Welcome to GemCorp.'

'See what I mean?' said Burr. 'It's just you and me in this one, Ricardo. Trust me.'

Ricardo trusted Burr, but he was not keen to become a violentology statistic, and this distinct possibility loomed large in his mind just two minutes into the cab ride from the hotel. Two minutes was the time it took Ricardo to suspect that they were being followed by a dark-windowed car. At first he said nothing, but when they moved outside the city centre the car was still there, and was joined by another one. The tails stayed behind the taxi on its winding route further from the centre and deeper into the poverty-stricken *comunas* around Bogotá. When he and Burr finally left their cab, four bulky men got out of the two cars and followed on foot.

Ricardo cleared his throat and said, 'Burr, I think we're being followed.'

'Yup,' said Burr. 'Since we left the hotel.' He didn't seem in the slightest bit perturbed.

'Who are they?' asked Ricardo.

'Not sure.'

'Oh. OK.' Ricardo lapsed into silence with a shrug.

They were walking through a poor neighbourhood of tenements and run-down houses. As the streets around them grew narrower, the alleyways darker, Ricardo glanced round to see two of their shadows draw a little closer. The other two seemed to have disappeared. Burr still appeared completely unconcerned, leading Ricardo through the twisting streets and out into a dusty little square. Ricardo could see the other two men already in the square, walking quickly ahead to cut them off. Burr turned right and walked towards a street that ran off the middle of the square between steaming piles of rubbish, on top of which a number of dishevelled figures were sitting in the sun.

'Hey!' Ricardo heard a shout behind him.

He looked back to see the two followers break into a run. The two in front began closing in too, but Burr walked briskly into the side street without a backward glance. Ricardo followed him, expecting any moment to be grabbed from behind and feel the muzzle of a gun in his back. But nothing happened. Ricardo glanced back to see the four men stop at the beginning of the street. He noticed that the figures on the rubbish heaps were men and women in rags, their mouths gaping, their eyes wide in the rictus of a drug high. Drunks lurched in the shadows. Dark doorways he and Burr passed contained stalls with guns and grenades for sale. On one table was a selection of tubes of glue and phials of crack cocaine. On the wall, Ricardo saw graffiti of bullets – cartridges of all shapes and sizes.

'Is this the . . . ?'

'Yup,' said Burr. 'The Calle del Cartucho. Enjoy!'

Ricardo shook his head in astonishment. '*The* Calle del Cartucho?'

Calle del Cartucho – 'Cartridge Street' – was notorious, a skid row gone bad. It was a no-go area for the authorities, the sink of Bogotá and one of the worst places in the world – a pit of insanity, violence, prostitution, drug addiction, delinquency, theft, rape and murder.

'That's the one. Don't you like it?'

'I'd like it better if I had a nine-mil in my pocket.'

'It's all right,' Burr reassured him. 'No police, rebels, paramilitaries, army, or even organized crime gangsters are allowed in here, only straight criminals and scum. We're pretty safe, I reckon. Hey!' He slapped down a filthy child trying to pick his pocket. He grabbed the urchin by the ear. '*El Chacal, donde está?*'

The boy struggled and squealed for a moment, then led them sulkily down the street. He stopped outside a crumbling building by an open sewer of stinking ooze. Burr quickly palmed the boy some coins and patted him on the back. 'Look after Señor Ricardo,' he said, then walked alone into the building.

The house was run-down and dark. It stank of faeces and vomit. Dirt or maybe arthropods crunched under his feet. Cockroaches scurried away from his approach. The walls were streaked with mould and filth. The floorboards creaked. Burr checked out a couple of rooms. In one, addicts lay around, slumped in a sea of drug paraphernalia. In another, a prostitute serviced her client. As Burr put his head round the door she looked at him over her client's shoulder with a complete lack of interest.

Stuck to the door at the end of the corridor was a poster – a photo sequence of a silverback jackal killing a baboon. Burr knocked on the door. After a short pause he heard a voice say *'Adelante!'* from within.

Burr went into a dimly lit room. Chacal was sitting behind a big metal desk. Burr could still see quite clearly that the little emerald dealer was tense, his right hand grasping something below the desktop. When he saw the visitor he raised his hand – empty – and waved Burr in.

'Hey, I remember you from Arroyo Blanco. You are the chief scientist! Señor Burr, no? What a pleasant surprise.' He put his hand up to his ear, thumb and little finger extended, 'Burrrrrrr! Burrrrrrrrrrrrr!' He laughed at his telephone imitation.

Burr gave a long-suffering smile and sat down facing the emerald merchant. On the desk was a large white blotter, a lamp, a magnifying jeweller's loupe and a small weighing scale with a digital read-out. 'Hello, Chacal,' said Burr. 'I need some help.'

'OK, OK. Just tell me why you're here. Keep it short. I haven't got much time – lot of appointments.'

Burr looked round the dingy room. 'Yes, I can see from the premises that business is booming.' He placed Tenoch's tied-up handkerchief on the blotter.

Chacal darted him a suspicious look, then turned on the lamp, which threw a bright white light onto the blotter. He began to untie the bundle, chuckling. 'You found some little butterflies already? I see you branched out quick from the science business, Señor Burr. Lucky you came to old Chacal to give you a fair price . . . *Madre de Dios!* His voice died off as he saw what Burr had brought.

Spangled green lights danced on Chacal's face, which took on an expression of wonder and greed. He screwed the loupe into his right eye and peered at them intensely one by one in silence.

After looking at each stone twice he looked up at Burr and said nonchalantly, 'Worthless rubbish. Fakes. Have you ever seen an emerald like this?' He held up a hexagonal stone of a clear, dark green that included what looked like a flower, its petals made up by arms of a lighter green crystal.

'Chacal,' said Burr patiently.

'I'll give you fifty dollars for them,' Chacal replied, yawning. 'It's paste. Good novelty stuff. Nothing special.'

'Chacal!'

'OK, OK.' The *plantero*'s look of indifference was replaced with one of almost childish eagerness. 'Where did you get these?' he asked.

'First you tell me about them.'

'Difficult.'

'Why?'

'Because these are . . . these are impossible,' said Chacal.

'What do you mean?'

'They are perfect. No emerald is ever perfect. These are . . . impossible emeralds.' Chacal was almost lost in wonder.

'Chacal!' Burr's voice cut through his reverie. 'What are you talking about?'

'Extraordinary chatoyancy,' Chacal murmured, picking up a smooth, rounded cabochon. 'See this,' he pointed excitedly at the bright green flash that ran deep across the heart of the stone: 'it's like the eye of a cat – *chat* in French. They call this cat's-eye effect chatoyancy. You get this when there is a fibrous inclusion in the stone, which causes the light to refract. I've never seen this level of pleochroism – of double refraction – in any gemstone before. I have been a *plantero* dealing emeralds for twenty-five years and I've never seen such a fine specimen.

'And look at these.' He picked up another emerald, in which light gleamed in the shape of a six-rayed star. 'Star emeralds. Again it is the inclusions that fracture the light into this estrellism, or star shape, deep in the stone. I've never seen such clear stones, or such bright, defined estrellism.

'This one,' he held up the hexagonal flower again, 'this is a trapiche emerald. The beryl crystal usually forms in this hexagonal shape. Here it has formed like the petals of a daisy.'

He went through some more jewels, then his voice fell to a whisper as he reached for a small stone – about the size of a fingernail – in a rectangular emerald cut.

'And this one?' Chacal asked. Burr's interest rose – he could hear the deliberate calm in the *plantero*'s voice. 'You got this in the same place, I guess? See, it has the same deep, clear sea-green as the others.'

'Yes.'

'This one mystifies me. You see, it is flawless. At first glance it looks fake, but it has none of the

259

wave-like clouds normally associated with artificial emeralds. No, it is absolutely flawless and it seems to have no inclusions.' He peered closely at the stone again, whispering to himself. 'No air bubbles, no fractures, no inclusions at all. *Es perfecta! Dios mío! Es un milagro* . . . It's perfect.'

After a while he put the stone down and turned back to Burr. 'You don't by any chance have anything like this, but larger?'

Burr shook his head. 'Not at the moment.'

'Well, just in case you do get hold of one, a really big stone – say, fifty carats – of this quality could sell at one hundred thousand dollars a carat. Even this stone, just three or four carats, must be worth at least six thousand dollars a carat. I have never seen a stone of this quality. To be honest, I am not sure what price to offer you for these . . .'

'I'm not selling, Chacal. Look, I'm doing some work for GemCorp and I want to know what is so special about these stones.'

'Special is right,' said Chacal. 'I have heard rumours of emeralds like these. I have never myself seen them before. These are not from the major mines of Colombia: Muzo emeralds tend to have a yellowish tint, Chivor emeralds a blue. Madero emeralds are normally a lighter green.' He pulled out a Chelsea Filter and peered at the stones through it. 'You see, they do not glow red. These stones are not coloured with vanadium; all other Colombian emeralds have traces of vanadium. They say these perfect ones – *las perfectas* – began to appear some weeks ago. It is said they have recently begun to filter in from the Madero region.'

'So they *are* from Madero mines, then?'

'No. The Madero mine produces decent emeralds, but nothing like the purity of this.' He held up the small emerald. 'And the Madero mine has yielded no star or cat's-eye emeralds.' He stared at the stone, enraptured, and continued almost dreamily. 'But GemCorp would know all this. You are not here on their behalf, are you, Señor Burr? If you are smuggling these stones, then look out. GemCorp cannot afford to allow this. It will have to act.'

'What do you mean?'

'GemCorp does not mind so much if the raw emeralds are mined and smuggled from Madero. In fact, dealers working for GemCorp buy most of them up from the rebels anyway. This costs GemCorp a little more, but the rebels sell the stones cheap and then GemCorp can still add most of the value by cutting and polishing. The thing about these emeralds you have brought me is that they are already cut. Perfectly finished stones emerging from the jungle? That will cut GemCorp out of the business.'

'Do they know about these emeralds?'

'They know, yes. And GemCorp are not the only ones desperate to locate their source. There are many fortune hunters seeking it. Also, they say it is Minister Ayala's personal obsession. Where did you get these?'

'I can't tell you that,' said Burr. 'But I think you can tell me more.'

'I see,' said Chacal thoughtfully. 'Well, listen. If you will give me these, I will tell you what people are saying . . .'

'Can't give you these, Chacal. They belonged to a friend of mine. He died for them.'

'And he bequeathed them to you?'

'Something like that.'

'Well, it sounds to me like they're hardly even yours . . .'

'Easy there, Chacal.'

The little *plantero* chuckled, with menace this time. 'You think a *Yanqui* can just walk into the Calle del Cartucho and out again, just like that, without paying a toll?' He moved his hand beneath the surface of the desk again and, keeping his eyes focused on Burr, called, 'Chulo!'

There were steps in the corridor, then the door burst open and a big shape Burr assumed was Chulo came flying into the room and landed on the floor in a limp, moaning heap.

Ricardo followed him in, dusting himself down. 'Everything all right, Burr?'

'A-OK,' replied Burr, who now leaned forward and turned the bright light on the table into Chacal's shocked face. 'Our friend here was just about to put his hands where we can see them and tell us everything he knows.'

Chacal pushed a drawer shut and put his hands on the desk in front of him. 'Look, I don't know much,' he said in a shaky tone. Burr grabbed him by the throat. 'Just that they say the Indians might be involved,' he wheezed.

'Indians?' asked Ricardo.

Chacal looked pointedly down at Burr's hand on his throat. Burr released him and Chacal made a show of spluttering and gasping for breath before going on. 'Yes, the Indians. The savages. Amazonians. There are backward tribes in that region. *Primitivos. Caníbales!* Until a month ago, there was only one known stone like this – in the National Museum.'

'I saw one stone like these before,' said Ricardo. 'The FARA had it.'

Chacal shook his head. 'Impossible,' he declared. 'The rebels have nothing like this. This is not from Madero. They must have got it from another source.'

Burr thought of the Indian he had seen in the forest. 'These Indians, could they have the technology to mine or cut anything like this?'

'No. Of course it is absurd, but where else do these stones come from? It's all fantasy, I'm sure, but the old tales die hard here. There is always the story of El Verde . . .'

'What is El Verde?' said Burr.

Chacal looked slyly up at him. 'Perhaps in return for one, tiny little emerald . . . ?'

Ricardo cracked his knuckles pointedly. 'Maybe in return for not ending up like Chulo . . .' he said.

From the floor, Chulo groaned again.

'Ah, I see,' said Chacal. '*Bueno*, I'll tell you about El Verde.' He took a deep breath and began, 'For centuries adventurers have been inspired to search for *El Verde* – the Green One. It is a lost city of emeralds greater and richer than El Dorado.' Chacal's eyes took on a far-away look as he described the mythical city: 'A fabled place where great jewels are strewn on the ground and can be picked from the trees. Conquistadors, explorers, *guaceros*, *planteros*, common treasure-hunters – many have disappeared in search of it. In 1540, even the great conquistador Don Rodrigo raided into the jungle, looking for the Green City.'

Filled with sudden excitement, Burr leaned forward across the desk. 'You mean Rodrigo de Ayala y Vivar?' he asked. Don Rodrigo was the same Spanish adventurer who had conquered the Mayan city at Xcalan.

'Yes,' said Chacal, surprised at Burr's knowledge. 'According to the stories, he had a great emerald from El Verde and wanted to discover its source. And people say he found it.' Chacal sighed. 'But we will never know, because, like so many others, neither he nor any of his men ever returned.'

Burr was amazed. The old fables fitted with what Tenoch and the Mayan *chacs* had told him: the emerald for the serpent's eye came from the jungles of the south. And if Chacal's version of the stories was true, the great emerald had indeed disappeared back into those jungles with Don Rodrigo.

Chacal looked up at Burr and Ricardo with wide eyes. 'They say the city is still out there, hidden in the jungle. Show me more emeralds like this and I might even believe it.'

As Ricardo and Burr left, Burr paused in the doorway and turned to ask, 'Do you know who Neman is?'

'No,' said Chacal sulkily.

Burr walked out, flicking something back over his shoulder. The *plantero* caught it with a sour expression and made a face at Burr's back. Then he opened his hand and looked at his catch. It was an impossible emerald – the perfect, clear one – and a wide smile spread across Chacal's face.

Burr and Ricardo exited the Calle del Cartucho from the other end and walked until they found a taxi. They appeared to have lost their followers.

'Where now?' asked Ricardo.

'Museo del Oro,' Burr told the driver.

'So now we're going sightseeing,' Ricardo complained.

They drove back through town to the historic Candelaria district and the museum. The Museo del Oro, housed in a striking, hypermodern building, was the pride of Bogotá. It contained a collection of pre-Columbian art second only to that of the Museum of Anthropology in Mexico City and an unrivalled treasure of pre-Columbian gold.

They wasted no time, making straight for the heavily guarded top floor and its displays of gold in the Salon Dorado. The darkened strong-rooms had muffling walls of thick, black velvet. The hushed vaults contained eight thousand priceless items plundered from indigenous Amerindian societies. The pieces were lit by spotlights on their glass cases. Images of lost civilizations – Muisca, Nariño, Calima, and Sinú – glinted in the beams. There were hieroglyphs covered in gold leaf, necklaces of gold and head-dresses of jade and gold enamelling. There were death masks of hammered gold and the lustrous, solid gold statues of jaguars and vanished gods. And there, standing on its own along one velvet wall, the sculpture they were looking for – a sculpture that Daniel had marked in a guidebook. It was a statue carved out of dark hardwood, gold-plated – the stylized figure of a naked man wearing a long feather in his hair. In the middle of his fore-head was a stone that flashed green in the spotlight.

The sculpture's caption read 'Amazonian Indian figure with emerald. Date and provenance unknown.'

The similarity with Tenoch's emeralds was obvious. Thanks to Chacal, they knew the stone was a chatoyant cabochon of great purity and fire, and they knew the provenance was Madero. Tenoch's hoard was the lost gems of the past coming to life. Ordinary emeralds had a potent enough fascination for man – no wonder people were dying over these. Burr wondered whether Daniel had died for them too.

They returned to the hotel, trying to make sense of what they had learned. They knew that Tenoch had somehow got hold of 'impossible' emeralds and that the old Mayan believed these 'small eyes' would lead him to a stone for the eye of the serpent. Thinking back to the carvings at Xcalan, Burr could see that the cat's-eye cabochon emeralds appeared to be smaller versions of the original stone that filled the serpent's eye.

Ricardo was still sceptical about El Verde and talk

about sacred emeralds, but he did see that there was a link between the emeralds and the mission. 'I guess this might explain the new emerald rush in Madero,' he pointed out. 'When Tenoch brought these cut jewels to the market in Bogotá, he sparked an outbreak of emerald fever.'

Burr agreed. 'And the new emerald rush helps explain GemCorp's eagerness to retake Madero. They must be desperate to trace the source of the perfect emeralds, especially if they think the rebels now have access to them. The company would want to cut off the supply.'

'And if we judge Elizabeth and Lester right, they will be wanting to get hold of the emeralds for themselves.'

But Burr still did not know where Tenoch had got the impossible emeralds or where they had been so expertly cut. He did not know who – or what – Neman was. And Daniel's disappearance, too, owed something to these emeralds. Burr was sure his partner had been to see the sculpture in the Museo del Oro. Burr could only hazard a guess as to why.

'In the meantime,' Ricardo reminded him, 'we've got a war to fight.'

Burr nodded and drained his glass. 'To a short war,' he said. 'We'll complete the Madero contract first. Then we'll try and find Daniel.' He didn't say it to Ricardo, but his plan would then be to follow up Tenoch's request: discover Neman and maybe find a stone to fit the serpent's eye.

* * *

Despite Ricardo's semi-amused disapproval, and the concerns of his own conscience, Burr's plan was also to take Leila to dinner that evening.

For much of that day Leila too thought about her date, with a mixture of excitement and apprehension. That morning she had woken up at six to the sound of a Jemberí banging on her window. She opened the curtain to check the length of the clinic queue and jerked back in surprise at the immensity of open sky from the seventeenth floor. She took a deep breath and looked out again tentatively. Months enclosed by the encroaching forest had left her almost agoraphobic. Gradually the perspective became less strange for her. The banging sound resolved itself into a jackhammer on the pavement below. Cars slid silently by on the Avenue.

Leila remembered she did not have to get up until later and promptly went back to bed, where she dozed blissfully in the sensuous cool of the air conditioning. Two years before, when Makepeace had first checked them into the five-star Fiesta Americana Hotel, Leila had thought it obscenely extravagant. But their pharmaceutical sponsors never complained and Leila had quickly relented at the sight of the hotel's opulent marble bathrooms. When she finally got out of bed, she treated herself to a long, deep foam bath and, in the scent of bath salts and lavender essence, forgot about the smell of creosoted cabins and damp earth.

After a leisurely breakfast, she took a cab across town to the Parque de la 93 and the studio of a left-leaning TV network. Leila's humanitarian work with the Jemberí had won her a lot of friends in radical Colombian circles. This was a great scoop for the channel and they gave her the red-carpet treatment. The editor also warned her to be ready for some media attention that night, since they were saving the story as the exclusive lead for their prime-time evening news show. 'I'll be fine,' Leila told him blithely, and she left for the laboratory.

The Madero project's pharmaceutical sponsors maintained a research lab at the University of Bogotá. Every couple of months Makepeace or Leila would bring in specimens collected in their fieldwork. Specialist pharmacognosists would then use the lab's state-of-the-art equipment to run a series of complex phytochemical tests. This time she dropped off some specimens of the *jomo* vine and – thanks to the Argonauts' canopy system and the gift from little Tupo – some flowering stalks of *kiragi* to test for the first time.

She then returned to the Fiesta Americana and a series of manicures, pedicures, facials and massages. She had her hair coiffed up in a chignon and she put on the one evening dress her mother had forced her to take to Colombia. For this one night, for the first time in a long while, she felt like not being a scientist or a doctor. In fact she did not want to be responsible for anything at all. She just wanted to be a woman.

Despite her preparations, the knock on her hotel room door took her by surprise. She was still sitting in front of the bathroom mirror, not quite ready. She took a deep breath and opened the door.

Burr was standing, surprisingly nervous, in the corridor. Seeing Leila suddenly framed in the doorway, for a moment all thoughts of war, of Xcalan, of Daniel, were driven from his mind. The only emeralds he thought of were the glowing green circles of her eyes, which twinkled at him with wry amusement.

'Are you all right?' Leila enquired archly of the speechless Burr. She was swathed in a full-length dress of beige silk mesh that revealed glimpses of her lambent, coffee-coloured skin. Close-fitting, the dress hugged her curves and flared slightly to the floor. Her black hair was up, accentuating a graceful neck and high cheekbones. Her face glowed with youth and vitality. Her eyes were darkened by a mixture of stress and a touch of kohl. Her lips were a subdued but definite lipstick-ruby. Her heart-shaped mouth was smiling but inside she felt a little uncertain, especially about the make-up – it was the first time she had worn any since her last leave in Trinidad.

Burr, realizing he must have been gaping, tried to speak. 'You look, uh, radiant,' he managed, suddenly sounding very Southern. 'What's going on?'

She responded with a charming, gurgling chuckle. 'Maybe it's just that I haven't been out for dinner with a man – well, apart from James – for ages.' She motioned him to come inside. 'Where are we going to go?'

'I've booked a table at Cielito Lindo,' he answered, 'overlooking the city.'

'That sounds wonderful, but I'm afraid I'm not quite ready. Will you excuse me just a minute?'

Burr couldn't imagine what more she needed to do – she looked perfect – but she slipped into the bathroom for some mysterious final feminine touches. A couple of minutes later she was still in there when the telephone rang. Burr left it for a while but it kept on ringing, so he picked it up.

'Burr,' he heard Ricardo's voice say.

'Yes?'

'Channel twenty-two.'

Burr switched on the TV to see a picture he recognized – a photograph taken by David on the *paramo*. It was of a hooded figure on a pile of bodies. The newsreader introduced the exclusive story with the caption 'The Bond – licensed to kill the cease-fire?'

'Oh, shit.'

'It gets worse,' said Ricardo. 'They're saying the proof of the story was brought by a research scientist from Madero.'

'Oh, shit.'

Leila's interview came up almost immediately. She looked wide-eyed and fey. She was interviewed holding a blood-stained rebel bandanna, 'belonging to one of the murdered guerrillas', as she put it. She accused the Bond death squads of being behind the deaths and, turning to face the camera, made a direct appeal. 'I believe that Minister Hernando Ayala is in control of the Bond. He must stop the killing or the people of Madero will continue to suffer and die.'

Burr was dumbstruck. He was not just disturbed by the fact that Lester must have sent Diaz the photograph. He was worried by what the image might give away. Leila thought the massacre had been carried out by the Bond, but Burr could see that, if Diaz was astute, there were clues in the picture that pointed to outside involvement. The Argonauts would have to be even more careful now.

On the line, Ricardo was calm and wise as ever. 'Listen, Leila is going to make some big enemies and attract a lot of media attention. The lobby is already full of journalists. If you're seen with her tonight, you're going to be on the cover of every newspaper tomorrow morning.'

Burr was livid. He cursed himself for being so interested in her. Ricardo had been right, and so had Anthony. Women were trouble.

'How could she be so stupid?' he said out loud.

'How could who be so stupid?' asked Leila as she emerged from the bathroom, putting on her earrings.

'I'm sorry, Leila,' said Burr awkwardly. 'I think I'm going to have to take a rain-check.'

Leila's smiling face screwed up in dismay. 'What do you mean?' Her gaze flicked from Burr to see herself on the TV screen. 'Oh, I see.'

'I can't risk our project becoming involved in any controversy,' Burr explained stiffly. 'I think Ricardo and I are going to leave town. We'll wait for you back in Arroyo Blanco.'

'Yes,' said Leila sadly. 'I understand.' Then she added bitterly, 'You're just like James. You only care

272

about your pet little project – your bloody butter-flies. Don't you think it's worth risking something for truth and justice?'

'That's not my job. I don't know what truth is, and I doubt you do either.'

Burr and Ricardo slipped out of the hotel by the back door and flew back down to Arroyo Blanco. Disappointed and confused, Burr found himself thinking of the forest. What had Makepeace told him? Only one per cent of light actually gets through to ground level. He felt like that. He was in the dark, surrounded by the riotous web of events. These things were somehow woven together, he suspected, but he could not find the thread. Magic, destiny, he did not want to countenance. But the possibility crept in. Why not? If there were impossible emeralds, what was one more? If there were small eyes, why not a large one? Perhaps Tenoch would not have died in vain.

After Burr left, Leila exchanged her gown for her jungle doctor's gear and laboured through hours of media interviews. When she returned to her room, exhausted, she found dozens of voice messages on her hotel phone. Most were from journalists; some were gruesome death threats. There was nothing from Burr.

Leila felt she'd been a bit of a martyr. She looked regretfully down at the evening dress laid out on the bed, at the black kitten heels alongside. She had planned to have a really romantic evening, but she had sacrificed it – and probably her relationship with Burr – for the greater good. Well, other people had sacrificed a lot more than that.

Leila was surprised and gratified by the extent of the media response, but the excitement wore off quickly. The next day, after a round of breakfast-show interviews, she sneaked off to the lab. While working she called Ayala's ministry at regular intervals, trying to get a meeting with the minister himself. None of her calls was returned. Leila became increasingly irritated, pacing the lab rest-lessly, unable to concentrate. She went down to the ministry building and waited for three hours, until the secretary told her that the minister had not come in to work that day.

Eventually, she ran out of patience. So she hired a car and drove up into the hills above Bogotá. The air there was warm, yet fresh and dry, which felt delicious after the constant dampness of the jungle heat. She had hired a convertible and the cool wind in her hair and the sun on her body made her feel light-hearted and daring. The road switched back and forth, up through tall conifers. Views of the sun-lit city below flickered through the trees. The astringent scent of pine mingled in the air with the rich perfume of roses. At the top of the climb was a lush plateau of bright green pastures and endless fields of chrysanthemums, carnations, daisies and roses – yellow, white and red, red, red. Colombia was such a blessed country, thought Leila. As well as yielding cocaine, coffee and emeralds, it was one of the world's biggest flower producers. According to

Burr it was also the world's biggest exporter of butterflies. She wondered with a wry smile whether the red roses had made her think of Burr. She was surprised how upset she had been when he cancelled their dinner. Still, she couldn't blame him. And they were going to meet up in Arroyo again for the return journey to Madero. Funnily enough, she had never seen herself with a scientist before. But then, as Makepeace said, Burr was different.

Little pastel-coloured villages clustered here and there between the vast *latifundia* – the scented estates and summer retreats of the Colombian elite. Their sprawling colonial mansions flecked the plains with stands of cypresses and whitewashed Spanish-colonial bell towers.

Leila found the minister's estate near the village of Santa Marta. Armed guards stopped her outside tall wrought-iron gates. They were adamant that she would not be let in. When Leila refused to leave, they called up to the house for guidance as to what to do with this determined, attractive woman who thought she could simply turn up on a weekend to see the minister without an appointment. The answer was still negative.

Leila got out of the car and waited in the warm sunshine. There was a constant buzzing of bees on the roses. The guards ogled her bare legs and winked at one another slyly. Maybe there were a few reasons why the minister would see her. After a while, a guard opened the gates.

'You're lucky, señorita,' he called, waving her through. 'The minister says he will see you.'

'And don't worry, the minister's wife's not at home,' sniggered another.

Leila smiled sweetly and spun the wheels, leaving the guards coughing in a cloud of dust.

The drive ran for about half a mile through an avenue of tall cypresses to the paved forecourt of the minister's residence. Leila was greeted by a valet who took her car and by a butler, who escorted her into the spacious marble entrance hall. The hall overlooked a Moorish courtyard with a bubbling fountain. Through an arcade on the other side of the courtyard Leila thought she caught a glimpse of a man in a wheelchair.

Leila waited in the hall for a while, then wandered out into the courtyard and into a high-ceilinged drawing room overlooking the grounds. It was hung with what looked like family portraits. There was a group portrait of a much more youthful Ayala, his wife and young son. Leila moved over to a grand piano covered in family photographs in ornate silver frames – first communions, weddings, a clean-cut young man (Ayala's son perhaps?) playing tennis, holding up trophies, making a speech, graduating from Harvard. Dominating the room was an old painting, a dark oil of a sixteenth-century Spanish aristocrat in armour. His goatee beard was an arrogant, jutting triangle. Looking up at the vast canvas, Leila felt dwarfed. The nobleman's eyes, staring out over the centuries, told of the self-belief and vindication of the conqueror. He was clearly a conquistador. His cloak was emblazoned with the crest of a dragon rampant, with a burning eye. One hand rested on a map of the vanquished New World. In the other he held a glowing green globe the size of his palm. It looked like a paperweight, she thought.

Leila moved over to the huge picture windows. The drawing room looked out on wide, rolling grounds. Arabian horses grazed in the distance. Closer to the house, on a manicured lawn, Leila saw the minister playing with a couple of young children. A blonde woman of around Leila's age sat at a table below a large parasol, watching and laughing. His daughter, Leila guessed, or daughter-in-law, perhaps – she did not look Colombian. That would make the kids Ayala's grandchildren. She smiled, lost in the idyllic scene for a moment, but then reminded herself that Ayala was the forest's – and her own – bitter enemy. She reset her look into one of mean resolve.

'Ahem.' The butler cleared his throat behind Leila, who jumped. 'The minister will see you now.'

The butler walked Leila through the house to a large study in an opulent, masculine style of dark wood panelling, bookcases and leather. On the wall behind the imposing mahogany desk hung a banner carrying the same dragon crest as in the painting of the conquistador. The butler indicated a tall-backed chair in studded brown Moroccan. Leila sat down.

After a moment, Ayala came in, smiling and mopping his brow with a handkerchief. 'Sorry to keep you waiting,' he said politely. 'My family is very demanding. Would you care for a drink?'

'No, thank you,' said Leila stiffly. Ayala seemed

taller close up than he did on television, more dangerous. Even in shirtsleeves, talking quietly in his home, he exuded an overwhelming charisma and sense of sheer power that startled her. Leila suddenly felt very frail and vulnerable.

'I must have some water if you don't mind.' He clinked ice from a silver bucket into two long glasses, filled them from the crystal water jug, and put one in front of Leila anyway. She drank from it nervously. Ayala drained the other glass and refilled it before turning to Leila. He did not sit down but leaned with casual elegance against the edge of his desk.

'So what can I do for you, Dr Walcott?' he asked in perfect English. 'I must say, you have caused quite a stir.'

'I stand by everything I've said, Minister. If you have the future of the people of Madero at heart, you will try to keep the peace.'

'It is not in my power to decide these things. And even if it were, your cause is not helped by using such strong language, or such unfounded accusations against the self-defence groups, against companies trying to protect their legitimate interests . . . and against me. You realize, of course, what can happen to people who attack my family name?'

Leila gulped. Her throat was dry, but she got the words out anyway. 'The accusations are not unfounded, Minister. Despite the cease-fire, violence in Madero is increasing. It is your responsibility to negotiate a peaceful settlement to this conflict, not to encourage warring armies to seize the National Park and rape it, one after another.'

'That is precisely why we agreed to the cease-fire. Which the FARA abuse. We have heard the tales of atrocities in Madero and we know that under Diaz there is unfettered exploitation of the forest. This is the very reason why we retain the option of annulling the cease-fire. If negotiations with the rebels break down, we must be prepared to recapture sovereign Colombian territory. It is our duty.'

Leila leaned forward eagerly in her chair and spoke with passion. 'But, Minister, we are talking about a private company, with a private army, killing people in cold blood. And it will only get worse. We believe GemCorp and the Bond are planning to retake the mines.'

'We believe?' Ayala exclaimed. He stood up again, towering above her. 'By "we" do you mean you and the rebels? There are many voices, señorita, who say that too many non-governmental organizations are aiding FARA. We know you act as the rebels' doctor. We know you carried this story to the media for that murderer Diaz. Perhaps your assistance goes even further than that. Do you perhaps provide the terrorists with funding, or with information? If I told you now about our plans, would you not tell it to Diaz? Perhaps those voices are right and you are in league with that Marxist pig, that hypocrite. Would you be interested in the size of his bank account in the Bahamas?'

Leila did not want to hear. Shaking with

adrenalin and fear, she remained steadfast. 'I do not support FARA. I am on the side of the forest and its people. Every day I see, and I deplore, the cruelty that the rebels inflict on the people of Madero, on the Jemberí, on the forest itself.'

'Indeed?' Ayala smiled and sat down again on the desk close to Leila. 'Remember the forest is on nobody's side – certainly not on yours. The Jemberí will steal from you without compunction, and they inflict cruelty on whom they please. Be careful, señorita: you have very few friends in this country to be making such a big noise. Let me remind you that my family has ruled this part of the New World for over five centuries. I will not allow my heritage, this great country, to be undermined by communists or by any other foreign powers. We will decide our own fate and how to use our own natural resources. We are independent and will not be bullied by the guns of Marxist fanatics, by the power of America, by the frenzy of Green activists, or even by the dollars of the pharmaceutical companies you work for.'

'But you are happy to take bribes from GemCorp,' Leila blurted out.

Ayala seemed thunderstruck. For a moment he was still. Then he replied with icy calm. 'I have my own interests in Madero. I take bribes from nobody.'

Leila could tell her accusation had infuriated him. 'What do you call it, then? Investment? Face it, Minister: you're angry because it's true. You put on these airs and graces – nobility, history. You talk about honour, about independence. Then you let an American – a Yankee – company buy you and your country's mineral wealth for a few meagre dollars.' She stood up and flung the blood-stained bandanna onto the desk beside Ayala. 'You sell them the blood of your own people.'

Ayala was speechless with rage. Then he spoke, controlling himself with visible effort, and his voice was thick with menace. 'There are clearly many things you do not understand, señorita. But hopefully this you *will* understand: given the publicity you have caused, it may not be wise to expel you from Colombia right now, but your project's licence expires in two months. Rest assured this licence will not be renewed and you will never work in Colombia again.'

Suddenly he leaned forward and took Leila's chin in his hand. 'You are a beautiful woman, and it is an unfortunate part of my character and my code – the airs and graces you mock – that I would not hurt a woman. That is why, so far, your excess of zeal has cost you only your current career path. But this is just the first lesson about the consequences of your actions. And if any more of your accusations come to my attention, nothing, not even your gender or your beauty, will protect you. Contrary to your flattering views of my power, there are forces out there that I cannot control, and more lessons will be administered, each one swift, severe and, if called for, final.'

He pressed a button on his desk and the butler entered almost immediately.

'Manuel, see Dr Walcott out.'

As she left, Leila felt her legs begin to quiver

uncontrollably. Pausing to steady herself against a pillar in the courtyard, she heard a brief commotion in an adjoining room. The butler tried to hurry her along, but Leila stayed put. She looked through an archway and down a marbled corridor, at the far end of which she saw a man walking towards her. He was a handsome man in his thirties but he walked with a strange yet somehow familiar wobbling gait, almost like a bizarre dance. She watched for a few seconds, then the man staggered and fell. Two attendants appeared immediately and helped him to his feet. The man moaned and jerked spasmodically as they lowered him into a wheelchair and hurried him out of sight.

Zona Rosa, Bogotá

Sashaying through the arcade of jewellery boutiques in the Zona Rosa, Chacal was exceedingly pleased with his work over the last twenty-four hours. Since the crazy American – who was a scientist as much as Chacal's grandmother was the Infanta of Castile – had turned up out of the blue, Chacal had become a wealthy man. For very little work, and at the cost of no more than a bruised throat, Chacal had made a small fortune. He had dropped heavy hints about his goods around the busy stalls of the emerald market at the corner of Avenida Jimenez and Carrera Siete. Now all the big dealers were chasing him to secure his merchandise. An Italian buyer had offered him forty thousand dollars for the emerald. He was confident that the next shop, a world-renowned French brand of *haute bijouterie*, would do even better.

He approached the glittering glass front of the store and rang the buzzer. The smiling manager let him in and relocked the door behind him. The air conditioning was cool, the carpet plush. Diamonds and emeralds winked at Chacal from the brightly lit cabinets. Nothing to match my merchandise, thought Chacal smugly. The manager ushered him to a chair in front of an ornate desk, then went into the back to fetch something. Chacal heard a mechanical noise behind him and felt a chill of doubt. He glanced round to see the shop's metal security screens rolling down over the windows. Chacal turned back to the desk to see someone sit down opposite him and he gulped with fear. It was a woman with a smile so false it chilled his blood. He knew her type. He had seen them in bars from Cartagena to Putumayo. A step behind her stood a man he recognized all too well from the tattoo on his arm. It was El Cangrejo. Everything Chacal had heard about his methods came rushing back. He had seen Cangrejo's tattoo and grin in all the weekend papers – on a pile of dead men. And here he was revealing his face to Chacal. Suddenly, Chacal was truly afraid. Dimly he realized that the woman was talking to him. She was asking for something. The stone.

'I don't know what you mean, señora,' said Chacal pathetically.

'It's señorita,' she purred. 'And I don't believe you. Lester!'

Cangrejo moved forward with surprising speed and grabbed Chacal's thin neck with a strong hand. He squeezed, the pincers from his crab tattoo closing on Chacal's windpipe. Chacal tried to struggle, but Cangrejo simply twisted his arm painfully up behind his back.

Chacal saw that the woman was holding out her hand. He scrabbled at his pocket, pulled out the stone and placed it in her open palm. Elizabeth nodded and Lester released his hold on Chacal's throat.

'It's beautiful,' breathed Elizabeth. She placed it on the white blotter on the desk and switched the light on. 'A perfect specimen,' she said, marvelling at the emerald's colour and perfect clarity through a jeweller's loupe. 'Just as we thought, Les.'

Elizabeth brought out another stone and put it next to Chacal's on the blotter. It was the stone Lester had taken from Cuchillo's body. 'These stones are from the same source.' She put down the loupe and turned the desk lamp straight into Chacal's face. 'Now, if you want to live, Chacal, tell us the rest of your little tale.'

'I don't know what—' wheezed Chacal, and instantly, with a nod from Elizabeth, Lester's pudgy hand was suffocating him again.

A few minutes later, Chacal lay whimpering on the floor after blurting out almost the entire story. He told them how he met Burr in the El Verde Bar in Arroyo, and how Burr and another man had visited him two days ago with the emerald.

'Did he say where he got this?' asked Elizabeth, holding up the stone.

'All he said was it came from a friend,' spluttered Chacal, 'someone who's now dead. He did mention someone called Neman.'

'And you're sure this was the only stone Burr had?'

With a bizarre spurt of bravery, Chacal looked her in the eye. 'Yes, I'm sure.'

Elizabeth observed him carefully, then stood up. 'Yes, you're lying,' she said. 'Too bad. Well, Les, we need to find out what our friend Burr knows. And maybe see if we can find the rest of these stones.'

'Uh-huh,' Lester said. Then he pointed at the sobbing Chacal. 'What about him?' he asked hopefully.

'We-ell, go on, then,' said Elizabeth, like a mother allowing her child an extra ice cream. 'I don't think it's good to have information like this floating around.'

'I don't think so either, Liz,' said Lester gratefully. He was so pleased. Ever since they found that emerald on Cuchillo's body, he had noticed a change in Liz. She was much more amenable to his way of doing things. He took off his jacket and bent down over Chacal, flexing his stumpy, perfectly manicured fingers and the crab pincers tattooed on them.

The terrified store manager came back in to see Elizabeth and Lester leaving.

Lester looked flushed. 'You'd better clean this up,' he said to the manager. 'The little *cacorro* soiled himself.'

On the luxuriant pile carpet, Chacal was no longer moving.

Arroyo Blanco to Madero, Colombian Amazon

After returning from Bogotá, Burr spent a couple of days in Arroyo Blanco, where, despite a show of reluctance, Ricardo was more than ready to show Burr the progress the militia had made. The latest training exercise was a helicopter assault. They ran through the drill for Burr and, despite some minor hiccups, Burr was impressed. The paramilitaries' helicopters came skimming low across the plain and hovered above the base. Dust stung the faces of Burr and Ricardo as the Bond's Jaguar platoon slid down ropes from the choppers. Led by Paul Hill, they deployed across the Landing Zone swiftly and professionally.

'Not bad fast-roping,' shouted Burr over the helicopter noise. 'No wonder Lester likes these guys.'

Ricardo agreed. 'Yes, they learned fast – had to get rid of a lot of bad Marine Recon insertion habits Daniel taught them. Daniel would have had them coming into the LZ attached to the rope like a

Christmas tree.' Ricardo was determined that his outfits would fight the Ranger way. The only exception was the pixellated Marine Recon combat dress. The pixels made you look like low-resolution computer printout, but in the forest you just disappeared.

When Leila arrived in Arroyo on her way back from Bogotá, she met up with Sven and Burr, and they drove back down to Madero. They talked in a desultory way, but the atmosphere between Leila and Burr was strained. They discussed some of Leila's data, and Burr pointed out some migrating green-and-black *Urania* moths. Otherwise, the drive passed uneventfully.

They studiously ignored Leila's adventure into the world of human rights and high politics. Leila also did not tell Burr of her visit to Minister Ayala, or that after her visit she had spent much of her time hiding from the media in the University of Bogotá library, though not in the Botany section. Prompted by what she had seen at the minister's residence, she had first got out some books on the history of Colombia from the Spanish Conquest. She had then moved on to the latest papers on wasting diseases and neurological disorders.

Both Burr and Leila wondered, independently, if they would be able to recapture the easy companionship they had felt when working together in the canopy. They knew it had been undermined, and neither was quite sure exactly why.

All along the forest road, the checkpoint guards

only stopped the vehicle to chat and alleviate their boredom and on the ferry crossing the rebel crew talked happily about how much they preferred the cease-fire to war. They would like to give up their guns and just be plain boatmen. It was a good living. They had heard what had happened to Cuchillo, but they hoped it was an isolated incident. They certainly did not see it affecting them. The Bond militia never dared to come that deep into the forest.

After dropping Leila at her research station, Burr arrived back in the Argonaut camp at dusk, to be met by David and Janine. Janine seemed worried and David was even more agitated than usual. They had already heard about the newspaper stories and the photograph from the *paramo*, but it wasn't that.

Janine did not explain at once but first gave Burr a quick and efficient report on the Argonauts' activity during his absence. Left in command, she had certainly kept the team busy. Using night-vision equipment, the team had begun to build up a good picture of rebel activity at night. Working in two-man foot patrols, the Argonauts had also scouted half the perimeter of Madero. On patrol they had carried butterfly nets. These had proved so effective as a cover that rebel guards had helpfully guided the Argonauts around booby traps. Pike also thought he had identified extensive minefields around the emerald mine itself. These still needed to be mapped, but it looked like they lay in a defensive circle on the forest side. So any move to capture the mines would probably have to come from the town.

'OK,' said Burr. 'Good work, Janine. Now, are you going to tell me what's eating you?'

'There's something you should see,' Janine replied.

'And how!' said David. 'Pike is freaking out completely. And so are we all.'

'You going to tell me what you're talking about?'

'Come on,' said Janine. 'Ahmad put it out in the forest.' She led them off through the thick layer of brush into the inky blackness under the canopy. Their torch beams played on the trees. Here and there they were reflected in the bright mirror eyes of forest animals – the green dots of spiders, the wide, yellow plates of kinkajous. Above in the canopy the night monkeys sang and whistled softly.

After only a few paces, Janine stopped. 'Here it is.'

'See?' David said.

At first, Burr was just aware of a bulbous shadow on a pole. He took a step closer and raised his torch beam to reveal a shrunken human head.

'Shit!' he exclaimed, looking away and lowering his torch. 'Any idea who it is?' he asked after a moment.

'No way, man,' said David. 'It's hardly human.'

Burr pointed his torch beam back at the object. The head was a grotesque black leathery thing. A shrunken bonsai face with empty eyes, it was the size of a large grapefruit and bore a grotesquely contorted expression. It was mounted on a smooth, black spear.

'This morning we woke up and it was planted in the middle of the fucking camp,' David said. 'I think somebody is trying to give us a message.'

Burr thought back to the Jemberí bowman he had seen in the forest. 'First the Indian lurking around the camp, and now this,' mused Burr. 'For sure, they're trying to tell us something. And it does look like a warning.'

'What could they be warning us about?' asked Janine. 'Have they somehow worked out we're not scientists? Why would that even matter to them?'

'I don't know,' answered Burr truthfully. He was thinking of what Chacal had said about Indians maybe having something to do with Tenoch's emeralds. *Primitivos*, he had called them, *caníbales*. Could Burr's involvement with the emeralds be the cause of the Indians' attentions? But the Indians had been observing the camp before Tenoch was killed.

'So we take the hint, right?' David said, interrupting Burr's thoughts. 'We're pretty much done here. Let's be warned and decamp. I mean, maybe these Indians gave the same warning to Daniel. And maybe he didn't listen.'

Burr averted his torch beam, consigning the head back to the darkness. 'What do the others say?' he asked Janine.

'Pike is complaining too,' said Janine. 'He says we should at least get a pay rise if we have to work surrounded by headhunters. Ahmad will go with David, of course.'

'Anthony?'

'What do you expect? He says nothing, as per usual. You know, I think he was surprised – and his professional pride was insulted. He was on watch when the thing was put in the camp and he doesn't like anyone being able to sneak around here without his noticing. My guess is he sees it as a challenge.'

David snorted. 'You know that freaky Georgia SNOB. He reckons he can kill anything before it kills him. The rest of us reckon we should leave.'

'No, David. We have a job to do. Leaving too soon just means we take casualties when we come back. We stay here until we have the complete picture.' Burr began walking back towards the camp.

'Burr!' Janine called. She turned her torch onto the head again and wondered if she should tell Burr of the horrible, irrational feeling that had troubled her since she first saw the macabre object. Something about it – Janine could not say what – made her feel the head was familiar. She decided not to mention it.

'Yes?' said Burr.

'What do we do with the head?'

Unsurprisingly, it was the ever-obliging Sven who ended up with the job. He snapped a salute, then went out into the dark, put the head in a plastic bag and buried it in the sandy soil. That night Burr increased the watch to two per shift and after dark he issued both with M4 rifles. Tenoch's impossible emeralds he hid among his scientific gear, in a selection of empty moth cocoons.

* * *

After Burr dropped her off at the research station, Leila found Makepeace bent over his desk in the field lab.

'So how did it go?' he asked, without bothering to look up from his microscope.

'Not so well,' admitted Leila. 'I don't think anything's going to change.'

'Do you think not? Despite all this?'

Makepeace pushed over a computer printout. It was from a website – images of Leila with her bloody bandanna.

'While I am quite impressed with your spirit, dear girl, I'm afraid that I am considerably unimpressed by your strategy. You've now made yourself the story. And you've insulted Ayala, in person, very publicly, and repeatedly. He could revoke our travel permits and close down the project in the blink of an eye. And now, thanks to you, he probably will. And –' Makepeace saw Leila bend pointedly down to look into a magnifying glass. He raised his voice. '– And, *listen to me, Leila*. Annoy him again, and Ayala could do a lot worse than just close us down.'

Makepeace snatched up the printout and began to read: ' "Dr Leila Walcott, twenty-five..." ' He looked up at Leila over the top of his glasses. 'We'll let that pass ... "from the Botanical Research Centre of Madero, insists that Minister Ayala has power over the paramilitaries. She conveys a plea to the minister from all who value peace and humanity to call off the Bond." ' Makepeace slammed the printout down on the table, setting the test-tubes

293

jingling and the chemicals rippling in their vessels.

'I was trying to do something at least,' she said miserably. She felt awful. The images of death had revolted her. She had been scared by Ayala and she was overwhelmed by guilt. She simply could not bring herself to tell Makepeace that he was right, and that Ayala was going to close the project down in two months.

'Leila, for some unfathomable reason you insist on seeing Diaz and the FARA as Robin Hood and his Merry Men. When will you realize that Diaz is a snake and his men are thugs? He may paint himself as a saintly combination of Che Guevara, Simón Bolívar and Toussaint L'Ouverture, but at heart he's a bandit and he would sell his grandmother, the people, *La Revolución* and Che's blessed memory if the price was right.'

'I don't think so,' argued Leila timidly. 'At least Diaz has a cause.' She was biting back tears now.

'Leila, darling, I hate to be the one to inform you, but the holy generalissimo is in it for the money. You've seen how he has his men work that mine – as hard as GemCorp did, night and day.' Makepeace looked sadly at his headstrong colleague. 'I can't believe you did his dirty work for him, Leila. And against my advice, too.'

Leila did not answer. She convinced herself that the shock of Ayala's threat might hurt Makepeace. It would be better to break it to him gently some time in the future. Perhaps the next time they were together in Bogotá. After all, she thought, things might change. The project had been threatened with closure before, and Makepeace had closed it himself at least once. He had always managed to bounce back.

Stiffly, she handed him some of the data from the lab tests and moved to her own microscope to look at some slides.

'You know something, Leila,' Makepeace said to her kindly, 'you'll save many more people by your ethnobotany than by trying to play politics. Stick to what you're good at. Find something useful in these plants, and that will be your best argument for preserving the forest.'

Secretly, Leila had come to agree. It would be a relief for her to stop struggling for human and forest rights for a while and concentrate on botany. Soon they were both talking animatedly about the recent confirmation of active secondary compounds similar to L-DOPA in a vine known by the Jemberí as *jomo*, which the Indians used as a hallucinogen. The presence of the active chemical was not a complete surprise to Leila, because the thorough Makepeace had already ingested a preparation of the plant in the name of science – with spectacularly weird results.

Leila was encouraged to see that plants which the Jemberí identified as medicinal were ten times more likely to contain active secondary compounds than a control group of randomly selected plants. The ratio appeared to vindicate the ethnobotanical premise that the traditions of the forest peoples were more than mere superstition and old wives' tales.

Still, the specimens included no miracle cures for the Jemberí wasting disease or any other. The latest lab analysis on the *kiragi* plant was interesting. It turned out that *kiragi* did contain alkaloids oddly similar to some of the chemicals in a sponge, *Discodermia panoplia*, which could inhibit the growth of some cancers.

'Look,' said Makepeace excitedly. 'Only the flowering specimens contain the alkaloids. That would explain why we've never found active secondary compounds in *kiragi* before.'

Leila nodded. She knew that the chemical composition of a plant can change at different stages in its lifecycle – such as budding and florescence. That's why watercress should be picked before it buds or it becomes bitter. Or if you want the best elderflower wine, the flowers should be picked as soon as they open in the morning.

Though Leila was encouraged, she remained glum. She had always trusted the Jemberí when they said *kiragi* was special. But now she had only two months to prove them right.

Since Diaz had received the vile message from the Bond about Cuchillo's demise, security and mining activity had increased in Madero. The mine was now operating around the clock. There was also increased diplomatic activity. A United Nations delegation turned up to try to maintain the ceasefire. Anthony saw them from the treetop OP in their white SUVs marked with the light blue 'UN'. Diaz had also assiduously sold off access to loggers, mineral prospectors and other parties hungry for Madero's resources. The newcomers felled trees and dug shafts, or *cortes*, to search for emeralds. The forest echoed to the boom of falling trees and the detonation of dynamite – seismic transects probably.

Leila did not return to the Argonaut camp. Burr was relieved, but also disappointed and a little apprehensive in case she did appear again. He would have liked to see her just once more as a scientist, before he returned to being a soldier for the attack on Madero. He had enjoyed their time together when he was a lepidopterist. But then again, he thought, the harmony would not have lasted after she discovered the true nature of his purpose. And the relationship would have been based on deception. Leila had made her feelings about mercenaries clear. As soon as she found out what Burr really was, that would have been the end of it. Not for the first time, Burr cursed his profession. What was he? he wondered. Was he a soldier? Was he a liar? For his work he had used deception many times. But that was just what he did, right? Not what he was. Would the real, essential Burr be defined by his deceptions or by, say, the time in the Collegiate final when he told the truth? How ironic, thought Burr, that one decent act had doomed his tennis career and brought him nothing. Rather, it had led him to years of violence and deceit.

One afternoon, Burr heard a vehicle drive up. He saw it was a white SUV and hoped it was Leila, but it was Cinco and some rebels, arriving to search the camp. The rebels now visited the camp two or three times a day. With the increased vigilance, all Argonaut intelligence-gathering was slowed down. In the enforced idleness, Burr convinced himself he could see Leila just one more time. Despite his misgivings, he decided to take up the invitation to visit her and Makepeace. If he got the chance he would mention that the canopy system had broken in a high wind and that Leila should stay away.

When Burr arrived at Leila's clearing, her welcome was so warm, her pleasure at his surprise appearance so fulsome and disarming, that Burr could not bring himself to say anything about staying away from the canopy.

In the field lab, Makepeace's greeting was more wary. Still, he seemed to take real pleasure in showing Burr the process by which the plants were pressed, dried and labelled for voucher specimens. The *kiragi* Leila had found in the canopy had been dried in the wooden press and mounted as the first complete specimen of the plant. The original flowering stalk that Tupo had picked was in water on the windowsill. Its flowers were gone and already the plant was drooping and withered.

Leila told Burr about how the flower had opened at dawn and that butterflies had appeared at the window when the flower had been open. Burr listened and examined the *kiragi* more closely. Its stalk really was a hollow tube, with the petals of the flower at the top hiding the entrance. He pulled them aside and looked down the tube.

'Have you ever found anything inside it?' he asked.

'Yes, as a matter of fact,' said Makepeace. 'Some non-flowering specimens contained tiny eggs. And in this flowering specimen, Leila found the remains of some kind of insect pupa attached at the bottom of the tube. Could you take a look?'

'It looks like a butterfly chrysalis,' said Burr, examining the cocoon Leila had found. It had a hard cap at one end. 'Presumably this end would face up the tube,' surmised Burr. 'That would seal off the cocoon from predators and provide a tough protection for the adult butterfly developing inside.'

Leila was perplexed. The infertile *kiragi* had insect eggs in the stem. The fertile, flowering *kiragi* contained a butterfly pupa. The flowering *kiragi* also seemed to attract the golden butterflies in some way. And it was the flowering plant that contained the active alkaloids. Somehow it all fitted together, but how? They pondered the mystery together as Leila walked Burr through the forest to the second clearing, to see her failed attempts at horticulture. The feelings they had for each other before the trip to Bogotá seemed to be returning. It was as if the forest itself made them forget the barriers that came between them.

'Some just die,' said Leila, showing Burr the forlorn, wilted plants. 'Some survive, but never become fertile – no fruit or flowers.'

'It might not just be the soil or sunlight, you know,' Burr said. 'It could also be due to much more complex interdependencies – like *Bertholletia excelsa*, for instance.'

Leila nodded. She knew about *Bertholletia excelsa*.

Their seeds, known as brazil nuts, are a valuable forest crop, but all attempts to cultivate brazil nuts in plantations had failed. Once the trees were taken out of their natural forest environment, they failed to produce nuts. Nobody knew why.

Burr bent down to look more closely at some of the struggling plants. 'My guess is that a lot of these species rely on specific birds or insects for pollination. When the plants are removed from their usual habitat, the insects can't find them. Or even if they can see or smell them, they can't get to them. Many rainforest species don't like bright sunlight, you know. Most species won't even cross a clearing to get to food. There is even a kind of ant that builds its own tunnels across open spaces to avoid direct sunlight. Perhaps you should try cultivating in the shade.'

'Not a bad idea,' said Leila thoughtfully. She was a little put out that a lepidopterist was giving her advice on botany, but she liked talking to him. And of course this was the rainforest, where everything was interdependent. 'Thanks,' she decided to add with a forced smile. 'I'll see if I can find some more up in the canopy and test your theory.'

Bending down beside the withered *kiragi* stalks, Burr smiled back up at her. Seeing her there above him, biting her lip and looking frail and strong at the same time, he suddenly wished he was telling her the truth. He wished he really was a scientist and not a soldier.

On the way back to the research centre, Leila took Burr via the forest dwellings of the 'civilized'

300

Jemberí. There were a number of the Indians wandering about. All of them seemed oddly lethargic. Some quivered and jerked as they walked, clearly quite seriously ill.

'Now you see why I am so desperate to find a cure,' said Leila. 'They call us ghosts, but look at them. They're like ghosts in their own land.'

Leila bent into a palm-frond hut and introduced Burr to a listless Maria and her subdued son, Tupo. Maria's arms were trembling slightly and once or twice she almost hopped with small spasms, as though performing some strange dance.

'What's wrong with them?' Burr asked as they left the hut and walked back towards the research station.

'We don't know,' said Leila. 'They seem to have some kind of degenerative disease. It's virulent and invariably fatal. The onset appears to be in the late twenties or early thirties. It seems to affect most of the Jemberí of that age we see here. Of course that might be because it's the sick ones who tend to come to us. We don't know what happens in the forest, but it's possible that the sick are expelled from the tribe and end up here. Until we have more contact with the Jemberí in the forest, we won't know. But among the "civilized Jemberí" it seems pretty pervasive.'

'It's genetic?'

'We presume so. Since reading up on this last trip to Bogotá I've been thinking it seems oddly similar to a wasting disease called Cruzeiro's. But Cruzeiro's is strictly a disease of the European gene pool. There are no reports of anything similar from any other forest tribes. At first we thought it might be an endemic virus, but there is absolutely no evidence of it being communicated to non-Indians and the consistency of the age-related symptoms suggests a genetic component. And a component isolated to this tribe. I would give anything to find a cure for it. These are the few Indians who have survived the white man's germs, and whatever they do this wasting illness will get them in the end. It really is a curse on these people.'

'There's no treatment? Don't they have any traditional cure?'

'Not that we know of.'

'So much for ethnobotany.'

Leila smiled wryly. 'Well, I have the feeling that they might know something, but won't tell me. I think it's taboo. They say that only the shamans know – and their shamans are all in the forest. To be honest, I feel that the problem with these people is that, once they have abandoned the jungle, they abandon the old ways, and it's almost as though they wipe the slate clean – they forget, or make themselves forget, what their life was like. There might also be an element of protecting tribal secrets, perhaps sacred secrets.'

'It's more than that,' said Burr, looking at two Jemberí men sitting together, staring vacantly into space. 'These people are not interested in surviving. They've lost the will to live.'

His attention was distracted by children's screams and he looked round to see two kids playing marbles in the dust. Like kids everywhere, he thought. 'The kids seem fine, though. And what about Diaz's Indian, Cinco? He seems fine – healthy, at least.'

Leila smiled. 'Yes, the kids are kids. And Cinco? Well, for a start, he is *mestizo* – half white, half Jemberí – so he could be less likely to inherit any genetic components of this disease. He's also from a different clan from these Jemberí, which is lucky, seeing as the rebels are happy to treat these people like dirt.'

'I've met a forest Jemberí,' said Burr.

'Oh yes?'

'I'd say he was in his early thirties,' said Burr. 'He seemed pretty fit to me.'

'What did he look like?'

'Pale, tall for an Indian, strong build, scars on his chest.'

'Oh, that sounds like Neman,' said Leila casually. 'The scars – well, they say the forest Jemberí cut their chest every time they kill a man.'

Burr took a deep breath, trying to hide his excitement. He failed. By chance he had discovered the identity of the mysterious Neman. 'Trust Neman,' Tenoch had said. 'Through him you can find a stone . . .' Now Burr knew who Neman was. It was another piece of the perplexing jigsaw of this mission.

'So Neman is an Indian?' he asked eagerly. 'You know him?'

'Sure. He's sort of in between for a Jemberí – half wild, half civilized. He was brought up by

303

missionaries but went into the jungle when he was a young boy. He reappeared a few months ago. He worked with the Argonaut Ecology scientists who disappeared. Neman helped with interpreting and sometimes with their research trips in the forest.'

'Did he help with their last trip?'

'I don't know, but I think you're the first person to have seen him since.'

Apart from Tenoch, thought Burr. He bet Neman had something to do with Tenoch's emeralds. Perhaps Neman had even given them to the Mayan. 'How often did Daniel and his team go into the forest?' he asked.

'Oh, very often. They might have been impolite, but they were quite intrepid. They would be gone for days at a time. That's why they weren't missed for so long. When they disappeared, for a while everyone assumed it was just another of their research trips.'

'This Neman,' said Burr, 'where do I find him?'

'I don't know. We assumed Neman had disappeared with Daniel. Anyway, you don't find Neman. He finds you.'

That evening, back at the Argonaut camp, Burr cursed to himself. He had forgotten to tell Leila to stay away from the camp. He would have to tell her in the morning.

'Company!' It was six-thirty a.m. and Madero was already heating up like an oven below lowering clouds. From the lookout post above the entrance, Ahmad's voice rolled over the Argonaut camp through the thick air. The company was Leila, arriving unannounced to resume work in the canopy. After Burr's visit she felt good. The walk in the forest had been more delicious than any dinner date in a fancy Bogotá restaurant. And that night she had drifted off to sleep in warm, sensuous imaginings of seeing him again. Now she waved up at Ahmad as she passed underneath him and parked at the edge of the clearing. She checked her face quickly in the rear-view mirror before walking through the camp towards the canopy winch. Passing Burr's tent, Leila saw the flap was open. On the spur of the moment, she bent down to look in.

She quietly pulled open the flap and peeked in to see a man sitting at a folding camp table, his back towards her. The man seemed to be examining and photographing some small items on the tabletop. Butterfly eggs, she imagined, or cocoons. Craning her neck, she looked closer and saw with a start that they were anything but.

Soundlessly, Leila let the tent flap fall. Then she turned away in a fury and drove off. She left so quickly she did not see Burr winching himself up into the canopy. He had no idea Leila had even visited.

Back at her research station, Leila slammed her car door and strode off into the forest. After a few angry paces she leaned against the mottled grey bark of a soaring rubber tree and breathed deeply to calm herself. She was surprised at the strength of her reaction. A glowing, azure-streaked morpho flitted past in the dim light, and she clenched her fists. She could kill that slimy larva of a fake lepidopterist. This is what comes from spending too much time alone in the jungle, she told herself. You get cabin fever, lose your judgement and make a fool of yourself over the first half-decent novelty that comes along.

It appeared that Makepeace was right after all. Burr and his team were not there for the wildlife, they were there for the emeralds. A voice inside told her that it was impossible – Burr knew far too much about butterflies to be faking it – but she pushed all quibbles aside. She had just seen the proof right there in Burr's tent. Makepeace had marked the last group of 'scientists' as emerald hunters too – 'More interested in geology than botany,' he had said.

It began to rain, a steady rain that would have soaked anyone without a waterproof garment in less than a minute. Leila knew this because when she had left for Burr's camp, in bright sunshine, she had done so without a waterproof garment. Now, after less than a minute in the rain, she was soaked. The rain beat on Leila's head, streamed down her face and neck, and trickled down the channels of her spine and breasts. It plastered her shirt to her body and her dark hair in rats' tails across her head. She felt devastated and suddenly, terribly alone. She cursed the forest with its appalling blend of abundance and deprivation. False promises, Leila thought. This jungle is full of them.

Standing there in the rain, an overwhelming feeling of defeat descended on her. The project was going nowhere. Her life was going nowhere. Madero was not paradise. It was more like hell, full of hardship and death. She was confused and frustrated. She did still believe that the jungle was hoarding great discoveries, but now the project had only two months. There was no more point to it. She might as well give up. Walking back to the lab alone, Leila heard a distant boom and felt the ground shudder, and she knew that another great gash had been cut out of the Madero National Park. Rebels or government, it was always the same. The mines of Madero would expand, the rebels would destroy the forest and the militia would perpetrate horrible crimes.

Leila was distraught. Makepeace had said she should be careful of Burr and he had been right, just as he had been right about the dangers of goading Ayala. She couldn't keep the secret from Makepeace any more. She would have to tell him that Ayala had decided to end the project. She stood there helpless, crying in the rain.

That was how Makepeace found her. He was carrying his umbrella as usual, though it afforded little protection. The rain was sheeting in from all angles, even from below. He took her arm and led her towards the shelter of the field lab. Leila looked up at him apprehensively under the umbrella. 'James,' she sobbed, 'I have to tell you something.'

Arroyo Blanco, Colombian Andes

Ricardo was worried. He tried to tell himself it was just in his nature and that everything was going well. The intel from the advance recon OP at Madero was first class. Apart from one last sector, Ricardo had been able to build up a complete, detailed map of the town and guerrilla defences, including information on strongpoints hidden within buildings and in the forest – information the best satellite images could not provide. The intel included the observation that most of the rebels drank heavily on pay nights – Fridays – and so were well below par the next morning. Anthony had also noticed that they were particularly slovenly and undisciplined unless Cinco was the officer of the guard. Burr estimated that an attack which took advantage of these facts might find the rebel defences at no more than fifty per cent normal effectiveness.

As for the Bond militiamen, Paul and Ricardo had improved their discipline and effectiveness beyond recognition. But Ricardo was still worried. He had not been pleased with Burr's interest in the Trinidadian ethnobotanist. And things had really got tricky around the time of his and Burr's visit to Bogotá. Ricardo was uncomfortable about the media stories of the *paramo* 'massacre' and he could feel that the militiamen were getting restive and impatient. Pumped up by the media circus starring his crab tattoo, Lester claimed they were ready to start offensive operations against FARA outposts. Ricardo opposed this, arguing it would alert the defenders of Madero, jeopardize the assault and put the forward recon team in danger.

And so when Elizabeth and Lester arrived from Bogotá, Ricardo was on his guard. He did not like the way Elizabeth had been dealing with the Argonauts. She was playing some sort of game. The Last Number Redial on Burr's sat phone showed that one of his forward recon squad had been talking to someone in GemCorp, Bogotá. Ricardo was sure that someone was Elizabeth. And now in Arroyo, Ricardo saw her talking more often than he liked to Craig Thynne.

Then Nicola told him that one of the Bond helicopters had left that morning and not yet returned. Paul reported that he had seen Lester and some of his Jaguar team drawing kit and ammunition earlier. Ricardo hoped to God they were not doing anything stupid.

He asked Elizabeth about Lester's absence. She reacted with unfeigned consternation to the news, but quickly recovered her awesome cool.

'Look,' she said soothingly, 'we are not planning

any offensive operations without Argonaut. In fact I'm glad you came to talk to me, Ricky. I wanted to show you this.' She pulled out a Polaroid photograph and handed it to Ricardo.

'Looks like an emerald,' Ricardo said, instantly recognizing the beautiful stone Burr had given to Chacal. 'Where did you get it?'

'You tell me. I think you know a bit more about it than that.'

Ricardo looked closely at the photograph. 'It looks like a good stone to me. How much did you pay?'

'Pay? All the emeralds from Madero belong to GemCorp, Ricky. Why should we pay for them? We didn't pay Cuchillo, did we? Now look carefully, Ricky. It's an emerald like you've never seen. Except you *have* seen it before, haven't you? In fact, Ricky, I bet you've seen all of these.' She passed over a computer printout covered in thumbnail images. The images were of Tenoch's emeralds.

'Looks like a nice selection of rocks,' said Ricardo, wondering how Elizabeth had got hold of the photographs. 'What's your point?'

'How would you like to get rich, Ricky?' Her voice had become low and husky.

'I am rich enough, *gracias*.'

Elizabeth smiled. 'No. I mean rich beyond your wildest dreams.' She came closer to him and was almost whispering now, as seductive as the offer she was making. 'If we can find the source of these, Ricky, we will be rich enough to own all Colombia. Now listen. We know you were in Bogotá with Burr.

We know that you went to the Calle del Cartucho. What's going on? Where do the emeralds come from?'

Despite himself, Ricardo felt the allure of the emeralds and the wealth they promised. The stones winked at him from the printout with all their mysterious power, and he thought of their glimmering beauty in real life. Elizabeth had made them imagine they could be his. His throat went dry. 'And if I can find the source of these emeralds for you,' he asked, 'what's in it for me?'

'A share in untold riches, Ricky.'

Ricardo thought of what he could do with untold riches. He thought of a new boat, he thought of Rosa and the children ... and there the dream ended. He was happy with what he had. And that included his friendships and his honour. 'Did you make the same offer to Daniel?' he asked.

Elizabeth paused. 'What if I did?'

Ricardo did not respond. Daniel had been a good soldier, but impetuous. If Daniel had been tempted with stories of El Verde, Ricardo knew he would have gone for it.

'I see,' he said thoughtfully. 'Well, thanks for the offer, but it's not exactly persuasive. I mean, look what happened to Daniel ... The answer's no, thanks, Elizabeth. As far as I'm concerned, Argonaut is here to do a job, take our payment and go home.'

Elizabeth looked at him slyly. 'As far as you're concerned maybe, but what about the others? Burr appears to have his own agendas these days. He

311

seems as interested in his Trinidadian doctor as in the mission.' She saw that she had struck a nerve and she licked her lips subconsciously before carrying on. 'Don't tell me you haven't seen how distracted he is? And just remember, all the emeralds from that forest are ours, whether they come from the mine or not. And we expect them all to be given to us. You just make sure our friend knows that. That is, if you can tear him away from that sweet little botanist.'

Ricardo walked away with his mind racing. Had Elizabeth approached any of the other Argonauts with such an offer? Paul would have rejected her, but someone like Craig, who Ricardo hardly knew, might go for it like a shot. He thought Pike definitely would. Maybe even David. It was definitely time to call Burr.

'We have to bring the attack on Madero forward,' he said firmly. 'Then, please God, let's take our money and leave these people to their own devices. I am starting to feel dirty working with them.' Ricardo explained his worries as cogently as he could.

Burr agreed. 'OK, Ricardo, we'll do it your way. Let's go in four days. That will be a hungover Saturday morning and the officer on duty will not be Cinco. The rebels on duty will be as slack as we're going to find.'

'Fine,' said a relieved Ricardo. 'Just make sure to stay sharp. Your mole is not just talking on the sat phone now. He's going through your stuff, and sending pictures.'

'What do you mean?' asked Burr.

'He's photographed Tenoch's stones and transmitted the images to GemCorp. Whoever it is, his first loyalty is clearly not to Argonaut.' Ricardo took a deep breath and said something he hated saying. 'Burr, you've got to look at David.'

It was nothing more than Burr was thinking. He couldn't believe that David would betray him, but David was the one with the digital camera. And it was David who had provided Lester with the now notorious picture of him on a pile of bodies. They had thought David sent it to Lester innocently, as a souvenir, but now that was doubtful.

Finally Ricardo added something he now knew for certain. Elizabeth had not stated it explicitly, but it had been clear from the Polaroid, and she had meant it to form part of her warning to him and Burr. For Ricardo it was the final indication of what sort of person Elizabeth really was.

'Oh, and by the way, Burr,' he said, 'Chacal is dead.'

Madero, Colombian Amazon

The conversation with Ricardo left Burr disturbed and angry, but bringing the assault forward meant that he had no time to dwell on it. He whipped the team into action, trying to finish preparations for the assault that very day. Ahmad and David completed the final patrol around Madero, identifying a hidden strongpoint in the jungle by the river. As an incidental bonus for Burr they captured a couple of localized mutant variants of the 'postman' butterfly, *Heliconius melpomene*. Burr kept an eye on David but could not see any indication of duplicity.

Burr then despatched all the team except Pike up to Arroyo Blanco, where the GemCorp assault force was gathering. Anthony and Sven were ordered to return immediately to Madero with the Barrett .50 calibre sniper rifle and the 60 mm mortar. Burr would have preferred to bring these heavier weapons in piece by piece, but he was confident that the Argonauts were now familiar enough not to be searched.

The ranges and target priorities for the sniper

rifle and the mortar were well established. Along with Pike's prepared explosions, their support fire would demoralize and decimate the rebel defences during the assault. When Anthony and Sven had returned to take up their positions, Burr planned to drive up to Arroyo to lead the attack.

Burr was not sure why Leila had not returned to the Argonaut camp, but her absence stood him in good stead with the Argonauts. They assumed that their commander had acceded to their request and told Leila not to come. Burr found that he missed Leila enough to pass by the Ethnobotanical Research Centre on the pretext of checking out the *kiragi* again. Neither Leila nor Makepeace was in when he arrived.

Burr was confident of seeing them again that evening, however. The occasion was the eve of the *Batalla de la Independencia*, Colombia's Independence Day. It was also one year since Diaz had ridden into Madero like Simón Bolívar and liberated the town. To celebrate this anniversary, Diaz had invited all the leading citizens in Madero, including the scientists and all foreign nationals, to a grand gala dinner.

Madero River, Amazon jungle

That same day, halfway between Madero and the Andes mountains, all was quiet on the river. The rebel crew on the paddle steamer were making their second ferry crossing of the day to the western bank. They were carrying a couple of trucks loaded with hardwood logs, some assorted pick-ups and the old scientist from Madero.

From under his battered bush hat, Makepeace watched the western bank approach without pleasure. Since Leila had told him of Ayala's threat to close his project, he had felt as though his world was crashing down around him. He had reacted angrily, shouting at her, damning her foolishness and disobedience. Losing the project would be a disaster not just for him, but for the Amazon, and for the world! He had decided to travel swiftly to Bogotá to try to repair relations with Ayala. He pulled a letter from his pocket that he had made Leila write and sign. In it she apologized to Ayala and promised not to get involved in anything like that in the future. It had been Makepeace's plan to take it to Ayala, to plead his case. He was also pleased to have a good reason to evade Diaz's odious party.

But now Makepeace was uncertain what he was going to do when he got to Bogotá. When he had left Madero, he had been adamant that he was not going to sacrifice his life's work for the self-righteous antics of one young researcher. Now, he wasn't so sure.

With a sigh he looked down the boat at his fellow passengers. There were some young Jemberí men carrying forest goods to trade in Arroyo Blanco. Leila was their doctor and their protector. She loved them and fought for them. What did he do? He tolerated them. Up at the front were two families of peasant settlers. They had been part of a migration programme taking the urban poor to the endless spaces of the forest. The government had sent them to Madero with promises of a lush paradise with land for everybody. It had been a disaster. After the trees were cleared, the sandy forest soil quickly became a desert. Crops failed and cattle died. Indians came out of the forest, stole their goods and, sometimes, murdered them. It was people like these settlers who cut the seismic surveys for a few cents a day. Now they were returning to the slums of Bogotá, or Medellin.

There were also some rubber-tappers, men who worked with the forest, protecting the environment to safeguard the source of their precious sap. And there were the truckers, driving the huge loads of hardwood logs torn from the forest. Leila was right, somebody had to try to put a stop to that. What was the point of spending his life working on the rainforest if it was all going to disappear?

Driving up through rebel-held territory he had witnessed what would happen to the National Park if nothing was done. First he had seen the tree fall – a giant *Ceiba pentendera*, perhaps two hundred years old. As he got closer he saw the work party, sweating peasants with machetes, hacking away at the undergrowth under the eye of overseers with hard hats and a few rebel guards. One guard was by the roadside, beating an Indian. Perhaps the man had protested. The labourers had carved a great gash in the forest. He knew that dynamite would be set every three hundred yards and detonated for the resulting shock waves to be analysed. It was a seismological survey. Oil and mineral prospectors performed them to judge the rock below, cutting tracts hundreds of miles long. If this transect continued in the same direction, it would go right through the area of Makepeace's research.

What had he done? He had not even stopped. He had allowed the guards to wave him past. He had driven on by as though he had seen nothing. He was ashamed. In this forest you could not stay neutral in an ivory tower. The world was crashing down around him whether his project continued or not.

All along he had been a fool, a stuffy, academic fool. Leila was quite right to care about the forest, to care about the evil of the Bond. They could not be allowed to go around murdering at will. He had been selfish and short-sighted. He had cared more about his precious bloody Crafoord Prize, which to be honest he never stood a rat's chance of winning. Tears ran down his cheeks. Makepeace pulled off his glasses to wipe his eyes. He had even been angry with Leila because of Burr. How could he have blamed her, a young woman, for becoming interested in a man? For two years she had done nothing but give her heart and soul to her research.

The ferry was close to the bank now, and most of the passengers went back down to their vehicles. Makepeace heard the engines start, but he did not move. He crumpled up the letter in his hand and flung it into the river. He had decided not to disembark. He would stay on board for the return crossing, then drive straight back to Madero. He would let Leila know she had his full support. If his project died, so be it. At least he would go down fighting.

Then, almost in slow motion it seemed to Makepeace, the boat ran a few feet up the mud bank and settled back slightly into the water. It was still for a few moments as the ropes were flung to the shore and Makepeace heard the shouts of the rebel boatman calling to the shore party to tie up. He waited for the ramp to fall and the vehicles to drive off, but nothing happened. Suddenly there were screams and a volley of shots. The ferry was tugged by the current and began to drift back into the stream.

Makepeace ran towards the front of the upper deck, only to be confronted by a man screaming and pointing a gun in his face. The man wore a black mask, with holes cut for the eyes and mouth, and, round his neck, a white scarf with the mark '07'.

There were Bond paramilitaries all over the ferry. They herded the crew and passengers onto the upper deck and lined them up along the rail. The rebel boatmen were clearly terrified, the Jemberí impassive. Other passengers pleaded loudly for their lives and the peasant settlers held their sombreros in front of them helplessly. Without a helmsman, the ferry drifted sluggishly out towards the middle of the river. The dripping paddle wheels rotated slowly backwards in the current.

One of the hooded militiamen then paced up and down the line of terrified captives. From the blue crab tattooed on his arm, Makepeace knew him as the Bond's leader, El Cangrejo, 'The Crab', the man whose picture Leila had given to the press.

Then Cangrejo chose a man from the line. Makepeace recognized a boatman who had talked to him on a previous trip; he remembered his saying how much he wished to give up fighting. Cangrejo dragged the man over to the stern, pulled his head back and slit his throat.

'No!' shouted Makepeace, trying to get to Cangrejo. 'Stop!' Two Bond men held him back. '*Sicarios*,' he spat at them. '*Cobardes!* Assassins and cowards.'

Cangrejo paid no attention. He finished mutilating the body and, leaving it for two of his men to fling overboard into the river, he walked through the viscous, spreading pool of blood on the wooden deck and pulled out another rebel. Two other guerrillas tried to jump into the river below. The *milicianos* shot one as he vaulted the rail. The other managed to plunge down into the water, only to be riddled by a hail of fire from the deck.

'No!' shouted Makepeace again, rushing forward, only to be jolted by a rifle butt in the belly. He fell to the deck, winded and panting.

'Stay down there, you fool,' snarled Cangrejo, bending over him. 'This does not concern you.'

'Oh, yes, it bloody well does,' wheezed Makepeace. He reached out a hand and plucked Cangrejo's hood from his head.

Lester looked down at Makepeace without expression. 'You shouldn't have done that,' he said.

Madero, Colombian Amazon

A few hours later, way downriver in Madero, Burr
left Pike in charge of the camp and went up to the
Mission Hill for Diaz's celebration dinner. On the
shaded patio by the edge of the hill, there was a
gathering of a few rebel officers and about a dozen
guests. There were a number of reps from oil
companies, some *planteros* sent by GemCorp's competitors to buy emeralds, and a delegation from an
up-and-coming cocaine operation. The ambassador
from the United Nations was also there – a portly
low-level bureaucrat in his fifties with two bright-
eyed young assistants.

Burr saw Leila instantly. She was laughing,
sparkling in the close-fitting dress he had seen so
fleetingly in Bogotá. It revealed elegant shoulders
and the swelling of her breasts. The late-afternoon
sun lit her skin with a golden glow. She was moving
gracefully around the terrace on the designer shoes
she had planned to wear on her date with Burr. He
thought she looked achingly beautiful.

Burr smiled at her. She responded in kind and left

Burr stunned. Her smile was cold and deliberately, completely false. Leila turned away and continued animated small talk with Javier Diaz and a good-looking executive from a logging company.

The pudgy Diaz was squeezed into a pressed military outfit topped off with a cap like Fidel Castro. Considerably shorter than Leila, he was basking in her attention. 'You look beautiful tonight, Dr Walcott,' he said gallantly.

'You know it's Leila, Generalissimo,' said Leila, a little too loudly, so that Burr could hear, 'and you look quite the picture yourself.' She flashed Diaz a smile and touched his shoulder lightly.

A long table lit by candles had been set under the passion vines, with a view down to where the dark waters of the Madero River looped close to the base of the hill. Burr sat at the other end of the table from Leila, who was on Diaz's right. She took careful pains to see that Burr noticed just how much attention she was paying the *comandante*, her gurgling laughter carrying to Burr through the general buzz of conversation. Burr found himself between a taciturn *plantero* and the female assistant of the UN envoy. She appeared to be a thoroughly discontented young woman, complaining about her boss, her colleagues and her mission as a whole. 'It really is a waste of time,' she moaned. 'These guerrillas will never see sense and this place is so awful anyway.'

Then Diaz stood and cleared his throat. 'Ladies and gentlemen,' he began, 'tonight is a great night for the people of Colombia. It is the anniversary of our glorious capture of Madero. Since then we have been able to save considerable portions of this great country's wealth for the poor and oppressed. And if I may, ladies and gentleman, I would like to request you join me in a toast to the poor of the earth . . . *los pobres de la tierra.*'

'*Los pobres de la tierra!*' The guests all drank solemnly.

Diaz wiped wine from his lips and went on. 'Next I would like to conclude with a toast to our glorious never-ending revolution, which will free the world from capitalist tyranny, but first . . .'

Burr yawned inwardly. He really was looking forward to getting rid of Diaz. On top of it all, the creep was a card-carrying Communist bore. Burr prepared to doze off in self-defence, but then he felt a sudden shift in atmosphere. He snapped to full alertness. He glanced up to see Diaz pause and look out into the dusk. Cinco came hurrying up the slope and whispered something in Diaz's ear.

'*Madre de Dios!*' exclaimed Diaz in a shaken voice. He turned away from the table and walked swiftly down towards the river.

'What's going on?' Leila called after him.

The party broke up in confusion and a moment later the guests began to get up and follow Diaz down the hill. Burr caught up with him in a knot of men standing round something on the river bank. He heard Leila scream.

Lying on the bank in the blood-red evening light was the wet, muddy body of James Makepeace.

'*Mira que bastardos!*' exclaimed Diaz.

There were appalling mutilations on the corpse. River animals, probably piranha, had fed on Makepeace while his body floated downstream from the ferry, but the human-inflicted damage was the more shocking. Burr felt the champagne sour in his throat.

'Look!' a man called, pointing at another white shape revolving silently downstream in the black water. Two men waded into the river to pull the body out. As they tugged, the sodden shape rolled over heavily. It was a corpse – a rebel from the ferry crew.

'*Dios mío!*' someone gasped.

'And another!' was called before the man's body had reached the bank. It was another young guerrilla. Soon Burr, along with Diaz and his men, were all involved in the grim work. A white-faced Leila joined in too, vomiting into the Madero, oblivious of the piranha and caimans, wading and swimming out into the dark current, grabbing the corpses as they floated silently down from what was clearly a massacre.

After half an hour there were twenty bodies lined up on the bank. As a doctor, Leila was not unfamiliar with death, but she had seen nothing as sickening as this. All the victims had suffered the same mutilation. Their throats had been cut and their tongues pulled down through the gash.

'Who did this?' stammered Leila. 'Why?'

Diaz answered quietly. His whole body was shaking with rage. 'It is a final message from the death squads – from the Bond.'

'How do you know?'

'You can tell by the way these people have been killed. It is a method called *la Corbata*, "the Necktie". It dates from a period of civil war in this country that we call *la Violencia*.'

'But why?'

'It is a direct warning from the Bond. If they had wanted the bodies to sink, they would have disembowelled them. They planned for the bodies to float downstream. They want to tell us that they are coming. That is unfortunate, very unfortunate – for you.' Diaz raised his voice. 'Nobody move!'

Diaz signalled to his men and they levelled their rifles at the distressed dinner guests. Burr understood the situation in an instant. He knew he could knock down the rebel next to him and be into the river in moments. But then an extraneous idea – 'save Leila!' – ambushed his calculations. Burr hesitated for the extra microsecond it took him to judge that she was probably just too far away to grab, and that, anyway, he should save himself. He tensed to make his move and felt the hard metal of a gun barrel under his ear. Then he heard Cinco's low voice, so close Burr could feel the *mestizo*'s foetid breath on his temple.

'*No te muevas, cabron,*' hissed Cinco. 'Keep still.'

Burr did as he was told.

A shaken Diaz explained the new developments. 'This latest outrage by the Bond leaves me no choice. In the face of this vile threat, our no-hostage policy no longer applies. I am afraid that, as of now, you are all my prisoners.'

There was a gasp of shock from the guests. The UN envoy and some others protested loudly. Burr did not move. He was watching Leila. She seemed to be barely aware of what was going on around her. She was sobbing uncontrollably, unable to tear her eyes from Makepeace's body. She continued to cry as guerrillas herded her and the rest of the captives back up the Mission Hill and into a barracks room.

'Stay calm,' ordered Diaz. 'If you remain quiet and do not try to escape, nothing will happen to you. Nothing, that is, if the Bond leave us in peace and, of course, if your organizations are willing to pay the bountiful ransoms which, no doubt, you so richly merit.'

Arroyo Blanco, Andes mountains

News of the massacre at the ferry and of the
hostage-taking reached Arroyo Blanco that night.
Ricardo and Elizabeth immediately met to discuss
the new situation and were together when an elated
Lester returned to the base. He walked gaily into
the briefing room. His uniform was stained with red.
He had rolled his right sleeve up and the crab tattoo
was only just visible through the caked blood.

'*Tosque, parceros?*' he asked in Colombian slang.
'What's up, dudes?'

Lester's jaunty step faltered as Elizabeth tore into
him. '*Tetra hijueputa! Idiota!* This time you have
gone too far.'

Ricardo stepped forward to confront Lester as
well. He was wary – Lester was clearly in the grip of
some sort of high, whether brought on by violence
or narcotics. 'You fool,' Ricardo said, standing eyeball to eyeball with Lester. 'Are you insane? What
have you been doing?'

'What we should have done a long time ago,'
snarled Lester, pushing Ricardo away violently, 'and

what we would have done if we hadn't been wasting time with you gutless mercenaries.' He swung a punch at Ricardo's head. Ricardo ducked, stepped in close and knocked Lester down with two precise blows to the solar plexus and jaw.

Lester dragged himself to his feet, rubbing his chin. He glared at Ricardo with loathing. 'Don't call me insane, Ricardo. What do you know of this place? Did you know that Diaz and his rebels murdered my family? Did you know that those Godless Marxist bastards burned our village? They killed our priest and burned our church. They burned our altar! It's too late to stop us, Ricardo. We have begun the offensive. I have watched the FARA steal our goods and rape our country for long enough.'

Ricardo shook his head in disbelief. 'I'm sorry about your family, Lester, and your village, but don't think you're the only one with a tragic story. My family has suffered from Marxists too – in Cuba. Your little bit of revenge today is not going to help your cause. Thanks to you, Burr and many others have been taken hostage. Their lives are in danger and our attack plans are ruined.'

Lester smiled coldly. 'They have taken hostages, eh? Good. Tell him, Elizabeth, what does that mean?'

Elizabeth was looking at Lester with an amazed expression. She answered slowly, realization dawning. 'It means . . . now that FARA has broken its cease-fire pledge not to take hostages, we have a clear right to move in with full force.'

Ricardo was furious. 'But the rebels only kidnapped them because of Lester's raid on the ferry. It is you who have destroyed the cease-fire.' Ricardo took a deep breath and tried to calm down. 'Look, what's happened has happened. Let's move forward calmly. Now, I have Anthony and Janine preparing for a covert insertion. As soon as they have pinpointed the hostages' exact location we can adapt the assault plan.'

'But, Ricky,' Lester said, soothingly, 'we already have your great attack plan. We should carry it out tonight. It is perfect timing. Tomorrow is *Batalla de la Independencia*, and it will be announced to great rejoicing everywhere that Madero has been recaptured for the Colombian state.'

Ricardo struggled to keep his temper. 'It's not a good idea. We should hold on and redraw the plan to co-ordinate hostage rescue with the assault. If we attack blindly, the hostages may be killed.'

'I am afraid that in this case,' Elizabeth said, 'strange as it may seem, I think Lester is right. An attack now will take the rebels by surprise. They think the hostages will keep them safe.'

'And that's it?' Ricardo was seething, clenching his fists ready to knock Lester down again. 'You don't care that the hostages may be killed, that Burr may be killed?' Ricardo glared at Elizabeth's impassive features. Lester was simply grinning. 'No, I guess you don't, but anyway, the plans have to change. Look, we're missing Burr, our commander, and Pike, who was going to blow charges in key places. Also, Anthony and Sven are now here in

Arroyo. Our original plan had them providing sniping and mortar support from the ground.'

'It's OK,' Elizabeth said soothingly. 'We have overwhelming force – five helicopters, the entire militia, including Lester's Jaguar commando platoon. That should more than make up for Burr and Pike.'

'I doubt it,' retorted Ricardo, desperately trying to work out what Burr would do in this situation.

Lester bristled. 'Are you suggesting that my men are not capable?'

'No, they're capable. I've trained them, remember? It's just that it's hard for any unit to make up for Burr's leadership.'

Elizabeth patted the Cuban condescendingly on the back. 'If anyone can do it, Ricky, you can.'

Ricardo struggled to remain calm. Elizabeth and Lester had made their decision. The attack was going to go ahead no matter what. Ricardo knew that after Lester's actions at the ferry, Burr would have called the whole operation off. He would not want to work with murderers. Ricardo would have done the same, except now Burr and Pike were captives. Their lives and those of the other hostages were at stake. It would be better to try to work with the militia, to try to minimize the mistakes.

'OK,' Ricardo said, 'but let's try some modifications to the plan. Oh, and Lester . . .' Ricardo paused, looking Lester directly in the eye, 'you better hope that things go smoothly.'

'*Ah, si?*' Lester sneered truculently – his beating at Ricardo's hands still smarted – 'and why is that?'

'Just remember,' said Ricardo slowly, 'if Burr is hurt during the attack – in any way at all – I will personally kill you.'

'Of course, of course,' said Elizabeth. 'Now, what are your ideas?'

She led Ricardo over to the wall map of Madero. They quickly worked out an alternative plan that Ricardo thought would maximize the hostages' chance of survival. Then the Cuban left to prepare for the assault.

Elizabeth turned to Lester and said thoughtfully, 'You know, Les, *querido*, this is not a disaster. We can make this work to our advantage.' She thought for a moment longer, then looked at Lester with a new expression. Lester could hardly dare to believe his eyes, but it looked like respect. 'This hostage situation,' she said slowly, 'even an idiot would have seen that killing the ferry crew could lead to the rebels taking hostages . . .'

'Maybe,' said Lester, uncertainly.

'. . . And that a particular person – Burr, for instance – would be among those hostages.'

'Maybe,' repeated Lester, still unsure whether she was going to scream at him again.

'You know, Les, I was angry with you about the Cuchillo picture. And today, when I heard about the ferry and the hostages, I could have killed you. But now . . .'

'Now you feel different?' he said tentatively.

'Now I feel different.' Her voice became low and soft. 'Tell me, Lester – the ferry. Did you do it for me?'

Almost in a trance, Lester moved towards her. Adrenalin and violence had made him bold. 'I did it for you, Liz,' he whispered.

'And this attack on Madero,' continued Elizabeth, breathing deeply, 'you know, I have the feeling that in this assault you will not have the survival of Captain Whitman at heart.'

'No,' agreed Lester, standing up against her, pressing his bloody uniform against her white shirt. He could see her nipples through the cotton and feel the excited rise and fall of her chest. His heart was pounding. 'It will be so sad if some hostages are unfortunately killed in the crossfire.'

'And maybe even some of the Argonauts,' murmured Elizabeth, closing her eyes and tilting her head backwards ever so slightly. 'So very sad.'

In a paroxysm of joy, Lester pulled her to him and kissed her violently.

Madero, Colombian Amazon

Hurtling through the swirling mist in the first glimmer of dawn, Nicola saw the lights of Madero flickering ahead in the dark. Below her the forest was a black-green blur. She was flying the lead chopper low over the treetops; her single-rotor Black Hawk contained Lester and a squad of para-militaries. Nicola hugged the contours of the forest and held course to hit Madero from the north-west. She had seen Burr's map of the guerrilla positions and knew that, if she took that approach and stayed below the level of the top of the Mission Hill, she could keep out of the 20 mm cannon's line of fire and probably the 12.7 calibre as well. Another Black Hawk and two Hueys, all packed with troops, were tucked in tightly behind her tail rotor. Nicola felt proud. The Bond pilots had responded well to her coaching.

Not far behind, piloting Argonaut's Chinook, Craig followed the formation as they swung round to the north-west. Craig was keeping the heavy, twin-rotor transporter a bit higher than the more nimble smaller craft. He was not quite skimming the canopy, but staying about fifty feet above it, just enough to avoid the odd monster emergent tree. Over his headphones, Craig heard Ricardo and the Argonauts in the cabin behind him singing 'Guantanamera'. Even Anthony was singing. The other Argonauts joined in across the airwaves in their different choppers, including Nicola and Paul on his harmonica. As the flight hit the outskirts of Madero, the two Hueys, carrying Paul and a platoon of militia, peeled off and headed for the mine complex. Nicola led the remaining force in a beeline for the Mission Hill.

Lying among the other hostages in the cramped barracks, Burr tried to think. He was appalled at the massacre on the ferry and at himself for being so blind as to work with the Bond. He was not happy about his predicament either, but he did not feel the hostages were in great danger. So far the guerrillas had treated their captives humanely, and Burr believed that Pike, still back at camp, would contact Ricardo, enabling a rescue to be mounted swiftly. Burr was more concerned about Leila, who seemed inconsolable. He squirmed across the floor and said how sorry he was about Makepeace, but she just turned her head away. She was in shock from Makepeace's death, of course, but she had begun ignoring him before she had known. He could not figure it out.

Burr's mood changed for the worse around midnight, when Pike was bundled into the barracks. In response to Burr's unspoken question, a shake of Pike's head indicated that the guerrillas had not found the Argonauts' hidden weaponry, so at least their cover as scientists was safe. Burr was still not overly concerned. He was confident that Ricardo could alter the assault plan to take in a rescue. The best option would be to infiltrate Anthony to establish where the hostages were being held. Then, at the beginning of the main assault, a squad of Argonauts could secure the hostages and lead them to safety in the disorder of battle. Easier said than done, thought Burr, but Ricardo would have it covered. Still wet from his immersion in the Madero, he shivered himself to a shallow sleep.

When he awoke it was still dark, but the Mission Hill was alive in an outburst of activity. The mine's alarm siren began to wail like an air-raid warning. Burr could hear guerrillas running about and shouting frantically. He forgot any expectations of planned rescue. This was too soon. Ricardo wouldn't even know where they were being kept. Then the doors to their prison were flung open and all twelve hostages had their hands cuffed roughly behind their backs.

It was raining heavily, but the guards, commanded by Cinco, hurried their captives out of the barracks, roping them together in pairs by the waist. The hilltop was turning swiftly into a sea of mud. Burr was soon wet through again. Leila found herself tied to the young oil executive, Burr to the grey-haired UN envoy.

'Scared?' Burr asked his neighbour.

The UN envoy shook his head. His face was white and perspiring.

'Me too,' said Burr.

A smattering of small-arms fire began. Diaz appeared for a second out of the downpour, then rushed off towards the shooting, pausing only to shout at Cinco something that sounded like '*Tres!*'

Burr could hear the thump of helicopter rotors clearly now amid the rattle of gunfire. Did Diaz mean three helicopters were coming in? Burr was pleased that none of the large-calibre weapons had fired yet. This suggested the choppers were using the intelligence Burr's team had gathered. They were sticking to the flight path Nicola had planned to avoid the anti-aircraft defences.

In front of Burr, Cinco turned to the hostages and pointed at a couple of *planteros* roped together. Two guerrillas raised their rifles and shot the emerald dealers where they stood. Cinco then pointed at the UN envoy's assistants – a young man and woman also tied together. They were dragged forward. The girl began to wail. Not a muscle moved in the *mestizo*'s impassive face as he shot the man in the chest. The body crumpled, pulling the wailing girl to her knees in the mud. The rebels cut the rope attaching her to the corpse and hustled her off down the hill with the other hostages.

Suddenly chaos was exploding around them. Blasts rocked the hilltop – rockets from the helicopters, thought Burr. Lines of tracer bullets criss-crossed the brightening sky and the sound of gunfire was everywhere. Leila, tied to the oil executive, stared at the dead bodies, speechless with shock and horror.

Burr was too angry to be scared. *Where were the Argonauts?* They should have been rolling up guerrilla units on the back slope of the hill, cutting off the rebels' escape route while the main attack moved up the front slope. Burr had no doubt Ricardo would have planned it that way. For some reason the planning had all gone to hell.

Despite his habitual singing, Ricardo felt uneasy as the attack began. He was concerned for Burr and the other hostages. The assault force had no idea where the hostages were being held and, unless the attack was pressed as swiftly and efficiently as possible, the captives' lives were definitely in jeopardy.

GemCorp's priorities had further undermined the operation, with Elizabeth and Lester insisting that the mines should be one of the initial objectives. That would take Paul's unit out of the main battle. Ricardo felt they should have concentrated their forces for a pincer attack on the Mission Hill, quickly overrunning the FARA nerve centre before the rebels had time to react. That would probably have kept the hostages in place and trapped the rebel high command. The mine would surrender after that.

But it was past time for worrying. Ricardo felt Craig cranking the helicopter up to top speed, the Chinook tilting forward, its engines screaming. 'Stay close!' Ricardo shouted in Sven's ear. Then the

Chinook was feathering back and plunging downwards. The Argonauts flung open the doors on both sides of the cabin. Even before the wheels touched, Ricardo was leading his squad out, yelling and looking for targets. Sven was at his shoulder, rifle at the ready. A little more gingerly, half of the militiamen in the Chinook followed them. Craig lifted off again immediately, taking the rest of the Argonauts and militia to another Landing Zone on the other side of the hill.

Even with eyes narrowed against the blown sand and buffeting downdraught from the rotors, Ricardo saw immediately that Craig had dropped them in an exposed LZ a long distance from the Mission Hill. Some way ahead of them, Ricardo could see, Nicola had landed Lester and a squad in the correct place, in the dead ground right at the foot of the hill. The commandos were spreading out and moving up the slope. Worryingly, Nicola's chopper had not taken off again. It sat still on the flat ground, rotors spinning slowly. Gunfire crackled nearby and some of Ricardo's militia troopers hit the dirt. He shouted at them to get up and led them forward at the double.

Paul's platoon took the mine in minutes.

The mine's main defences were two medium machinegun emplacements by the gate. Despite their overwhelming numbers, the paramilitaries hung back. Paul was forced to take out the emplacements by himself, crawling forward under fire and lobbing grenades over the sandbags. Once the machineguns were eliminated, the paramilitaries rediscovered their courage. They charged forward, whooping and blasting away. The rest of the rebel guards fled into the jungle.

Looking back from the mine, Paul could see that the main assault was still moving slowly up the Mission Hill, but many of the assault troops had been landed too far off and were still some way from the hill itself. He also realized that the failure to surround the hill had left open for rebel forces a natural escape route along the road to the jungle. Paul saw a chance to close the gap and ordered his militiamen to come with him. They ignored him. He was stunned to see that most of them had already thrown away their weapons and were rushing into the mine shafts and sifting feverishly through the piles of newly mined pegmatite. In the midst of battle, they had begun a frantic search for emeralds.

Eventually, Paul coaxed a few sulky militiamen away from their frenzy of greed and bullied them into accompanying him back down towards the battle in the town.

On the edge of Madero, by the main road, there was a sandbagged emplacement that would provide a great blocking point. Paul recognized the outpost. Burr had marked it as being held only by kids with antiquated weapons. He could see the quivering barrels of their rifles sticking up over the sandbags.

'Wait,' Paul ordered the men with him. 'Hold your fire!'

'Surrender!' he called to the checkpoint. 'You are surrounded. There's no hope.'

Quickly one, then two, then about nine clearly terrified boys and girls stood up dejectedly with their hands raised. Paul led his men over and took possession of the post. They tied the hands of the young rebels and sat them down in a huddled group by the sandbags. A few minutes later, a wild-eyed Lester emerged from the smoke with a grimy group of *milicianos*. They were covered in blood and dirt. When the child prisoners saw the crab tattoo they moaned in fear and jumped up to escape. Paul's men shoved them back onto their haunches.

'We said: no prisoners,' said Lester, looking directly at Paul.

On the other side of Madero, Janine knew things were going wrong as soon as they exited the Chinook. Commanding Anthony, Ahmad and David plus a sizeable militia force, her mission had been to attack up the back of the Mission Hill and surround the rebels, catching them in a trap. But, somehow, Craig had put them down too far from the hill. It was going to take time to link up with Ricardo, Lester and their frontal assault force. In the meantime, escaping rebels would be able to slip past them. Guns were firing from the hill, but the frontal attack was obviously still hidden on the far slope.

There was some fighting going on around the mine, where the wailing alarm siren was adding to the din of battle. That would be Paul. If he secured the mine quickly enough, he might be able to close the trap on the rebels. There was gunfire everywhere. For a moment Janine's head whirled.

Nicola should have been flying her chopper in gunship ground-support. Where was she and where had the other choppers landed Lester and his men? Jesus, it was all a fucking mess. She fanned her men out into a line and led them forward. They moved swiftly through the town towards the hill, pouring controlled, concentrated fire at any guerrilla resistance. Ahmad spearheaded the attack, firing his M240 from the hip.

'Janine!' she heard through her helmet mike. It was Ricardo.

'Yes, Ricardo.'

'What's your status?'

'We landed too far from the hill,' Janine replied. 'We're still moving towards the objective.'

'It's too late for that. We're on the hill and it looks like the rebels are withdrawing. We've found three hostages dead. The rest are gone. The rebels are running for the forest. Swing round and block their line of retreat. See if you can link up with Paul over towards the mine. You might be able to cut off the rebels and the hostages.'

'Can't Nicola get round there in the chopper? Keep them back with machinegun fire?' There was a crackling silence on the circuit. 'Ricardo?'

'I just passed her chopper,' Ricardo came back. 'Nicola's dead.'

'Jesus, I wish we had Burr,' Janine said.

'Affirmative to that,' responded Ricardo. 'Cut off the escape route in time and we might be able to get hold of him.'

They needed to move fast. Janine decided to

342

ditch the militiamen and ordered them to move towards the Mission Hill, mopping up resistance. Then she and the three Argonauts turned and moved swiftly off through the town.

Led by Cinco, the guerrilla guards jogged their hostages out through the back streets of Madero at a swift pace. The sounds of battle were confused in the warren of narrow alleys. A militia Huey powered overhead, door machineguns firing at unseen targets in the direction of the Mission Hill. At the edge of town, the rebels and hostages paused by a checkpoint full of dead child guerrillas. There was heavy firing on all sides, and between the checkpoint and the forest was a bare, sandy area with no cover.

Burr saw with disgust that the child soldiers had their hands tied behind their backs and had obviously been executed. Lester's work, he guessed. He wondered if this mission could produce any more horror. He had to wonder for only a few more moments. Beside the sandbags Burr saw a body in pixellated camouflage fatigues. It was lying face down in the dirt. With mounting concern, Burr crawled over to get a closer look, tugging the unwilling UN envoy with him. The dead man had been shot in the back. Burr nudged the body over with his knee and found himself staring into the lifeless face of Paul Hill. Before he could react, the guerrillas wrenched him and the other prisoners to their feet and sent them in a helter-skelter dash towards the forest.

The light was stronger now and some militiamen

must have spotted them. Bullets whipped across the open ground, cracking through the air and kicking up puffs of dust. One of the rebel guards fell and did not get up. Nobody stopped to help him. To his right Burr felt the UN envoy panting and struggling to maintain the pace. Then away to his left Burr heard what sounded like an M240 machinegun being fired in sharply controlled bursts. That was almost certainly Ahmad. He looked left and saw, a few hundred yards away, a four-man squad strung out in a loose fighting line. They advanced steadily and swiftly, pouring an intense fire directly into guerrilla defences. He heard a constant rattle of three-shot bursts – two in the chest, one in the head, Special Forces style. They could only have been Argonauts. They were in completely the wrong position, but at this moment Burr didn't care. If only he could draw their attention . . .

Two grenades exploded as he watched, and the guerrilla forces opposing the Argonauts broke and fled. Burr squirmed under the grasp of a guard and tried to run towards his men, shouting wildly. But the UN envoy behind Burr froze with fear. The rope connecting them brought Burr up with a jerk. A guerrilla guard knocked Burr back into line with a rifle butt and stuffed a red bandanna in his mouth to stifle his cries.

Then the hostages plunged into the forest.

By late afternoon, all rebel resistance in Madero had ceased. Fires smouldered and bodies lay scattered in the streets. The militiamen got drunk and went on the rampage – raping, looting and gleefully shooting Indians and alleged rebel sympathizers.

Lester was in a state of bliss. He almost clapped his hands in glee as he stood on the Mission Hill, savouring the screams and crackle of gunfire that carried up to him on the heavy air. Later he thought he might even go down and join in.

'So things are good,' he said to Liz. The rebels had been given a real bloody nose. Diaz had run so fast he had left behind his huge stash of malt whiskies and fine wines. And, most importantly for Lester, he and Liz were back together. 'And I guess GemCorp will be happy that the mines are secure.'

For some reason, Liz didn't seem quite as happy. 'Yes,' she said acerbically, 'and the mine could even be working again in a few days if your crazy militia don't massacre too many of the workers.'

Some things had been spoiling Elizabeth's enjoyment of the victory. First, Diaz had got away with the emeralds – all the emeralds produced by the Madero mines in the last six months. And second, well, second was that Burr and the hostages were still with the rebels and probably still alive. The hostages were no more than a nuisance to Elizabeth, but since her rejection by Burr her feelings towards him had developed into something close to hatred. She honestly would not have been unhappy if Diaz had done away with him. Unfortunately, Diaz had killed only three hostages, none of whom was Burr. But Elizabeth thought she now had a solution for these problems – a solution that might be better for everybody.

'I think I may have an idea, Les,' she said. She outlined the plan to him. Lester didn't really understand it, but he had learned to trust her. 'This is our chance,' she urged him, 'our chance to really make it – one chance, then we are out of here. Out of Madero, out of Colombia.'

Lester beamed. He was happy as a puppy. He just loved the 'our'. 'Hawaii?' he asked. 'You and me?'

'Sure. Why not?'

He was in ecstasy. His psychotic brain rushed into visualizations of the paradise she was promising, then jumped to its logical conclusion. 'And so, Liz . . .' he hesitated, '. . . will you marry me?'

She patted him on the cheek. 'Why, Lester, how sweet. But first things first, yes? Let's get these Argonauts out of the way and finish our business here.'

Lester wasn't sure if 'how sweet' was a good answer to a proposal, but he accepted it for the moment.

She walked across the hilltop to talk to the waiting Ricardo Martinez. She could start to put her plan into action right away. Lester looked at her in admiration. She always had it worked out. It really was amazing how he could never see these options, not until she pointed them out. Then they were obvious, of course. They were a great team, him and Liz.

As far as he could gather, the point was that William Walls had paid all the remaining money for the Argonaut contract and all other expenses directly into an account controlled by Liz. She was apparently now telling Ricardo that Argonaut had not yet fulfilled their part of the bargain and she would not pay out the money until the contract was complete. Until then, a few million dollars would stay in her account. Lester wondered for a minute how that would benefit him. But he trusted her, and they were back together, right? So he didn't worry about it, even if he didn't quite understand it.

He did understand that Diaz had got away with a lot of GemCorp's emeralds, and that somehow Elizabeth planned to get hold of those as well. Though she had also said something about not giving them to GemCorp. Lester wasn't sure that double-crossing Walls at this stage was a particularly good idea, but Liz knew best. It all made his head hurt, but that's why he left that part to her. At least, that's what she told him.

He turned away from the view over the burning town to where she was lecturing Ricardo on a terrace shaded with flowering climbers. Lester couldn't believe the poor Cuban was resisting. Didn't he know it was pointless? Liz always got her way.

'Look, Elizabeth,' Ricardo argued, as calmly as he could. 'We've done our job. You've got Madero. We would like full payment and release from our contract. Fast. We need to get Burr and Pike.'

'Ricky, Ricky, Ricky.' Elizabeth was shaking her head sadly. 'I'm afraid you still have some work to do for us. Your contract was to get the stones back. Until you do that, you get nothing. Anyway, why do you need the money now? You can't spend it in the jungle.'

Ricardo insisted stubbornly. 'It should be wired into the Argonaut account in Miami. I checked with Carlo. He says the balance of the invoice is due on capture of Madero. There is no mention of retrieving any stones. Diaz is bound to make a ransom demand for Pike and Burr. Carlo might have to pay it. For that he needs the cash.'

'Ah, yes,' said Elizabeth, 'poor Burr. I'm afraid I can't get worked up about Pike – he never had the same effect on me. The question is, can you afford to sit here and wait for a ransom request? As long as Diaz thinks Burr is just a scientist, he won't be in danger and the ransom will not be that expensive.' She paused. 'But what if Diaz discovers – somehow – that Burr and Pike are mercenaries like you? I don't think they would last very long then. No, Ricky, I'm afraid you're going to have to be more proactive.'

An angry and frustrated Ricardo left the hilltop and walked down to where the Argonauts had set up a defensible area in a derelict school next to the dusty soccer field. The Chinook waited in the heat next to a vacant classroom, where Ricardo called the team together. On the desk in front of him were Nicola and Paul's personal effects.

'I will tell Nicola's folks when we get back,' said Ricardo, looking at the sad collection of name tags, Nicola's iPod and Paul's harmonica. 'Anybody know Paul's family?' asked Ricardo.

'Ain't got none,' said Anthony.

Ricardo reported what Elizabeth had told him. The deal was that if the Argonauts brought back the emeralds, then GemCorp would pay the contract in full, and also give them a share of the recovered stones. To help them, Elizabeth had provided the co-ordinates of the main FARA base.

'It's bullshit,' burst out David. 'Doesn't it strike you as strange that two of us were killed and that they were the only ones who had no Argonaut back-up? I don't trust those assholes. They're never going to pay.'

Ahmad agreed. 'Paul is dead. Nicola is dead. This whole mission is finished.'

'Ain't no question,' added Anthony. 'Crab Man and Witch Woman had this planned all along. I say we kill them right now.'

'I'm with Anthony,' agreed Janine. 'We can take 'em. They're a bunch of amateurs.'

'Simmer down,' said Ricardo forcefully. 'Cool it. Look, I'd like nothing better than to take them out, but we can't be sure they killed Nicola, or Paul. And let's face facts. They have one hundred and fifty troops here. We are just seven. They have the high ground, the helicopters and some heavy weaponry; also, we're low on ammo.'

'I don't mind the odds,' said Janine.

'If Burr was here, he would take them,' muttered Ahmad.

'But he's not here,' Ricardo retorted. 'So what do you suggest we do, Ahmad?'

'First we get back to Arroyo, pick up the mortar

and more ammunition. Then we infiltrate close to the rebel base and get Burr and Pike. We take all Diaz's damn emeralds too. Then we come back here to deal with these Bond sons of bitches.'

David looked at Ahmad admiringly. 'Not bad, Maddy: simple, effective and not at all bad – especially for an A-rab. Come on, let's vote on it.'

'Hey, friend,' said Sven quietly, laying a massive hand on David's shoulder. 'There is no vote here. We are still in a combat situation. Sergeant Ricardo decides.'

'Thanks, Sven,' Ricardo said. 'Before we decide, I think we should hear from the pilot.' He turned to Craig, who looked a little nervous. 'What do you think, Craig? We would need to be dropped in close to the rebel base. You would have to exfiltrate us in a few days.'

'Could be done,' Craig mumbled. 'We can take some gas from one of the choppers here to help get us back to Arroyo. There we can refuel with enough to get me all the way to the rebel base, then back here to wait until the extraction.'

'OK,' said Ricardo, 'this is what we're going to do. We fly out of here in the Chinook, re-supply at Arroyo, then launch an attack on the rebel camp. We bring out Burr and Pike, and take the emeralds from Diaz. We deliver them to Elizabeth and Lester. That will complete the contract. We get paid and then, if we still want to, we get even.'

'Makes sense to me,' said David.

Craig nodded. 'I guess I'll infiltrate you near the rebel base by night and return to exfiltrate at a time and place to be designated.'

'It's a little rushed,' Ricardo admitted, 'but I think it's our only choice. The rebels will be off balance after their eviction from Madero and, although its location is pretty well known, their base is deep in the jungle and nobody has ever dared to assault it. They won't be expecting anything.'

The Argonauts' meeting broke up and the team prepared to move out.

David and Ahmad went over to Nicola's helicopter where it sat on the far corner of the football pitch. Shooing away a Bond guard, they siphoned the contents of its fuel tank into jerry cans. While the high-octane fuel was glugging out, Ahmad looked at the cockpit of the Black Hawk.

'You see anything strange about this?' he asked David.

'Like what?' asked David, after peering closely at the glass.

'Nicola was killed in her seat, right?'

'Yes. Round right in the side of the head.'

'That would mean the bullet had to have come from over here.' Ahmad stood by the co-pilot's door.

'That's right.'

'Do you see any bullet holes?'

David shook his head slowly, comprehension dawning. 'No, Maddy. No, I do not.'

On the other side of the soccer field, Craig got into the Chinook and performed some hasty checks. Then he slipped out of the far side of the chopper and scurried across the open ground into a stand of brush at the foot of the Mission Hill. He paused to see if he had been spotted, then walked swiftly up the slope towards what was now GemCorp HQ.

Craig didn't like Lester. He liked Elizabeth even less. In fact Craig thought they were a couple of jerks who would sell their mothers if the price was right. Craig realized that he was hardly being the paragon of honesty with the Argonauts, but he dismissed this as not being the real him. It was just a phase, a brief turn. Maybe betrayal was a virus and he was catching it from Elizabeth and Lester. The means of transmission was clear, though – it was money – and Liz and Les paid so much of it. That's what made them so damn contagious.

When Craig came back down the hill he was, in theory, two hundred thousand dollars richer, and pleased that he would be making just a couple more flights before leaving Madero for good. He slipped back into the cockpit, confident that the Argonauts had not noticed his brief absence.

A few minutes later, Anthony came strolling down the hill. He went into the old schoolhouse, where Ricardo was cleaning his M4.

'Well?' prompted Ricardo.

'Well, what do you think?' Anthony asked.

'My guess?' Ricardo closed one eye and looked down the barrel of his rifle. 'I think he went straight to Elizabeth and Lester.'

'He sure did. An' then they fuelled up a chopper and loaded her with air-to-airs.'

Ricardo gave a slow nod of understanding.

Anthony spat into the dust. 'So now what?'

'So now we need a change of plan.'

Amazon jungle, south-east of Madero

As soon as the hostages entered the muffling forest, the sounds of fighting at Madero faded quickly behind them. Burr was still tied to the UN envoy. A few yards behind, roped to a taciturn *plantero*, Pike was complaining about not having any cigarettes. Leila stumbled along in a daze, still distraught at Makepeace's death. Cinco marched them all day, until just before sunset, when they reached a small clearing with a rubber-tapper's hut by the river. There they ate from a guerrilla food cache and Cinco allowed them a short rest. To the prisoners' relief, their aching arms were now cuffed in front of them.

The clearing appeared to be a rendezvous point. Some guerrillas fleeing from Madero were waiting there when the column arrived and over the next few hours more survivors of the rout turned up in groups of two or three. Some of them were wounded. Diaz did not appear.

Burr pretended to sleep, listening carefully to the guerrillas. They were in an ugly mood, cursing the government and the murdering *Yanqui* mercenaries who had fought with the attackers. They had seen them – white men and women, dozens of them. And black men too, someone else said. They seemed to know exactly where all the strongpoints were. The rebels' big guns had not been able to find a target. There must have been treachery, spying! One of the guerrillas said that Cinco thought there might be spies amongst the hostages. The guards looked at their captives with hostile eyes.

By five o'clock in the morning, they were on the move again in the permanent twilight of the forest floor. Burr judged that they were heading south-east, deeper into the endless reaches of the Amazon jungles. They crossed valleys and forded a series of muddy streams. One of the latest additions to the group, a hulking straggler from Madero, took up a position directly behind Leila. In the moist air, her dress was permanently damp, and the man stared at her body, clearly outlined by the clinging material. Now and again he pursed his lips and made sucking, kissing noises. A few steps back, Burr saw Leila turn round to look at the man, who winked at her and rubbed his crotch. She spat in his face. The man cursed and fell back for a moment as he stopped to wipe off the spittle. Then he rejoined the line, muttering and glaring at her back.

Just after sunset, Cinco called another halt. The hostages were pushed to the ground where they stood. Some of the guerrillas got drunk on the *aguardiente* they carried in their hip flasks. Their *mestizo* officer let the captives drink his water – a few sips each. It was almost pitch-black in the forest. No moonlight penetrated the canopy. Leila and the oil executive sat with their backs against a huge fig tree. Leila could only sense Burr sitting a couple of yards away. Exhausted, she passed out in the thick, soft layer of leaves and detritus that coated the forest floor.

She was awoken by a weight, and by the reek of stale sweat and alcohol. A heavy body lay on top of her and a hand was pulling up her sodden dress. Leila tried to push him off, but the man was too big, too strong. Nearby, some guerrillas were still awake. She could hear them laughing and singing drunkenly. They must have lit a lamp, for there was a dim light in the undergrowth. Leila drew breath to shout and the man hammered a fist into her solar plexus. Pain transfixed her body and her plan to shout was replaced by the urgent need to breathe. As she wheezed desperately for air, a strong hand clamped down over her mouth, muffling her cries. She writhed in the man's grip. Her cuffed hands beat uselessly on his back. Her attacker pulled his hand away again and punched her in the temple. She fell back, stunned. Her head lay on one side, cushioned – nicely, she thought – in the carpet of leaf mould, twigs, fruit seeds and the carcasses of dead fauna that formed the natural compost of the rainforest. She acutely felt the tiny feet of insects and arthropods crawling on her bare skin. Vaguely she was aware of the man forcing her legs apart with his knees. She pulled on the rope that joined her to the oil executive and looked over at him. Just a few inches away, she saw his staring eyes, his corneas dim white pools in the darkness, wide open in terror. Big as a kinkajou's, she thought. He just lay there. Leila could still hear the sound of the rebels' drunken singing. She felt her attacker rip her dress, and her mind fled deeper into itself, further away from the here and now. Then, from above her, she heard a shout, which turned into a shrill scream. The man jerked away and she felt a warm wetness on her thighs.

Leila came to her senses and screamed too, pulling away from the man who was rolling on the ground and wailing. Out of the corner of her eye, she saw Burr and the UN envoy shuffling back to their place between two massive buttress roots. Cinco and some guerrillas rushed over with torches. In the torchlight she saw that the warm liquid drenching her legs was blood, and that her attacker was the guerrilla who had leered at her on the march. He was now writhing in agony, his trousers round his ankles. Blood was gushing from a gaping wound in his groin. A long sliver of bamboo jutted from the gash. At the edge of the pool of light, Leila could see, Burr was wiping his cuffed hands on some fallen leaves. He carefully turned the leaves over before settling back next to the shaking United Nations man.

'Fool,' hissed Cinco at the wounded rebel. 'Diaz will kill you if you harm any of them, especially this one.'

The would-be rapist was carried away. Cinco gave

Leila some water and leaves to wipe off the blood, and a thin poncho to cover herself. He examined her closely in the torchlight, pointing the torch into her eyes and feeling the bruises on her temple and stomach. He then ran the beam carefully over all the other hostages. The beam went past Burr, hesitated, then returned to him. Burr sat, roped to the fat UN man, with his back against a fig root, legs bent, hands resting on his knees, clearly in view. There was no blood on them.

Leila sat shivering and sleepless for the rest of the night. She felt a mixture of shock at the assault and massive relief at her narrow escape, but there were other things troubling her racing mind: the trauma of Makepeace's death and confusion over Burr. She doubted whether an emerald hunter could have acted with such cold violence, and if there was any lingering hope in her mind it had certainly gone now.

Whatever on earth he was, treasure hunter or worse, she knew for sure that Burr was not a scientist.

Madero, Colombian Amazon

In the Chinook at the foot of the hill, Craig started up the rotors. He was pleased. He was going to make a lot of money. Just the flight up to Arroyo for supplies, then back to drop off the Argonauts near the rebel base. The plan agreed with Ricardo was for Craig to wait in Madero, then return to pick up the Argonauts in a week. Craig was also to be standing by for emergency extraction at any time. The alternative plan he had agreed with Elizabeth and Lester was that he would drop the Argonauts in the jungle and just leave them there. Even if the Argonauts survived the jungle, the guerrillas and the Indians, the Bond would take care of them when they called for extraction. By then the mercenaries would be in no state to cause trouble. Frankly, whatever happened to the Argonauts after he dropped them off just did not bother Craig in the least. For the two hundred thousand extra dollars he had been promised, it would take a lot to bother him.

Craig felt a tap on the shoulder and turned to see

the little Jew wearing the pink shower cap give him a thumbs-up. Damn, the guy looked like such a dork! Craig gave him a fake smile. 'All set?' he asked. David nodded, grinning like an idiotic gnome. He slapped Craig a little too hard on the back, grinned again, then ducked back into the cabin.

'Here we go,' said Craig into the microphone of his headset. 'Hold on tight.' He sped the rotors and eased the chopper up and forward. The load was light this time and they rose swiftly up into the night sky. Below them some of Madero still burned after the battle. He swung the chopper above the houses and out over the forest, banking slowly back towards the mountains. He settled into a westward course. Ahead of him the heights of the Andes still glowed red in the sunset.

The rotors settled into a smooth rhythm and the cabin noise came through on Craig's headphones. 'All right back there?' he called.

There was no answer for a moment, then he heard Ricardo start to sing 'Guantanamera', just as he had during the assault on Madero. Apparently that smart-assed Cuban always sang that stupid song when he was going into battle. Well, he'd fought his last battle now, and he didn't even know it. What a jerk! Even if the poor fool survived the jungle, he would not survive the extraction. Craig grinned and envisaged the surprise Ricardo would get in a week's time when, instead of Craig in a Chinook, a Black Hawk gunship turned up and sprayed him and his men with five thousand rounds per minute. Smiling, Craig even hummed along to 'Guantanamera' as Paul joined in on the harmonica. Looking down, he could see the Madero River snaking below him, glinting in the moonlight.

Something was bothering Craig. He stopped humming. The song still sounded in his ear. The aircraft felt fine, the throb of the rotors right on song. He checked the instruments – everything seemed right. And yet... He could hear the harmonica playing 'Guantanamera'. Paul always played along ... But Paul— Craig slammed the chopper into hover and, turning round, pushed open the door to the cabin.

What he saw there sent him white with fear. In a panic, he grabbed the controls and yanked the helicopter into a steep turn. Out of the corner of his eye he caught movement down by the river, then he saw something rising out of the forest straight in front of him. In a blinding flash of light Craig saw the matt black angles, machineguns and rocket pods of a Black Hawk. The canopy of the attack helicopter glinted with a dull sheen in the moonlight and the cold faces of the pilots behind the glass seemed to stare right at him. Then the flash of light faded, leaving just a bright trail of fire heading straight towards the Chinook.

Craig screamed.

From the Mission Hill, Elizabeth and Lester saw the Chinook stop suddenly, hover for a moment, then go into a desperate, banking turn. Flares and electronic chaff spewed from its anti-missile defence pods, but to no avail. Moments later Lester flinched as the helicopter disintegrated in a ball of fire. Bits of bodies and shards of burning debris mushroomed from the explosion and fell to the ground like a bursting firework.

Amazon jungle, south-east of Madero

The guerrilla column moved off again just before dawn. Cinco waited behind, and when the column was out of sight he scoured the place where the prisoners had lain. He made sure to turn over leaves in between the enormous buttress roots of the fig tree where Burr had been sitting. Scavenger insects had already been eating the evidence, but, looking closely, the *mestizo* could see the red marks on the leaves and smell the blood.

The guerrillas and their captives were now moving steadily downhill, crossing gorges and rivers that flowed down from the uplands of Madero. Burr figured they were making for the rebel base. The normal practice would be for the hostages to be held there until ransomed. He was not desperate to escape. The guerrillas generally treated prisoners well, and when ransoms were paid they returned their hostages in one piece. Also he felt that Leila and the others would be safer with him around. In any case, stumbling along tied to the UN envoy, Burr saw no opportunity to get away. He tried to commit as much as possible to memory, just in case, but there was a dreary, obstinate sameness to the forest, which yielded no notable landmarks. At midday, the guerrillas and their prisoners ate from another guerrilla food dump, this one hidden in the hollow of a colossal *Jatoba* tree, around which the forest floor was covered in the emptied husks of its seed pods.

Burr was happily surprised when Leila crawled over and addressed him for the first time in days. 'Who are you?' she whispered.

'What's got into you?' he retorted.

'James was right. You're not a lepidopterist, are you?'

'*Dryas julia*,' said Burr, pointing at a bright red butterfly fluttering around her hair, 'commonly called *flamme de flambeau*. And what are you talking about?'

Leila was not amused. 'Look, I don't know who or what you are, but I think you may be something I don't like, and that disturbs me. Because for a brief while I thought I might like you – a lot.'

'And I—' He wanted to say he thought the same.

'Don't bother,' interrupted Leila, 'but thank you anyway – for saving me last night. Let's just leave it at that.' She turned away.

Later that afternoon, the column picked up a faint path and followed it for about an hour before coming to a ragged halt. After a short pause the prisoners were waved on again. The cause of the hold-up was a vehicle – in the middle of the wilderness. As the rebel guards hustled him past, Burr could see it almost up-ended in the bush, twisted against a tree. It had gone down off the path and been abandoned. Burr and Pike exchanged a meaningful glance. It was a white Land-Rover and it looked armoured. It was almost certainly Daniel's. Some of the rebels were still poking at it dubiously as though to test if it was dead. Through the open rear door, Burr saw the interior had been ripped apart and soiled. The seats had been torn open and the stuffing strewn around. There appeared to be no sign of occupants.

Cinco led them on along the increasingly well-trodden path and that night they simply slumped down on the trail where they stopped, too tired to speak or move. Next morning they struck a track where some vehicles were waiting. The hostages were pushed roughly into the back of a rickety truck and driven off. For hours they bumped along the narrow road, which switchbacked steadily downhill out of the sierra, and then the vehicles crawled through the night without lights to avoid detection from the air.

At some time in the small hours they stopped in a large clearing. The concealed lights of an extensive camp glowed in the trees, leaking through chinks in tents and shutters. The prisoners were untied from their partners and shepherded out of the truck into what looked like a large farm storeroom with breeze-block walls and a bare concrete floor. One end was piled high with bulky plastic sacks.

'Marijuana and coca seeds,' said Pike, examining the sacks, 'and fertilizer.'

Burr paid no attention. Finally free of the bulky UN envoy, he checked the place thoroughly. The door was crude but strong, made from a single panel of iron, bolted and closed with heavy padlocks. Close to the door was a small window, at a man's eye level, with heavy metal bars. Through the window, Burr could see that the door opened onto an area enclosed by high double fences. In the moonlight these appeared to be topped with barbed wire. Between the two fences ran a couple of large Dobermann guard dogs.

Before slamming the door closed, the guards came in and unshackled the women. The men were left with their hands cuffed. The guards took their lamp with them and the worn-out prisoners were left in total darkness.

The next morning the hostages were allowed out into the enclosed area outside the storeroom door. The chain-link fences were high, and were inter-woven and topped by thick strands of razor wire, confirming Burr's impression from the previous night. The daylight also revealed the setting of the rebel base. Lying in a lush fold in the hills, most of the camp was hidden under trees, with camouflage netting spread over the wooden cabins and gun emplacements. The base was surrounded by fields of coca and marijuana plants. Soon some Jemberí women appeared, bringing the prisoners a breakfast of beans and manioc.

'Where are you going?' Leila said in Jemberí to the girl who ladled beans onto her plate.

The girl looked at her with that frank lack of interest the Jemberí could display even for the most fascinating of events and went away without saying anything.

The hostages had been put inside again when Diaz arrived in the camp. His unmistakably shrill voice could be heard shouting orders, raving about the murder of his men and cursing the '*hijueputas de mercenarios Yanquis*' who had taken his emerald mine.

From the window, Burr saw Cinco go over to Diaz and point back at the storeroom. Diaz seemed to have a fit, shouting incoherently. Then a group of guards headed towards the prisoners.

Burr dropped down from the window and pulled Pike aside. 'Listen, I think we could be in trouble. Whatever you do, don't admit we're combatants. Just stick to the story, OK?'

Pike nodded, biting his lip. 'I'm calm,' he said, his voice shaking noticeably.

The fence gates were swung open and Diaz called the hostages out. He was filthy, unshaven, and haggard from lack of sleep. His fatigues were torn and marked with burns, smears of blood and mudstains from days slogging through the jungle.

'Which ones are the spies?' he shouted. 'Which of you are the *hijuepuerca* mercenaries?'

Nobody responded.

Diaz pointed at Burr and Pike with a wicked smile. 'You two!' he yelled. His men moved through the gate, dragged the two Argonauts out and pushed them to their knees in front of Diaz. 'My men tell me there was a black mercenary and a very big man and a woman. You had a black man, a very big man and a woman working with you. Where are they?'

Burr looked around meaningfully. A number of Diaz's men were black. There were quite a few women and at least two guerrillas could easily have been called 'very big'. Burr waited until the point must have sunk in, then said, 'The rest of our team were in Arroyo Blanco, getting supplies.'

Diaz stepped forward. 'You lie. You are mercenaries.'

'No,' said Burr.

Diaz slapped him across the side of the head – hard. There were gasps from the other hostages.

Burr saw stars and tasted salt blood. He shook his head vigorously to stop the ringing in his ears. 'Well, they always say the truth hurts.'

Diaz hit him again.

'Still no,' said Burr.

'What about you?' said Diaz, turning suddenly towards Pike and punching him viciously on the mouth, splitting his lip.

'We're not mercenaries,' spluttered Pike. 'We work with Argonaut Ecology, out of Miami.'

'You lie. I'll—'

'General Diaz,' Burr interjected, 'remember that day on the hill? You said you knew we were obviously scientists.'

Diaz looked at him suspiciously. '*Si*, I remember thinking that at the time.'

'Well, I also remember you saying you were never

wrong,' said Burr. He grunted in pain as Diaz kicked him in the stomach.

'That's true enough,' said Diaz. 'Your problem is, Cinco doesn't trust you, and he is never wrong either.'

Diaz turned to Pike. '*Venga muchacho*. Tell me what you know.'

'About what? I am an orchid collector. I can tell you about orchids.'

The guerrilla leader nodded his head at one of his men, who stepped forward and smashed a rifle butt into Pike's face. Pike went down, moaning.

'The negro mercenary,' Diaz said: 'he was the same negro working with you, no?'

'No,' Pike groaned. 'I don't know.'

The guerrillas kicked him ten, eleven times in the stomach and back. He gasped with pain each time. Burr heard some of the hostages sobbing. Others cried out in protest. Was that Leila shouting for them to stop? He hoped so.

Diaz ignored her pleas. 'So, Señor Pike,' he said, smirking, 'you know so much about orchids, tell me what kind our little Juanita is wearing in her hair.'

Cinco grabbed Pike's head and twisted it to look at Juanita. She was a pretty girl with big eyes, her beauty lessened for the Argonaut by the AK-47 she had pointed straight at his head.

Pike gulped. He looked desperately at Burr, who shrugged. We're screwed, he was thinking. He had no clue about orchids and, as far as he knew, neither did Pike.

'No, I won't tell you,' Pike wheezed, spitting blood.

Juanita reversed her rifle and smashed him in the chest with the butt.

Pike groaned. 'I mean I can't tell you.'

The girl shouted at him. '*Porque no sabes. Porque eres un Yanqui, un coño de mercenario Yanqui!*' She looked expectantly up at Diaz, then beamed when he nodded approval at her tirade.

'No. Please believe me,' moaned Pike. 'It's not an orchid. Believe me. Look at it.'

Diaz ordered Juanita to give him the flower. She glared at Pike as she took it out, releasing her hair, which fell in long black tresses over her shoulders. She handed the flower to her commander and he began to laugh.

'Very good, Señor Pike. Very good. I am satisfied.' He threw the flower in Pike's face and it fell to the ground in between Pike and Burr. At the base of the stem was the clear white imprint MADE IN TAIWAN.

Guards dragged them off to a small hut on the other side of the clearing.

'Nice work,' Burr complimented his fellow Argonaut. 'Not sure how you spotted that, though.'

Pike gave a bloody smile, wincing with pain. 'I may not know orchids, but I'm an explosives man. I know my plastic.'

They lay in the sweltering hut for hours without food or water. When food was finally brought to them, Cinco came in before they could eat. In each hand he held a waxy leaf wrapped round a small yellow and black frog. The black stripes of one frog were slightly wider than the other. Holding one over Burr's plate, one over Pike's, he squeezed the two frogs. Oily liquid sweated from their pores, ran down their backs and fell in drops as large as tears.

'I thought General Diaz believed us,' said Burr tiredly.

'I do not believe,' said the *mestizo*. 'Choose!'

'What's going on?' moaned Pike.

'Well, I think you'll find frogs like this are brightly coloured because they are advertising the fact that they are poisonous. These ones resemble examples of *Phyllobates terribilis*, though I can't be sure. They're known as arrow-poison frogs, by the way. They're just about as poisonous as anything can ever get.'

Pike moaned in despair.

'Now, these look like two mimic species. They could both be poisonous – examples of Mullerian mimicry, when different poisonous species evolve similar warning colours. But my guess is that one of these is a harmless Batesian mimic. The harmless species takes on the strident colours of poisonous species to deter predators. The question is, which is which?'

'What?' said Pike. 'Your *guess*? Have you gone crazy? Which is which? I don't know anything about frogs!'

'Eat!' ordered Cinco. 'Choose!'

Burr hesitated, then plunged his spoon into Pike's food and took a large mouthful. He chewed it slowly and deliberately, then swallowed, staring all the while at Cinco's heavy-eyed, expressionless face. Nothing happened. Cinco seemed satisfied. He nodded and left.

Pike breathed a sigh of relief. 'How could you tell?' the explosives man mumbled, still white with fear.

'I couldn't,' said Burr. 'I don't know anything about frogs either. Still, I'd take fifty-fifty rather than let that bastard Cinco have his way. Not only that, I'm damn hungry. Want some?'

Pike shook his head and watched, white-faced, as Burr wolfed down his food.

Sometime in the night, the door of the hut opened and Diaz looked in. 'Put them back with the others,' he said with a yawn. 'I always knew they were scientists.'

Pike and Burr were a mess. They were bleeding, bruised and filthy, their clothes torn. Leila rinsed their cuts with water, checked their injuries and found that Pike had a couple of broken ribs. He winced in pain. 'Anybody here got a cigarette?' he pleaded.

When their dinner was brought round, Leila found some fresh guavas and chocolate on her plate. 'Good life,' the serving girl muttered to her in Jemberí. Her name was Tokom, she told her. She had been to the clinic at Madero, where Leila had treated her and her family.

'You remember my sister's son?' she said. 'He gave you *kiragi*.'

'Tupo? Tupo is your nephew?'

The woman nodded. 'He is my sister's son. Maria

lies in Madero, where she dies. Tupo will be well. He is going to the warriors in the jungle.'

Leila was pleased that at least Tupo was safe, but she was deeply saddened to hear about Maria.

Then Tokom went on. 'You are in danger, Plant Doctor. This man Diaz. He enjoys using women and he enjoys killing people and ghosts of all kinds.'

Leila shared the food among the hostages, giving the injured Pike the largest chunk of chocolate. A slender figure, somewhat bedraggled, she moved over to where Burr stood by the fence, looking out through the wire mesh at the rebel camp.

'Here,' she murmured kindly, 'have some.'

'A peace offering?'

'No chance.'

Burr thanked her anyway and ate the fresh, bitter chocolate mechanically, wincing from a bruised jaw. 'I'm sorry about Makepeace,' he said. 'He was a good man.'

Leila went white at the mention of Makepeace. 'How dare you say his name!' she hissed. 'He was murdered by the Bond, your death-squad friends. Maybe your men even helped.' She looked away, trying to suppress her grief, anger, and, thought Burr, some other emotion that he couldn't quite gauge. She was hiding something.

'Diaz was right, wasn't he?' Leila continued quietly. 'I should have listened to James from the start, not to you – someone I knew nothing about. I can't believe I liked you for a minute. A lepidopterist? You're not even an emerald hunter. You're worse. You and Pike are mercenaries, aren't you? Well, aren't you?' Burr flashed her a warning glance but she persisted. 'And the previous group – what was his name? Daniel and his team – they were mercenaries as well. Tell me!'

Burr looked around to make sure nobody was in immediate earshot. There was a sudden barking as the guards released the attack dogs into the space between the two fences. 'We like to call it private military services,' he said quietly, 'and we try to work only for the good guys.'

'And who are the good guys here? Your militia friends who slit children's throats?'

Burr nodded. 'Fair enough. Though, believe me, my men would have had no part in those killings.'

'Is that all you have to say?' Leila looked at him fiercely.

Burr looked at her, mud on her face, her hair unwashed, tied back roughly from her face. He thought of her as she opened the door to him, fresh and smiling, in the Fiesta Americana Hotel. Burr wondered if he would ever hear her gurgling laugh again. He moved closer to her and spoke with feeling. 'Look, I admit that working with the Bond was a mistake. Believe me, I hope to get the chance to put that right. But just because the Bond are bad, that doesn't make Diaz and his gang the good guys.'

'OK, so Diaz isn't all I cracked him up to be, either. What's that got to do with you? He's not your problem. I don't mind killers in the military where they belong. But how can you come here and kill people of your own accord? America is not at war here. You're as bad as the Bond.'

'You think Diaz should just be allowed to get on with it? Don't people like him also have to be stopped?'

'Not if it's just to replace him with someone just as bad – like your GemCorp friends. I mean, there are other authorities, proper channels, legitimate international organizations . . .' Her voice petered out. Dark was falling swiftly as it always did so close to the equator. Two guards were approaching with burning hurricane lamps. Any minute the hostages would be locked up for the night. 'Why do you do it?' asked Leila out of the gathering gloom.

Burr could hear a note of hope in her voice. Perhaps she expected him to have an honourable excuse. For a moment there was silence.

'I don't exactly know. I want to find Daniel; I wanted to help the Mayans . . .' He shook his head slowly. Then he said flatly, 'Truth is, I do it because it's my job.'

'How much are they paying you?'

It was dark now, but Burr could still see Leila's green eyes glint in the starlight. 'Believe me, I figure that if I'm going to sell my soul, it's going to be for a lot of money.'

'That's fair enough,' said Leila sadly, 'if your soul's for sale in the first place.'

Miami, Florida

In the Argonaut Headquarters, Carlo put the phone down with a shaking hand. The shocking call had come from Colombia. A professional Colombian hostage intermediary had told Carlo that the FARA rebels were demanding a ransom of one million dollars apiece for Pike and Burr. The middle man would of course make sure that proof of life was provided before any ransom was paid. Luckily the rebels still thought the two were zoologists. They had called the number dedicated to the cover company, Argonaut Ecology. Carlo had coolly kept the scientist cover story going and had promised to raise the ransom money.

How Carlo was going to do that, he had no idea. It was a disaster. A few weeks ago everything had been going so well. Then Daniel had disappeared. Burr had joined up, true, but then Walls had come along. Next thing you know, news came of Burr's kidnapping, followed by reports of Nicola and Paul's deaths.

Then Elizabeth had called, saying that due to

Ricardo's inefficiency Diaz had escaped with six months' worth of emeralds from Madero. GemCorp would not pay a penny more unless these emeralds were regained. What's more, Ricardo and the remaining team members had dropped out of contact as completely as Daniel ever had. It was so unlike Ricardo that Carlo had to prepare for the worst.

He had just managed to fend off worried queries from Ricardo's wife, Rosa, when he received the most shocking news of all: Elizabeth reported the fatal crash that had killed Ricardo and the six team members with him.

Carlo was devastated. It meant his girlfriend Janine was gone. He could not summon up the strength to tell Rosa.

And now, on top of everything, the rebels were demanding a ransom for Burr and Pike. If he couldn't pay, they too would be killed. At first he felt he didn't care. Part of him even blamed Burr for letting Janine down. Carlo had trusted him to look after her. But as the initial shock wore off – to be replaced by a wrenching grief – Burr's rescue emerged as something he just had to achieve. But where would he get the money from? Carlo had expected GemCorp to pay the balance of the contract fee when Madero fell. Now that Elizabeth was refusing payment, what could he do? He couldn't send in the boys – they were all dead. If Burr was going to be freed, Carlo needed cash fast.

And then there was Xcalan and Burr's goddamn

beach. Appalled at his own actions, Carlo found himself wondering whether he even wanted Burr to come back from Colombia at all.

FARA *base, Amazon jungle*

Burr was woken up by the clanging of bolts on the storeroom door. It swung open and two guards entered, flanking the expressionless Cinco. The night was black behind them. The guards carried paraffin lamps and the prisoners blinked sleepily in the glow.

'You,' Cinco said, shaking Leila awake. 'You come with me.'

'What for?' she asked groggily.

'For what? For El General of course. To lie with him. Come now.'

'You're joking, right?' said Leila, suddenly wide awake.

'No joke. El General says he needs a woman tonight. He wants you. He tells me to explain this: you will be allowed to walk free in the daytime. You will be able to wash. He says to think of the cool water on your skin and that he has soap of a flower called lavender.'

For some reason Leila caught Burr's eye. He was looking at her intensely.

'Fuck off, Cinco,' she said, holding Burr's gaze.

The *mestizo* showed no emotion. 'Come,' he repeated matter-of-factly, 'or I must make you.'

'No! Take me!' The miserable girl from the UN delegation jumped up. 'Please take me.' She moved towards the rebel officer, standing as straight as she could, pushing out her bust. She looked a pathetic sight. The UN envoy tried to pull her back but she shook free of his grasp. Cinco looked at her with frank disgust. He felt her bust and rump roughly. '*Bueno, por qué no? Vamos.*' He pushed the girl through the door and the room was plunged back into darkness.

Next morning, the prisoners were in the fenced area outside the storeroom when the UN girl re-appeared. She looked none the worse for her night with Diaz. In fact her ordeal had left her rosy-cheeked and smiling. She had washed herself and her clothes. Diaz had given her a cotton dress, some cosmetics and toiletries. The other prisoners watched her enjoy the freedom of the camp during the day, wandering around ostentatiously, talking with the rebels and ignoring the hostages, with whom she now clearly did not want to be identified. Proud as a fiancée with her engagement ring, she flashed a chunky, uncut emerald which the rebel leader had given her.

'Where does she think she is,' complained Pike, 'fucking Stockholm?'

To her chagrin, the UN girl's extreme and rather sudden case of Hostage Identification Syndrome went into sharp remission that night when she was locked up again with the rest of the hostages. She did not sleep, though, instead sitting expectantly ready in the corner. Burr heard her brushing her hair in the dark, prettying herself for Diaz.

That night the rebel leader himself appeared. It was about midnight. 'Good evening, friends. So whose turn is it tonight?' he asked jovially. He stank of *aguardiente*.

The UN girl got up and stepped forward, smiling. Diaz slapped her heavily across the face. She staggered away in shock and collapsed, crying and holding her cheek. Leila gave Diaz a look of hatred, went over to the girl and tried to comfort her.

'You,' Diaz pointed at Leila drunkenly. 'You come with me.'

Leila ignored him. She was examining the girl's face, which already showed a swelling bruise on the cheekbone.

'Hey, Doctor!' Diaz slurred behind her. 'It's your turn.'

Despite the pounding of her heart, Leila ignored him again. A stony silence fell. She looked round to see Diaz pointing his gun at her. Fear and revulsion rose in her as she stood up to get some water and a cloth to cool the forehead of the whimpering girl. The rebel commander's face reddened and he shook with rage. The barrel of his pistol quivered as it followed Leila across the room and back. His finger tightened on the trigger.

Watching in anguish, Burr calculated the angles and distances and poised himself to jump. He could knock Diaz down, perhaps jarring the gun from his hand. If Pike was feeling up to it, he could be closest to the gun and might be able to grab it and fire off a shot or two at the guards in the doorway. Burr looked across at Pike, who was watching him carefully. Pike followed Burr's eyes to Diaz's gun hand and the spot where the pistol might land. Pike gave a slow and almost imperceptible shake of the head. It was hopeless.

Then Diaz fired a shot, which struck chips from the wall by Leila's head and ricocheted into the bags of marijuana seeds. She stiffened for a moment, then knelt down again and continued to treat the sobbing girl. Still she did not even look at Diaz.

'Talk to me!' he shouted. 'Or the next one's for you.'

Leila kept her back to him. Her hands trembled as she dabbed gently at the girl's bruised face. 'Hello, Diaz,' she said.

'You little fool,' he hissed. 'Why deny yourself a little pleasure?'

'It is more of a pleasure to say no to you.'

He chuckled. 'Dying for your honour is pleasing to you, I see. But what about one of your friends dying?'

Leila said nothing.

'I mean it,' he threatened. 'Turn around, you bitch, or I'll kill one.'

'You bastard,' yelled Leila.

'How about him?'

Leila looked round to see the pistol pointed straight at Pike, who tried to glower defiantly but ended up shrinking away from the inebriated rebel leader. Diaz moved the gun off Pike, running its aim over the prisoners sitting round the room. They quailed as the black hole of the barrel passed over them. He hesitated for a moment over the oil executive, who covered his face, whining. Watching her eyes, Diaz stopped waving the gun about and pointed it straight at Burr.

'How about Señor Mariposa? I think he has a soft spot for you.'

She clenched her fists by her sides and looked Burr straight in the face. 'Kill him if you like. What do I care about him?'

Diaz tightened his finger on the trigger again, then laughed and pointed the gun straight at the UN girl. 'How about her?'

'You're too drunk to hit anyway.' Leila stared at Diaz defiantly. 'Makepeace was right about you. You are scum. I would never do anything with you. It would be bestiality.'

'Shut up!' Diaz bellowed. He hauled the whimpering UN assistant to her feet and jammed the pistol against her head. 'Am I too drunk to miss from here? Well, am I?' He turned to Leila. 'You have three seconds,' he shouted. 'One! Two—'

'Stop,' said Leila. 'All right, enough.'

Fighting down a rising feeling of nausea, she got up and strode out of the room without looking back. Diaz brushed his slickly oiled hair into place and sniggered. The door closed again and the room was dark. In the blackness, Burr could hear the UN girl sobbing. He also heard the grinding of his own teeth.

Burr could not sleep. His handcuffed wrists burned. His entire body ached from beatings and fatigue. His mind raced with fruitless plans of escape. When he thought about Leila with Diaz, a knot twisted in his guts.

Across the compound, the rebel *comandante* had ushered Leila into his hut with exaggerated gallantry. He was singing gaily, slurring his words. His room was simply furnished: just a bed, small table, chair and desk, with hurricane lamps for lighting. On the table, bottles of spirits stood beside a revolver and a couple of grenades.

'Leila,' he said. 'That's an Arabic name. Are you Arabic?'

'I am from Trinidad. One of my grandfathers was a Muslim, from Bombay.'

'Aha! I knew you were not a *Yanqui*. That's why I like you so much.' He leered at her. 'Well, one of the reasons. There are a few others. Would you like to show them to me?'

Leila did not react.

'Hmmm. Well, we can do this hard or easy,' he said. 'It's up to you.'

Leila's mouth was dry. 'Let's keep it easy,' she said, 'but how about a drink first?' She stepped towards the desk.

Diaz's eyes flicked to the gun and despite his inebriated state he moved swiftly to intercept her. 'Allow me,' he said. He took a bottle and poured them both a drink. He raised his glass. '*Salud!*'

Oddly, Leila found herself noticing how she

automatically clinked her glass against his as if it was a normal social situation. It's like shaking someone's hand, she thought. If they extend a hand, even if you loathe them, the natural reaction is to shake it. It's so ingrained.

Diaz eyed her lasciviously over the edge of his glass as he drained it in one gulp. He had just put it down and moved towards her, when there was a commotion in the camp.

Burr heard the noises too. Voices were raised – some sort of alert perhaps. There were doors slamming, vehicles coming and going. For a moment his hopes soared: perhaps it was the rest of the Argonauts, come to negotiate their release. Burr stood up and glued his eye to the chink in the shutter over the small window. He became even more elated to see what looked like an Argonaut Land-Rover drive into the moonlit camp. There seemed to be three figures inside. Flanked by rebel vehicles, it was flying a white flag. Perhaps it was Ricardo, come to buy them back.

Burr saw rebels bang on the door of Diaz's hut and the FARA leader emerged, buttoning up his jacket. Burr could not see Leila inside the hut, but he caught a glimpse of a rumpled bed. Despite his relief at the arrival of the Argonauts, his heart turned over. He pushed aside aching thoughts of her with Diaz, and wondered whether Ricardo could meet the FARA ransom demands. If GemCorp had paid up, then it should be fine. Burr was already calculating how much he would have left and whether Carlo could squeeze anything out of the business to

384

pay for Xcalan, when the passengers got out of the vehicle.

There were no Argonauts in the Land-Rover. The occupants were two very nervous Bond paramilitaries – and Lester. Burr was not sure whether to be glad or not. He vaguely hoped Elizabeth had sent her sidekick to arrange their release, but then why had the Argonauts not come themselves? Perhaps this was a diversion, and the Argonauts were planning a simultaneous attack. 'Pike,' he called softly, 'something's happening. It's Lester.'

'Oh,' Pike mumbled. He sounded unconcerned. Burr guessed he had had all the caring beaten out of him.

Lester disappeared into a building with Diaz. Burr saw Leila emerge from the rebel leader's hut. She stood there awkwardly, arms folded across her chest. Nobody seemed to pay her any attention. After a while, Diaz and the others came out of the building. The tension between them was evident, but they were shaking hands as if to seal a pact. Lester noticed Leila and pointed at her, saying something, at which Diaz nodded. Then the guerrilla *comandante* sent a group of his men over towards the prisoners' building. Burr slid back to his position on the floor as the door was opened. The guerrillas dragged him and Pike out. They were unceremoniously flung down in front of Lester.

'Here, I believe, are the remaining two mercenaries you were seeking,' said Diaz. 'I always knew they were not scientists. And so, my non-scientific friends, be the first to greet my new ally.'

Burr sat up in the dirt. 'Hey there, Lester!' he said brightly. 'So you guys are working together now. More money in it that way, I guess. Are you doing this with GemCorp's backing, or are you free-lancing? And what about you, Diaz? You don't mind working with El Cangrejo? Even after what he did to your people?'

'Quiet,' snarled Diaz. 'Actually, that is another crime that you will pay for. Lester has told me it was you hired killers who murdered Cuchillo and his men.'

A few paces away, Burr caught sight of Leila staring at him. He couldn't tell if her look was one of pity or revulsion.

'Señor Lester,' Diaz went on, 'feel free to approach these *Yanqui* worms. I assure you they are not nearly as dangerous as they might once have seemed.'

'No,' said Lester, chuckling. 'So let's not waste our opportunity. I'm going to enjoy this.' He took out his pistol and pointed it at Pike.

Pike now gave up any semblance of bravery and grovelled desperately. 'You can't do this,' he whined. 'I did everything Elizabeth asked me. I watched Burr for you. I reported his movements. I told you he was going to Bogotá. I sent you the pictures of the emeralds. You promised me a share.'

Burr knew he was next in line for Lester's pistol, but at that moment he felt no fear. Instead he was swept by a wave of anger at Pike's betrayal. It had been him using the sat phone all along. He found himself wanting Lester to pull the trigger.

Lester laughed again. 'Yes, and thanks for all your good work, Billy, but the deal's changed, I'm afraid. Not much point in giving you a share now. You can't take it with you.' He shrugged. '*Chupa me la verga*,' he said, shoving his pistol into Pike's pleading mouth.

'No!' Diaz waved a hand and his men pulled Lester back. 'Not now. These two are mine and at present they are highly valuable.'

'How much do you want for them?' said the frustrated Lester. 'I'll pay you right now.' From his pocket he pulled out a handful of emeralds. Burr recognized them immediately as Tenoch's stones. He had left them hidden in the Argonaut camp. 'Oh, and by the way, Pike,' said Lester, 'thanks for telling us to look in the cocoons. We would never have found these otherwise.'

Diaz's eyes glittered with naked greed at the sight of the stones, but he restrained himself. '*Tranquilo*, Señor Lester,' soothed Diaz, 'calm down. These two are not for sale today. News of captured American mercenaries will really embarrass the US military. And it will make great public relations for *la Revolución*. Let us get our ransom money first. After that we'll sell them to you.'

'So we all get what we want.' Lester pushed the snivelling Pike aside and looked down at Burr with a snigger. He holstered his pistol. 'Oh, and by the way, Burr, I bet you're thinking that your buddies will be coming to get you, no?'

'Don't know about that,' drawled Burr. 'But they'll be coming for you, that's for sure.'

Lester put on a baby voice. 'Oh, *pobrecitos*! Poor little Burr doesn't know, does he?' He and Diaz began to laugh uproariously.

'Know what?' asked Burr.

'Ha, ha, ha, ha!' Lester was crowing with laughter. 'That . . . that they're all d-d-d-dead! Ha, ha, ha, ha, ha!'

Diaz nodded, panting for breath between spasms of laughter. 'Yes, I'm afraid it's true. They are just *marracos* in the jungle – all corpses. All dead. Lester tells me that two of your mercenaries were killed in the assault on Madero. It appears the rest wanted to come and rescue you, as I'm sure you expected. Unfortunately their helicopter met with a tragic accident.'

Burr couldn't hide the extent of his shock. 'All of them?' he gasped.

'Oh yes,' giggled Lester, wiping tears of laughter from his eyes. 'Paul and Nicola were killed in the attack. Then in the Chinook, everyone else. We sent a squad out to check. They found all the bodies – or parts of them.' He giggled again. 'Put them all together and you could have made – what? About six white men, two white women and a black man. Remind you of any particular unit?'

'You're lying.'

'Oh yeah?' Lester walked across to the Argonaut SUV and reached into the glove compartment. He came back holding a collection of small items, which he threw onto the ground in front of Burr. Burr saw an iPod covered in blood, a harmonica and a handful of cloth strips – printed name tags. *Hill*, one read. Burr had already seen Paul's body in Madero. Then there was also *Cohen*, *Masri* and – oh Jesus! – *Martinez*. Some of the tags had burns and bloodstains, but they were all there. All nine of them.

'There's still Carlo,' muttered Burr.

Lester put on a scared face. 'Oooh, I'm so frightened of Carlo,' he said, then burst out laughing again. 'You moron! Look where you are. You're in the middle of the fucking jungle. What the hell is that accountant going to do for you? What the hell is anyone going to do for you?'

Burr could hardly hear him. He was punch-drunk with a bitter mixture of relief, anger and grief. In a few seconds he had narrowly escaped death, found out that Pike had been working against him and learned of the death of his team. All his men were gone. Anthony was dead. Ricardo was dead. In his mind's eye he saw Rosa and the children. He saw Anthony's aged mother, so proud of her son, the decorated soldier. Burr had been the Argonauts' leader. They had trusted him and he had led them only to failure and a pointless end. And soon he and Pike would follow.

A short way off, Burr saw, Leila's look changed to one of horror. He struggled to remain calm, to rationalize, to find something to give him hope. All he could think of was Carlo. Carlo was a civilian, but he was intelligent. He would think of something, wouldn't he?

389

Miami, Florida

Carlo was having trouble living up to Burr's expectations. When the kidnap intermediary called again, he provided proof of life – a brief recording of Pike and Burr. That was a relief. But the middleman also explained that the Argonauts' cover was blown and that the ransom demands were now two million dollars – each.

Carlo became desperate. Frantically, he worked round the clock to try to raise the ransom money. He tried everybody he knew, every bank and loan shark. Nobody would advance him or Argonaut any more credit. Eventually, he reached for the phone and made the call he had tried everything to avoid. He called William Walls.

In an amused voice, Walls agreed to meet him, and he received Carlo lounging on a vast sofa in the drawing-room of his sprawling Key Biscayne mansion.

Perched on the edge of his armchair and fighting to overcome his nerves, Carlo got straight to the point. 'Mr Walls, I need payment for our contract immediately. We have recaptured the mine for you. But unfortunately Burr and another member of the team have been captured. We need the money to ransom them.'

Walls did not look upset. 'Whitman's been kidnapped?' He nodded slowly and an expression of mock concern spread across his face. 'Well, that's a cryin' shame.'

'I hope I've been clear,' said Carlo, frustrated. 'If we don't get the money to the rebels, they could kill Burr. Especially as they now know he's not a scientist.'

'Well, Carlito, in that case maybe not even the ransom will save him. And anyway I'm afraid it's out of my hands.' The oil tycoon shrugged. 'I've delegated authority to Elizabeth. She is now controlling all the funds allocated for Argonaut. And I trust her. Now, if she hasn't paid out, it's because your side of the bargain isn't fulfilled yet.'

Carlo flushed. 'Truth is, you're quite happy to see Burr stuck down in Colombia, aren't you? That was why GemCorp could offer us so much money, wasn't it? You just wanted to get Burr away from Xcalan.'

Walls smiled coldly. 'That's your version, Carlito.'

'But it's true, isn't it?'

The Texan laughed. 'It is entertaining. Burr thought he could mess with the big boys. And I must admit he has caused a bit of a ruckus over the Xcalan project. He's drummed up quite a lot of environmentalist support. He's even had questions asked in Congress. But in the end it wasn't so hard to get him off the beach. We just dangled some money in front of him and off he went. You should encourage him to avoid environmental politics and stick to what he's good at – killing people.'

A terrible suspicion began to dawn on Carlo. 'And Daniel? Did you pay them to get rid of Daniel, just so you could hire Burr?'

'Daniel's disappearance did create a very convenient vacancy,' mused Walls. He leaned forward, his posture stiffening. His voice took on a harsh tone of command. 'Now listen, Carlito, you are going to do as I say. I know that Burr's plan for Xcalan has been cleared to join the sealed auction. So has my Walls Oil plan. Soon it will be time for the sealed bids. Only one plan can win, Carlito – understand? When that time comes you will go on down to Xcalan again and work with the Maya just as you did before. Feel free to take their bid to Chetumal if you like, but just make sure that you also deliver this bid for me.'

Walls handed Carlo a large, sealed manila envelope and stood up to signal that the meeting was at an end. One of his bodyguards appeared and opened the door behind Carlo.

'The guide price for Xcalan,' Walls said, 'is eight million dollars. Nobody will bid more than nine. And in this envelope is a bid for ten. Walls Oil will own Xcalan, Carlo. And there we shall drill for, find, and extract, millions of beautiful barrels of light, high-quality Yucatán crude. And you will be handsomely paid. You can ransom Burr then.' Walls stepped closer and patted Carlo on the shoulder. 'Till then, if you want him alive I guess you'd better try and stall.'

FARA *base, Amazon jungle*

When Lester left the FARA base, Diaz, Cinco and a truck full of rebels went with him. Diaz and Elizabeth were to meet in the jungle to plan their next moves. The news was that an unofficial truce had been negotiated with GemCorp, or at least with their local representatives. Burr wondered if GemCorp's owners would have been happy with developments. Before he left, Diaz told Burr and Pike that Carlo had been contacted with an increased ransom demand, and that payment was required in forty-eight hours. Just in case Argonaut demanded proof of life, Burr and Pike would be allowed to remain alive precisely that long.

Lying curled up in the dark, Leila refused to speak to Burr, or even look at him. She felt a strange brew of conflicting emotions. Humiliation at her experience with Diaz mixed with relief that nothing worse had happened. She could not feel much sympathy with the other mercenaries' deaths, but she could not deny that the threat of Burr's death appalled her. When it had looked as though Lester would kill him and Pike, Leila had felt real panic.

On the other side of the storeroom from Leila, Burr heard someone crawling over to him in the blackness. He recognized the strong body odour.

'Stay away, Pike. Handcuffs won't stop me breaking your neck.'

Burr could hear Pike swallowing nervously before he spoke. 'I want to say sorry, Burr. About the spying. About the emeralds. I didn't enjoy doing it.'

'And what about on the *paramo*?' Burr asked bitterly. 'Were they already paying you when you shot those guerrillas who were trying to surrender?'

'Yes. They said they wanted no survivors. Really, Burr, believe me, I'm sorry.'

Burr was too drained to hate Pike. He felt only disgust and pity. 'You damn well should be. It's the one rule you never break, and you know it. You never sell out your buddies.'

The little demolitions man moaned in anguish. 'Forgive me, Burr, please . . . We can still get out of this, can't we?'

'Forget it. You've committed suicide. All the guys are dead. There's no way out of here and there's no way they're going to let us live.'

'Wha–what do you mean?'

'Get real, Pike. Even if Carlo pays the ransom, Diaz is going to kill us. If he doesn't kill us, he's going to sell us again – to Elizabeth and Lester. And they *will* kill us.'

Burr could tell Pike had reached his limit. Beaten, his ribs broken, and shaken by his close brush with death, his nerves had gone. His voice quivered with fear. 'But the ransom ... I thought these guys usually played by the rules. If they get the ransom and kill the hostages, they'll never be paid again, right?'

'Usually right. But we're different. We're combatants, not civilians. They hate us. Also, they're not fools. They have no choice but to kill us.'

'Wha— why?'

Burr sighed and rolled over, trying to find an unbruised part of his body to lie on. 'Because if they don't, sure as hell I'm going to kill them.'

That shut Pike up. The room was silent for a while, except for the UN envoy, who had developed a racking cough, and someone – the UN girl perhaps – sobbing steadily. Then Burr heard Pike speak again.

'Burr?'

'Go to sleep, Pike,' said Burr tiredly.

'But I think I can get us out of here.'

Burr was suddenly very much awake.

Pike's idea was appealing, but it had some major flaws. 'Such as,' whispered Burr: 'can you do it in handcuffs, in the dark?'

'In the dark, no problem,' said Pike. 'Practised it at Fort Bragg with my eyes closed a hundred times. The cuffs? Well, I guess we'll see.'

'Another fundamental problem,' Burr went on: 'diesel?'

'I can help,' whispered a disembodied voice from the darkness, startling them. 'Sorry,' came the voice again, 'didn't mean to scare you.' Burr could make out the soft Trinidadian brogue. It was Leila. She had crept closer and had been listening without their noticing. 'I can get you some diesel,' she said. She was close enough that Burr could just make out her shape in the dark. Her jasmine scent came to him faintly, too.

'How?' asked Burr.

'The woman who makes the camp food – Tokom. She is Jemberí and will help us.'

'Us?'

'I'm not staying here another night with Diaz.'

'Leila, do you know the risks of escaping? One, we may be shot in the attempt. Two, they might hunt us down. Three, we may not survive the jungle. We will be without any equipment, supplies or assistance. It will be dangerous and difficult.'

'So it's semi-suicide. No problem. I'll be feeling pretty suicidal if I have to visit Diaz again. Are you finished?'

'As long as you're clear.'

'I'm clear, thanks. Now, you had better be clear about some things too. I might want to escape with you, Burr, but that doesn't mean I like you. In fact you people disgust me. You're nothing but killers for hire – *sicarios*.' Leila's voice had become a bitter hiss.

'We were just doing a job,' mumbled Pike plaintively.

'Well, and very professional you've been about it. The whole forest is in turmoil. The chances of a peace settlement are completely destroyed. God knows how many people have been killed. The rebels still have all the emeralds mined in the last six months. Your team is all dead, and you're prisoners. In Trini we say: "Spit in de air, it goh fall in your face!" Great job, boys.'

The Argonauts were silent. Everything Leila said was true.

'Also, Burr, or whatever your name is, you lied and made a fool of me.' She cleared her throat. 'Now,' she went on, businesslike again, 'any other problems we need to solve?'

'Yes,' answered Burr: 'a big one. What do we do about the guards? We're not going to be able to muffle the explosion. And if we do get away they will send a search party, for sure, so we will need to get as big a head start on them as we can.'

'True,' said Pike. 'What's the answer, Burr?'

There was a long silence. Then Leila spoke again. 'Well, actually I have an idea for that too.'

At breakfast the next morning, Leila spoke to Tokom. The girl looked scared, but scurried off to consult the other Jemberí women. She returned after a while and nodded in agreement.

Leila went over to Burr, who was sitting in the doorway of the storeroom. 'Good news and bad,' she muttered. 'Good: they can do it. Bad: they will need two days.'

'That takes us beyond the payment deadline,' said Burr.

'They have to cut enough vines and pound them to extract the juice. Tokom says they can do it by tomorrow night. She will put the mixture into the guards' supper. Actually, it might just get them high before the forty-eight hours is up.'

Burr couldn't help but admire Leila. Despite the pressure of the situation, she had been observant enough to notice the vines growing in the jungle fringes behind Diaz's hut. They were *jomo*, the powerful hallucinogen that Makepeace had tested in Madero. It had sent him tripping for about eight hours.

That night Tokom slipped Burr and Pike two small leather knapsacks containing water bottles, some food and a full bottle of the fiery *aguardiente*. When she came to collect the plates, she passed them a container of diesel, siphoned from the rebel vehicles. Pike hid it among the sacks of coca seeds. To Leila, Tokom confirmed that she and some other Jemberí women were gathering the *jomo* vines. They would be ready to proceed the next evening as planned.

Diaz and his men returned to the base in the afternoon. The self-styled generalissimo was feeling smug. He had always known his forces could not hold on to a town as large as Madero for long. And despite losing control of the mines, things were going well.

At a jungle meeting on the way to Madero, he had negotiated a good deal with GemCorp, or at least with Elizabeth and Lester – it appeared that they were working on their own behalf for a while. Well, that was fine by him. The deal was simple. Diaz had agreed to share the emeralds FARA had taken from the Madero mine, but in return GemCorp would cease its offensive and would give FARA a free hand to operate in the province. GemCorp and FARA would divide up the region between them, operating a profit share on the proceeds from emeralds, logging, oil and drugs. Everybody won.

Most exciting for Diaz were the emeralds that Elizabeth and Lester had taken from Burr. Diaz was able to fill in part of the puzzle, identifying Tenoch the *guacero* as the carrier of the emeralds. Elizabeth had wondered if anyone knew of a Neman who had been mentioned in connection with the emeralds. Cinco had told them that Neman was a wild Jemberí. They deduced that he was the source of the stones. And they were all in agreement that where there were some emeralds, there would be more.

So they had agreed to exterminate the Indians and mount a joint expedition to find the source of the impossible emeralds that were coming out of the forest. Diaz had not said it at the meeting, but he believed the source was the fabled city of El Verde, and that untold riches were out there waiting for him.

And despite the deal, Diaz nursed a deep, festering rancour towards the Bond. The fascists had inflicted heavy losses on the rebels at Madero and he would never forgive the massacres they had carried out on the *paramo* and at the ferry. Once they had discovered El Verde, the rebel leader was looking forward to an indulgent revenge. He would end the alliance and take everything. He looked forward with great pleasure to killing Cangrejo.

Some more good news was that sizeable ransoms for the UN employees and some others had already been paid. Diaz informed them that they would be released soon and amused himself by reminding the rest of the prisoners that their ransom deadlines would pass sometime in the small hours. He also savoured telling Leila just how much he looked forward to seeing her again that night. 'And tonight,' he whispered in her ear, 'I can promise you we will not be disturbed.' Leila gave him a look of such profound disdain and hatred that it almost ruined his enjoyment of the moment. But then Diaz comforted himself with the knowledge that she would soon change her tune. The idea of being on top of her naked Creole body was highly arousing. He suspected that, unlike most of his partners, she would be special enough to be given regular access to his bed.

The prisoners were locked in at about seven that evening. Pike and Burr immediately got to work. Clumsily, with their cuffed hands, they pulled down a sack of fertilizer from the stack. It fell with a thump onto the concrete floor of the darkened room.

'What are you doing?' asked a voice trembling on the edge of hysteria. It belonged to the UN girl. 'Are you going to escape? We'll all be killed. I'll tell the guards.'

'Shut up!' her boss hissed. 'Leave them alone, you little fool. The rest of us will be ransomed and released. They will be killed if they do not escape.'

Burr nodded gratefully in the darkness and ripped the sack open. Painstakingly, working blind, Pike began his task, pouring out the fertilizer onto the concrete floor, then by feel trying to get a mixture of twelve parts ammonium nitrate fertilizer to one part diesel. He kneaded the diesel and fertilizer into a gooey mass, then scraped it back into a plastic fertilizer sack and packed it tight. While Pike worked, Burr went back to the piles of marijuana and coca seeds and dragged the bulky sacks aside to leave a gap against the wall of the block. Then he sat back, tense and sweating, eyes peeled for a glimmer of light under the door, ears straining for approaching footsteps.

Around ten, the door opened without warning.

There stood Diaz's lieutenant, Cinco. He lifted a gas lamp and peered round. In the shadows at the far end of the room, Burr and Pike lay down hurriedly over the heap of fertilizer and diesel. The shadow of Cinco's feather flickered on the ceiling. He seemed to see something suspicious and moved towards the Argonauts, bringing the circle of lamplight nearer. If the light fell directly onto them, the mess would be clearly visible. Burr held his breath, pretending to be asleep. He heard the *mestizo*'s footsteps approaching closer and closer. Any moment the light would reach them.

'Wait!' It was Leila's voice. 'I know you've come for me.'

Cinco stopped, the rim of the lamplight playing just at the very edge of the fertilizer spread round

Pike and Burr. Another step and he would see everything.

'I'm ready,' she said flatly. Burr opened his eyes to see her standing up. She held herself straight and tall, staring Cinco straight in the face. She looked determined and scared. Her eyes glowed in the lamplight. She walked out without another word. The rebel gave the room another cursory look, then followed her out.

In silence, Pike and Burr redoubled their efforts, scraping the ingredients together, their fingernails breaking on the concrete floor, then pushing the concoction bit by bit into the plastic sack. The other hostages did not interfere. It seemed to take hours. And every minute, Burr was thinking about one thing only.

Cinco led Leila across to Diaz's hut and pushed her inside. Leila stood in the corner of the room and waited. She was worried that the *jomo* vine was not having an effect. Cinco seemed fine and none of the guards had been acting oddly. And, damn it! she could see Diaz's supper sitting untouched on his desk.

The FARA leader had not eaten the hallucinogen, but he had been drinking again. He came stumbling into the hut a few seconds after the smell of alcohol announced his arrival.

'Shall we pick up where we left off last time?' he asked her, pouring drinks for both of them. This time she did not join him in the toast, but held her glass in front of her like a barrier.

Diaz drank his whisky and took the glass from her hand. 'Dance for me,' he slurred, lying back on the bed.

'In a while. Why don't you have something to eat first?' suggested Leila coyly.

'Very well.' Diaz took a few mouthfuls of his food, then turned back to her. 'No, Doctor, I find I am only hungry for you. Now dance!'

'There's no music.'

'Music doesn't matter,' he snapped impatiently. He began to unbuckle his trousers. 'Dance!'

Leila closed her eyes, swallowed, raised her arms and began to sway awkwardly. She tried to find a *soca* beat in her head and think good thoughts of liming to a steel band at carnival in Port of Spain. It didn't work.

'Stop!' shouted Diaz. 'You are an awful dancer.'

Leila ignored him, hoping that dancing would postpone anything worse. Also, it was possible that the drug in the food, or the sheer volume of alcohol, would knock him out.

'How about a cigarette?' she asked.

Diaz ignored her. Then he waved a finger in the air. 'Aha!' he exclaimed. He clumsily reached over to the desk and switched on the radio. A crackly salsa beat filled the room. 'Better, no? Now you can dance. And remove your clothes at the same time.'

'No. Why should I?'

'Typical,' said Diaz, laughing. 'Always defiance at first. But you know you have to give in eventually. And the best is that you will come to enjoy it. They always do. Not always the first time, but they do. I believe it is my skill in lovemaking.' He executed a mock bow. 'But then, let's not get ahead of ourselves. You will be in a position to judge very soon. And remember, if you perform well, you will be getting one of these.' He ducked underneath the bed and reappeared with a cloth bag. He poured the contents out onto the bed, creating a coverlet of uncut emeralds.

'From Madero,' said Diaz. 'This is just one month's produce – I have almost six months' worth here. Choose one.'

'Not interested.'

'You might as well, Doctor. Be sure that you are going to earn it.' He swept the emeralds back into the bag and replaced it under the bed.

Leila was beginning to panic. She wondered how long it would be before the bomb went off. She wondered if the hallucinogen would ever kick in at all.

'Now take off your clothes and dance.' There was no more playfulness in Diaz's voice. He pulled his pistol from its holster and pointed it at Leila.

'All right, all right.' She held up her hands. 'You win, but why not let me undress you first?'

'Very well.' He grinned. 'That's more like it.'

The rebel *comandante* lay back on the bed and Leila removed his boots and gun belt. He kept hold of the gun as she unbuttoned his shirt, revealing a chest covered in thick hair. Like a gorilla, she thought. She gave him a phoney smile and slowly pulled down his trousers. He lay there leering at her, his stomach bulging over his underpants.

'Are you sure you don't want something more to eat?' she tried again.

'Just get undressed,' he ordered impatiently.

Leila turned her back and slowly began to unbutton her dress.

'Look at me,' he commanded.

She turned reluctantly towards him as the dress opened and she let it slowly slip from her shoulders to the floor.

In the oppressive heat, Leila had long since shed her underwear, and so she stood naked in front of Diaz, one arm over her breasts, the other between her legs. Utterly humiliated and helpless, she felt her resolve begin to crumble. The tears finally came, running in rivers down her face and across her chest.

'Now dance.'

Leila began to sway to the music coming from the radio. It was now playing a song by some Spanish crooner – Julio Iglesias perhaps.

Diaz gestured with the gun that she should move her arms away and with a gasp she did, first revealing her breasts and then, slowly, her sex.

'*Muy bien*,' said Diaz, taking a swig of *aguardiente*. '*Qué fufurufa, qué zunga rica* . . . What a beautiful bitch . . .'

She danced for a few minutes, moving her body sinuously to the music, turning her back to her captor as often as she could. The bomb still did not go off. She felt shamed and nauseous, but she could bear it. If only she could keep him entertained until the bomb went off, then she would . . . It would be better if he would put the gun down, she thought.

'Do you still need that gun?' she asked, in what she hoped was a husky voice.

'Shut up and dance,' responded Diaz.

A new song started – 'La Bamba' – and Leila turned round again. She took a deep breath and prepared to expose herself for another few minutes. Surely that would be long enough and Burr would come.

Then Diaz did put down his gun and things suddenly got a lot worse. He grabbed Leila from behind and bent her arm behind her back. She struggled but he was too strong. He forced her to her knees in front of him. He thrust his bulging briefs into her face and she gagged. '*Chúpeme la picha*,' he ordered in gutter Colombian.

Leila's mind raced and she began to panic. The bomb has failed, she thought. I'm going to be raped.

He twisted her hair viciously and she gasped in pain. 'Come, come, Doctor, it won't be the first time you've seen one.'

Fighting down her revulsion, Leila pulled down his pants to be confronted by Diaz's semi-flaccid penis.

In the storeroom, Burr inched the bomb-sack across the floor and into place against the far wall. Pike sat back against the wall, favouring his damaged chest.

'Now pull off my left shoe,' Pike whispered.

Burr shuffled round and grasped a boot.

'The *left* one,' came the exasperated whisper.

'All right, all right,' murmured Burr. He pulled off the boot and pushed it into Pike's hands.

Pike worked his finger down the inside of the shoe to the built-up sole and pulled up a flap. Carefully he removed two small detonators and a matchbook, all wrapped in tied condoms. 'Not just a vain dwarf after all, eh?' he said quietly.

'I guess not,' said Burr.

Pike inserted the detonators deep into the explosive mixture, then he and Burr packed layers of seed sacks tightly round the bomb to smother the blast. From the bottle provided by Tokom, Pike poured *aguardiente* onto the fuse – a torn strip of cloth that ran out between the sacks from the top of the detonators.

Burr squinted out through the shutter again. He could see no activity in the camp, but he couldn't put that down for certain to the effects of the *jomo*. His field of vision was quite narrow. He could see the feet, toes up, of one of the guards outside the storeroom fence, which suggested he had passed out on the ground. Good – that would allow them to get the keys and unlock the cuffs. Burr looked up across the compound to where he could see a light flickering in Diaz's hut and what looked like a shadow moving rhythmically on the wall. Burr imagined what was going on in there and clenched his fists. Diaz was a dead man at least three times over.

'OK,' he whispered to Pike.

All the hostages curled up in foetal positions in

the opposite corner, hands over their ears. The little explosives man struck a match. The cloth flamed, burnt right up to the sacks, then died.

Pike swore and crawled over to the sacks of marijuana and coca seeds.

'There's still a bit of the fuse sticking out,' he said. 'I can just about light it.'

'You're mad,' whispered Burr. 'You'll blow yourself up.'

'Yeah, maybe. But at least I'll go out on grass and coke.'

Pike struck another match and the room exploded in a blinding, deafening flash-boom and a storm of flying seeds.

Gingerly reaching for Diaz's slowly swelling penis, Leila looked up to see the rebel leader's triumphant leer change to an almost comical expression of surprise and disbelief. The hut shook and dust fell from the thatched ceiling as the camp echoed to the thump of an explosion. For an instant Diaz was transfixed in shock. Immediately, Leila twisted his penis with one hand and punched him in the testicles with the other. Diaz screamed soundlessly and doubled up in pain. Leila kicked him in the stomach, then grabbed for his fatigues. Shooting exploded in the camp and in less than a minute Burr burst through the door, uncuffed, a rifle in his hands – and a machete in his belt. He saw Leila standing half-naked and defiant over the guerrilla leader, who was curled on the floor, wheezing and clutching his genitals. For an instant Burr and Leila stood there in silence. Her eyes blazed in the lamplight like green fire.

Leila pulled on Diaz's combat jacket. 'Don't ask,' she said.

'Don't talk,' retorted Burr, ignoring the helpless Diaz. 'Where are the emeralds?'

'Under the bed.' The jacket was a better fit than the trousers, which were a bit loose, though the length was fine. Leila grabbed a pack of cigarettes from the table and stuffed them into her trousers. Burr pushed the supine Diaz out of the way and turned the bed over. The rattle of shooting outside was constant now. Pike appeared, panting, in the doorway. He was splattered with blood, and, like Burr, was covered in seeds.

'You all right?' Leila asked him.

'I'm fine ... just blew me across the room – me and a couple of fingers.' Pike lifted his arm. The last two fingers were missing from his right hand. Blood was pouring from the stumps. 'You work with explosives, it goes with the territory,' he said. 'Done well to get this far without losing any.'

'What about the other prisoners?' Leila asked.

'They all seem fine,' Pike answered. 'They're just going to stay put and wait to be ransomed.' He glanced round anxiously. 'Now, can you damn well hurry up. Some of the guards are still just about functioning.'

Right on cue a wild-eyed rebel staggered into view, vainly spraying bullets. Pike fired a short burst and the man fell into the dust. From another direction an AK-47 opened up and bullets tore through the roof of the hut.

'May I enquire as to how long you intend to be?' Leila asked Burr.

'Don't talk,' repeated Burr, stuffing the bags of emeralds into a small knapsack.

Leila shook her head. 'Stealing, eh? You really are charming.'

'Come on,' Pike urged. He could see guards approaching groggily from different corners of the camp.

On the floor, Diaz was moaning. 'No, no. *Mis esmereldas!* Leave my emeralds.' He squirmed towards his pistol. Burr knocked him out with a blow from his rifle butt. Then he picked up Diaz's pistol. In his mind's eye Burr saw Tenoch's face swelling and choking as he died. A dull emptiness came over him and he aimed the pistol at its unconscious owner.

'No, Burr!' shouted Leila.

'Sorry, Leila, he's dead.'

Leila shook Burr violently. 'No, Burr! He's not worth it. Let's go!'

Burr glared at her for an instant, then tossed her the pistol. Leila caught it and stuck it in her trousers. Then she turned and ripped the sheets off Diaz's bed.

'What's that for?' asked Burr.

'Don't talk,' Leila said, and she ran out of the door.

Burr shrugged, grabbed a couple of grenades off the table, gave Diaz a farewell kick in the groin and fled with the others towards the treeline. The *jomo* had done its job. All over the camp, guerrillas were slumped on the ground, asleep, or rolling about in waking narcotic dreams. Some guards were less affected, though. A number of them had even managed to orient themselves after the explosion, and work out that an escape was in progress.

At the edge of the camp, two guards stood up groggily in front of the fugitives, rifles pointing vaguely towards them. Burr killed them with two precise three-shot bursts – two rounds to the chest, one to the head – and ran past, pausing only to snatch a couple more magazines. A few wild bursts of fire came close to the escapees, ripping through the leaves. Then they were into the forest, running as hard as they could. Bullets flicked through the branches and buried themselves in the trunks of trees. Leila tripped over a fallen log and yelped in pain. Burr helped her to her feet and they stumbled off into the blackness of the forest. They had escaped, but Burr knew their trials were just beginning. Leila had said that escape was semi-suicide. Well, thought Burr grimly, she might have been half right.

Amazon jungle, south-east of Madero

Around the perimeter of the rebel camp, much of
the undergrowth had been cleared for coca fields.
The going was easy and the fugitives made good
time. With the adrenalin of the escape still strong,
Burr made them keep up as fast a pace as he could,
trying to put distance between themselves and the
rebels. He hoped that by the time the guards came
down from their *jomo*-induced trips, the fugitives
would be hidden deep in the jungle. Three people
left a much bigger trail than two, however, and Pike
was leaving a blood spoor – good as a homing
beacon to a tracker.

After a while they moved into secondary jungle,
where the vegetation had been cleared and recently
regenerated. Here the trees were small and the
undergrowth thick. Their progress slowed to a
crawl. Burr walked in front, hacking a path. This
would also leave a trail, but they had no choice, and
at least from leaving such a visible sign of their passing they would know if they were going round in
circles. It was hard enough orienting yourself in the

jungle by day, but at night, with little moon, it was virtually impossible. Burr would have to rely on sheer instinct and a sense of direction honed by Pachal's jungle training and many night operations.

Burr relied on leading them uphill in what he felt was the direction of the Madero sierra. He wanted to hit one of the rivers they had crossed on their trek to the rebel camp. There he planned to use the water to put any trackers off the scent and strike off in a different direction. It was very tough going. Vines and roots tripped them up; thorns tore at their limbs and clothing; branches impeded them and huge fallen trees blocked their path. After two hours, Burr called a five-minute rest. They slumped, panting, to the ground and drank some of the precious water. Leila pulled the bed sheet from her bag and ripped a strip off it. She used it as a bandage on Pike's bloody hand.

'Well, at least it's not raining,' she said.

Right on cue, it began to pour. They were soaked through in seconds by an unrelenting heavy torrent. The temperature dropped sharply and they all began to shiver.

Pike groaned. 'In future, Leila, would you keep your weather forecasting to yourself.'

'Actually this rain could help,' said Burr. 'It will help wash away our tracks, especially the blood. Let's keep moving.'

The downpour soon stopped, but the ground had turned to mud. They slogged through it, out of the dense secondary jungle growth and into more open virgin primary forest. Here no human hand had affected the vegetation and there was little under-growth beneath the tall canopy. This meant fewer shrubs and thickets at ground level, but there were still trees everywhere, with buttress roots and dangling networks of lianas. And here it was even darker, the treetops having linked overhead like a roof. Too tired to speak, they stumbled on through the dark. Night monkeys cooed above them and invisible creatures slithered off as they passed. Once they surprised a dozing tapir, which crashed off into the undergrowth.

Every hour Burr ordered a rest – a five-minute break that soon stretched to ten. When he heard the cries of howler monkeys signalling the approaching dawn, Burr assessed the situation. It would have been better to press on, but the way was now leading distinctly uphill and they were exhausted and already suffering from dehydration. Leila was limping heavily and Pike was obviously in trouble. His bandage had been torn and his hand was bleed-ing again. His damaged ribs had him wincing with every other step.

'OK. Let's rest here,' Burr said when they reached a flat, dry spot, well curtained by bamboo and interwoven vines. It even seemed relatively free of ants. 'Just an hour or so,' he added, then he moved off, looking for a climbable tree from which to get a view over the forest.

'I wish I had a cigarette,' grumbled Pike.

'Oh, yes,' said Leila. 'I forgot. I took these for you.' She pulled Diaz's crumpled cigarette packet from her pocket and tossed it to Pike.

His look of amazement turned to a broad smile. 'I owe you one,' he said, carefully extricating a cigarette and lighting it with one of his lovingly protected matches, 'a big one.'

Burr came back soon afterwards without having found a tree to climb. Pike was already asleep and Leila was re-bandaging his wounded hand with another strip from Diaz's bed linen.

'The wound's not closing,' she whispered. 'He needs stitches.'

Burr nodded.

'But then, I guess you knew that, didn't you? You probably know plenty about combat medical procedures. I suppose they teach you a lot of that in – what? – Delta Force? Special Forces?'

'Something like that.'

'The way you shot those men in the camp . . . so easily . . . You killed them without a second thought. It . . . it's grotesque.'

'They would have killed us. Sometimes you have to shoot first.'

'You would say that,' Leila said coldly. 'You're a killer.'

'Not a killer, Leila. A soldier.'

'There's a difference?'

Burr sometimes wondered the same thing. There had to be a difference, otherwise, well, otherwise his life did not bear thinking about. 'Look, Leila, I know you disapprove of what I do, but this is not the time to deal with this. I am your only hope out here, so if you want to survive you'd better stow the bleeding-heart liberal angle. This jungle could be as much an enemy as the search parties that will soon be on our trail. We have to work together.'

Leila opened her mouth to speak.

'Shhh,' Burr said, more gently. 'You sleep for a while. I'll keep watch.'

Burr let the others sleep for just over an hour as the light swelled to the dim shadow of day beneath the almost unbroken canopy far above. They drank the rest of the water and ate the small pack of manioc and beans that Tokom had prepared for them. Leila checked Pike's hand. It was trying to scab over, but he was still in considerable pain, and she was worried about infection setting in. She was also worried about her foot. With some remaining shreds of sheet she had tied a support around her ankle, but she was still limping as they set off north and west, away from the rising sun.

The day was warm and humid, but under the trees it was cooler than in the direct sunshine of the rebel camp. Now and again it drizzled, though they could tell only by the rustle of the rain on the leaves of the canopy and the trickle of rivulets running down the tree trunks. Hardly any moisture penetrated to the forest floor. They were moving uphill and Burr hoped that over the ridge they would find the land sloping down to a river.

It was thirsty work, but Burr kept them supplied from a type of thick, brown liana which grew quite commonly in this area. A two-yard length of this vine gave out about half a pint of safe, fresh water. They walked up the ridge and down into the valley on the other side. There was a meagre stream at the bottom. The water was dirty and Leila said they shouldn't drink it. They splashed themselves and walked upstream for a while to hide their tracks before turning up the other side of the valley. At the top of that slope they stopped for another rest.

'Any vines?' asked Pike. 'I'm thirsty.'

'None that I can see,' said Burr.

'Don't know how you tell,' grumbled Pike. 'All look the same to me.'

'What about the bromeliads?' suggested Leila, pointing up into the trees.

'OK, good idea,' said Burr. 'Help me up, then.'

Pike and Leila gave Burr a leg-up to a low-hanging branch and he climbed on towards the canopy.

'The fuck's he doing?' wondered Pike.

'Tank bromeliads,' Leila explained. 'They're epiphytes – plants that grow on the branches of trees. The bromeliads trap water in their own cisterns. Relatives of the pineapple, actually.'

'I'd prefer a pineapple,' said Pike glumly.

Burr clambered into the upper branches, which were festooned with vines and lined with epiphytic flora, including bromeliads. He crawled out among the plants on one massive branch until he found a bromeliad with a brimming reservoir. The small pool contained a number of aquatic insects, so he filtered the water through his shirt into the water bottles. Before making his way back to earth he climbed a few feet higher, right up into the canopy, and looked back down the valley they had just crossed. He saw nothing but the mute green carpet of trees stretching in all directions. There was no sign of pursuers.

But he knew they were there.

For the rest of that day they moved gradually northwards, back up into the sierra. The terrain became more mountainous, the valleys deeper, their slopes steeper. The fugitives' lungs were burning. Their pace was slowing perceptibly and Burr could see they needed to eat. It wasn't just physical exhaustion that was the problem. Hunger worked on the mind and the morale. The hungrier they were, the more they would make mistakes, the more they would lose hope. He and Pike could try to hunt with their rifles, but that might give away their position, and anyway the forest seemed devoid of game. Burr kept an eye out for food of any kind, but the rainforest is generally a very clean place – any fallen fruit or carrion is swiftly disposed of by myriad armies of recyclers. Fortunately, Burr had been taught about the forest by Pachal in Yucatán and he knew there would be food if you looked hard enough.

Whenever they passed fallen tree trunks, he bent his head to the wood as if listening.

'*I talk to the trees*,' sang Pike teasingly, dredging up a tune sung by Clint Eastwood in the musical *Paint Your Wagon*. 'Do you think they're going to tell you where to get some food?'

'Kind of, but actually it's only palm logs that are really worth listening to.'

Leila wondered if Burr was showing the first signs of a delirium brought on by exhaustion and dehydration. After a while they did find a small tree with a few unripe papayas. Burr picked one and ate just a little.

'I wouldn't eat too much of this if I were you,' Leila advised Pike, who, ignoring her, consumed four in a flash. A little later he was spitting blood, complaining of a painful, raw tongue.

Leila patted him on the back. 'Green papaya – high in papain. The Jemberí use it as a meat tenderizer.'

She tried to help by cutting a liana for water, but when she chopped down a length and put it to Pike's mouth nothing happened. It was empty. 'Damn it!' she cursed, 'I'm sure that's the right vine.'

'Yes, it is.' Burr took the machete from her hand. He cut the vine at the top, then the bottom. The water gushed out. 'Got to cut the top first, see? Or the plant sucks all the water right up.'

They were tiring fast when Burr put his ear to a fallen palm log. It seemed to please him.

'So this one's told you where to get food, right?' asked Leila sarcastically.

'Uh-huh. Listen.'

She put her ear to the log and heard a rustling sound. 'Oh no,' she said.

That night they forced down a meal of fat, juicy termites, raw and wriggling.

'Well,' said Leila ruefully, in broad Trini, 'I guess what don't kill does fatten.'

419

They spent a fitful night, Leila shivering with cold and Pike coughing in a shallow sleep. When they woke at first light, Burr asked Leila about her ankle.

'The ankle's fine,' she said. 'Doesn't hurt a bit.'

Burr went off looking for food and Leila lay back in the hollow, her ankle hurting dreadfully.

Pike lay back and lit a cigarette.

A short way off, Burr found an emergent Suriname greenheart tree, encircled with corkscrewing lianas. Using the natural rope ladders of the vines, he carefully climbed into the upper branches to get his bearings. Up in the sierra to the west was a glimmering golden cloud, and he thought back to watching the morning butterflies in Madero with Leila in that short period when he had been a scientist. It had been mysterious and, well, romantic. That time was over now. He wondered if he would ever get the chance to explain, or even to report the butterfly phenomenon. His thoughts drifted to Ricardo and the others – all gone – and ranged on to the disappearance of Daniel and the end of Xcalan. He sat there for a while in a mood of regret and self-reproach. Then a movement caught his eye. Looking way back down the valley he saw a figure come out of the forest and stand beside the river. There was a splash of colour – a feather perhaps – in his hair. He was followed by a dozen or more others. The first man crossed and moved up and down the far bank, pausing here and there, stooping almost as though to sniff the ground. Then he disappeared into the forest. After a few minutes, he reappeared and the line of men stood up, crossed the river and started up the valley in the direction Burr and the others had taken the day before.

Burr cursed and slid down the tree. He returned swiftly to the others, with nothing but some fleshy custard apples.

'Spit out the seeds,' said Leila as she and Pike began to wolf down the sugary fruit. 'They're poisonous.'

They ate in silence for a while. Then Burr asked, 'Which of you has been smoking?'

'Er, well, me,' admitted Pike. His face looked haggard as he wiped his mouth and looked up at Burr guiltily.

'Very stupid,' said Burr. 'I could smell the smoke right down the valley. A trained nose could probably smell it miles away. Have you smoked any others since we escaped?'

'Well, yes. I had a couple yesterday when you left us.'

'What did you do with the butts?'

'What?'

'What did you do with the butts?'

'I didn't throw them away,' said Pike indignantly. 'Leila wouldn't let me litter the forest.' Out of his trouser pocket he pulled a few yellow cigarette filters.

'Well, that's something. Still, you might as well have left them an invitation.'

Pike looked embarrassed. 'Sorry,' he mumbled.

'No, it's just as much my fault,' said a tired Leila. 'I brought them. Anyway, won't the rain destroy the smell?'

'Yes,' replied Burr. 'But the rain doesn't penetrate everywhere, and where there's little wind a smell can linger in this forest for days. An expert guide like Cinco can track you by your body odour alone. There's no need to give him extra help.' He held out his hand. 'Give me the cigarettes.'

Sheepishly, Pike handed over the packet. Burr glared at him, then urged them to their feet. 'We have to move,' he said.

'No more breakfast?' asked Pike plaintively.

'They're on our trail.'

'How far?' asked Leila anxiously.

'Close. Cinco is tracking us. We'll have to increase our pace.'

'No problem,' said Leila with a wan smile. Burr saw now that she had weakened in the night. A sweaty Pike managed to stand up unaided, but Burr had to help Leila to her feet. She swayed alarmingly for a moment before taking a deep breath and straightening up with visible pain. 'See?' She grimaced. 'All fine. Let's go.' She hobbled off as fast as she could.

By the evening, Burr could see they were at the end of their tether. They were moving, but semi-comatose. Even Burr could feel himself 'droning' in and out of awareness like Rangers at the end of the exhausting induction course. The temperature had dropped dramatically and they were all shivering from cold. He knew they had to rest and have a proper meal. He led them down to a river. The streams were low and the fish would be easy to find. Soon he came on a shallow lagoon, cut off from a slow river. Silver flashes in the water revealed that the muddy water was seething with fish.

'But how do we catch them?' asked Pike. The prospect of food brought back the leery grin of the old Pike for a moment. 'I know,' he said greedily: 'we could grenade them.'

Burr ignored him. 'We could make spears, but you need to be able to see the fish to hit them. The Indian way is to poison the fish, but I don't know how to find the poison.'

'*Hura crepitans*,' said Leila.

'What did you say?' Pike asked.

'*Hura crepitans*,' she repeated, pointing at the tree Burr was leaning on. An hour later, after scarring the trunk, gathering the sap and pouring it into the water, dead fish were bellying up all over the pond. With heavy armoured heads, long feelers round their mouths and bat-like fins, they looked like hideous prehistoric catfish.

'*Carachama*,' said Burr. 'Good to eat.' Then he began to pile dead wood to make a fire.

Leila looked worried. 'Won't it give our position away?'

'I don't think it will make a difference. They are on our trail anyway. And we're weak. If we don't get a proper meal they're going to catch us for sure. In fact, if we don't eat, we might die whether they catch us or not. This weather is a *friaca* – a cold front that comes up from Patagonia. We need warmth tonight.'

Pike offered Burr the matchbook, but there were only two matches left.

'Save them for your cigarettes,' said Burr kindly. From a stand of bamboo, he chopped a length of tube and cut it in half. It was dry inside. He whittled a stick to a point, then scraped the pointed stick rapidly back and forth in the groove of the bamboo. Friction built up next to a little pile of kindling made of cotton from a kapok seed and splinters of dry bamboo pith. Leila knelt down to blow on the kindling and a small fire sprang into life. Once they had set the fish cooking, Burr led them in building a shelter. 'All right, tonight we're going to sleep in more comfort. Leila, you get some branches and lay them lengthways together on the ground as if you were going to make a raft – one wide enough for us all to lie on.'

She collected the branches and carpeted them with palm leaves. 'Why don't we just put the palm leaves on the ground?' she complained.

Burr ignored her, weaving palm fronds together to form a simple plaited roof and wall. They devoured the flame-grilled fish, then huddled together in the shelter to sleep. It started to rain. Leila saw immediately why they had laid the branches on the ground. The rainwater ran between the branches. If they had been lying on the ground they would have been soaked. Pike slept, shivering and feverish. Against her protests, Burr gently rolled up her trouser leg to reveal her ankle. It was red and swollen.

'Broken?' asked Burr, his fingers carefully probing round the injury.

Leila winced. 'Bad sprain, I think. But it's going to get worse. I can't go on at this pace.'

Gently he laid her foot back down. 'I'm not sure any of us can.'

'Why don't you leave us?' Leila asked. 'You could make it on your own. Why are you trying to save us?'

'I'm not rightly sure. I guess there are just some things you do and some you don't do. That's just the way it is.' Burr didn't say what had actually occurred to him and what he had known since the night of Diaz's abortive party: that he did not want to be anywhere but with her.

Beside them Pike moaned in a delirious dream and woke up. The stumps of his fingers had begun to suppurate. Part of the wound had become infested with unpleasant-looking worms. Pike could feel them writhing in his flesh and it was driving him mad.

'We should get rid of that,' said Leila.

Burr nodded. 'I could cut them out.'

'I think you'd cause more damage with that thing.' Leila pointed at Burr's rusty machete.

Pike cleared his throat. 'Doesn't the patient get a say in this?'

'Sure,' Leila reassured him. 'What do you want to do?'

'I don't know,' he said miserably.

They fell silent, the roar of the rain cutting out all other sounds.

'May I have Pike's cigarettes?' Leila asked Burr politely.

'Now you want to smoke my last cigarette?' Pike quipped. 'This really is a bad day.'

Leila smiled. 'Sorry,' she said, lighting a cigarette

with one of the precious matches. She held Burr's machete just above the burning end, allowing the smoke to condense on the end of the blade. She then applied the blade to the wormy part of Pike's wound. She repeated the operation a number of times, and within minutes three or four bloated grey worms wriggled out, shrivelling and dropping to the ground.

Pike shook his head. 'And I put all that nicotine into my lungs.'

'I guess you were right to bring the cigarettes,' said Burr. He smiled, but he knew that Cinco would have continued moving through the rain. They would soon be caught.

A little later, Leila felt a hand gently shaking her shoulder. She woke up with a start to see Burr kneeling beside her. Pike was sleeping again. Burr picked up his rifle and the two grenades and took a handful of emeralds from one of the leather bags. He handed the other bags to Leila.

'Now, listen. I'm going to leave you for a while. You head up the valley for a couple of hours, then cut down to the river. Cross over and stay heading upstream towards the high ground. Keep going along the river bank as long as you can, then camp just inside the forest, close enough to see the water. I'm going to try to lead them off course. I'll double back to the river and move up the bank, looking for you.'

'You're mad,' she whispered. 'You'll never find us.'

'Just do as I say. And one of you had better be

awake and watching out for me. I don't want to miss you in the dark.' He looked at her silently for a moment, then began to move off the way they had come.

'Burr!' Leila called softly.

He stopped.

'I'm sorry,' she said. 'I shouldn't have judged you. It was unfair.'

'Don't apologize,' he replied. 'Maybe you were right.'

He moved off into the trees and followed their trail for a short distance, covering the signs of their passing as best he could. Then he turned in a new direction, away from the river, breaking stems and branches to leave obvious signs. A few steps down the new, false trail, he dropped an emerald. Moving swiftly away, now and again dropping an emerald, Burr was swallowed up by the forest.

Twenty-four gruelling hours later, an exhausted Burr was back on the sandy river bank. Not more than a mile upstream from where he had left the others he heard a loud snoring from the undergrowth. He turned in to find Leila fast asleep over Pike's rifle. It was Pike snoring as he tossed and turned in a shallow dream.

Burr did not wake them, but sat quietly in the eaves of the forest, looking out at the river. Some Queen's Page swallowtails, *Papilio androgeus*, were puddling by the stream in yellow and black clouds. A rainbow of mealy parrots and macaws was gathering across the river to feed on a mineral-rich bank of clay. Down the beach, a turtle finished laying her eggs in the sand and slid slowly back into the water.

Leila woke with a start to see Burr sitting guard over them. Feeling immediately safe, she smiled and relaxed back into a doze. She could not make him out. He was a soldier, for sure, a killer – she had seen it. He represented everything she hated – that she should have hated. Her mind tried to think of all the things she loathed and she realized they had always been abstract concepts such as 'racism' and 'injustice'. The number of real people she hated was tiny. Oh, she had detested plenty of people in angry moments – boyfriends, parents, poor James Makepeace, a thousand times – but never coldly or for very long. She never hated them the way she hated people she had never met – like dictators, say, or those models who wore fur. If she met them, Leila thought, they would probably be very hard to hate. And here in front of her was no abstract notion of a killer, but a man, a man who was struggling to save them.

Looking at Burr now, she feared that over the last day and night he had given his all. He looked gaunt and sapped. His eyes were dark hollows sunk deep in his skull. His clothing had been torn to shreds by thorns and clutching branches. His body was covered by dozens of inflamed lacerations and grazes.

Leila reached out and touched his shoulder gently. He seemed to stiffen slightly before looking round. 'We didn't get very far yesterday,' Leila said. 'I'm sorry.'

'Don't worry. I didn't expect you to.'

'This river water is the clear, black water. It's clean. You should wash.'

'Yes.' Burr laid down his rifle and Leila averted her eyes as he walked down to the river bank and stripped naked. The water had that dark clarity that marked the rivers running down off the oldest Andean rock, long scoured clean of its silt and minerals. This pure water washed the exhaustion of the night away with a shock that was piercing cold, though nothing like as strong as the jolt he had felt to his very core when Leila's hand touched his shoulder.

Burr came out of the river a little downstream and walked back up the river bank, naked in the sun. From the shadows of the forest, Leila watched him with frank interest. He looked like a beaten-up version of a dream of hers from a long time ago. His shoulders were not as imposing, but they still formed a wide V with his narrow waist. He had a hard, wiry frame, with that taut, sinewy musculature that comes from tough use, not from the gym. Old scars shone white on his bronzed skin, criss-crossed by the livid scratches and bruises of the last few days. His penis, which swung easily from side to side as he walked, may not have had quite the disproportionate scale of her dream man's, but it would do for a living, breathing human. And besides, her dream man never got any closer than the hazy middle distance. He certainly never turned up with an armload of fresh turtle eggs.

Burr pulled his trousers on, came back into the

trees and laid down his haul of the soft, leathery eggs. Then he began to pile wood to make a fire. There was a distant boom and a shiver ran through the forest. Monkeys howled and the macaws lifted, squawking, into the sky in a perfect formation of red and green.

'What was that?' asked Leila.

'Something I left for them on the trail,' said Burr. 'Good. They won't be smelling anything for a while now. And if they've only reached the grenade trap, they're far enough away for us to risk a small fire.'

They devoured the turtle eggs, then obliterated all traces of the fire and moved on through the brush along the valley floor. All day they followed the river gradually uphill into the high sierra. Burr feared they were moving too slowly. Pike was still weak from his wounds, but now it was Leila who was holding them back. Burr had fashioned a branch into a stick to help her walk, but she was hobbling badly.

Well before sunset she was white and tottering. Burr called a halt. He found a spot with a view back down the river and soon, on the other side of the valley, high up on the ridge, he saw a thin plume of smoke rising into the air. As the light faded, he could clearly see the flickering pinprick of a fire under the canopy.

'Well?' asked Pike when Burr came back to their small bivouac.

'They're there. They're not even bothering to conceal themselves any more.'

'What are our chances?' Leila asked him levelly.

She was white-faced and sweating. Her Trinidadian accent was pronounced.

'Unless they decide to turn back, the likelihood is that they will catch us sometime tomorrow. Pike and I will kill some of them, but there are too many.'

'So there's no hope?' Pike looked resigned and helpless.

'There's always hope,' said Leila fiercely. 'We'll make it.'

Burr nodded, impressed by her yet again. 'We'll do our best.'

Pike lay down and was snoring in an instant.

'You can move quicker without me,' said Leila. 'Leave me here.'

'Not a chance.' Burr wiped her perspiring forehead. 'You still haven't found your miracle cure. There are people out there who need you.'

'Look, I have severe heat exhaustion,' she went on. 'Headaches, cramps and nausea. Skin, pale and clammy. Pulse, weak and rapid. I need rest and salt rehydration.'

'Thanks for the self-diagnosis, Doctor, but it sounds like a mild dose of flu. You'll make it.' Burr tried to sound as convincing as he could.

'So now you're a doctor as well. Thanks for the second opinion.' She gave him a wan smile. 'You know, I just can't work you out. What makes you tick? I don't believe you're doing this for the money.'

'To be honest, I just can't tell any more. I might be doing it because it's the only thing I know. You couldn't simply give up practising medicine, could you?'

'You're right, I couldn't. And the butterflies?'

'I *do* know about butterflies. I specialize in *Heliconius* and its interaction with *Passiflora*. I have had peer-reviewed papers published in scientific journals and I do in fact farm butterflies on an island called Xcalan, in the Yucatán.'

'The island is real?'

'It's real all right. Though it feels like a bit of a fantasy right now. And unless I can get out of this, it's going to be ruined.'

Leila looked at the ground. 'Listen, Burr,' she began timidly. 'There's something I have to tell you – the reason why I've been so awful.'

'Don't worry. I know you've been upset about Makepeace, about all the others – about everything. Anybody would be affected by all this.'

'It's more than that.' Leila began to cry softly. 'It's guilt. I said I blamed Makepeace's death on you. And partly I do, but it's more my fault. I have no right to criticize you for interfering. If I hadn't taken that photograph to Bogotá for Diaz, if I hadn't got involved in things that didn't concern me . . . If I hadn't accused Ayala of running the death squads . . .' She paused and wiped the tears away. 'Ayala was going to cancel the research project. I told James and it devastated him. That was why he was on the ferry. He was going back to Bogotá to see Ayala. He would not have been killed if it wasn't for me.'

Leila smiled weakly and closed her eyes.

Deeply moved, Burr fought his exhaustion, trying to keep alert. He told Leila of his own guilt. He told her of the people he had killed, of the things he had done that he was not proud of. He revealed it all and he realized there were no more secrets between them, though he was not sure how much she heard as she struggled to stay awake with him. He saw her green eyes blink, then close just for a moment, then for longer. Then she was asleep. If he listened carefully, he could hear soft breathing amid the night sounds of the forest. A tapir stomped through the undergrowth. A jaguar coughed in the shadows close by. Strangely, he thought he heard human voices too, but he dismissed them as hallucinations. From now, he decided, no more dissembling, no more secrets – ever. The embalming dark weight of the forest crept up round him. A soft rain pattered like a lullaby onto the palm leaves. Glow-worms circled in the blackness. And he slept.

Leila opened her eyes. She felt calm and determined. She knew what to do. She leant over and kissed the sleeping Burr gently on the forehead; then, stifling a spasm of coughing, she stood up and hobbled out into the night.

A while later Burr awoke suddenly to a burst of gurgling laughter – Leila's laughter. 'Shhh!' he said sleepily. Then he realized Leila wasn't there. It was still night. He leapt to his feet as he heard a deep, rolling growl like a saw – a jaguar – then sounds of a struggle somewhere in the forest. The laughter died away and was followed by another growl and a profound silence. There were no more human noises.

'Leila!' Burr shouted, starting to run. Pike grabbed him, putting a silencing hand over his mouth. Burr's desperation dissolved into grief. He sank to the ground and for the first time in years he wept.

After a while he got up and went out quietly into the dark. The night echoed with strange deep hooting sounds, almost like whale-song, the blowing of conch-shells or the calls of loons. Burr searched back and forth for a while but could see nothing. He returned to their makeshift shelter and sat by the ever-weakening Pike. They huddled together helplessly, with nothing but millions of useless dollars' worth of useless emeralds.

In the morning, led by the loud buzzing of flies, they found a pool of blood on the forest floor, less than two hundred yards from where they had slept. The undergrowth had been broken and flattened in a struggle. They sat for a few minutes in sombre silence. Burr wanted to say something, but the words wouldn't come.

'Come on,' said Pike. 'We both know why she did it. Better not let her down.'

Burr nodded. He estimated that Leila's self-sacrifice might buy them a day of grace, but unless they found river or road transport in that time, he was sure that Cinco would overhaul them. Without Leila, their pace did improve significantly, but Burr felt leaden, drained of strength and purpose. After less than an hour he sat down wearily. Pike tried fruitlessly to pull him to his feet. Then Burr blinked his eyes, wondering if he had gone delirious. A new branch had sprouted from the tree trunk in front of him. He gazed at it curiously. It was straight and smooth and seemed to have sprung out of nowhere. And it was feathered at the end. He reached out to touch it and another branch thudded into the tree just by the first. Arrows, he realized. They were arrows. Then there was a rustling of leaves and grinning warriors appeared from every direction. Burr and Pike were surrounded.

Pike raised his rifle. 'Don't move!' murmured Burr. 'You won't get two paces.'

'Don't worry. They're not guerrillas,' said a voice that sounded like Leila's, 'they're Jemberí.'

Burr thought he was hearing a ghost, but there she was – a living Leila, being supported by a Jemberí warrior. Her colour had returned and she was smiling broadly.

'Where are you going, Butterfly Soldier?' said a tall, pale Jemberí, who seemed to be their leader.

Burr recognized the man now. He had been distracted initially by profound joy and relief at Leila's reappearance. Then he had been distracted by the severed head impaled on the end of the warrior's black wooden spear.

'This is Neman,' said Leila, trying not to look at the grisly trophy.

'Where are you going, Neman?' responded Burr carefully.

'Have you food?' Neman enquired. Two fresh cuts were bleeding beside the line of scars on his chest.

'No, and we are hungry.'

'Hmm. That is unlucky, because we are hungry

too. We have some glory, though. The plant doctor made us keep them.' He made a signal and some more beaming Indians appeared with three bound captives. The only survivors of the pursuing rebels, their red bandannas had been stuffed into their mouths. Around their necks the heads of their comrades had been strung like demonic pendants. Two of the guerrillas were wriggling and protesting desperately into their gags, their faces sweaty, their eyes bulging with disgust and fear. The third prisoner was Cinco. He seemed relaxed and accepting of his fate.

'You are lucky, Butterfly Soldier,' said Neman. 'We smelt cigarettes two days ago so we knew there were ghosts in the forest. Then we heard the plant doctor crashing about in the night. The jaguar heard it too. Fortunately we were nearby – our shaman had told us to expect you. We drove off the jaguar. This one,' he gestured in the direction of Cinco, 'heard the plant doctor too. But he is grown lazy and stupid. He did not hear the Jemberí.' The pale warrior chuckled. 'Let us go and shrink heads.'

PART III

THE JUNGLE TAKES SIDES

With the poor of the earth will I cast my lot.

From *Versos Sencillos* by José Martí
Words used in the song 'Guantanamera'

Amazon jungle, south-east of Madero

The Jemberí village was a cluster of wood and palm-thatch dwellings in a grove of smooth-trunked trees. The huts stood on stilted platforms about four feet high. They were scattered on clear, grassy ground under a high, dappled canopy. Neman showed the fugitives to an empty hut and they climbed up onto the platform to find hammocks strung from the palm-trunk rafters. Pike and Leila fell into their hammocks and passed out instantly. A weary Burr went outside and looked round.

What did the Jemberí call them? Ghosts. This was a village where he was a ghost. And it was a ghostly place. It was eerily empty. There were no women or children. Burr looked about carefully, and through a stand of *Cecropia* trees he saw a figure whose gait looked vaguely familiar. It took him a moment to realize who it was. But the context was wrong. In fact it was impossible – the Jemberí might refer to all white men as ghosts, but this really was a ghost. After Leila, it was the second he had seen that day. 'Ricardo?' Burr said; then, louder, 'Ricardo!'

'You're alive!' he exclaimed moments later, from the depths of a Ricardo Martinez bear hug. He was overwhelmed with joy and relief. A massive weight of grief – and guilt – had been lifted from his shoulders.

'*You're* alive!' retorted Ricardo.

'The others?'

'Nicola, Paul and Craig are dead. The rest are here.'

'But they shot down the Chinook. You were all inside. They found the bodies . . . your name tags . . . Nicola's iPod . . . Ricardo, are you crying?'

There were cries of surprise and happiness as the rest of the Argonauts appeared and ran towards them.

Ricardo shook his head and quickly wiped the wetness from his eyes before the others got too close. When things had calmed down after a noisy reunion, Ricardo explained what had happened to them. Enough had gone wrong with the mission to make him highly suspicious of everyone, especially Craig Thynne. Ricardo figured that Elizabeth and Lester had no desire to keep Craig around either. Finally, when Anthony saw that GemCorp had armed a helicopter with air-to-air missiles, Ricardo deduced that all the Argonauts together in one vulnerable aircraft would prove too tempting a target. Without telling Craig, Ricardo and the team had loaded the Chinook with the bodies of their dead comrades and other cadavers taken from the battlefield. The bodies were the right number, complexion and size to pass as the Argonauts they replaced – at least after the effects of a mid-air explosion. Apparently the deception had worked.

'But we still had to convince Craig that we were all in the chopper,' broke in David, still wearing his pink shower cap. 'The problem was Paul's harmonica, you see. Nicola had recorded us all singing with her digicam, remember? We set Nicola's iPod to play "Guantanamera" into a head-set microphone, so that Craig would think we were on board. Unfortunately the version Nicola had recorded also had Paul playing on the harmonica. And Paul was already dead.'

Ricardo smiled grimly. 'Craig would have realized after a few minutes. I can just picture his face when it hit him and he looked back into the cabin. He would have seen he was flying dead men.'

Woken by the voices, Leila and Pike emerged sleepily from the hut to another round of back-slapping and story-sharing.

'Served that scumbag Craig right,' said Pike, 'for working with those bastards.'

Burr shot Pike a warning look and he shut up quickly. Burr saw no reason – if Pike behaved – to tell the others about his spy work for Elizabeth and Lester, but for Pike to complain about others' treachery was pushing his luck.

'Ma'am.' Anthony nodded to Leila.

'Hi, Leila,' said Ricardo. 'Good to see you again.'

'Hi, Ricardo. And is this the whole of your *scientific* team? How are the monkeys, Sven?'

'Hey, hey,' said Sven, shyly. 'Er, I am sure they are fine.'

'What about Professor Makepeace?' asked Ricardo.

'I'm afraid he's dead,' said Leila. 'The Bond killed him at the ferry.'

'Those bastards have got a lot to pay for,' declared Ahmad, to general agreement.

Burr nodded. He was pleased to see the Argonauts, but he thought they still seemed a little subdued, maybe even uneasy. And they appeared to be unarmed. After a while, he walked aside with Ricardo. 'What's wrong?' he asked quietly. 'Where are your weapons? And where are all the Jemberí?'

The village was still almost deserted. Neman had now appeared with the few warriors who had found Burr in the forest, but they were the only Indians to be seen.

'Quarantine,' explained Ricardo. 'They're afraid of catching an illness from us. They keep us in this part of the village. There are two more areas: the main part of the village a bit further on, then another outlying hamlet in the forest on the other side of the main village. They've left this hamlet to us. Of course the Jemberí are very inquisitive. They have a hard time keeping away. Some of the women did come back yesterday, but when you arrived they all took off again. I guess they'll reappear if none of these guys get sick because of you.'

They looked for a moment at Neman and his warriors, who had now sat down in a circular communal space covered by a conical, palm-thatched

442

roof. A fire was burning in the centre of the circle and the smoke was rising through a hole in the apex of the roof. The Jemberí were happily chatting and shrinking heads. One man was whistling as he cut the back of the scalps from neck to crown and peeled the entire face off the skull. Another then began sewing the skin together and filling the head with hot sand. A third warrior was preparing a tanning potion, presumably to dip the heads for shrinking and preserving.

Ricardo grimaced. 'You're right, Burr. There is something wrong.' The two friends walked a little way off to the edge of the village. 'I think we're in trouble,' Ricardo said. 'We had been in the jungle almost three days, moving well, when the Jemberí captured us. Surrounded us without a sound. They took our equipment and all our weapons and we haven't seen them since. We have heard some shots being fired, though, and a few explosions. We thought maybe the Jemberí were testing the guns. We've been here a few days now and the Jemberí seem friendly, but we're definitely more prisoners than guests.'

'They haven't bothered to tie you up? Lock you in?' Burr asked.

'Well, they have no locks, and they're confident that the jungle will keep us in. We tried to get away a couple of days ago. We went about one a.m. in three groups of two, each group in a different direction. By ten the next morning they had brought us all back here. They found it highly amusing.'

'So why are we in trouble?' asked Burr. 'The Jemberí rescued us. And they hate the rebels and the Bond. And, believe me, so do I.'

'Amen to that. Listen, Burr,' Ricardo's voice dropped to a whisper. 'I know what happened to Daniel.'

Burr was frozen to the spot for a moment. 'Well?' he prompted.

'Come with me.' Ricardo beckoned him towards the forest. 'It's not far,' added the Cuban, in response to the tired Burr's querying glance.

With an attempt at nonchalance, Ricardo wandered into the jungle. From the hamlet where the Argonauts were housed, he led Burr along a faint path over towards the village centre. He crossed a small stream and skirted round the main settlement. Through the trees Burr glimpsed the wide, thatched roofs of large dwellings. Behind the village rose a ridge of steep, wooded hills. The two Argonauts could hear the sounds of voices and women pounding manioc with wooden poles. They heard the laughter of unseen children who skittered through the undergrowth at their approach. Ricardo followed the path past the main township and, after traversing another stretch of virgin forest, led Burr to the final outlying part of the village. He stopped by a small hut just inside the forest. The thatched hut, built of latticed bamboo and raised on a platform of wooden poles set on stilts of palm, stood slightly away from the other dwellings but was otherwise identical.

Ricardo climbed the short ladder onto the platform. He swallowed, looked down at Burr anxiously and beckoned him up. With a heavy sense of foreboding, Burr climbed the ladder and entered the hut.

As he passed the threshold, he recoiled in shock. He turned back, took two steps and vomited.

Burr stood outside for a moment, leaning on the bamboo wall, the bile burning his throat. After a series of deep breaths he went back inside.

One part of the mystery was solved. From the roof of the hut hung a head with bright red hair. Daniel's shrunken face had been shaped into a savage snarling grin. Five further heads dangled alongside his from the roof beams.

'Didn't Daniel have six men?' asked Burr.

'Yes. Apparently the missing head was planted in your camp – as a warning. When Janine saw these heads she remembered who he was – some guy from Detroit she knew from Marine Recon.'

They stood in silence for a moment. Burr's mind was full of memories of Daniel, the scrapes they got into, his crazy superstitions. He felt sadness for Daniel, which gradually matured into a slow-burning anger. He spun round as a voice from behind him interrupted his thoughts.

'You like our spirit house?' It was Neman, standing in the doorway with a palm-wood spear. Two warriors flanked him, similarly armed. One of them wore a helmet with pixellated camouflage. The helmet microphone dangled from round his neck like a pendant.

'You killed them,' Burr said coldly. 'Daniel was my friend. You killed him, then you mutilated him.'

Neman nodded. 'Yes, we did kill them. We did not mutilate them. We preserved their heads as we do those of all we kill. It is a way of avoiding bad luck.'

'Just like that. Like I throw salt over my shoulder if I spill it? Why did you kill them in the first place?'

'They came to take our land, along with the GemCorp miners and the rebels and the militia and all of the ghosts. For this we send warnings – like we sent to your camp. But they took no notice. Like you took no notice. Then they came into the forest, looking for the place you ghosts call El Verde.' Neman wandered up and looked into Daniel's dead face. The weight of his footsteps set the heads swinging gently. 'I thought he could help us, but I was wrong. We did not want to fight, but when we fight we are the bravest people in the world. We made the killing spears. We are far braver than the ghosts. In the forest we fought them. They killed ten of the Jemberí. We killed all of them.'

'And us?' Burr enquired.

'Many of the people say we should kill you too. They think we should kill all ghosts who come into the forest. Satán says this.'

Hearing his name, a squat Jemberí standing in the doorway smiled broadly and nodded. His teeth were brown and worn down.

'So why haven't you killed us too? What are you waiting for?' Burr looked up at the gruesome ornaments. 'Not ready to redecorate?'

'You are not like those men. I believe you can help us. I ask you now, will you help us?'

Ricardo snorted derisively. 'You must be mad. You killed our friends. You probably ate them too.'

Neman looked offended. 'Only the flesh of this part,' he said indignantly, gripping the inside of his upper arm. 'We do not eat any other part. It is bad luck.'

Ricardo went white. '*Madre de Dios*,' he whispered.

Neman smiled confidently. 'I think you will help.'

Ricardo shook his head. 'You're mad.'

'You are good men. That is why you are with the plant doctor. You have come to find and to save, not to take and kill. You are not like the other ghosts who want to destroy our forest – they are our enemies. These ghosts have tried to destroy you – so they are your enemies also. We could join to fight against our enemies. More men like these will come.' He gestured at the swinging heads. 'The *malditos*, the cursed Bond, will come. *El malo* Diaz will come . . .'

'What will you give us if we help?' asked Ricardo. 'Do you have emeralds?'

Neman had a quick discussion with his two companions in Jemberí, then replied, 'We gave all the emeralds we have to Tenoch. These stones have brought us nothing but ill fortune. However, we can give you something else of green. Why is it the ghosts give so much value to the green?'

Neman gestured and Satán went to a corner of the hut and pulled away a large mat of woven palm

447

leaves. Underneath were piles of rotting green paper. It was money: American dollars, many thousands of dollars, in disintegrating green bills. Most of the notes were covered by virulent fungus and moss. Huge holes had been gnawed by worms and termites. Ants crawled through a network of tunnels chewed out of the nutritious cellulose.

Ricardo reached down and picked up a twenty. 'Worthless. Not even Pike will be excited by this.' The bill disintegrated in his grasp.

'Yes,' said Neman. 'We cannot understand how ghosts live from this paper. Tenoch brought us this in return for the green stones. It is worse than useless. Two children played with the green papers and they died. We had to kill two peasant colonists to appease the spirits. If this paper is no good to you, we have nothing to give. The green stones bring only evil. We promise nothing except the gratitude of the Jemberí – and of the forest. Perhaps I could explain it like this. If you help us, you will become one of us.'

Burr had remained quiet and thoughtful, listening to Neman and Ricardo. Now he asked, 'And if we don't help?'

Neman smiled ruefully. 'We will let you go. You have – how do the ghosts say it? – my word.'

'Yeah, and I bet you gave Daniel your word as well,' said Ricardo. 'Don't trust them, Burr. These guys will kill you for a joke. Isn't that right, Satán?' Ricardo smiled at Satán, who, not understanding a word, grinned crazily back, laughing and nodding his head.

Burr was in a turmoil of grief and anger at Daniel's death. But part of him had steeled himself for this. He had known, without admitting it to himself, that Daniel was unlikely still to be alive. He had been missing for too long. And Burr could guess what had happened. He had seen the new Daniel in Miami, seen how greed had eaten him up. Burr could picture Daniel's reaction when he heard the rumours of El Verde. It would have appealed to his lust for adventure, his impetuousness. Daniel had made the wrong choice. In any case there was no time to lament him now. Burr had to decide his own course of action.

'Can we give you our answer tonight?' Burr asked Neman cautiously. 'I need to consider my own answer, and in any case I cannot speak for all of my friends.'

'Very well,' agreed Neman.

'And, Neman, I have three more questions.'

'Ask then.'

'Where are all our weapons?'

Neman nodded. 'We will show you. They are safe. What else?'

'Where did the emeralds come from, the emeralds you gave Tenoch? And what do you know of the serpent's eye?'

Neman looked at Burr oddly. 'Of the serpent's eye, I know nothing. The emeralds...?' He seemed to reflect for a moment. 'The emeralds came from El Verde of course.' He said this with a straight face, which then creased and crinkled as he tried not to laugh. After a moment he gave up and a tremendous guffaw burst out of him.

Then his two warriors joined in and within seconds all three were doubled up, crying with unstoppable laughter. The vibrations shook the hut and the roof poles. Burr turned away, with the image of Daniel's obscenely grinning head jiggling at the end of a string.

At an order from Neman, Satán led Ricardo and Burr through the forest to the towering hollow trunk of a strangler fig. In this cavernous space, below humming nests of *Polistes* wasps and a twittering colony of predatory *Vampyrum* bats, was what was left of the Argonauts' equipment. Ricardo and Burr sifted through the mess. The weapons had been thrown willy-nilly into the pile of leaf fragments, bones, dried blood and bat guano. Many of the bullets had been fired off. The body armour, helmets and most of the electronic equipment was missing. Insect larvae and beetles seethed on the surface of the bats' leftovers amid scattered 5.56 mm and 7.62 mm rounds. Some of the guns were badly beaten up and Burr wasn't sure about the radio.

'I think we can salvage some of the rifles, the Barrett and the M240,' said Ricardo. 'This is finished.' He held up the mortar tube, bent beyond repair. 'Still, we'll easily have enough firepower to fight through a couple of contacts on the way out.'

Burr said nothing.

A terrible thought occurred to Ricardo. 'I hope you're not thinking of staying here,' he said suspiciously.

Digging a couple of M4 magazines out of the muck, Burr still did not reply.

Ricardo slumped back against the inside of the trunk. 'Oh no, Burr. You're going to stay, aren't you?'

'With the Barrett and the M240, I could do a lot of damage,' said Burr. 'Of course we'll have to see how much ammo there is.'

'Jesus Maria Joseph, Burr! You can't. You suddenly think you're some kind of eco-superwarrior who can save the noble savage? It's that damn woman, isn't it? She's got you in the palm of her hand, Burrito. You would do this for her?'

'Not just for her, Ricardo. And anyway, what's so bad about that? What would you not do for Rosa?'

'Rosa's my wife, Burr. Correct me if I'm wrong, but the Trinidadian doesn't even particularly like you. Look, we've been through a lot together. Remember Kandahar, Burr? Remember Faluja?'

'I remember, Ricardo.'

'We did them, Burr. We did them all, but don't expect me to stay through this one. I miss my family. Every night I picture myself kissing my wife, tucking the children in. And I've had my fill of all . . . of all this. I will never come on another mission, Burr. Madero was ugly.' Ricardo's voice cracked. 'They murdered Nicola in her cockpit. They shot Paul in the back. They slaughtered children, for God's sake.'

'That's why I'm staying,' said Burr grimly. 'But not you. You're getting out of here. Take a share of the emeralds, then go home to Rosa and the kids. That's a direct order.'

'What about you? What about Xcalan?'

'You may be right about the Trinidadian, Ricardo, but it makes no difference whether she likes me or not. I'm not just staying for her. And as for Xcalan . . .' A distant look came into Burr's eyes. '. . . Shall I tell you something, Ricardo? The Maya never wanted me to come. They said it was wrong to save their island by inflicting violence elsewhere. I ignored them. And they were right. Protecting the Maya is pointless if I'm helping to destroy the Jemberí. It would have been better to rely on magic.'

He patted the dripping grey bark of the hollow trunk. 'You see this tree? It's a strangler fig – *Ficus urostigma*. The strangler grows up round its host tree and eventually kills it. The original tree rots away, leaving the hollow central shaft. This tree is a world, Ricardo, a world of its own. Its small crevices provide homes for *Anolis* lizards, or *Polistes* wasps. Bigger cracks might hold birds' nests, or the nests of stingless bees. During the day the fig provides its fruit for parrots and monkeys, which then distribute the fig seeds throughout the forest. At night the whip scorpions – amblypygids – will patrol the trunk and land snails will leave their trails of mucus. The main hollow is home to these bats, and a whole ecosystem lives off the bat leftovers. There will be hundreds of interdependent species reliant on this tree, which in itself is part of the vast, interdependent web of this forest. Destroy this tree, destroy any part of it, and the rest disintegrates. In the past we've fought, we've killed, for far less than that.'

Ricardo shook his head in frustration. 'That's all very well, Burr, but you've seen how these Indians live. They are ignorant, superstitious, untrustworthy. They have been killing innocent peasants for fun – and harmless emerald prospectors. They killed Daniel. Burr, their life is terrible. You want to perpetuate it?'

'I want to give them a choice. They should have the choice, Ricardo. And by the way, Daniel was the most superstitious person I ever met.' Burr bent down and continued to rummage for working weapons and ammunition.

Ricardo grabbed his arm forcefully. 'Don't do it, Burr. Come back with me. This one is suicide. I can feel it.'

Burr looked up from where he knelt among the steaming bat droppings and scavenging insects. 'It's too late. Listen, Ricardo, they say you can tell a man by his friends. Well, I guess with friends like you, I can't be all bad. But if you lay the good and bad of my life onto the scales, I have a rotten feeling I know which side is heavier. I've fought enough fights that I'm not proud of. This time I've really got the chance to fight for something right.'

That night Burr gathered the Argonauts round a small campfire in the Jemberí hamlet and explained the Indians' request. Twenty yards behind him, the Jemberí warriors were performing the final rites of their head ceremonies, dancing and singing to the sound of drums and wooden pipes. In all the excitement, the Jemberí's quarantine discipline had begun to slacken and a group of naked young boys sat scraping the seeping fat from the heated heads. The yellow grease was squeezed out through the pores of the skin as the heads continued to shrink.

'You really think we should stay and help these guys?' asked David, looking at the cavorting Indians. 'I mean, look at their hobby. You wouldn't exactly take them to see your grandmother. And have you forgotten about Daniel? The guy with the red hair – you know, who's been *hanging around* here lately. Guy with the reeeally small head.'

'*Mira*, David,' said Ricardo. 'Look, apparently Daniel and his crew went a bit wild. When the stories about El Verde started to spread, they got excited. Lester and Elizabeth told them about the rumours of strange emeralds and they decided to try for it on their own. They thought these Indians had some mythical treasure and they wanted to come and take it. The Jemberí stopped them.'

Leila spoke up. 'Yes, but the next attack will come with bombs and helicopters and machineguns and grenades. It's hopeless. All the Jemberí will be killed. All of you will be killed. Burr, there's no point in any of you staying. Fighting achieves nothing anyway. And you can't possibly win. Can't you just negotiate? You could go back to GemCorp. I could try going back to Ayala. We could stop the killing.'

'Believe me, Leila,' said Burr, 'I've had my fill of killing, but how do you propose to stop it? Do you think you could buy them off?'

'You could hand over the emeralds you took from the rebels. They belong to GemCorp.'

'And we *will* hand them over – but only to the GemCorp top management. Elizabeth will not get a thing from us. And, believe me, even if we did give them the emeralds, that wouldn't be enough. Greed is what started all this off in the first place. And it's not ordinary greed. I don't believe in curses, but if anything is cursed it's these goddamn stones. These things have a power over some people. It's far beyond their value and it drives men mad. I'm sorry, Leila, but there are some things you should understand. If Diaz and the others come here, it will be to destroy. The only way to stop them will be to fight.'

Leila appeared unconvinced.

'Look, Leila,' Burr went on, 'you seem to think that it's politics and mysterious social forces and faceless "corporations" and military–industrial complexes that cause problems. It isn't. It's individuals. People like Diaz, like Lester and Elizabeth. Real people with real motivations – such as greed and hate. And we are fighting against those people right now. There is only one way to stop them now – to destroy them.'

'There is always another way.'

'Not here, Doc. Not now.' It was Anthony's rolling Georgia tones. 'Sometimes you've just gotta deal.'

'And you deal in lead, right?'

'Guess so.'

There was a pause. Then Leila shrugged and sat back. Burr turned to the Argonauts with an expressionless face. 'So now you know the score. I've said I'll pass on the Jemberí's request to you,

455

but that's all I'm going to do. I'm not asking any of you to stay. In fact, I think you should all go home. Everyone will get a weapon and a fair share of these emeralds, worth, say, three times their contracted payment. It's no more than we are owed by GemCorp.'

Leila smiled. '"Tief from tief make Gawd laugh", we say in Trinidad.'

'Just so,' said Burr. He looked round the firelit faces. 'As for me, I've thought about it and I'm staying put.'

Beside Burr, Ricardo cleared his throat and said quietly, 'Well, I've thought about it, too. And I'm with Burr.'

Burr turned to him, ready to remonstrate, but he saw the steely look in his friend's eye and knew there was no point in arguing. 'Anthony?' he asked.

'You say the Barrett's OK?'

Burr nodded.

'Well, then, I'm fixin' to stay, Cap'n.'

Ahmad was sitting beside Anthony. 'I am Palestinian. I know about losing land,' he said, 'but the reason I stay is for Paul and Nicola. The Bond betrayed us and we should pay those dogs back.' He looked over at David expectantly.

'Are you all nuts?' burst out David. 'You're going to help these Indians. These guys are fucking cannibals, man. I mean, they killed Daniel. They *ate* him.'

Ahmad shook his head. 'Daniel and his men turned bad. They came to take from these people. The Indians were defending themselves.'

'OK, so maybe you believe these cannibals. OK, so maybe Daniel didn't have their best interests at heart. Still doesn't mean it's right for him to be killed and eaten. And anyway, if these Indians can do such a great job defending themselves, they can carry on doing it without me. Me, I don't want to end up eaten, Maddy. I mean, check that one out – he looks very hungry.'

They all looked across to where the wizened Jemberí shaman was squatting nearby, putting the finishing touches to a six-foot blowpipe. He was eyeing the Argonauts with what could indeed have been a ravenous look. David waved at him and he waved back with a gap-toothed grin.

'I want to leave too,' whined Pike. 'One, I don't want to spend another minute in this shitty jungle and, two, these Indians might eat me and shrink my head. Unless . . . Burr, what about all this El Verde stuff?' A greedy glint came into his eye. 'I mean, we've heard a lot of talk about emeralds. What if it's true? What if these Indians do know where El Verde is? We can make a mint.' His voice dropped to a whisper. 'We agree to help them, get them to tell us where the stones are, then we take them ourselves and, bam! we're outta here.'

'You see any evidence of treasure lying around?' David looked about theatrically. 'Oh, let me see . . . Oh, of course, we could sell the shrunken heads of Daniel and our other buddies to the Smithsonian ethnography department. And then there are those green piles just lying about everywhere – they must be the emeralds of El Verde. Oh, sorry, they're *leaves*! Face it, they gave all their emeralds to Tenoch, like Neman told Burr. The only emeralds here now are the ones Burr took from Diaz. I say we divide those up and get the hell out of here.'

'You may be right,' said Janine. 'I figure we've got back Madero, so we've done our job. I'll take my pay in emeralds and go back to Carlo. That share would be enough to set us up pretty well. Sorry, Burr, but I guess I'm out too. I can't see us winning this fight. Not against FARA and the Bond combined.'

'Sven?' Burr turned to the big Swede.

Sven was silent for a moment, then said slowly, looking at the ground, 'I have always trusted you, Captain. But this time, it would be foolish to stay.'

'That's four of us leaving, then,' said Pike, 'and I think we should get going straight away.'

'You're not going anywhere yet, Pike,' said Leila. 'You're resting for a few days. You'll never survive out there.'

Pike began to protest but was cut off by Ricardo. 'No discussion, Pike. You heard the doc. She can take you as soon as she says you're fit to move.'

'There's no hurry for us to leave,' said Janine, a little shamefaced. 'We'll wait until Pike is fitter. We could help you prepare some defences for the village. And I'll see if I can repair the radio.'

'And don't you dare think I'm going anywhere either,' said Leila fiercely. 'I'm staying whatever.'

The Argonauts' meeting broke up. The warriors were still dancing. It appeared that the threat of infection no longer scared the villagers. The rest

458

of the tribe had been unable to resist the spectacle of the head ceremony and a row of women and children were gazing, mouths agape, from the far side of the hamlet.

As Burr watched, Sven came up behind him and cleared his throat sheepishly.

'Captain, there is something I have to tell you.'

'What's that, Sven?'

Sven bowed his massive head. He seemed ashamed. 'I want to apologize,' he said. 'I was never ... I was never ...'

'A *Fallskärmsjägare*? I know.'

'Yes, Captain. I wanted it all my life, but I was never in the Special Forces. Except, well, except after I left the army, I went on a few courses for civilian enthusiasts. I was only in the army for one year. They let me go for indiscipline, after I hit an officer. I am now a nightclub bouncer in Malmö.'

'That's all right, Sven.'

Sven looked at Burr with a mournful expression. 'But please, Captain, tell me, how did you know?'

'Up on the *paramo*, with Cuchillo, you didn't fire your weapon, did you?' Sven shook his head slowly. 'Most soldiers never fire their weapons in combat, you know. It's the biggest difference between regular soldiers and Special Forces. In this case I guessed you were probably scared of hitting me and Ricardo. He also knew that you weren't experienced. That was why he told you to stick close to him in the Madero attack.'

Sven was now distraught. 'Have I let you down, Captain? Have I shown any indiscipline?'

Burr put his hand on Sven's shoulder and smiled at him reassuringly. 'No, Sven, you have been a good, brave and disciplined soldier. Ricardo told me that you performed well at Madero. You would be an asset to any unit. You have not let us down.'

As the forest darkened, the Jemberí finished their celebrations. The last dollops of secreted grease were scraped from the shrunken heads, the sand was poured out and they were filled with heated pebbles before being buried for the night. The tribal leaders came with Neman from the main part of the village to hold a council of war. Satán and many of the warriors advocated separate surprise assaults on the rebel camp and on the Bond forces at Madero. In the firelight they relived their recent successful small actions against unarmed peasants, rebels and Daniel's team.

'It might make sense,' observed Ricardo. 'They won't be expecting an attack, and we could hit them before FARA and the Bond can unify their forces. We hit them repeatedly and keep them off balance: classic guerrilla tactics.'

It was the logical plan, but for some reason Burr was not persuaded. He caught the eye of the Jaguar shaman looking at him piercingly. Two toucan feathers stuck up from the shaman's long, braided hair and a memory bubbled up in Burr's mind.

He found himself thinking back to a day on Xcalan. He had been learning from Pachal about becoming one with the forest. He had climbed a gigantic tree – a *Ceiba pentendera*, he remembered.

He felt himself drifting back there now, felt how his mind had floated with the sunlit leaves, the salt breeze and the warm, faintly swaying ceiba wood underneath him. After a long while, Burr had opened his eyes and found himself looking directly at the shimmering, iridescent green of a quetzal. The rare bird, revered by the Maya, was perched on a branch not two yards away. It was sitting stock still, the only movement the faint ruffling of long, drooping tail feathers in the breeze. Entranced, he realized that the quetzal was hunting. He watched it wait patiently, unmoving, repeatedly ignoring smaller prey, until a six-inch praying mantis stalked within reach. Then the quetzal struck with blurring speed and a flash of crimson breast.

'Aha!' the Jemberí shaman said with a smug grin, bringing Burr's thoughts back to the present.

'No, Ricardo,' Burr said, slowly, averting his eyes from the fiendish-looking holy man. 'Minor guerrilla attacks don't achieve anything. And for us to mount a decisive offensive would need overwhelming force, which we do not have. Anyway, I'm sure that FARA and the Bond are all working together already. No, we must be patient and fight them on our own ground. We must lure them in and destroy them.'

'I don't see how,' said the Cuban. 'The Jemberí can muster about fifty able warriors, maybe one hundred with boys and old men. We're outgunned and outnumbered. And now, I can tell you, some of those filthy paramilitaries are pretty well trained. I should know. I trained them.'

'What about the jungle?'

Ricardo shook his head. 'The rebels are used to fighting in the forest. And anyway, remember what Bully would say in jungle training: "The jungle is neutral." '

'Not with the Jemberí, it isn't,' said Burr. 'This jungle just took sides.'

That night, roped to a palm tree in the forest, Cinco heard his Jemberí guards talking about the fabulous, mythical El Verde and its wealth, which they swore never to let fall into anyone's hands. His sharp ears also heard them discuss what weapons and tactics they would most fear. The ghosts had said something called a cluster bomb was the worst. They had also said that they could endure anything except a mass assault in numbers.

An hour or two later, the guards appeared in the village without their captives. Laughing uproariously, they went up to Neman, who was sitting with Leila and the Argonauts, and told him what had happened.

'The prisoners escaped!' cried Neman, laughing along with his warriors. 'Cinco and his men bribed our warriors with emeralds.'

'But that's terrible!' exclaimed Leila. 'They will tell Diaz and the others where we are.'

'Hope so,' said Burr.

'Well, that's just great!' Pike moaned. 'Now they'll be down on us like flies on shit. I've really got to get out of here.'

The laughing guards opened their hands to show

462

the corrupting emeralds – they had been bribed with the stones Burr dropped to lead Cinco and his men off their track. The Jemberí tossed the uncut emeralds carelessly into the forest as if they were worthless pebbles. Pike gasped; then, suddenly full of energy, he jumped up and, despite his ribs and missing fingers, scrabbled after the stones in the undergrowth. He came back filthy, having found just one small, dull emerald. 'The way I see it is this,' he said, the covetous, scheming look coming over him again: 'if that's how these Injuns treat emeralds, they must have a whole bunch lying around here somewhere. I've got a hunch this whole El Verde thing is true. I don't care if every goddamn fascist death squad or communist rebel in the whole of the Amazon turns up here, I'm staying.'

The following day, Argonauts and Jemberí set to work together on the village defences. Neman calculated about seven days for Cinco to reach Madero, then perhaps about the same for any ground forces to make the return journey. The settlement already had some early-warning systems and traps in place. These were enhanced and new ones set up, both on the ground and above it. Wooden stakes were cut and placed between trees to block approaches. Vines thick and strong as steel girders were woven into impenetrable barriers to funnel attackers into predictable directions.

Burr and Neman worked mainly on preparing defences in the canopy. They tied pliable vines into ladders and knotted others into climbing ropes.

They strung cables of lianas from tree to tree, creating a cat's cradle of rope bridges. In pre-arranged spots, lighter lianas were cut, tied with a noose at the end, then left coiled and ready for action. Up in a big Spanish cedar, Burr noticed a flannel moth. It reminded him of something from his school-days in Alabama. He asked Neman if there were many of that type. Neman looked at him curiously for a moment, then laughed with under-standing and nodded happily.

In front of the main village lay an area of open woodland with wide patches of grass. There was a bridge over the stream here and it was the most obvious approach to the village. Ricardo detailed Ahmad to cover this. David helped him set up the M240 machinegun, building up next to the bridge a protective breastwork made of hardwood logs so tough they would blunt a nail. They camouflaged the nest with dirt and leaves and paced the ground in front of the gun, noting the likely lines of attack. David was still urging Ahmad to leave with him. 'Come with us, Maddy. Don't stay here, man. You'll never get out.'

'I am afraid,' said Ahmad, 'but don't you think we should fight these people?'

'OK, OK, so I don't like that they tried to kill me. But revenge is a dish best enjoyed cold – not when *you're* cold. It doesn't work if you're dead.'

'Sorry, Davey, I stay. But, look, you go and no hard feelings, OK?'

Ahmad beckoned over some Jemberí women and together they cleared away much of the undergrowth to give a better field of fire. David walked the forest in front of the gun and pointed out to the Jemberí spots where attackers might take cover – good places for the warriors to plant unpleasant surprises. Standing in the machinegun nest, Ahmad watched David regretfully. He was trying to forget that the annoying little *Yahudi* would not be with him during the battle. He might be irritating as hell, and an Israeli to boot, but this was going to be a tricky fight, and in a tricky fight there was nobody better to cover your back than David.

Satán for some reason had adopted Anthony. And the hyperactive little warrior accompanied the taciturn Georgian as he scouted for sniping positions. Anthony had wanted to get rid of him, but when Satán slyly brought out a gourd of *kicha* Anthony looked at him with a new-found respect. He gazed at the slimy, saliva-preserved alcohol with longing. 'I won't have mine now,' he said, sorely tempted, 'but I sure appreciate the gesture.'

Anthony set up his forward post in a leafy mahogany overlooking a clearing that Ricardo had pinpointed as a likely LZ for helicopters. He chose a second sniper's nest back on the edge of the main village, and in case it was overrun he set up a final post on one of the small hills behind. With Satán's help, he camouflaged the positions. Then he prepared a range card for each one. He imagined lines of enemy approach and painstakingly marked various trees with range signs on the side facing him. With Leila's help he also explained to Satán that he would like to know whether the trees were hardwood or soft. And Anthony marked the soft-woods with the red juice squeezed from berries.

While some constructed defences, other Jemberí men chiselled new blowpipes from the smooth black wood of the shunta palm. They carved new ten-foot-long war spears and tied toucan feathers to the hafts. They cut sheaves of blowpipe darts and bamboo arrows, flighted with hoatzin feathers. Their shaman brought vines from the forest and boiled them in a secret potion, chanting mystic incantations. When it reduced to a thick, black paste, he dipped the missiles into the potion, coating their tips with the lethal poison *curare*.

'This should even up the odds,' said Ricardo.

'Oh no,' said Neman. 'The *curare* is for hunting. We never use poison in war. It's bad luck.'

Spending time in the village, Leila was finally able to begin working with the Jemberí in their true natural state and in the process experienced a world that no modern man had seen before. She also found some interesting items: one of her stethoscopes worn as a necklace, and, abandoned in the dust, one of Makepeace's microscopes. James had been right, she thought: the Jemberí really were terrible thieves.

Leila met Tupo, the child whose mother, Maria, lay wasting away back in Madero. The little boy hugged her quickly then ran away, overcome with shyness. Initially Leila found the female side of Jemberí society a little suspicious and hard to talk to, but Tokom, the woman who helped the escape from the rebel camp, had also turned up in the village. With stories of how the plant doctor's magic had cured so many Jemberí in Madero, she quickly convinced the women to make Leila welcome.

With Tokom's help, Leila began working with the women, preparing medicinal plants and dressings for the wounds they knew would come. She observed the women's activities and medicaments with excitement, but after a day mixing pungent potions the fumes gave her a thumping headache.

'Do you know a cure for headache?' she asked hopefully.

'Oh yes,' said one of the women.

'Of course,' called another, laughing. 'We have cures for everything.'

'What must we do?' Leila enquired keenly, wishing she had a pen and paper to write down the remedy.

A woman turned to her, looking very serious. 'First you must go to Madero.'

'Ye-es?' said Leila, surprised.

'Then you must go to the pharmacy and ask for something called Advil.'

Madero emerald mines, Colombian Amazon

The shriek emanating from the cabin by the mine gates showed that Mr Sticky Fingers was hard at work again. Elizabeth gave a satisfied smile as she looked round at the bustling activity. Just days after its recapture, the Madero mine was fully operational again. She took a deep, contented breath. Wasn't it nice when things worked out just the way you wanted?

The mines were producing emeralds again and she had negotiated a deal with Diaz to take most of the rough gems FARA had mined in the last six months. Walls and the GemCorp management would never know. She would just tell them the stones were lost in the chaos. Add the millions GemCorp had put at her disposal for the Argonaut contract and she was already a very wealthy woman. And all this would be nothing compared with the riches waiting for her in El Verde. She had seen Tenoch's emeralds and felt that they were but a fraction of what the Jemberí were hiding. It was so thrilling, she could almost taste the money. In fact the night before, lying in Diaz's old bed with Lester, she had put some of the emeralds into her mouth and rolled their glassy smoothness round her tongue.

'How do they taste?' Lester had asked.

'Priceless,' she had said.

By the time Walls realized things were going wrong, Liz would be far away and out of reach. She would never return to her original life in Medellin. She had come too far for that. It would suit her best to go back to Miami; she liked the high life there. But that would be impossible. She would have to stay clear of the States – of the Americas, in fact. She would go to Madrid perhaps, or Paris, somewhere a wealthy woman could live a sophisticated lifestyle. Not for the first time, she wondered how Lester fitted in with her plans. She was fond of him, yes, and found him useful, but beyond that she didn't know. They had slept together a couple of times recently and it had been fun. She had her needs like any woman and Burr had not obliged. Lester was clearly still devoted to her, but, truth to tell, for some of the time they were actually doing it she had been thinking about that Burr Whitman. Anyway, Elizabeth just couldn't picture Lester as part of her future. That gross tattoo, the foul language, the mule-like stubbornness . . . They had tried to live together before and it had been impossible. It was a worry to her. She had come to rely on him. Also, he would not be easy to get rid of.

There were other issues too, which meant she could not be too complacent. She could not trust

Diaz, of course. He and his squalid guerrillas would have to be eliminated as soon as El Verde was captured. It was all she could do to prevent Lester from killing him now. And then of course things never went precisely to plan.

First Burr had escaped from Diaz. Then Cinco had emerged from the jungle with the troubling news that Ricardo and the other Argonauts had not died in the helicopter crash. In fact, they had joined the Indians. Luckily, Elizabeth liked thinking on her feet.

Diaz and Lester had been incensed to learn that the Argonauts were still alive. But after the initial dismay, Elizabeth made them see the bright side. 'With one, decisive attack we can take care of a number of issues,' she pointed out. 'We get the emeralds and impose the final solution for the Indians and Burr Whitman.'

'Kind of like killing two Burrs with one stone,' Lester had joked.

When Cinco explained how he had heard the Jemberí talking of the vast riches they were hiding, Diaz and Lester had no more doubts. The rumours of El Verde had been confirmed. An attack should take place at once. They would conquer the Jemberí and find the lost city itself. The *mestizo* had taken seven long days to reach Madero. He estimated that with vehicles to take them part of the way, they could get back to the village in four.

Elizabeth thought it would be just fast enough. She knew that Hernando Ayala was the big problem. So far she had managed to dissuade him from coming to Madero, saying that things were still too unstable for a Colombian government presence to return. But Ayala was shrewd, and thanks to Lester's grandstanding he was already suspicious of their activities. Elizabeth knew the minister would not let them operate unhindered for long. It was only a matter of time before he brought in the army to reoccupy the town.

In this small window of opportunity, the new alliance in charge of Madero had to pillage as much as possible from the province. Elizabeth looked down from the mine to see a convoy of trucks and SUVs moving off into the National Park. The convoy was commanded by Javier Diaz and contained a joint FARA/Bond ground force. They resolved to drive as close as possible to the Jemberí village, then Cinco would guide them the rest of the way. When Diaz and his infantry attacked, Lester and Elizabeth would lead a simultaneous helicopter assault. The Indians and remaining Argonauts stood no chance.

Jemberí village, Amazon jungle

Neman accompanied Burr up one of the small conical hills behind the main village to show him the lie of the land. The trees there were short and stunted. The ground was scattered with quartz and white stones. Below him, close to the foot of the hill, he could see the open circle at the centre of the main village. Despite the thick canopy enclosing it, rising wisps of smoke and glimpses of thatch gave away the presence of clustered huts. Glimmers to the east of the village reflected off the surface of the small river where Ahmad had set up his machinegun post. The river ran along the edge of the village, forming a natural barrier. Beyond the stream, a good three hundred yards of thick jungle separated the village centre from the outlying hamlet where the Argonauts were staying. Any column advancing from Madero was expected from that side, so the Argonauts' hamlet would be in the front line.

Looking the other way, Burr could see the second outlying part of the village, which included the spirit house and its grisly contents. It lay a few hundred yards off, protected from a rear attack by deep ravines.

Behind the hills, Burr was surprised to see a large lake. It looked very square at the edges, as though it might have been man-made. He noticed that the water was bubbling. A slight sulphurous smell drifted up on the humid air. There was another line of four forested hills on the other side of the lake. They also had a curiously regular shape. When he squinted at them, they looked almost like pyramids.

Then his attention was seized by something else he saw – something that enthralled him as it had in Madero.

'What is the matter?' Neman asked.

'What is that?' mouthed Burr, spellbound.

'Oh, this is the blessed cloud, the *kiragi* dance.' Neman laughed, then he went on cryptically, 'It is the blessing of the forest on our people. It lifts our curse. It is a fickle blessing that disappears if the forest is disturbed.'

The next morning, Burr went to wake Leila at first light. She moaned softly in protest and rolled over in her hammock, still cosseted in the warm, familiar dream of Maracas Beach and a man. Except this time the man had actually reached her, and she had touched the muscle on his chest. It was burning to the touch and iron-hard.

Burr shook her again. 'Come on, Leila. You must see this.'

A few minutes later, a bleary-eyed Leila was wrapped around with fat lianas and winched up through the morning mist by heaving Jemberí. She was irritable and resentful. The mist was damp and she shivered with cold. At the top, Burr unwove her from the lianas, grasped her hand and led her to a fork in the upper branches. His grip was light and utterly reliable. She felt suddenly like one of the butterflies he had held for her in Madero, fluttering in his cupped palm. It was a delicious feeling, like being trapped and free at one and the same time. She clasped his hand tighter, and there, holding fast to Burr on a high branch among dripping leaves and epiphytes, opened her eyes wide in amazement and delight.

They were in the middle of a golden cloud of butterflies dancing and swirling in the morning mist. There were thousands, tens of thousands of them, soaring and dipping in waves and spirals like a darting flock of birds. Then, impossibly, the sun broke through the clouds and added a rainbow to the scene, the colours leaping from the hill behind and arching through the golden cloud. Like God's signature underlining His work, thought Leila, as she forgot that Burr had woken her unfairly, forgot to blame him or herself for Makepeace's death, forgot that he was a mercenary and an untouchable. In the midst of the golden cloud, sharing her joy and wonderment, he was like an accomplice at some secret initiation rite. She clung on to him for dear life and wept like a child in his arms.

For a while they watched, speechless, the butterflies cavorting round their heads. In Madero they had seen the cloud only from a distance, but here they were right in the middle of the dance. Burr held out his arm and in an instant it was coated in a quivering layer of butterflies, perching on his tanned skin. The butterflies were about the size of Leila's palm. Their wings were golden, with red whorls on the rear pair. They reminded Leila of something. And then she placed the scent of tuberose she had noticed down in the village.

'*Kiragi*,' she whispered. 'They look like *kiragi* flowers.'

'Yes,' said Burr. 'The Jemberí call this the "*kiragi* dance". They say it is a blessing that lifts their curse.'

'Look!' exclaimed Leila. All around them the butterflies were beginning to flutter back down through the misty leaves as the sun rose. They seemed to be clustering round some un-distinguished, grey epiphytes with tubular stalks and small yellow and red flowers.

Descending from the canopy, Leila and Burr were caught in a torrential rainstorm. As soon as they reached the ground, they scrambled, laughing, into the nearest hut. It was empty and they sat quietly on the raised platform, under the dripping thatch.

'Why are you really staying, Burr?' Leila asked eventually.

'I don't really know,' he answered, pulling off his soaked shirt and wringing it out. 'I've been wonder-ing myself. My mother was a bit of an idealist, I suppose. I think she always wanted to save the world. Maybe in some ways I was trying to do it for her. The army was my father's idea, of course, and I always saw it as a noble cause. But I guess it all went wrong somewhere. I was in Afghanistan, in Iraq and a dozen other places where they told us we were saving the world, but we never did. And you're right, Leila. I've been involved in plenty of wrong things. Things I'm not proud of . . .' He gave a rueful smile. 'I guess everybody is looking for something. Just, most people aren't sure what. Take me. I came here for a contract and to search for Daniel, but maybe I was really meant to search for Tenoch, and an emerald.'

And maybe, he thought, looking at Leila, to search for you. She sat with her legs bent up, arms round her knees, leaning slightly forward. Her slender feet were bare. Her green eyes sparkled and the wet shirt clinging to her breasts and stomach had become transparent in the rain.

'And, I, I've been looking for a miracle,' said Leila.

But I've found a man, she thought.

Burr leaned back easily next to Leila against the palm-trunk wall of the hut. 'One thing Neman said made me think as well. He said if you help us, then you will become one of us.'

Leila nodded, her eyes taking in the way his body flexed. The water on his wet torso gleamed like oil. 'For the Jemberí that is very special. It's like saying you will become alive – you stop being a ghost and become a human being.'

The rain drummed louder on the thatched roof and gushed in rivers from the eaves. Burr and Leila sat hidden as if behind a waterfall. After another short silence, Burr spoke again.

'I'll tell you why I'm staying. I've fought to save the world all my life. Under orders and for money and in my own head I've tried to do right. Now, you can dream of saving the world all your life and you will never get the chance to do it. I guess that here I've got a chance to save the world. Well, not *the* world – maybe just *a* world. If I can help save this world, these people . . . It may not tip the scales in the greater scheme of things, but it will add something to the good side. And that's enough for me.'

Leila looked at him searchingly. 'You really mean it, don't you?' she said. 'You're a real green soldier, a true eco-warrior. Maybe we environmentalists need more of you Special Forces operatives.' She laughed her charming, bubbling laugh.

'You're laughing at me,' said Burr.

'No,' she said sweetly, 'but I just thought – well, it gives a whole new meaning to the term "Green Beret".' Burr smiled and Leila touched his arm kindly. 'It's the same for me, you know. Dreaming of saving the world, looking for some miracle drug to save mankind – it doesn't happen.'

'Maybe not, but you may find something that will alleviate one symptom, make one person's life better. Even that is worth it.' He looked at her. 'I just stopped myself saying something corny then.'

Leila looked at him sitting next to her. Above the village, the sky was clear, though the rain continued. Her eyes were like big green pools in the sunlight

477

refracted through the wall of water pouring from the roof. She leaned over and kissed him.

'Will that unstop it?'

He nodded slowly, savouring the taste of her. 'I'm warning you,' he said, 'it's really corny.'

She kissed him again, warm and soft, tasting like honey.

He cleared his throat. 'Believe me, you change my world. You're my miracle cure . . .'

Her laughter gurgled playfully as she kissed him again to shut him up, and this time he kissed back and pulled her against him and they fell back slowly, slowly, onto the palm-leaf matting.

Watching in the rain with knowing eyes that could see through darkness, rain and even wood, the Jemberí shaman chortled to himself and nodded with approval.

Cocooned in the rain, wrapped in each other, Leila and Burr slid back and forth between love-making and sleep in a kind of waking dream. Sitting cross-legged like a guardian gargoyle, the shaman kept visitors away from the hut with a hiss.

Leila moved slowly over Burr's lean, hard body, tracing and reading the criss-crossing of old scars like a treasure map leading to the buried secrets of his life. Part of her expected speed and violence in the act, but while she might have predicted his strength and precision she was surprised that he was so unhurried, sensitive. She surmised that his nature was dualist in all things: yin and yang; a soldier who would kill you in an instant, a scientist who could spend an hour measuring a butterfly's wing. He investigated her body thoroughly and creatively, making relentless, haunting love to her in ways she never knew she hungered for.

Late in the night, Burr awoke to find himself entwined in a hammock with Leila, her lithe body softly wound round his. A waning moon had risen and Burr saw two small white moths sipping moisture from Leila's eyes. Burr shooed them away. And Leila woke, blinking, her eyes stinging, full of tears.

'They like your eyes,' said Burr. 'Not surprising really.'

Leila smiled like a stretching cat and put her arms round him. 'They're after the salts in the tears, right?'

'Er, yes.' Burr looked at her with an affection and admiration that surprised him. 'What does "Merry birds does mess dey own nes" mean?'

Leila yawned contentedly. 'It means we shouldn't be too happy, I guess.'

'Did you know you speak Trini in your sleep?'

She gave a husky chuckle. 'I know I dream about Trinidad.' She was quiet for a moment, then she whispered, 'Burr?'

'Yes?'

'Have you noticed something remarkable here?'

'Yes,' he answered, idly caressing the tips of her breasts. 'A few things, as a matter of fact.'

She looked down at his hands on her, at the silver sheen on her skin, and marvelled at the perfection of it. 'No, I mean with the Jemberí.

They seem different from the Jemberí at Madero.'

The same thing had occurred to Burr. 'You're right. They all seem happier, stronger, more purposeful. I guess these people are all still living the way they want. They haven't lost their will to live.'

'That's all true, but I think it's even simpler than that. These Jemberí are healthy.'

Burr thought about it for a moment. 'You're right,' he agreed. 'There's no sign of the wasting disease. And there are plenty of old people about too.'

'Burr, I think they have a cure, and I think it's to do with the *kiragi*.'

Leila and Burr walked out of the hut to giggles and knowing glances from Jemberí and Argonaut alike.

Anthony shook his head. 'Woman means trouble,' he said.

Ricardo grumbled and huffed and puffed. He gave Leila a dirty look and pulled Burr away quickly, complaining that they had lost valuable time working on the village defences.

Leila went back to working with the Jemberí women and tried again to broach the subject of the wasting disease. This time she tried a different tack. Rather than asking – as she had back at the clinic – about a disease, she tried asking about black magic and 'the great curse'. She was amazed when the women told her immediately, and quite openly, that, yes, there was a curse on the Jemberí. It affected both men and women and it struck when they were in their prime. It was like opening a door into

480

Jemberí culture. The concepts and the vocabulary were difficult for Leila to make out, but she was reaching a whole new level of understanding. For the first time she felt like a true ethnographer. This must have been how it was like for Pierre Clastres among the Guayaki Indians, Colin Turnbull among the Mbuti Pygmies. The Jemberí claimed the black magic had been laid upon them long before by a ghost. The curse almost destroyed the Jemberí, but Pacha Mama, the forest spirits, took pity on the tribe and sent the daily blessing of the golden cloud, the *kiragi* dance. The *kiragi*, the women insisted, was the only way to ward off the curse and the *kiragi* was useless without the cloud.

Of course! Leila realized she had mistranslated 'golden cloud' as 'storm of gold'. Somehow the secret of *kiragi* lay in the golden dance, in the symbiotic interrelationship between butterfly and plant.

'But,' Leila said, 'I have tried to find the magic in *kiragi*. It does not work. The leaves are poisonous.'

The women laughed at that. 'It is the *kiragi* flower that is the cure.' They began eating *kiragi* flowers from their early twenties, they explained. The flower had to be specially prepared with the juice of a certain vine. Also, the flower had to be picked just after dawn, while it was still open, immediately after the blessing of the dance.

'But why do the Jemberí who leave the forest still fall sick?' wondered Leila.

'It is bad luck to leave the forest,' the women explained. 'The curse will come upon them. You see, there is no golden cloud outside the forest, in the land of the ghosts. And in any case, for the *kiragi* to fight the curse it must be chewed up and spat out with the saliva of a true Jaguar shaman. Otherwise it will never work.'

Leila looked over to where the shaman sat without speaking. He finished his blowpipe and gave it to Satán. Then the shaman started on another task. He took a long, smooth bole of shunta palm, its dark wood heavy and hard as iron, and began to scrape.

Later on, watching the shaman, Leila and Burr finally pieced together the puzzle – a story of co-evolutionary interdependence developed over millions of years.

Eggs and caterpillars had been found only on non-flowering *kiragi*, so they deduced that the butterfly larva is born inside a non-flowering *kiragi* plant. The *kiragi* is the caterpillar's host plant – its home and its source of nutrition. When it is ready to become an adult – after feeding on the *kiragi* leaves for a few weeks – the caterpillar crawls deep into the plant's tubular stalk and spins a cocoon at the bottom of the tube.

Burr surmised that the spinning of the cocoon then somehow primed the *kiragi* to produce pollen and buds. These developed on the outside of the stalk, round the entrance to the tube. Meanwhile, inside the stem, hidden in its cocoon, the caterpillar pupa developed into a yellow and red adult butterfly. When the imago, the adult butterfly, emerged, it was always at dawn. While the imago crawled out of the stem and unfurled its wings, the *kiragi* flowers also opened into full bloom.

'That's it!' exclaimed Leila. 'It's impossible for the escaping butterfly not to pick up pollen all over its body.'

Burr nodded. 'The butterflies then fly up to look for mates in the golden dance. When the sun rises, the butterflies are too fragile to bear it, so they return to shelter in the nearest *kiragi*, which they then fertilize with pollen from the *kiragi* where they hatched. The females lay eggs in the stalk, and the whole cycle is repeated.'

Leila carried on: 'And although a *kiragi* plant might bloom many times, each individual flower dies back straight after dawn. The lab tests showed active compounds only in flowering *kiragi*, and what the Indians say supports that: if *kiragi* is to be effective as a medicine, it has to be picked during the morning display. That's the only time the plant's chemical composition will be effective against the wasting disease.'

'Do you have any more ideas about the disease itself?' asked Burr.

'Well, I did some research on neurological diseases in Bogotá and I'm pretty sure this looks like some variant of Cruzeiro's disease – though Cruzeiro's is a European disease. It's inherited and otherwise not contagious, so I've still got no idea how it might have infected the Jemberí. If we're right about the *kiragi*, it could be a real break-through – not just for the civilized Jemberí but also for thousands of Cruzeiro's sufferers worldwide.'

Burr looked across at Leila tenderly. 'For

someone who's just made a remarkable ethno-botanical discovery, you don't seem very happy about it.'

'I am happy. But all I can think about is whether we can get a cure out fast enough to save Maria. And anyway, we could both be dead in a few days. Then soon the forest and the *kiragi* and the golden cloud will be destroyed. Nobody will ever know about this cure. And that'll be that.'

A week after Cinco's 'escape', Neman and Burr declared the defences as ready as they ever would be. David, Sven and Janine left the village the same day. They were given provisions by the Jemberí – guavas, bananas, golden tomatoes and black potatoes – the original strains of staple foods now grown the world over. Burr gave each departing Argonaut two big handfuls of the uncut emeralds taken from the rebels – GemCorp owed them at least that much, he reckoned. He also allowed each of them to take a precious firearm. He gave them the pistol Leila had taken from Diaz and the two AK-47s that he and Pike had stolen from the rebels. Burr kept all the Colt M4s. The Argonauts in the village would have interchangeable ammunition for all but the sniper rifle and the machinegun.

The three Argonauts, guided by two Jemberí teenagers, set off after a brief farewell. 'Will, courage, endurance,' Burr said to Sven as they shook hands. The big Swede choked, snapped a farewell salute, then spun on his heel before he began to cry.

Ahmad also struggled to hide his dejection at David's departure. He stood watching mournfully until the small group disappeared into the brush.

For two days the Jemberí youths led the three Argonauts away from the village on paths they could hardly see. The guides hunted constantly and the group gorged themselves on peccary – wild pig – on the buck-toothed aquatic rodents capybara, big as dogs, and on *paujil*, the fat forest bustards. The second evening brought the first signs of the impending assault: helicopters clattering above the canopy. And on the third morning of their march, their guides became extremely agitated. They led the Argonauts in among a thicket of ferns, hanging vines and aerial roots and indicated that they should remain quiet. Soon even the Argonauts could hear sounds. They were indeterminate at first, but then resolved into many separate noises – the crackle of a radio, crunching leaves, breaking branches and voices, lots of voices.

First Diaz's lieutenant, the half-Indian Cinco, came into view. A couple of minutes later, a long line of panting men followed. Heavily laden with arms and supplies, they were hacking their way slowly along the trail. They trudged past only a few yards from the hiding Argonauts. The force was a mixture of guerrillas wearing the red scarf with star and paramilitaries wearing the white scarf with the 07 motif. Janine recognized the squat form of Javier Diaz in the middle of the column.

The watchers kept silent until the sounds of the passing column had died away.

'About a hundred and fifty at least,' said Janine.

David nodded. 'I made it nearer two hundred. Then you have to add in the helicopter support – four choppers – another fifty maybe.'

'Captain Burr and our friends do not have a chance,' said Sven, with a worried expression.

'Lucky we got out in time, then,' said David. 'Come on.'

'Should we not go back?' wondered Sven miserably.

'Are you crazy!' David exclaimed. 'They made their choice. This is precisely why we left. You think we could make any difference? No way, man! It's suicide.'

'At least one of us should go back to warn them,' insisted Janine.

'Already done,' David said.

Janine looked around. Silently, one of the Jemberí guides had slipped away. The remaining youth smiled at her uncertainly.

'Well, I guess that's it, then,' she said. 'Let's go.'

And their remaining guide led them on away from the village, towards civilization and safety.

Diaz plodded onwards in the advancing column. He had forgotten how awful the deep jungle could be. It was uncomfortably hot and sweaty – and the insects! He cursed himself for getting so soft in Madero. Then for the hundredth time he reminded himself he was a FARA rebel leader. Discomfort meant nothing to him. Also, he reminded himself, this little campaign had the potential to prove unimaginably profitable. It was worth a little unpleasantness. El Verde! He had heard rumours of it since childhood – everybody had. And now it appeared to be real.

The emeralds Tenoch had been trying to smuggle were just two of many. Elizabeth and Lester had shown him their stones. They were indeed the rumoured *perfectas*, like the two gems he had taken from Tenoch's empty eye socket. One pocketful of those exceptional cut jewels was worth as much as a sack of the light-green rubbish they mined from Madero. And Cinco swore that when he was being held by the Indians, he had heard them talking about the thousands of shining green stones that they had to protect from the ghosts. Oh yes, the rewards would be well worth a little unpleasantness.

Diaz slapped at an annoying fly and scratched at the elastic of his underwear where a number of itching chiggers had congregated. It did rankle with him that Elizabeth and Lester were going to lead the helicopter assault in comfort. He imagined the cool breeze through the helicopter doors and grumbled at the dank, stagnant humidity of *la selva*. He could never understand what people saw in this place. It was good only for hiding in. He himself hated the rainforest. When it came to power, *la Revolución* would abolish the forest and its reactionary inhabitants. The FARA had tried to explain Marxism to the ignorant Indians a thousand times, but they had never listened. This campaign would be a good step towards solving that problem. What did they call it – 'ethnic cleansing'? Well, the world would be a lot cleaner when they had mopped up these primitive Jemberí. And the *jodido* Bond militiamen too. His guerrillas outnumbered them, and once the battle was won, the filthy fascists would be eradicated at the same time. Oh, he could smile at Lester, sure, but he hated him. He gathered that the FARA had killed most of Lester's family way back when. Well, Javier Diaz would be very happy to finish the job. Then, after distributing some to his men, he could take the bulk of El Verde's emeralds for himself. He would be a very, very rich man.

Cheered by thoughts of greed, double-cross and genocide, Diaz shouted encouragement to his men and sent word up to Cinco to increase the pace.

Three days after Janine and the others had departed, one of their young scouts stumbled into the Jemberí village. He had run for twenty-four hours and was in the extremes of exhaustion. He reported that an enemy column was in the forest and approaching. Ordered to describe it, he took a deep breath. His eyes glazed over and he recited solidly for about ten minutes.

'It's incredible,' Leila murmured: 'he remembered everything, every detail.'

The boy described a column of about two hundred ghosts. He could not have given the number – the Jemberí did not count beyond ten – but he described each man individually. They were clearly mixed guerrillas and paramilitaries, heavily armed, and led by Cinco – 'half-ghost with the toucan

488

feather in his hair' – and 'the fat ghost with the red hat' – Diaz in his beret.

There was a murmur of consternation from the Jemberí.

'It is bad news,' said Ricardo. It was a lot more than the Jemberí's hundred fighters, all told.

'Yes, it is very bad,' agreed Neman in dismay.

'Two hundred is many. And more will come in helicopters. We will be significantly outnumbered.'

Neman shook his head. 'Oh no. The Jemberí do not mind that. The warriors' complaint is that they will have to build new spirit houses for all the heads we will take. Warriors do not like building. They are very lazy.'

The shaman showed no reaction to the news. He simply continued shaping his block of wood. It was now a ten-foot-long shaft, thick as a man's calf. Over the next day, as scouts reported the column advancing closer and closer, Leila watched him at work, unhurriedly shaving the block down, unmoved by reports of the enemy's approach. Leila felt she was watching an artist. In the way a sculptor searches for form in his block of marble, so, she felt, the shaman was seeking something in the wood, coaxing it from the very heart of the tree.

Eventually the scouts reported that the ghosts had camped within an hour's march.

'They will come tomorrow,' said Burr. 'Every man must be in his position by dawn.'

The mood round the village was apprehensive. The warriors sharpened their four-foot bamboo arrows one more time, made final adjustments to the toucan feather fletching and performed the ritual invocations to the capricious forest gods. By the campfire that evening, even the shaman stopped whittling to listen as Ricardo sang a haunting rendition of 'Guantanamera'.

Annoyingly for Javier Diaz, the fighting actually started before dawn. At least it did for his mixed ground force of guerrillas and militia. Diaz had set them marching when it was still dark, and their first casualty was a man whose foot was punctured by a simple trap – a covered hole filled with sharpened bamboo stakes. That had been irritating enough, but now in the dim morning light the rebel commander was standing in front of a *miliciano* who had been impaled by another primitive device – a swinging stake. The man was clearly dying, pinned through the chest to a broad tree. At least he was only one of the fascists, thought Diaz, not one of his guerrillas.

He pointed at the quivering form. 'See what happens when you don't look where you're going,' he warned his men. Then he waved them forward again.

With Cinco in the lead, Diaz's troops picked their way cautiously through the trees and snaking vines. All round them the forest echoed with the weird hoots of the unseen savages. The *mestizo* guide raised a hand to bring the line to a halt. He pointed at the ground: 'Eggshell leaves,' he said to Diaz, who nodded with understanding. The brittle leaves were the Indians' version of a motion-detector alarm. The headhunters always laid a carpet of them round their camps. When stepped on, the leaves crackled and crunched loudly, warning of jaguars – or raiders. It meant that they were very close to the objective. Diaz radioed to Lester that the ground force had arrived in the village and could the high-and-mighty, first-class aerial passengers damn well hurry up.

In the village, the Jemberí fighters slipped quietly into their positions before first light. Apparently still oblivious, the shaman sat on the platform of his hut, where he had been ensconced for a week. He had laboured all night and his creation was almost finished. It was now a long pole. Its smooth haft was slender as a woman's wrist, but hard as marble. It was not absolutely straight, but slightly irregular and snake-like, following the long, sweeping curves of the unbreakable shunta grain up to the tip, on which the shaman was now working with infinite concentration.

Leila tried to get him under cover as the dawn approached, but the old man simply ignored her. When the attack came – at daybreak, as predicted – he was still there, oblivious, whittling minutely.

Burr was high in the treetops to greet the sunrise. All round him swelled the blossoming golden cloud of *kiragi* butterflies rising up through the mist in their dance, accompanied by the booming morning cries of the howler monkeys. Suddenly the howlers became uncertain, quieter. Gradually their calls petered out altogether. For a moment or two, the forest was utterly silent, as if holding its breath. Then a dull buzzing grew in the distance. The noise approached rapidly and two turboprop ground-attack aircraft roared out of the mist. They flew low over the treetops, straight through the swarm of butterflies. Vortexes of red-gold and mist swirled from their wingtips into the slipstream as they made a pass over the village, their wings laden with bombs. The planes turned back and flew overhead again, this time releasing half of their payload. The bombs plunged down and detonated among the trees with dull thumps, followed by a thousand minor explosions.

Ahmad looked out over his well-protected emplacement. 'Cluster bombs,' he said, as smoke carrying the acrid smell of explosive drifted through the trees. 'Nice one, Ricardo.'

Crouching beside Ahmad, Ricardo nodded grimly. He had planned for Cinco to hear that the defenders feared cluster bombs most of all. Cinco – and the militia – had obviously bought the story, but the weapons, lethal against troop concentrations in open ground, were useless in the confines of forest. The thousands of small bomblets dispersed on impact simply wasted their violence against the branches and tree trunks. High explosive would have been much more deadly. Ricardo patted Ahmad on the back and moved off to check for casualties. There were none.

Unable to view the effects of their attack beneath the trees, the planes turned back for another bombing run, with the same results. Then after a couple of strafing passes, firing blindly into the canopy, the aircraft turned for home.

The whine of the disappearing propeller engines dwindled and was replaced by the rhythmic throbbing of massive rotor blades. 'Here they come!' shouted Burr, and Neman, beside him in the canopy, barked out orders.

Anthony slid a round into the chamber of his Barrett with quivering hands. Hidden by a curtain of lianas, he was in his advance post – the giant mahogany tree overlooking a small clearing. He had already let some of the attackers pass underneath him unhindered. He was waiting for bigger prey. Next to him, sitting happily between some bushy epiphytes, the twitchy Satán grinned and slid a dart into his blowgun. Last night the two of them had got roaring drunk with a gang of warriors and Anthony was now feeling the after-effects. He had tried to shoo Satán away, but the Jemberí would not go. He tried to push him out of the tree, but Satán was a real tree Indian, whose prehensile big toes splayed outwards almost at right angles from his feet after a lifetime of climbing. Satán had cackled with laughter and stuck like a limpet. Then he had brought out his gourd of *kicha* and taken a deep swig. Anthony felt his hands stop quivering.

'I guess you're fixing to stay there, you crazy little varmint,' muttered Anthony. 'Well, OK. You make sure an' keep that bottle safe for later.' He just hoped Satán would not give away his position before he had time to get off a couple of shots.

Further back towards the village, from high in the

canopy beside Neman, Burr could see four helicopters, two Hueys and two Black Hawks, troops crowding their doorways. A Jemberí called up to Neman that the enemy was moving forward on the ground as well. It was going to be a combined air–ground assault – in force. So far the co-ordination looked impressive. Burr had a moment to wish that Daniel and Ricardo hadn't trained the sons of bitches quite so well.

Then all hell broke loose.

The helicopters bellied up over the village and hovered there like predatory aerial dinosaurs. Then they opened up with their machineguns, pouring thousands of rounds indiscriminately down into the trees and huts. Without visible human targets this overwhelming firepower was not going to cause great casualties, but it had its desired effect – fear. The torrent of bullets seemed to reach everywhere. Men huddled into cover helplessly as the unrelenting lead ripped holes in the thatched roofs and stripped leaves and even branches from the trees. Water spouted from the punctured reservoirs of bromeliads, bees rose angrily from riddled hives, and a tribe of howler monkeys fled, bawling, through the trees. The broken bodies of birds, monkeys and two Jemberí warriors tumbled down from the canopy. Then the lead helicopter, a Black Hawk, added a volley of ground-attack rockets, the missiles roaring down through the trees and exploding on all sides. Paying no attention to the mayhem, the Jemberí shaman sat calmly, concentrating on his carving, while all round him shrapnel punched holes in his flimsy hut.

Then lines were flung from the leading chopper and the Bond's elite Jaguar platoon began to fast-rope expertly down into the forest. The first commando passed close to Neman, who stabbed out through the leaves with his long spear and hit the man in the chest. The blow spun the commando around on his rope, but did not penetrate his body armour. Burr reached out, grabbed the cord and pulled the disoriented militiaman into the tree. Neman slashed his throat with a bamboo knife and gave a deep-throated hoot as the man plunged, life-less, to the forest floor.

Burr began firing careful short bursts from his M4, knocking down a couple of paramilitaries. His first shot was the signal for a hail of darts and arrows to fly from defenders in the canopy. Some bounced off the bullet-proof jackets of the attackers, but two commandos were hit in their legs and arms. They swung wildly on the ropes, spraying gunfire at their unseen attackers and shouting. In a few cases the arrows and darts hit their mark and the militiamen fell, flailing, to the ground.

Under intense fire, Neman shinned out along a branch close to another dangling line. He let the commando slide past, then slashed the cord, send-ing the man crashing to the base of the tree, where he was quickly despatched by a couple of warriors.

The guns in the Black Hawk opened up again, peppering the trees around to beat back the ambush. The defenders took cover for a moment, then Burr waved a signal at two warriors in a neighbouring tree. The pair crept out from behind the trunk and moved nimbly along a branch towards the helicopter. They were carrying a large brown object in a sack. The sack sounded like it was humming. One man pulled the bag away and the other instantly lobbed the large football-shaped object into the open door of the helicopter.

Noticing the movement, the door gunner swivelled his gun towards the Jemberí. Burr watched the bullets sweep along the branch, brushing it clean of epiphytes and vines, and catching the two warriors. They disappeared in a mist of droplets of blood and flesh, almost vaporized. The gunner punched the air in triumph, but then jerked strangely and began to flail crazily at the air around him. The helicopter began to rock violently in its hover. The Bond commandos still on the ropes yelled and clung on for dear life. Then the Black Hawk was rising steeply backwards and spinning, scraping some militiamen off against jutting branches.

As the aircraft spun round, Burr could see the pilots scrabbling at their faces and screaming, struggling to escape from their seatbelts. The chopper seemed to be full of smoke. Out of control, the heavy rotor blades began to clip the treetops. One of the pilots tried to bring the craft back under control, but whatever the Indians had thrown inside was too much to bear. He abandoned the controls and joined the rest of the crew. They jumped from the chopper in all directions, clutching desperately for vines and branches, pursued by a smoky cloud of enraged wasps. Unmanned, the Black Hawk drifted away, slowly tipping over, pulling the remaining commandos with it, still dangling on their ropes. Screaming, they released their grip as the helicopter ploughed into a massive tree and disintegrated. The Jemberí in the treetops yelled in delight.

Meanwhile the second helicopter, a Huey, had hovered slowly over the trees, discharging its own barrage of machinegun fire. As it came into Anthony's line of sight, Satán squawked and dived behind the tree trunk to escape the shower of bullets. The gun's traverse swept past them then, through a web of branches, leaves and lianas. Anthony's hand was steady as he coolly shot the door gunner in the forehead with the Barrett. The man pitched halfway out of the door and hung limply in his webbing. The Huey swerved away, and Anthony carefully put two more .50 calibre rounds into the engine housing, apparently without effect. The chopper then swung round out of Anthony's vision and dropped ropes closer to the village for another commando assault.

Below the Huey, a Jemberí warrior ran out on a branch, swirling a liana like a lasso. A militiaman shot him from the helicopter, but not before the warrior had managed to launch the liana, thick as a ship's hawser, so that it looped round one of the Huey's skids. A crew member leaned down to remove it but jerked back as he was hit in the nape of the neck with a bamboo arrow two yards long.

A commando climbed down onto the skid, but

before he could remove the vine another noose flew out of a different tree and caught the skid on the other side of the helicopter. A third liana, aimed to loop round the Huey's tail, was sliced up by the tail rotor. The aircraft began to pull upwards, but another liana, then another and another, sailed out of the trees. They hitched around the skids and held the helicopter fast. The Huey tried to climb clear of the forest, but found itself trapped like a fly in a web. The pilot boosted the power, snapping one vine, but four or five more were thrown, adding to the net that now held the helicopter fast. The gunners in the doorways laid down a withering fire, but the Jemberí took cover. Then they began to pull.

Inch by slow inch, the Huey was dragged down towards the treetops. Desperately, the pilot sent the engine to maximum lift, and the machinery screamed as the rotors strained against the cat's cradle of lianas. For a moment the defenders and the Huey were in equilibrium in this bizarre tug of war. Then, imperceptibly at first, the Jemberí began to gain. The paramilitaries bailed out, followed by the crew, leaping to safety in the trees or sliding down ropes to the ground.

The pilot held on until the last moment, his craft's motors whining in protest, screeching at an increasingly high pitch. Minced leaves and twigs flew in all directions as the weighted rotor tips began to shred the treetops. When the blades started to smack solidly into the thicker branches, the pilot flung himself out of the door. The Jemberí pulled the helicopter down into the thicket of boughs and foliage until the blades buckled, broke and spun violently off in different directions. The body of the Huey, its engine still roaring, tail rotor still turning, plummeted like a diving whale and smashed, a smoking wreck, into the forest floor.

When the helicopters came juddering overhead and opened up with their Gatling guns, Diaz kept his men back, away from the storm of lead. He could see beams of sunlight break through where the bullets had slashed great gaps in the canopy. Figures began to charge through the undergrowth towards his line and his men began firing frenziedly. Some wild pigs burst from the brush in front of him, squealing, fleeing madly from the shooting and explosions. 'Hold your fire!' Diaz screamed as a tapir barrelled past. The charge was only forest animals, startled by the noise. Then the shooting died away and Diaz stood up. 'Attack!' he shouted into the sudden silence.

His mixed force of militia and guerrillas rose and moved forward with a shout, past the bodies of tapirs and a couple of peccaries. Then silent arrows and darts were whipping through the air around them. Two of Diaz's men fell. Ahead, he saw, figures were moving on the ground among the trees and in their branches. He knelt and fired a long burst into a tree ahead of him and was satisfied to see a body fall to the ground. They advanced a little and he discovered it was a howler monkey.

In the first line of the ground defences, Ricardo

hummed 'Guantanamera' as he watched the attack begin. He immediately realized that the Jemberí were inflicting casualties but hardly slowing down the advance. He began shooting, adding the firepower of his assault rifle to the Indians' more primitive weapons.

Diaz heard gunfire from up ahead and saw some more of his men mown down. There was shooting above in the canopy too. Then a Black Hawk was spinning overhead and bodies of the crew fell, screaming, through the trees. When the helicopter exploded, the attack ground to a halt.

'*Hijueputas de mercenarios!*' cursed Diaz. It was not going to be as easy to take this village as he had thought. '*Adelante!*' he shouted. '*Vamos!*' Diaz moved forward at a crouch and his men followed hesitantly. They were firing blindly into the brush ahead at defenders who were fast and elusive. The headhunters flitted like ghosts between the trees, striking silently with knife and spear and dart. Suddenly screams and a burst of gunfire sounded to the rear of the attacking force. Diaz spun round, but could see nothing there.

'Paco is gone!' shouted one of the paramilitaries. 'He was just here!' The man held up Paco's discarded weapon. Then more shooting and screams came from the vanguard. Another attacker had disappeared. '*Caníbales*, coming from the trees!' one man was yelling. 'He flew down and took Manolo!'

Then a corpse came cracking down through a tree, bouncing limply off branches and landing in the midst of the attackers. They yelled in horror. Paco's broken body had no head.

Burr was perched high overhead, next to the struggling Manolo, who he had gagged and lashed to a branch with lianas. He looked down with grim satisfaction through the leaves as Diaz and his terrified troops began firing indiscriminately up into the trees. Burr waited until they had passed below him, then leaped from his perch. He plunged sixty feet through a channel between the branches, down to the ground behind the main attacking force. This time he did not grab a guerrilla to take with him, but fired a burst from his assault rifle as he fell. He saw an attacker go down, then, as Burr's feet hit the ground, he buckled to take the impact and the elastic vine that attached him to the branch stretched then contracted, yanking him back up into the tree like a bungee cord. By the time the enemy had turned round, he was hidden in the foliage again.

Diaz struggled to keep his men calm. The unseen Indian defenders had them wavering. And worse, the rebel commander could hear another helicopter in trouble. Its rotors screamed, then there was a horrible breaking sound, a large crash, and silence. A moment later the attackers heard the Jemberí whooping loudly in celebration. An armed figure appeared in the branches of a nearby tree. Diaz and two of his men gunned him down, only to see that it was a paramilitary who had escaped the helicopter wreck. A few more survivors came scrambling down as Diaz reconsidered their plan of attack. There was no sign of Lester. Diaz decided to split his force. He sent Cinco at the head of a strong unit of guerrillas to make a flanking attack, then he continued his advance.

Standing in a towering sweet cedar, Burr flicked a short length of rope over a liana that stretched like a bridge over to a neighbouring tree. He slipped his wrists into the ready-made loops and slid silently across into the canopy of a broad-leafed *Cecropia*. He could see Cinco advancing below with a large group of attackers. Burr unhooked from the vine and ran smack into somebody's face. He jerked back in shock, teetering on the branch and raising his gun to fire. It was a sloth! He had bumped right into the animal, which was hanging upside down from its claws, completely undisturbed by the uproar all round. About the size of a large dog, the sloth was beautifully camouflaged with a tint of green algae growing in its fur. It looked at Burr balefully, its jaws munching slowly on some of its favourite, juicy *Cecropia* leaves; then, losing whatever vague momentary interest it had in anything other than food, the sloth turned back to concentrate on its breakfast.

Burr moved on through the branches and came upon two elderly Jemberí who were sitting patiently in the tree with a number of large sacks. Eating grubs and chatting idly, they looked up when Burr appeared. They took hold of the bags, which seemed to be writhing and squirming. 'OK!' Burr said to the two aged warriors, giving them the thumbs-up. They grinned at him toothlessly and made the same sign. One of them gave a chirruping bird call, which was answered by similar calls from nearby trees. Below, Cinco looked up sharply and shouted a warning to his squad, who began to shoot wildly up into the canopy.

To draw their fire, Burr hurled himself in another slide along a vine leading down to a slave wood tree covered in bright-red berries. Cinco spotted him and pointed, screaming orders. The *mestizo* and his men shifted their fire towards Burr as he slid across the vine, bullets cracking through the air around him. In the trees Burr had just left, a dozen elderly Jemberí opened their sacks and tipped the contents down onto Cinco and his troops below.

Thousands of spiky, multicoloured caterpillars tumbled down from the trees. The writhing mass carpeted the ground and coated the attackers' clothing, falling and crawling in their hair, squirming inside their shirts. The spines of some of the caterpillars were sharp and highly toxic. Many of these fell directly onto the attackers and jabbed into them, causing intense pain. Others stung them on the hands or the body as they tried desperately to swat them away. Most damaging were the little lions – beige furry balls of caterpillars like tiny Pekinese, which Burr knew from the southern USA. They were the larvae of flannel moths. Burr had remembered how a plague of them had once shut down his school in Alabama. Now their myriad toxic hairs floated round the attacking force like a cloud of poisonous gas, irritating the eyes and causing choking and agony to the nose and throat.

The attackers panicked. Screaming with revulsion and pain, they retreated in confusion. A number of them, repeatedly poisoned by stings, their lungs choked by the urticating hairs of the little lions, had to be dragged away. The Jemberí shot two men full of arrows as they staggered backwards, blinded and helpless. A third man was left quivering on the ground in toxic shock, his body a crawling rainbow mass of caterpillars. In the trees the elderly Jemberí pointed and chortled while they watched in glee. Burr congratulated them with another thumbs-up. The first phase was going well. But he knew that the battle was just beginning.

After witnessing the fate of the first two helicopters, the pilots of the remaining pair – a Huey and a Black Hawk – had swung them round to a small clearing a little way back from the village and come down low to disgorge their complement of assault troops. Ricardo had forecast the attackers' movements to a T. Now they were landing just two hundred yards from Anthony Robinson. At that range, they might as well have been standing next to him.

As the Huey feathered back to land, one pilot slumped in his seat. A star-shaped hole had appeared in the cockpit glass, matched by a gaping hole where his left eye used to be. The co-pilot grabbed the controls and kept the aircraft steady as the militia squad jumped out. Then the co-pilot too was knocked back with bullets in his head and throat. Anthony caught sight of a furious Lester screaming in the cabin of the helicopter, but could not get a shot at him as the craft crunched heavily to the ground and sat there like a paralysed insect. Anthony fired three times into the motor for good measure. The Black Hawk also came in to land and its complement of paramilitaries leaped out. Anthony was surprised to see Elizabeth emerge with them, carrying an automatic pistol. Two more militiamen fell dead with massive wounds from the .50 calibre rounds as Anthony aimed and fired in a remorseless rhythm. The surviving attackers dived into the undergrowth as the helicopter took off again, its guns firing wildly into the treeline at the unseen sniper.

Anthony remained invisible. He fired only one more shot – to remind the attackers of his presence. He was playing a massive part in the battle by keeping around twenty attacking troops pinned down in the clearing. Satán was impatient, however, and after a few minutes of non-action he suddenly jumped out onto a branch and loosed an arrow in the general direction of the enemy. The arrow landed harmlessly in the grass, but Satán had been seen, and the remaining helicopter, along with the men on the ground, turned all their firepower against Anthony's tree.

When the little Jemberí broke cover, Anthony cursed and immediately abandoned his hide. He turned for a split second to grab the gourd of *kicha* and that was a split second too long. A storm of rocket and machinegun fire erupted around him, leaving the soaring tree a broken stump. He tumbled through the branches and slid down the bole, then, still clutching the sniper rifle, he leaped face first into the muddy leaf matter and fungi on the forest floor. Feeling a burning pain in his shoulder, he reached back to find a solid three-inch splinter of hardwood jutting from his upper back. He picked himself gingerly off the ground and limped back towards the village and his next hiding place. He wasn't sure if he would be able to take it up, though. Any clear lines in the battle had disintegrated. The shooting seemed to be coming from all sides.

Diaz was apoplectic with rage. The attack was in tatters, thanks to a bunch of crazy Indians and those has-been, fucking, *jodido* mercenaries. At least two of the Bond helicopters were down and Cinco's flanking attack had been pushed back by caterpillars – by *caterpillars*! Diaz could see that the problem was the trees. The damn savages were running about up there like monkeys. 'You're half one of them,' he snarled at Cinco. 'You get up there.'

Diaz's *subcomandante* nodded obediently and quickly found one of the knotted vine ladders set by the Jemberí. He shinned up into the branches and soon came across a militiaman. The man was clinging for dear life to a branch eighty feet above the ground. White with fear, he was the one surviving man from his helicopter squad. 'Let's go down,' he said in a trembling voice.

Cinco looked round carefully and shook his head.

'No, you come with me.' The *mestizo* unhooked his belt and looped it over a liana. The *miliciano* watched fearfully as he leapt out into the air and slid along to the next tree. 'Come on, you fool!' Cinco hissed.

The trooper gulped and followed suit. Moving slowly from tree to tree, the two men made their way towards the sounds of fighting.

Not far away, Burr was also moving through the trees. He had lost touch with Neman and the others, but was still trying to pick off targets from the cover of the canopy. It was harder now. The attackers were wise to the threat from above and were watching the trees. There was still at least one helicopter overhead as well. He could hear its rhythmic roar rising and falling as it roamed about, its Gatlings opening up now and again – presumably where the guns could be brought to bear on visible defenders. He heard a sound like a car door slamming and cursed under his breath. It was a mortar. The door slammed again, just before the first shell exploded. The barrage seemed to be dropping accurately in the outlying hamlet and all along the front line. Burr hoped that Ricardo and the others were keeping their heads down.

He clambered through a large fig, the fruit of which was buzzing with wasps, and slid over on a prepared vine bridge into the purple cloud of a huge jacaranda. His nose filled with the heady scent of its blossom. And there, draped across the branches among the flowers, was the body of a Jemberí. The warrior had been stabbed repeatedly in the back.

Someone was in the tree. He heard the crack of a twig in the canopy and dived head first off his branch just as a burst of gunfire ripped through the leaves around him.

Burr tumbled down through a blur of purple-green and breaking branches, snatching desperately for a handhold. He managed to grasp a drooping vine and swing himself to safety on a lower branch. Lying prone among some thick bromeliads, he looked up to see his attacker climbing down towards him – a Bond trooper. The man fired a burst at him that only narrowly missed. Burr pulled his rifle round and fired back. The *miliciano* screamed and fell from the tree. Then Burr heard a mighty crack above him in the jacaranda and a huge figure blotted out the sky as it plummeted through the snapping twigs and purple blooms. Burr rolled over and pulled the trigger of his Colt. It clicked – empty! The falling form smacked into him like a block of mahogany.

Cinco landed on Burr's solar plexus, driving the air from his lungs. Burr was helpless, but for a split second the big *mestizo* had to regain his balance. He teetered critically for a moment on the high branch, and that moment gave Burr the chance to roll aside, avoiding the knife that Cinco plunged deep into the branch where his throat had been. Before the rebel could pull the knife free, Burr, his arms tightly wrapped round the branch, kicked him viciously in the belly. Cinco staggered back, arms waving to keep his balance.

Burr shuffled down the branch towards him. A

vision of the *mestizo* throttling Tenoch flashed in his mind and he was filled with a cold rage. He lashed out again ferociously, kicking Cinco from the branch. In desperation, the *mestizo* grabbed Burr's leg, giving himself the chance to clutch the branch, and, with immense strength, he swung himself back up to Burr's level. Cinco then crept back along the limb, holding on to a higher branch for stability. He stamped on Burr's leg and kicked him in the head and stomach. Stunned, Burr could not react as his adversary pulled him up and punched him repeatedly in the face. Bruised, bleeding and disoriented, Burr was helpless. In the first show of emotion Burr had seen him give, Cinco guffawed. Then he picked Burr up to throw him from the tree.

With the last of his strength, Burr groped out blindly. His numbed fingers found a drooping vine. It was coated with wickedly sharp spines but he clutched at it desperately nonetheless; and when Cinco flung him from the branch, Burr looped the vine over his head. Burr plunged from the tree, still clinging to the vine, and his weight wrenched the viciously barbed noose tight round Cinco's massive neck. The *mestizo*'s bellow of pain was cut short as the air supply died in his throat. His face went red and puffy; his eyes bulged as he shook his body violently and plucked frantically at the spiked garrotte that was suffocating him. Perplexed, Cinco's thoughts turned slowly from horror and fear to simple amazement at the unfair and unpredictable turn of events.

Dangling below, Burr clung on for dear life, his

hands bloodied by the spines on the jerking vine. Above him he felt the struggles weaken as the *mestizo* subsided slowly to the wide branch and lay still except for the few, final nervous spasms of violent death. Inch by painful inch, Burr pulled himself back up the liana. The dead face was now swollen and blue. The eyes, though clouded with burst blood vessels, stared down at him with an aggrieved look. By the time Burr pulled himself onto the branch beside the corpse, tiny *iuturi* ants were already crawling up into the nostrils and open mouth. A five-inch-long cockroach, *Blaberus giganteus*, began gnawing at a warm fingertip. Burr rinsed his face and bloodied hands with water from a tank bromeliad. Then he took the dead man's knife and moved back towards the sounds of battle.

In the air and on the ground, the attackers had suffered heavy casualties, but they were still advancing. They had numbers and firepower on their side. Outgunned and running out of surprises, the defenders withdrew to a second line of defence.

Dug in by the stream that ran along the edge of the main village, Ahmad and five Jemberí were holding off a flanking attack by a large group of paramilitaries. Prone beside his M240, Ahmad was using his ammunition sparingly, trying to make each burst count. Beside him a Jemberí was slumped to the ground, his head pulped by a high-velocity round. A hand grenade exploded and another Jemberí died, clutching at terrible wounds in his chest. One by one the remaining three Jemberí around Ahmad's position loosed their arrows, then melted away. There were just too many attackers. He heard a series of loud thumps and he dived to the bottom of the emplacement. A deafening mortar barrage fell round the position, sending fountains of earth and vegetation up into the air. Ahmad could see the attackers gathering for a rush and he knew that any instant he would be overrun. He tried to think about his life and found that he had only two regrets: one was not making the pilgrimage to Mecca, and the other was that David was not with him.

Then the attack came. The men moved forward on a wide front, slipping through the trees and pinning him down with grenades and gunfire that smashed the emplacement into smithereens. Then suddenly the shooting seemed to falter. Ahmad heard a crashing through the trees to his left, accompanied by staccato three-shot bursts from an AK-47. He peered over the remnants of his log barrier to see two of the attackers fall. The rest had turned away from Ahmad to face a new enemy. They were sitting ducks and Ahmad didn't pass up the chance: he loosed off a series of lethal bursts from the machinegun.

'Maddy!' a voice was shouting. 'I'm coming, Maddy!'

There was another gunshot and a guerrilla toppled from where he had been hiding behind a tree trunk. Ahmad saw a blob of pink zigzagging towards him through the trees. It resolved itself into a figure that ran straight at Ahmad's emplacement

511

and launched itself over the breastwork in a flying dive. The attackers had recovered from their surprise and an intense fusillade chased him, kicking up clods of earth and knocking jagged chips out of the hardwood barricade.

'Hi, Ahmad,' said David, panting and huddling down out of the storm of gunfire. Sweat was pouring freely from under the shower cap.

Ahmad glared at him. 'You took your time, you Zionist freak.'

'So that's all the gratitude I get. I just saved your Islamic fundamentalist ass.'

'I don't need your help,' said Ahmad sulkily. He turned back to his machinegun and fired a burst into the trees. 'Just get lost.'

There was a moment of calm. Then David spoke quietly. 'Sorry, man. I'll never do it again. I mean it, Maddy. We're a team.'

Ahmad snorted. 'Great fucking team. You left me here!'

'But I came back, didn't I?' He raised his head over the parapet, fired two quick shots and ducked down again.

'Why did you come back? I thought you were scared of these cannibals?'

'Yeah, but I reckoned that if they were going to make a goy stew out of you, it should at least be seasoned with some good Jew.' David saw a fleeting smile on Ahmad's face, quickly suppressed. 'And I mean it,' David repeated. 'Never again.'

Ahmad looked at him suspiciously. 'Never?'

David shook his head.

512

The firing on their position intensified and they heard the paramilitaries yelling as they whipped themselves up for another assault.

'Partners?' asked David, extending his hand.

'Partners.' Ahmad smiled, gripping David's arm. 'Now shut up and fight.'

David grinned and lay down next to the machine-gun. He deftly fed a new belt of ammo into the breech and replaced the M240's barrel, grumbling that Ahmad had let it get far too hot.

Grenades exploded round the emplacement, bullets fizzed and cracked and punched splinters out of the surrounding tree trunks. They heard the war cries of charging men. Amid the shower of dirt and shrapnel and lead and shards of wood, Ahmad and David looked at each other and nodded. Together they yelled in defiance and jumped up over the parapet, firing like demons.

Ricardo had been moving constantly round the battle since the first shots were fired, encouraging, organizing and lending firepower where needed. Now, under the mortar barrage, he quickly ordered the abandonment of the front line and the outlying hamlet. Cursing Sven for training the militia mortar team so well, he worked desperately to ensure a steady, disciplined withdrawal towards the second line of defence. When most of the Indians had taken up their new positions, he grabbed Pike and set off on another tour of the shrunken perimeter. They stopped at each group of defenders, boosting morale and laying down some brief bursts to convince the enemy that there were plenty of armed men lying in wait.

From the far left of the line, Ricardo could hear the controlled bursts of Ahmad's machinegun. In the centre, the Cuban found Anthony. He had retreated to his second defensive position with some seasoned Jemberí fighters and Satán, who had somehow survived the destruction of their first post and was now firmly glued to Anthony's side. They were holding off a considerable number of the enemy. The sniper had brought down perhaps a dozen men with the Barrett. His colour-blindness meant he saw the attackers clearly, even in the low light under the trees. He was running low on .50 calibre ammunition.

'Wish I had a better spotter than this little crittur.' He nodded at Satán. 'Might even have bagged me Liz and Les a few minutes ago. But, no, we're too darn slow, so both the sons a' bitches still runnin' around.'

'Elizabeth is here?' exclaimed Ricardo. 'Shit, they must be confident. Think you might get another shot?'

Anthony didn't respond. He squinted into the sight of the Barrett and Ricardo could almost see his body relax into absolute stillness as he focused on a target. While he slowly exhaled, his index finger squeezed imperceptibly on the trigger and the big rifle bucked with a deafening bang. He peered down through the sight again. 'Check it,' he said, handing Ricardo the weapon.

Ricardo looked through the sight and saw a dead

guerrilla toppled out from behind a tree, blood all over his chest. There was a hole drilled in the trunk of the tree at about chest height. The trunk looked about five foot thick.

'Balsa,' said Anthony. 'See the red mark on the tree trunk? Tree could've been twice as thick and with this baby he'd still be dead.' He patted his rifle with a smile.

Ricardo and Pike moved off along the line. Satán watched them disappear into the trees, then pulled out the *kicha*, took a swig and offered it to Anthony.

'What the hell,' he said and took two long swigs of the slippery liquid. Satán nodded crazily. Soon he and Anthony had drained the flask. The sniper was drunk. Satán, like all Amerindians, lacked an enzyme vital for metabolizing alcohol, so he was almost comatose. He drunkenly pulled out another gourd, but dropped it. It rolled out from their hiding place behind a tree and immediately two attackers jumped up and riddled it with bullets. The *kicha* sprayed everywhere. Anthony rolled out of cover and brought down the attackers with two swift shots. He rolled back behind the tree to watch rue-fully as a glugging stream of white *kicha* soaked into the forest floor.

A little way off, Ricardo and Pike came upon Ahmad's machinegun post. It was empty except for mounds of cartridge casings and two dead Jemberí. Guerrilla and paramilitary dead were piled high all round the position. 'Look,' Pike said. He picked up David's shower cap. It had a bullet hole in it. Ricardo had no time to digest the implications before there was the roaring of a helicopter above them and a Gatling gun swept the area. Ricardo dived for cover as the bullets kicked up the dust round the nest and riddled the heaped bodies. The helicopter swept over and on to the village.

'*Mierda!* Stay here, Pike!' shouted Ricardo, jumping to his feet. 'If they come this way they'll just walk into the village.' He ran back towards the village in the wake of the helicopter.

Suddenly alone, Pike nodded glumly, then threw down his empty Colt M4. He scavenged an AK-47 and some magazines from the bodies and lay down in the machinegun nest amid the silent, stiffening dead.

Back in the clustered huts of the main settlement, Leila was worried about Burr and the other defenders. She was far too busy tending the wounded to be afraid for herself. She was using whatever rudimentary treatments she could, and also trying to keep women and children safe from the fighting. As the enemy advanced, Leila had moved her charges back towards the middle of the village, keeping the retreat as orderly as possible. She had just gathered Tupo and some other children into one of the huts surrounding the village's open central gathering area, when the last remaining helicopter reared up over the trees and flopped down into the bare, circular space.

The helicopter began to revolve, turning slowly on the spot, firing blindly into the houses. The multi-barrelled Gatling guns spun furiously, spewing hundreds of metal casings out onto the hard-beaten earth of the village. It was going to be a massacre. Leila saw the bullets coming closer and closer, ripping the walls of hut after hut. At any moment, it would come round to theirs and the children would be slaughtered. Now the bullets were just starting to punch through the side wall. Leila could see the holes appearing as if by magic. Little dots punctured the side of the hut, each penetrated by a ray of light. The wall was becoming a sieve. The noise was deafening, drowning the screaming of the children, who she gathered into a huddle in the far corner. Leila put her arms round the crying Tupo and covered his eyes.

Then two figures – one huge, one slight – ran, crouching, from the wreckage of the huts behind the helicopter. In amazement Leila recognized the smaller figure as Janine, the larger as Sven. Janine raced towards the open door of the helicopter but fell in a heap before reaching her objective. Sven's bulky form ran to the back of the helicopter. He ducked under the rear rotor and wrapped his massive arms round the fuselage where it narrowed towards the tail. The hail of bullets crept ever closer. Leila could feel the disturbance of their passing in the air. She pulled the children closer and wondered what it was going to be like to die.

But Janine had pulled herself to her feet and was staggering close to the helicopter door, one arm dangling uselessly. With a roar Sven dug his feet into the ground, bracing himself against the helicopter's rotation. It took a superhuman effort from that immense frame, but the helicopter stopped turning. The storm of bullets continued but held steady just an inch or two from Leila. She exhaled. The children stopped screaming. Then there was a sudden, deafening silence as the chain guns ran out of ammunition. They whirred on silently for an instant. Then, appalled, Leila saw the helicopter pilots jerk in their seats and bursts of red spatter onto the inside of the cockpit. Janine must have shot them. The engines slowed, the helicopter tilted and the rotors smacked into the ground, one by one, digging deep into the bare earth and breaking off in a series of shattering bangs. Sven was violently knocked down as the helicopter turned over and burst into flames with a rending crash.

Ricardo was still running back towards the village when he heard the explosion and saw the fire. He moved in quickly to take a look, peered round a hut and was astonished to see Sven trying to free Janine's limp body from the burning wreck. A couple of Diaz's men appeared among the houses on the other side of the open space and began shooting at the Swede. He ignored them, concentrating on pulling Janine from the wreckage.

Ricardo opened up a covering fire and hit one of the guerrillas. The other ducked out of sight, but more of his comrades were arriving. Among them Ricardo thought he saw Lester and Elizabeth. Ricardo cursed. 'Come on, Sven!' he roared.

The big Argonaut wrenched Janine free and moved towards Ricardo, who was laying down suppressing fire from behind the wooden stilts of a large hut. One of Sven's legs seemed to give out suddenly. He staggered but lurched onwards, dragging it in the dirt. Then he went down as though poleaxed. For a moment Ricardo feared he was dead, but the big Swede moved again – his arm jerked out and a grenade flew in the direction of the hut where the guerrillas were hiding. It exploded in a welter of screams, scraps of clothing and bits of flesh. Ricardo broke cover and tried to run out to the wounded Argonauts, but a storm of fire drove him back. Then Sven got up again. Amazingly, he lifted Janine and made a few more paces. But then Lester moved out from behind a hut and fired a burst from his automatic pistol.

Ricardo watched in anguish as the Swede's huge frame collapsed on top of Janine. They lay motionless just yards away.

When he heard Lester's 'Yee-ha!' he yelled back in anger and blazed away at him. The squat militia-man dived for safety.

Then Pike arrived and flung himself down next to the Cuban. 'Too many back there,' he panted. 'Diaz and the main force. Lester and Elizabeth are around too.'

'Are you all right?' Ricardo asked. There was blood all down Pike's leg and on his hand where the vibration of the gun barrels had opened the wounded stumps of his fingers.

Pike forced a wan smile. 'Nothing a few million dollars won't be able to fix.'

'OK, then,' said Ricardo.

'OK.' Pike grimaced. 'And, Ricardo, I should tell

you . . . I didn't always play straight with you guys. Burr already knows.'

'Stow it, Billy,' ordered Ricardo gruffly. 'You try and hold them off here. I'm going to get Burr.'

Aching all over, his palms shredded by the thorns of vines, it was Burr who found Ricardo on the edge of the last outlying hamlet. There was a lull in the battle as both sides regrouped, but Ricardo's assessment was bleak. The attackers had lost their air support and suffered significant casualties, but inevitably the advantages of numbers and firepower had begun to tell. Over in the main village, huts were burning round the wreckage of the helicopter Sven had destroyed. There were hardly any defenders still there – most of the surviving Jemberí had pulled back to the final hamlet with the spirit house. The remaining defenders were almost completely out of ammunition and had only a few darts and arrows between them.

Few of them were unwounded. Every one of them was exhausted. Burr could feel it too – the tide had turned. The attackers were winning.

Suddenly they heard a voice over a loudhailer. It was calling out in Jemberí, promising no harm to those who surrendered, and rewards to those who revealed the emeralds of El Verde.

'What does he say?' Burr asked Neman, who had come down from the trees with a bullet through his shoulder.

'He lies.'

Anthony loped in with Satán on his heels. The

sniper was covered in mud and his back wound was oozing blood. There was no sign of Leila, Ahmad or Pike.

Anthony was missing his rifle. 'I'm out. Anyone got anything that shoots?'

Burr handed him a pistol. 'All I've got.' He and Ricardo had long run out of ammunition for their Colts and were using AK-47s and ammo taken from the attackers.

'They came back, you know,' Ricardo told Burr. 'David, Janine and Sven. They came back. I think they're all dead.'

For a moment Burr was silent. He felt proud and at the same time numb with grief. His Argonauts had returned knowing it meant almost certain death. He nodded grimly. 'Can't say I'm surprised. You?'

'No.'

'They were good men. What about Ahmad?'

Ricardo shook his head sadly. 'No sign.'

'Leila?'

'Left her with Pike and some non-combatants. But I think they're cut off. Diaz came across the stream in strength on that side.'

Burr gave his friend a wry smile. They both knew it was all over. 'I'm sorry, Ricardo.' He put a hand on his friend's shoulder. 'I'm truly sorry.'

'Sorry for what?' Ricardo gripped Burr's arm fiercely. 'I stayed for my own reasons. And it has been a good fight. Anyway, you'll get us out of here. You always do.'

Grimy, covered in their blood and that of others,

they sat for a while in silence. The echoing sound of the loudhailer faded. Smoke from the burning village drifted overhead.

'What now, Cap'n?' asked Anthony, looking at Burr hopefully.

Burr felt exhausted and drained, but he refused to admit defeat. He could not abandon Leila. And when he saw the expectant looks on his men's faces, he knew he could not let them down. Despite everything, Ricardo still believed in him. Anthony still trusted him. But they had all trusted him, and look how he had repaid that trust. He pushed aside his doubts and tried desperately to think of something, anything.

'What would Staff Sergeant Bullford have said?' he asked.

'Old Bully?' Ricardo chuckled. 'What a time to think of him. Well, he would have said, "My left is overrun, my right is outflanked, my centre is giving way . . ."'

Burr finished the maxim with him in unison. '". . . Excellent! I attack."'

'Attack,' Burr repeated thoughtfully. 'Yes, maybe we attack.' He passed the suggestion to Neman, who discussed it briefly with his warriors. They agreed that it was the only option. Charging the guns of the attacking force might prove suicidal, but they had nothing more to lose. The Jemberí were on the verge of extinction. Wearily, and with little real belief, the defenders began to prepare for their final, hopeless gesture, the last heroic act of a doomed people.

It was then that the elderly Jemberí shaman strode out of the forest. Previously aged and bent, he now stood straight and proud, daubed in multi-coloured paint, with burning eyes. On his head was the polished skull of a jaguar, its jutting incisors yawning wide. A lush yellow and black jaguar skin draped him like a cloak. White, three-inch jaguar claws were tied to his fingers. In his hand he held his carved work so long in the making. It was a killing spear, black as night and lustrous as obsidian. Bird-of-paradise feathers ringed the haft just below the honed, razor-sharp point, polished smooth and bright as a mirror.

The shaman waved the spear and shouted defiance. With one voice, the remaining Jemberí yelled it back.

Burr and Ricardo nodded at each other, smiling. 'We attack.'

Still trapped in the main village, Leila noticed that the shooting had died down. Shell casings, spent arrows, broken spears and bodies lay strewn among the trees. Flames crackled loudly from where the helicopter lay blazing amid the debris of burning, broken huts.

She could hear a loudhailer calling through the forest, but it was too distant to make out the words. With a sinking heart, Leila suddenly realized that the battle was lost. Her priority had to be to save as many of the Jemberí as possible. Hiding with her among the huts she now had a swelling group of terrified children and some women, including

Tokom. They had been cut off from the Jemberí warriors and the only man with them was Pike, wounded in the leg, but fighting doggedly.

'Here they come again,' he called to Leila as a squad of attackers broke cover, firing from the hip at his position as they sprinted towards a nearby tree. Pike pulled back behind a hut, then rolled out again just long enough for a burst that knocked down one man. The others made it into cover, though, and Pike could see more troops moving forward from the other flank. Looking under the hut between tree trunks and stilts of houses, he glimpsed the legs of the attackers and, firing underneath, he brought down another couple of men with careful bursts. His wounded fingers were bleeding again and he was running out of ammunition. There was no sign of reinforcements. Jesus, he thought, I am actually going to die here, in this goddamn jungle. And for nothing. He realized that he didn't really believe all that El Verde talk. Idiot that he was, he had stayed in the village because it had seemed like the right thing to do. Oh well . . . 'There are too many,' he shouted to Leila. 'They're moving in from both sides. Get the kids away.'

Leila hesitated.

'Go on,' Pike urged, firing to left and right. 'Hurry!'

Leila knelt down beside him, wincing at the noise pounding her eardrums. 'Look, I don't think I ever thanked you for getting us away from the rebels.'

Pike squinted up at her. 'Don't mention it.' His

sallow face broke into a grin. 'Anyway, the cigarettes were more than enough. And it's not me that got us this far. It's Burr you need to thank. Now get the kids away. Keep moving till he gets here.'

It struck Leila then that she had never doubted for one moment that Burr would come. 'All right, but we'll need you with us,' she replied, helping Pike to his feet. She turned to the gaggle of frightened women behind her. 'Come on,' she yelled. 'This way.' They hurried the children off, but after a few paces she noticed Pike wasn't with them. She turned to call for him, but he was firing again at the advancing enemy. A grenade exploded close by and Leila shouted his name.

The smoke and dust cleared. Beside Leila, Tupo lay dazed where he had been knocked off his feet by the grenade. She saw that Pike was tottering. His left side was a bloody mess. He was shaken but still alive. 'Go!' he coughed, waving her away. A guerrilla charged, screaming, around the corner, aimed his rifle at the kids, then fell dead – shot by Pike.

Leila helped the petrified Tupo to his feet, then looked back to see the short figure of Javier Diaz appear behind Pike. She screamed as Diaz fired a long burst. The Argonaut's body jerked like a puppet under the impact, before collapsing in a lifeless heap. Leila was rooted to the spot in horror. Then Diaz saw Leila and slowly, deliberately, raised his rifle.

A strong hand wrenched her behind a hut just as Diaz opened fire. The bullets snapped by. Leila saw that her saviour was Tokom. 'Run!' she said simply, and Leila dashed after the fleeing knot of Jemberí women and children. They ran into a group of guerrillas and screamed, fleeing in different directions. The attackers had now penetrated the village in force and seemed to be coming from everywhere. Sprinting around the corner of a house, a Jemberí woman in front of Leila was cut down by a burst of fire. Leila spun round and rushed back the other way, only to be knocked to the ground. She looked up, panting, to see Javier Diaz standing over her with a triumphant look.

'So, Doctor,' he sneered, 'are you still an ethno-botanist or are you now a mercenary too? Whatever you are, rest assured my laissez-passer is with-drawn. You no longer have the right to be in this area.' Somewhere in the battle he had lost his beret, and his thinning hair stood up in crazy spikes, sticky with drying blood. His eyes were wild and he was raving. He could taste the victory and its heady tang had sent him almost demented. 'What?! Still here? In that case you will have to be punished.' He hesitated. 'The only question is whether at last to rape you before I kill you.' He seemed to muse on this for a second before adding, with a shrug, 'Actually, come to think of it, after will do. You play too hard to get when you're alive.' Leila was sur-prised to find that even as the generalissimo pointed the muzzle of the rifle at her face, she felt no fear, merely revulsion, and some vague regrets about questions never fully answered and things left undone.

* * *

Diaz's finger was tightening on the trigger, when there was a sudden crescendo in the gunfire from the other side of the village, mixed with a terrible wailing. He looked up, distracted, and the line of men advancing round him hesitated, listening apprehensively. They heard screams and yells. Then they saw Elizabeth and Lester, along with a group of militiamen and guerrillas, running helter-skelter back through the trees. Some of them were flinging down their weapons in fear. One or two men fell, pierced in the back by darts and arrows. The eerie, whooping death-calls of the Jemberí filled the air. The men round Diaz faltered as their comrades fled past them without a second glance. Then they were confronted by a terrifying sight.

The dwarfish shaman, ten-foot spear in his hand, face set in a berserk battle snarl, was crashing towards them through the forest at the head of a wild charge of Jemberí. Covered in blood and garish whorls of war-paint, cloaked in jaguar skins, claws on their hands and gaping jaguar skulls on their heads, they yelled like banshees. With them charged Burr and the remaining Argonauts, snarling and screaming with the best of them.

Calling on his men to hold fast, Diaz opened fire on the charge, hitting two Jemberí warriors. In that instant, Leila grabbed an abandoned bamboo arrow lying beside her and jabbed the four-foot shaft up into the rebel leader's groin with real venom, going for the femoral artery that ran down the inside of the thigh.

Diaz staggered back, bellowing in pain. He

527

plucked out the arrow with a wail and looked down, aghast, at the hole in his leg. At the same time the Jemberí charged straight in among his troops, stabbing, slashing and clubbing. Leila had missed the artery, but Diaz had turned away from her, looking round desperately. After a short, bitter hand-to-hand fight, the attackers broke. On every side they dropped their guns and fled in terror. In a rage, Diaz pointed his gun at Leila once again. Then his expression changed to one of pain and disbelief. A jet-black palm-wood spear point appeared just below his ribcage. The spear twisted in the wound like a screw and pushed further out. He looked down at it protruding a full foot from his torso. A voice behind him gave the inevitable hoot of the Jemberí when they killed a man. But this voice was high and childish. Diaz opened his mouth wide but before the scream could come he was dead. The FARA *comandante* toppled over to one side, revealing the stout form of Tokom and her nephew Tupo, still gripping the spear they had just thrust through Javier Diaz with all their joint strength.

Leila felt a strong hand on her shoulder. 'You all right?'

She looked up to see that it was Burr, his eyes burning white in a face covered in dirt and blood. He noticed Diaz's body but did not give it a second glance. For a moment he and Leila were frozen there in the midst of the battle. Around them the Jemberí rushed past in a frenzy, chasing the militiamen and rebels into the forest. Shots and explosions signalled that some of the enemy were still putting up a fight.

'I'm OK,' Leila said, putting her hand on his. 'Pike's dead. How are the others?'

'We'll only know when it's over.' In the mêlée Burr had lost touch with Ricardo and the other Argonauts. Burr kissed Leila on the forehead, then moved off in pursuit of the retreating invaders.

The deep, eerie hoots of the Jemberí resounded through the jungle as the Indians hunted their enemies through the trees and hacked them down one by one. They found the guerrilla Manolo still alive, tied to the tree where Burr had left him – and took his head. There were women among the defeated invaders, but it made no difference to the Jemberí. They caught them and decapitated them just the same. Neman himself ran Juanita through with a spear, pulled her raven hair back and sawed her still-breathing head off with a bamboo knife.

Ricardo and some Jemberí found themselves pursuing Lester, Elizabeth and a group of *milicianos*. As the militiamen were shot down, one by one, the ecstatic Indians with Ricardo kept stopping to take their heads. When he finally caught up with his quarry, Ricardo was alone.

He worked his way round ahead of them, then stepped out into their path as they ran out across a small clearing.

'OK, Lester,' he called, covering them with his rifle. 'Time's up.'

'*Chinga tu madre*,' spat Lester. 'Do it right now. There's no way these savages are getting El Cangrejo alive.'

Ricardo's finger hovered over the trigger. One burst could end it. He could take revenge for the Argonauts murdered at Madero, for Makepeace killed at the ferry, for all those – Indians and Argonauts – who had died that day. He would also, he guessed, be avenging many other mute victims of Bond massacres unknown.

'No,' cried Elizabeth. She looked grimy and frightened. 'Mercy! Don't shoot, Ricardo, please.'

'Shut up, Liz,' Lester shouted. 'If he doesn't do it, someone else will. I'd rather get it over with than be skinned alive by some fucking cannibals.' He turned back to Ricardo. 'Come on, you coward *chimbo Cubano*. Do it!'

Ricardo's heart thumped. Adrenalin surged through his body. He steeled himself against pity, thinking of Nicola, shot in the head, of Paul assassinated in cold blood. Then suddenly he hesitated. He saw his wife and kids smiling. If he shot these two now, he wondered, would he ever be able to look his family in the eye again? He felt shattered and shriven. There had been enough killing. He waved his rifle at Elizabeth and Lester. 'OK. Surrender to me, you'll keep your heads. I'll protect you from the Indians.'

'And what then?' asked Lester suspiciously.

Ricardo shrugged. 'Burr will decide. But if you survive as far as Bogotá, I'm sure there are plenty of courts that would like to get their hands on you. Not to mention your employers at GemCorp, who might feel you owe them more than just a few explanations.'

Lester was unconvinced. 'Might as well do it now,' he repeated.

'No, Les, this is our only chance,' Elizabeth pleaded. She dropped, crying, to her knees. 'Thank you, Ricardo,' she sobbed. 'Oh, thank you.'

'Now drop your guns,' the Cuban said, unimpressed.

Lester looked over at Liz. His heart ached to see her so scared and defeated. She nodded to him, and they both threw down their automatic pistols and raised their hands in surrender.

Ricardo wondered if he really would be able to stop the Indians taking their heads. He would try, because he had said so. But if he failed, he doubted he would lose much sleep. And he certainly would not guarantee to protect them from the other Argonauts.

'OK, you two,' he gestured with his rifle in the direction of the village, 'let's move.'

In the hours following the battle, the fighters returned from the chase in ones and twos. At first the mood was subdued. Anthony, usually elated after a good fight, was grimly silent as they searched for their comrades. The victory had come at a cost. The forest was littered with corpses – Jemberí, guerrillas and militia. And Argonauts. They found Sven in the heart of the village, his broken form lying like a massive shield over a still breathing

Janine. They found David too, with Ahmad beside his body, weeping like a child.

There was little rest for Leila after the battle. First she had to look after the wounded at the makeshift clinic she set up, complete with operating table topped with palm leaves. All the Argonauts required some sort of treatment. Janine needed a splint for a broken arm and bandaging for a gunshot in the side. Anthony needed a chunk of mahogany removed from his back.

Worryingly, Ricardo did not reappear. Burr heard rumours that he had captured Elizabeth and Lester, but he was almost frantic when nightfall arrived and there was still no sign.

When word came of Ricardo's approach, Burr was overwhelmed with relief. Neman said he was coming with a large group of warriors led by Satán. When Burr saw them emerging from the forest, he laughed and hurried over to greet his friend.

He was filled with a sense of foreboding when he saw that the Jemberí were moving slowly and sombrely, carrying a stretcher of vines. Peering at the stretcher, he froze for a second, then reeled back in shock. Cradled on the woven vines lay the shattered body of Ricardo Martinez.

'What happened?' blurted Burr, walking beside the stretcher and gripping Ricardo's hand. In the darkness he told himself that his friend's injuries did not look so bad.

'Woman means trouble.' The Cuban smiled weakly, red froth bubbling from his mouth. 'I had them cold. They pretended to surrender. Then

Elizabeth threw a grenade. Pretty dumb of me, no?'

As they carried Ricardo over to Leila's rickety operating table, Burr thought back to his escape from the rebel camp. He had not been able to kill Diaz in cold blood either. He shook his head. 'Not really so dumb, *amigo*. Anyway, you're going to be fine.'

Leila was not so sure. The Indians had built up fires to light her work, and in the flickering flames the Cuban's wounds looked much more critical. She extracted some jagged grenade fragments from his abdomen and strapped poultices to some of the wounds, but her despondent looks told Burr that this would not be enough.

Amid the great trees of the forest, next to the smouldering wreck of the last helicopter, the Jemberí celebrated their victory. They lit huge fires, swilled *kicha* and danced, festooned with the heads of their enemies. Ragged slices from their foes' upper arms sizzled and spat in the cooking fires.

As the night went on, in a turmoil of hope and fear Burr kept vigil beside his friend. The Cuban lay watching the victory rites calmly. Now and again he coughed blood. They talked of family. 'You should get one,' Ricardo told him. 'They're something really worth fighting for ... What about her?' He looked over at where Leila still laboured beyond exhaustion, extracting bullets and setting broken bones.

'I don't know,' said Burr. 'Maybe.'

'Maybe? You love her, Burrito. That's the truth. You don't give it a shot, you'll never get what you want. You may not know it but you need her – you'll need her to live in Xcalan. You need someone like her to truly live. Don't be too proud. Don't cut yourself off.'

'Too proud?' Burr protested. 'You're the proudest man I know.'

Ricardo smiled. 'Well, I got a lot to be proud about. My family . . .' His voice trailed off. A few minutes later, without warning, Ricardo looked up at Burr fiercely. 'Well, why do you think I'm so proud? You say you can tell a man by his friends. You have been my friend.' He coughed again and sighed in pain. 'Now listen, Burr: give my love to Rosa, to Ricardito and to little Paula.'

Burr felt his heart was breaking.

With a movement of his chin, Ricardo gestured towards his chest and Burr pulled a dog-eared family picture from his friend's pocket. He passed the photograph to Ricardo, who held it up close to his weakening eyes. Then Ricardo took a few deep breaths and stretched out a hand. Burr grasped it tightly, tears welling uncontrollably.

Silence fell. The Jemberí had stopped their celebrations. Then softly, on their wooden pipes, they began to play 'Guantanamera'. Ricardo was humming it, smiling faintly, when he died.

That night, with great reverence, the bodies of the four dead Argonauts were laid onto wooden pyres and burned. In the light of the flames and the moon, the Jemberí sang their spirits across to the heavenly forest, where there are no ghosts, where the grubs are always fat, the wild pig always plentiful, and the arrows of the hunter never miss.

The next morning the Argonauts collected the ashes of their colleagues into four carved boxes of shunta palm. Burr felt drained. War was always like this. And this one was not over yet. The Bond and FARA threat to the Jemberí had been ended, but Elizabeth and Lester's heads were not among the substantial collection currently being filled with hot sand by grumbling Jemberí warriors. And if Ricardo's murderers had survived, they could raise another force. They would be back.

Burr knew it would take Elizabeth and Lester a few days to get out of the forest. When they did emerge, Burr planned to be waiting for them. Nursing his bruised body, he went down through the forest to check out the surviving paramilitary helicopter. The Huey had sat quietly in its clearing since Anthony had taken out its crew. The rounds he had put into the engine had caused a little damage, but nothing that couldn't be patched in a day or so using the tools on board. Jemberí kids had done more harm in their victory celebrations, smashing dials, soiling the cabin and running spears and arrows into the exhausts and any other hole they could find. Burr reckoned he could have the chopper ready to leave as soon as Janine was fit to travel. It contained just enough fuel to get them back to Madero.

Janine could move in a couple of days, said Leila, who was working incessantly. It seemed that every

Jemberí, wounded or not, wanted to be treated by the famous plant doctor's magic. That night she slumbered, exhausted, in Burr's arms. He lay unable to sleep, his mind racing with memories of Ricardo and worries about Xcalan. Deep in the night there was a fluttering round Leila's head. Silver-green wings glinted in the moonlight and settled on her eyes – some of the parasitic moths had found her again. Burr shooed them away.

Next morning, Leila's impromptu clinic was still in full swing when he left her to gather some pupae of the grey-green tear-vampires for study. He was on his own among a stand of palms when Neman appeared. He was walking stiffly, his shoulder bound by Leila with palm twine and an antibiotic mould. There were five fresh cuts on his heavily scarred chest. 'Come,' he said. 'I have something to show you.'

Neman led Burr into the forest, veering in the general direction of the lake. After about half an hour walking along invisible paths, the Jemberí stopped. 'From here the forest spirits are evil,' he said; 'if you see them, they will be angered.' He covered Burr's eyes with a dark cloth. They continued, the Indian warrior murmuring a lilting, almost fearful chant to appease the malign forces round them. Though blindfolded, with the Jemberí's strong hands guiding him Burr seemed to move faster, with fewer snags and scratches than when he saw for himself. They went down a short slope and up another one. Burr sensed a change in the jungle about him. He felt stone under his feet.

It seemed as if the trees withdrew and the sounds of the forest dwindled. They stopped and Burr smelt burning oil. They walked a little further. The air became stuffy and heavy. Burr breathed in a dank, musty smell. Neman ceased his chanting and the sound of their steps began to echo as though in a cavern.

Again they halted and this time the blindfold was removed. Burr blinked in the yellow glare of a burning torch held up by Neman. Its flickering light showed that they were in a wide windowless tunnel, constructed from gigantic blocks of stone. The vast slabs were perfectly smooth, cut with precision and fitted together perfectly without a crack.

Neman led him further down the corridor, up and down a featureless maze of stairways and smaller passageways. Eventually, they came to a dead end. The stone wall in front of them was covered in complex, carved reliefs. In the light of the guttering torch, Burr saw that in the first images huge, bearded men with swords and armour rode on wild-eyed horses over the bodies of bowing Indians. Towards the bottom of the wall, the men were reduced in size and rode upside down, their bodies full of arrows. The final relief showed the Indians holding the bearded heads of their shrunken enemies.

The Jemberí pressed an unseen mechanism and a massive stone door opened in the wall. It swung back soundlessly to reveal a shadowed black space beyond. Neman stepped through the doorway and his torch illuminated a small, square room. Burr gasped as the flaming torchlight glittered and sparkled everywhere. It was like walking into a kaleidoscope. The light jumped back red and silver off rusting metal, white off bone, yellow off the stone walls and everywhere green – sparkling, dazzling green – off the piles of impossible emeralds. The countless gems were heaped everywhere, lying in the dust amid crumbling fragments of swords and skeletons of men in armour.

Neman turned round with the torch and the lights whirled about the two men. Burr was stunned. 'El Verde,' he whispered in awe. The shards of green light danced and shimmered on the walls. He could see the stones were worked and polished like Tenoch's hoard – emerald cuts, cabochons, hexagons, trapiches, and the mysterious cat's-eye emeralds, strewn everywhere like pebbles on a beach. The myths were true. This place was the source of the serpent's eye.

Neman nodded. 'It is what you ghosts call "El Verde". There were once many rooms like this. Pacha Mama has reclaimed most of them.'

'You lied to us, Neman. You could have told us of this before.'

'Maybe so, but we decided it was not wise. Consider this: we have learned that dealing in these stones brings only death and – how do you call it? – greed. The Jemberí have no word for this. I learned about this from your friend Daniel. He asked me about El Verde and I told him we had stones, if he could help us. But Daniel cared only for the stones. If we had told you of this place before, would not some of your men have been tempted to take the stones by force?'

Burr had to admit that Neman was right. 'And yet now you show them to me freely.'

The Indian nodded gravely. 'You are no longer ghosts to us. You are people, like the Jemberí. We trust you. Take what you can carry for yourself and your followers. Once you have taken, we will close this room and it will never be reopened.' Neman looked down at the treasure with loathing. 'We believed the green stones could help us, but opening this place only angered the forest gods. It brought evil. Through Tenoch we tried to use the stones. We chose him to help because he was not like the others. He did not seek money for greed, but searched for something to help his people. We thought with his help the stones could provide the means for us to change the fate of the forest. But the money he earned brought only more wickedness, more ghosts, into the forest.' The warrior bent to pick up a handful of emeralds. 'These things are a useless, dead, evil green. Good green is living green.' Disdainfully, he let the glassy stones sift through his fingers like worthless beach sand.

Burr nodded. 'We thank you,' he said, and began to stuff his pockets with the magnificent jewels. Burr was pleased. The emeralds would not bring back Ricardo or the others, but it would at least make sure that everyone got paid. When his pockets were full he took the rusty helmet from the skull of a conquistador and filled it to the brim with winking stones. Without making a dent in the trove, he had gathered enough gems to buy Xcalan many times over, enough to make every Argonaut – or their surviving family – very wealthy indeed. And all the while he was hunting for one stone, a stone that would complete Tenoch's quest and fit the serpent's eye.

Rummaging amid the shining green, his eye caught a flash of scarlet and he bent down to pick up an ancient journal bound in silver and thick hide. He brushed off the dust to see a crest of a dragon rampant, with a fiery eye. Carefully opening it, he saw the inscription of the author, and after blowing off the dirt he could just make out the name Don Rodrigo de Ayala y Vivar. On the next page he saw a sketch, the faded colours still just visible.

Burr showed Neman the page. 'Have you anything like this?' he asked.

Neman looked at him with hooded eyes.

'Poor Pike,' said Leila, when Burr returned to the village with the emeralds. 'He would have been in seventh heaven.'

Burr's team accepted their windfall with good grace, but without great glee. It came at too heavy a price. The Argonauts were curious, of course, but they could tell Burr did not want to talk about it, so restrained themselves. Leila was more excited, not by her new-found riches, but by the discovery itself. It was simply fascinating to her enquiring mind, but beyond that it seemed to offer potential answers to some important questions, missing links in a chain of deduction. However, when she drew breath to ask Burr 'where?' and 'how?' Anthony, Janine and Ahmad silenced her with meaningful looks.

Leila did convince Burr to climb the hills behind the village again. He could not tell where the treasure room lay, but, looking with new eyes, he could now discern the layout of the ancient city under the forest – the square ceremonial lake surrounded by the palaces, temples and pyramids. The sulphurous smell from the lake now reminded Burr that emeralds were formed by volcanic activity, such as that in the geothermal vents of hot springs. He realized that the fragments of rock strewn about the jungle were similar to the rocks of the Madero mines: volcanically formed, emerald-bearing pegmatite.

Leila was also caught up by the voice from the past – the voice of Don Rodrigo de Ayala y Vivar. While Burr, Anthony and Ahmad spent the afternoon repairing the helicopter, Leila read the faded journal avidly.

That evening, she tapped a drowsy Burr on the shoulder. 'Listen to this!' she said excitedly, and began to read. Burr was amazed to hear the story of the serpent's eye. In the year AD 1537, Don Rodrigo had plucked the 'Great Emerald' from the 'dragon of Xcalan'. Three years later, he wrote, 'Now, I lead my men to raid southwards through the endless jungles of the new continent. We seek the source of the stone – El Verde. It is a legendary city where men can pick emeralds from the trees.'

'I guess he found it,' said Burr, yawning.

'Yes, he found it!' Leila was thrilled. 'He calls it "a city of green gold, of green fire".

'Hmm, not a modest man,' she mused as she carried on reading. ' "Like a god, I Don Rodrigo came upon the heathen Indians. Like a god I rule in splendour from the fastness of the great stone pyramids. I have taken many wives ... I have accumulated wealth beyond measure."

'Something must have gone wrong,' Leila said, reading quickly ahead. ' "The sickness of my kin has come upon me ..." he says. "The cursed sickness saps my strength ..."' A notion occurred to Leila and Burr looked at her curiously. She felt a dawning sense of understanding as she read of the curse that destroyed the conquistador in the prime of his life. ' "The illness devours me from within. My limbs quiver uncontrollably and my vital force ebbs away. Now I can barely lift my sword. My hands tremble and I forget the names of my wife and heirs."

'The journal peters out in about the middle of the year 1546. The script is shaky, like that of a very sick man. It's quite hard to read. "As I weaken, the savages become restive ...We cannot rely on our weapons. In the damp of these damned forests, our powder is never dry ... Today they killed Manuel, faithful Manuel. A poisoned dart struck him in the neck and he died, paralysed, in my arms ... Now El Verde burns. My men are being slaughtered like cattle. José and his pikemen tried to escape. They killed them in the ball court below the temple pyramid."' Leila paused. 'Odd. His hand becomes steady again. "Now at the end, I clearly remember my wife and children. May whoever finds this journal tell them I say a fond goodbye. From below in the sacred ball court, I hear the faint dying cries of my soldiers, and the inhuman hoots the heathen only give when they kill a human being. Soon they will sound for me . . ." '

Leila closed the journal thoughtfully. Beside her, Burr was asleep.

Almost five hundred years after Don Rodrigo's death, and some four days after the battle for the Jemberí village, Leila and the remaining Argonauts made their way down to the helicopter. Janine, still too weak to walk, was carried on a stretcher of woven vines. All the Jemberí stood around to say goodbye. Satán gave Anthony a flask of his best, slimiest *kicha*.

Leila took Tupo as a passenger, and some gourds of curative potion freshly distilled from the flowering *kiragi* by the Jemberí shaman. If she got the concoction to Tupo's mother, Maria, in Madero, Leila still believed there was a chance of arresting the advance of the wasting disease. She huddled with Tupo in a corner of the helicopter cabin and prayed it was not too late.

As Burr climbed into the pilot's seat, Neman pressed a small palm-leaf package into his hand. 'For you,' the warrior said, 'and for Tenoch.'

Burr guessed what it was. His voice choked as he clasped his fist tightly round the magnificent gift.

'Tenoch is honoured. And the Maya of Xcalan will thank you.'

The Jemberí smiled. 'It is we who are grateful. Maybe the ghosts will now leave the people in peace.'

Burr started the engine, which whined as the blades slowly began to spin.

Neman crouched well out of reach of the turning rotors and spoke to Leila. 'Oh, and when you return, Plant Doctor . . .'

'Yes?' she shouted over the din.

'Bring many Advil.'

'Good life, Neman,' murmured Leila as the Jemberí melted back into the trees.

Burr cranked the helicopter carefully off the ground and pointed it towards Madero.

PART IV

THAT'S JUST THE WAY
IT IS

From the shoulders of beautiful women
I have seen wings unfold.
From the piles of waste
I have seen butterflies soar.

From *Versos Sencillos* by José Martí

Madero, Colombian Amazon

The Madero mission station appeared oddly quiet and deserted as Burr brought the helicopter in for a bumpy landing on the hilltop. There was an Argonaut Ecology Land-Rover parked outside Diaz's old HQ, however.

Burr sent Anthony and Ahmad into the building. They reappeared with a cowed, dishevelled Elizabeth and Lester. Ahmad was holding their automatic pistols.

'What do we do with them, Cap'n?' drawled Anthony.

'I think we should kill them,' called Janine from the helicopter, sitting up on her stretcher. 'Think of Paul and Nicola. Think of Ricardo.'

Burr was thinking of nothing else. He put his hand on the knife he had taken from Cinco, but, before he could even draw it, at some unheard command dozens of Colombian Army soldiers stepped out from hiding. Armoured cars roared up the hill and attack helicopters hovered into position overhead. There was no chance of escape.

Anthony and Ahmad retreated towards the helicopter, fingers on their triggers. They glanced at Burr for orders. He looked at Elizabeth and Lester and his hand closed on the knife again. Perhaps he could take one or other of them before he was killed. Just one would be worth it, he thought. But if the troops opened fire, they would all die. Burr looked round to see Leila standing anxiously just behind him. Beside Janine in the helicopter, Tupo peered out with big, trusting eyes.

Then a tall, perfectly groomed figure emerged from one of the buildings. He wore a suit and despite the heat he looked quite cool, as though he walked in an aura of air conditioning. Leila gasped as she recognized Hernando Ayala. The minister spoke coolly too, with an air of absolute, effortless control and superiority.

'You could kill one of them, Captain Whitman, but you too would be killed instantly.' He gestured at Lester and Elizabeth. 'This low type is not important. GemCorp itself is but a subsidiary of a far larger multinational conglomerate. You are quite powerless against them and against me, let alone against the Colombian military.'

'That's right, you *hijuepuerca* son of a bitch,' said Lester, pulling himself off the ground. 'Low type!' he grumbled. 'I'll show him.'

'And did you know, Burr, that this conglomerate also has interests in the oil business?' Elizabeth smirked. 'And did you know that this conglomerate is called . . .'

'Wait for it . . .' Lester laughed.

'Walls Oil,' murmured Burr, aghast.

'Correct!' guffawed Lester. 'The very people who want to do open-heart surgery on your *isla bonita*.'

'And suck it dry,' Elizabeth added.

Ayala silenced them with a wave of his hand. 'Now, Captain Whitman, you will hand over the stones. Drop the weapon too.' He nodded to two of his men, who approached cautiously.

Burr dropped his knife in the dust and the Argonauts surrendered their rifles. Lester and Elizabeth retrieved their handguns. Ayala's soldiers frisked the Argonauts and searched the helicopter, taking every emerald they found. The troops piled the bags up in front of Ayala. The minister gave a sign and the emeralds were poured out in front of him. First the rough emeralds the rebels had mined in Madero – pounds of stones and chunky crystals cascading from leather bags to form a glittering pyramid of uncut emeralds two feet high. Then on top of that rained the emeralds Burr had taken from El Verde.

'*Dios santo!*' exclaimed Lester, suddenly religious. Ayala's men gasped in amazement as the treasure of El Verde was revealed. The cut stones poured out, sparkling in the sun, millions of dollars, thousands of carats, of the finest emeralds in history.

Burr did not even notice. After everything he had been through, after all the loss and destruction, he could think only that Walls Oil and GemCorp were partners. Had Daniel known? he wondered. Had he been hired deliberately? He felt sick to his stomach. He had been duped and lured away, abandoning

Xcalan. And now the stones that could have bought the island were being poured away in front of him. At least, Burr thought, he still had Neman's great gift.

Ayala nodded with satisfaction as each bag disgorged its contents, but it was clear from his face that he was still looking for something. 'The stone,' he said, when all the bags had been emptied. 'Did you bring the stone?'

'The what?' Burr was incredulous. 'What are you talking about?'

'I am Don Hernando de Ayala. And I must have that stone. It is mine. My family will never stop searching for it. Nothing will prevent me or my descendants from scouring the forest until we find it. No law, no human being, no force of nature will prevent it. It is the only way to lift the curse of our blood. Now tell me: where is the stone?'

Leila looked at Burr, who felt something crack inside him. He thought of Isaiah explaining that the salvation of his people lay in the green eye. He saw the terrified Tenoch calling out to him, Tenoch who died searching for a stone to replace that great serpent's eye. He felt the power of Neman's gift to him. Now he would have to betray them all.

Burr stepped forward and undid Leila's hair where it was tied in a knot at the back. From the middle of the dark tresses he pulled out a palm-wrapped object the size of a golf ball. He unwrapped the bundle into Ayala's waiting hand. There on the minister's palm lay a gleaming, many-faceted emerald globe, set like an eye in a golden clasp shaped like a dragon's head. The emerald was a deep sea green, clear and flawless. Only at its heart had the perfect beryl crystal twisted in mysterious fibrous ways to catch and refract the light into a burning slash, like the eye of a cat, or a snake, narrowed against the sun. There was only ever one stone like this. Burr was giving up the stone of the Maya – that very stone which the conquistador Don Rodrigo de Ayala y Vivar had plucked from the plumed serpent of Xcalan half a millennium ago. Burr had seen it painted in the frontispiece of Don Rodrigo's journal. Now the conquistador's descendant, Don Hernando Ayala, Minister without Portfolio, took the jewel from Burr with a trembling hand and held it up in awe and hope. It flashed with green fire.

Elizabeth and Lester watched in frustration. She was irate that Ayala had the jewels and she did not. Lester had hardly registered the financial loss. His whole being had simply been overwhelmed with a desperate desire to finish Burr Whitman once and for all. He pointed his gun at Burr and spoke to Ayala. 'And now you've got your little treat, Minister, you won't mind me killing this sonofabitch.'

Burr said nothing. At that moment he did not care whether he lived or died.

'Stop!' shouted Leila.

Lester laughed. 'Need your girlfriend to save you? Where are all your pretty moves now, eh?' He walked up to Burr, his crab tattoo flexing as his finger tightened on the trigger.

Leila turned to Ayala in desperation. 'For God's sake, Minister! It's cold-blooded murder – stop him!'

Ayala shrugged. 'My family has its stone back. The rebels in the region have been exterminated. That politically embarrassing Bond militia is also gone. The mines are safe and producing again. What is between you is no longer any of my business.' He turned and walked away.

Two soldiers grabbed Leila again, pulling her back. She struggled in their grasp. 'No, listen!' she yelled frantically. 'Wait!' Ayala ignored her and carried on walking. She stopped fighting, took a deep breath, and said, as clearly and calmly as she could to the minister's departing back, 'Listen, Don Hernando! Kill us, and you will never know what we know. If you kill us and destroy this land, then the blight on your family will never be lifted. Your grandchildren will die a terrible death!'

Ayala stopped dead. He remained motionless for a moment, then turned round, a look of suspicion and incredulity on his face.

He stalked back towards Leila. 'Wait, wait.' He waved his arm and two soldiers edged Elizabeth and Lester away. 'What, what are you talking about?' he asked, his voice cracking with a mixture of hope and doubt.

She cleared her throat. 'I am talking about the health and survival of your family. I am talking about the fact that this forest holds the cure for a lethal illness.'

Burr and the others watched with amazement as

Ayala's face contorted. 'Tell me,' he pleaded, 'tell me!'

'The forests of Madero contain a cure for Cruzeiro's disease.' It was Leila who was calm now. She glanced at the men holding her. With a nod from the minister, they released her. 'We're going to make a deal,' she said carefully. 'I'll give you something that might cure Cruzeiro's disease. You have to promise two things.'

'What the hell is she talking about, Minister?' moaned Lester. 'She's jerking you around, you let her talk to you like that.'

'Shut up, you fool!' said Ayala coldly. He turned back to Leila. 'What are the two things?'

Leila tried to keep the fear out of her voice as she explained, 'One: you prevent any further invasions of the Madero National Park, whether for emeralds, logging or any other exploitation. And two: you agree to help me develop a cure for Cruzeiro's disease from the *kiragi* flower. And – oh, actually, there are three things – number three: you don't kill us. Any of us. At all.'

Burr groaned inwardly. Leila's desperate gamble had revived his hope. It was probably their only chance – and she was doing well – but he feared she had just made a fatal error. He just hoped nobody would notice.

Elizabeth laughed. 'Oh, sure. And we will all live happily ever after. It is a nice *Yanqui* fairy tale, but I see a different ending.'

Ayala seemed thunderstruck. 'How? How?' he was mumbling in confusion.

Lester looked at him as though he was mad. 'What's this Cruzeiro's crap? Are you sick? Got some kind of cancer?'

'No,' said Leila, more confident now, knowing her guess had struck home. 'No, Lester. The minister is fine. Cruzeiro's strikes in your twenties or thirties. If he had Cruzeiro's, he would be dead by now. No, it's his son who has it – and very badly. It was your son I saw at your house, wasn't it, Minister? The man in the wheelchair – that's your son.'

Still unable to speak, Ayala nodded helplessly.

Leila went on. 'Cruzeiro's disease is not a cancer, Lester. It is a neurological wasting disease that deforms the nervous system and the brain. It may be too late for his son, but now Don Hernando is worried about the next generation, about his grandchildren.' Leila reached into her bag and gently pulled out the leather- and silver-bound journal. 'Cruzeiro's disease is inherited, you see, and Minister Ayala is descended from Don Rodrigo de Ayala y Vivar, who also suffered from Cruzeiro's. He describes the symptoms in his journal, which I have read.'

'It's not possible,' whispered Ayala.

Leila handed the journal to the dumbfounded Ayala, whose numbed fingers failed to grasp it. The book fell into the dust. The rampant dragon crest lay face up, plain for all to see.

Gaining in confidence, Leila continued. 'Your ancestor, Don Rodrigo, died in this forest five hundred years ago. But he had lived among the Jemberí for years before he died. He took Jemberí wives, and through their children he passed his genes on to them – many times in fact. That is why, like Don Rodrigo's white descendants, the Jemberí have Cruzeiro's disease in their gene pool. They suffer the same curse as your family, Don Hernando – in fact, they *are* your family. While the civilized side of the lineage has suffered for centuries, the Jemberí have developed a cure.'

'Fine,' said Elizabeth carefully. Her pointed tongue darted out again in its subconscious mannerism. Burr had once found the flicker sensual. Now he saw it as snake-like. Alert as ever, she had noticed the fatal flaw. She licked her lips. 'That all sounds very interesting. But in case you didn't notice, Minister, she mentioned this wonderful thing's name. Now that we know it's this *kiragi* stuff, let's kill them anyway.'

Jesus! Burr thought, Elizabeth had picked up Leila's error. The minister would agree with her for sure. That meant they were all dead. Calmly, deliberately, he tried to relax his muscles, slow his breathing and focus his racing mind. Anthony and Ahmad behind him were disarmed and held at gunpoint. Janine was incapacitated. What could he do?

'Ah, you see, Liz has a point,' said Lester proudly. 'Why should the minister protect you, or the National Park, or those moronic Indians? He can simply take these *kiragi* plants and cultivate them for a cure.'

Idiot! Leila cursed herself, desperately trying to think up another way out.

'Well, Minister?' Elizabeth asked confidently, raising her pistol in anticipation.

Ayala was quiet for a moment. He seemed to be focusing his thoughts.

'You can't kill us, Minister,' said a voice.

This time it was Burr who spoke out.

'What now?' asked Ayala impatiently.

'It won't work,' said Burr, stepping forward to Leila's side.

'And what, precisely, will not work?'

'Trying to use *kiragi* on your own. It simply won't work. To prepare the medicine, you need to pick the plant at a certain point in its life cycle, even at a specific time of day. You also need the Jemberí Indians to tell you how to pick and prepare it.'

Elizabeth laughed. 'A knife to the gullet can extract that information.'

Burr ignored her. 'And even if the Jemberí would tell you – which they would not – you also need the services of a certain kind of butterfly to pollinate the *kiragi* plant. And this butterfly is found in one place alone: the Madero forests. This butterfly's caterpillars eat nothing but *kiragi*, which grows only in certain habitats. These habitats cannot exist without a complicated web of resources and symbioses with plants and animals, present nowhere but in Madero. Also, this butterfly is fragile. It can endure only small doses of direct sunlight and will not even cross a small clearing. It cannot tolerate open spaces and it cannot survive the disturbances that human settlement and exploitation bring. If its ecosystem is disturbed, this butterfly will simply become extinct.'

'Why should I trust you?' asked Ayala. 'You would invent anything to survive.'

Burr could see him wavering between scepticism and belief.

It was one of those moments when the skein of time and its complexities meet and are knotted. Small events from long ago had rippled chaotically through time. Only now was their effect fully felt.

'It's the truth,' said Burr simply. 'That's just the way it is.'

Lester snorted derisively, but Ayala hushed him instantly with a decisive motion of his arm. All sound and movement seemed to halt for a moment. Ayala was staring at Burr with a bizarre expression.

'What did you say?' he whispered. He mouthed, 'That's just the way it is.' Then he began to repeat Burr's name. 'Burr Whitman. Burr Whitman. Burrell Whitman . . . *Dios mío!* You are Burrell Whitman.'

'Oh, for God's sake,' blurted Elizabeth in exasperation.

Lester agreed. 'Burr, Burrell, what the fuck difference does it make?' He looked like he always did at his beloved Elizabeth for the decision. And she nodded back.

Before Ayala's troops could react, Lester yelled and shot at Burr.

Elizabeth opened fire at Leila.

Burr dropped to the ground, ducking Lester's shots and barging into Leila. He shouldered her aside a fraction too late to stop her crying out in pain as Elizabeth's bullet hit her. An instant later Burr grabbed his knife from the dust and spun it up into Lester's gaping, shouting mouth. The point went up through his palate and the blade buried itself deep into his lower brain.

For a critical instant, Elizabeth hesitated as Lester's crab tattoo spasmed and the gun fell from his suddenly limp grasp. Aghast, she watched a trickle of blood well up in the bottom of his open mouth. It overflowed through his teeth and ran down his chin. For a moment Lester's dead body teetered upright. 'Les?' she uttered. Then his body simply crumpled. Elizabeth was shocked and surprised to find her whole world crumpling with him. 'Lester, *mi amor*?' she moaned. There was no response. She wailed in anguish and the circle of onlookers dived for cover as she fired her pistol on automatic. The shots kicked up dirt all round Burr as he rolled aside, grabbing Lester's fallen pistol. He steadied himself for a split second on his elbows and shot Elizabeth between the eyes. The surrounding soldiers kept their heads down as Elizabeth collapsed, her spasming trigger finger spraying the remainder of her magazine wildly in all directions.

Burr scrambled over to where Leila lay, blood soaking through the clothes on her left side. He took her in his arms and she looked up at him with big eyes.

'Just a nick,' she said bravely. 'Looks worse than it is.'

Burr ripped the material of her shirt sleeve to see the groove the bullet had ploughed across her upper arm.

'Burr?' she said absently.

'Yes?'

'Can you get a new job? Your current one is a little too exciting for me.' She gave a wan smile, then passed out.

Ayala had not moved. He was still silently mouthing Burr's name and seemed to be in some sort of trance. He gave no sign of noticing the gunfight or anything else going on round him. Then he said, 'I agree to all your terms.'

Burr was amazed at the change. He wondered what had come over the minister, but it was not the right time to indulge his curiosity. 'OK,' he said. 'It's simple: you must guarantee that there will be no more exploitation of the Madero National Park. No logging, no more seismic exploration and no drug cultivation. And the emerald mines will not expand to damage the Jemberí or the National Park in any way.'

'Guaranteed,' responded Ayala.

'In return we can promise that the Indians will never undermine GemCorp's business by trafficking in emeralds. The Jemberí just want to be left alone.'

'Guaranteed,' repeated Ayala. He was pulling himself together again and his authority returned. 'Very well. Of course, if any emeralds do happen to emerge from the forest, they must be sold to the authorities. And as for Gemcorp, I will be revoking their concession. The state will be taking over the mines. And we will return more of the profits to the local people.'

He gestured to his troops and they pulled

Elizabeth and Lester's bodies away. The only reminders of their passing were the faint tracks of their dragging heels in the dusty earth of the Mission Hill.

Minister Ayala's occupation force had brought Madero firmly under control. The FARA hostages were ransomed and brought into the new mobile army medical centre. The wounded Argonauts were also treated there. For a change Leila received some medical care not provided by herself. After her arm had been bandaged, Burr tentatively asked her what she wanted to do next.

'I'm not sure,' she answered. 'I am fond of the jungle but I think I've seen enough of it for a while. The research centre will feel empty without James and right now I'm not sure I could cope alone.'

'That makes sense,' he agreed lamely. 'I guess you need a break.' Burr was thinking about what Ricardo had said – that he loved her. He realized he desperately wanted her to come with him. 'Where will you go?'

'Well, maybe I'll go home to Trinidad for a while. My parents have a cottage above the beach at Blanchisseuse. I could plan a project to harvest *kiragi* perhaps, maybe start trials on the *kiragi* potion as a cure for Cruzeiro's disease. I might even find some crazy botanist willing to take up Makepeace's endless survey work. Then I might consider coming back to the forest.' Even as she spoke, Leila realized she needed out. Not for good, but for a rest. She looked up at Burr. 'No. I think I'll come with you,' she said. 'For a while. If you'll have me.'

Relieved, Burr smiled his assent.

Leila had given Ayala some of the *kiragi* potion to try on his son. Burr and Leila then took the rest to test on the 'civilized' Jemberí. They went with Tupo back to the Ethnobotanical Research Centre. Though only a few weeks had passed since Leila had left, the place looked as though it had been derelict for months. The buildings had been pillaged and some of them were gutted by fire. The plant press was smashed and all the windows in the lab were broken. Despite the absence of Leila's clinic and Makepeace's regular handouts, there were still a few Indians camping there. They moved around as listlessly as ever. Their kids were playing marbles in the mud. They found Tupo's mother, Maria, bedridden and pale in her shabby hut. Tupo ran to her, chirruping like a happy bird. When she saw her little boy, she sat up and hugged him with arms that had begun to quiver uncontrollably. She could only just manage to lift him.

Leila gave her a few sips of the *kiragi* potion. A look of joy and confidence came over Maria when she heard what it was. She drank and fell into a tranquil sleep, cuddling her young son.

'I know what you meant,' Leila told Burr, looking at the sleeping mother and child: 'why you stayed and fought with the Jemberí. I might not be able to save the world, but I can make a discovery that could change the life of one small boy, or a few families.'

Burr nodded. 'Or a few thousand people whose

lives would be ruined by a terrible illness. It may not be saving the whole planet, but it's still worth it.'

'Exactly. And anyway, who wants to save the world? Half the time, the people who want to do that are a major cause of the world's problems in the first place.'

When the Argonauts left, two days later, the *kiragi* had already had a remarkable effect. Maria was walking again, not straight and tall, but hobbling by herself. When she waved goodbye to the departing Argonauts, it was with a broad smile and an arm almost as steady as her young son's.

Looking down at the broad, brown curve of the Madero River passing beneath them, Burr wondered what difference it all made for Madero. With the other Argonauts, he had passed by their OP the day before. It had been ransacked again and was already being reclaimed by the relentless forest. Burr had managed to rescue some of his insect specimens. Janine had lamented how her neat lines of white stones were already smothered in creeping clouds of purple morning glory. The 'crying eye' wasps had again colonized the warm tin roofs of the huts.

The emerald mines were in full operation once more. Hundreds of *guaceros* still tramped the mud, heads bowed, like lost souls in their endless search for emeralds. In the squalid mine gatehouse, Mr Sticky Fingers was still flexing his rubber gloves.

Up on the Arroyo airfield, the usual chill wind was blowing off the Andes as Ayala escorted the Argonauts and Leila across the roughly mown apron to his sleek Gulfstream G450 jet, which would fly them back to Miami.

'My son has been drinking from your *kiragi* mixture,' Ayala told Leila eagerly. 'Just two small sips, morning and night, as you recommended. Last night he sat unaided at table. He cut his food for the first time in three years.' His voice cracked with joy and gratitude. 'I know he may never recover fully, but thank you, Dr Walcott. I hope to welcome you back soon. You will have any resources that the Colombian government can provide. In the meantime, the army will rebuild your research centre.'

Burr was the last to board. When the others were inside the jet, Ayala held him back at the bottom of the small flight of steps.

'One moment,' he said. 'I have something for you.' The minister handed Burr a bulging leather pouch. 'These are for all of you. With my thanks.'

Burr opened the bag to see hundreds of cut emeralds – millions of dollars' worth. He sifted through them, observing that they included the pick of the treasure of El Verde, though not the serpent's eye.

'That I cannot give you,' said Ayala, reading his thoughts. 'It is an heirloom of my lineage and my country. Its discovery has lifted the curse on our family. It is a symbol for healing and for the rejuvenation of the forest. It will be displayed in the Museo del Oro, where it will be a boon for all Colombians.'

'Fair enough,' said Burr stiffly. He knew that the superstitious Mayans of Xcalan would be bitterly disappointed when he appeared without the gem.

Still, the emeralds in the bag could help raise money for the island. And there were enough gems for all the Argonauts to retire as multimillionaires.

'And something else.' Ayala handed Burr a newspaper. 'I have been checking up on you, Captain Burr Whitman, and I think you should read page five.'

Burr nodded his thanks and started up the steps. At the door of the plane he stopped again and turned back to Ayala. 'I don't get it. Why the plane, the emeralds? What made you suddenly trust us? We were your enemies. You had no reason to believe us. That whole *kiragi* story could have been invented. We gave you no proof.'

Ayala took a deep breath. 'Listen,' he said, his voice filling with emotion. 'My son is in the advanced stages of Cruzeiro's disease. He has fits. He is a cripple who can hardly walk. But before the disease came, he was a fine figure of a man – a scholar and an athlete. He was at university in America and was a successful collegiate sportsman – a tennis player, and a very good one. I watched him play in junior tournaments round the world. In the final of one of them, I saw him play you, Burrell Whitman.'

Wrapped in memories, Ayala's eyes lost focus as he looked out from the mountains over the cloud-covered forest. 'I was beside the court that day my son won the Collegiate Championship. You could have accepted the linesman's call and won the title, but you did not. The ball was in and you called it in. I remember thinking: here is a man to be trusted.'

Ayala's face lost its distant expression and he looked Burr straight in the eye. 'When you told me the truth in Madero, I recognized it. And I recognized you.'

Burr nodded without surprise. 'That's just the way it sometimes is.'

Miami, Florida

Burr and the exhausted Argonauts slept in the plane. Leila sat next to Burr, her head pillowed on his shoulder. His chest still aching from its bludgeoning by Cinco, Burr drowsed restlessly, unclear about the next few weeks. In theory, the plan was simple: take Leila to Xcalan and lie on the beach – on their beach – in peace. He hoped that she would not see the previous woman's sneakers. Perhaps he could get rid of them before she opened the cupboard – he hoped she would want some wardrobe space. In practice he could not believe that this plan would go right. Very few plans had over the last few weeks.

Somewhere high over the Gulf of Mexico, Burr awoke and remembered Ayala's newspaper. Extricating himself from under Leila's head without waking her, he pulled out the paper. It was a copy of the *Wall Street Journal*. He turned to page five and his plan changed. Halfway down the page was a column on Walls Oil. They were planning to strike a new offshore field within the week, in the waters off a Yucatán island called Xcalan. The story also said that the island and its onshore drilling rights were up for sale by sealed bid in four days' time. Burr looked at the date on the newspaper. It was two days old. With a chill, Burr realized that meant the auction would take place the next day.

Trapped in a luxury forty-five-foot cabin, eight miles above sea level, Burr felt everything he had worked for begin to shrivel. He could only hope that Carlo had things in hand. But first Janine, then he, had already talked to Carlo and told him they were on their way home. He had not mentioned anything about Xcalan. That made Burr anxious.

Back at Miami-Dade, there was no ticker-tape, no fanfare, no celebrity for the saviours of the Jemberí. Carlo was the Argonauts' entire welcoming committee. Burr could see tears of relief in his eyes as he took the bandaged Janine gingerly in his arms.

Anthony just nodded a silent goodbye to the group and turned away. 'Here, Carlo,' he said, giving him Satán's *kicha*, 'a souvenir. I'm finished with this stuff. You and Janine go and have a party on me.' After a few steps he paused. 'Next time you have a little job down in Colombia, Cap'n,' he drawled, 'please make sure not to call.' Then he laughed. 'You always were the best damn liar I've ever known, Burr. Little yellow butterflies, my ass. Little yellow butterflies ... Man, Ricardo would have dug that one.' And Anthony walked off, chuckling to himself.

Fighting back tears, Ahmad shook hands with everyone and hugged Burr.

'Where are you headed?' asked Leila.

'I am taking David's emeralds to his mother in Israel. And his ashes. He always wanted to be buried there – in Jerusalem, on the Mount of Olives.' Ahmad moved away as stolidly as ever. As his back turned, the tears came.

'So what's the story with Xcalan?' Burr asked Carlo, once the others had gone.

Carlo's happy look changed to one of concern. 'It ... it's all under control, Burr. I'm due down in Chetumal tonight. The final bids have to be submitted tomorrow morning.'

Burr heard the worry in his voice. Something was not quite right. 'It's all right, Carlo. I'll go.'

'No, no, no,' Carlo insisted. 'I've got it all prepared. You take it easy. No need for you to rush down there. Absolutely not.'

'Fine, but make sure that you've got everything factored in. Including these.' Burr handed him a bag bulging with emeralds. 'Eight million will be enough? You're certain we're bidding the right price?'

Carlo took the emeralds with a look of consternation. 'Sure of it,' he answered, managing to flash a confident smile.

Burr smiled back, but he had a sinking feeling. He hoped that after all the betrayals of the last weeks the real enemy was not closest to home. Looking at Carlo, so transparently happy to be reunited with Janine, Burr could not bring himself to suspect him. 'I trust you, Carlo. You go down and finish the job. In the meantime, I know what I have to do.' He turned to Leila. 'Will you come with me to Xcalan?'

Xcalan Island, Mexico

Twenty-four hours later, Burr was home. But it was not the homecoming he would have wanted.

'Well, I'm sure it's paradise out of rush hour,' said Leila ironically.

The narrow sand track leading to Xcalan was blocked by a line of massive Walls Oil trucks. Burr and Leila abandoned their vehicle and walked up past the exhaust fumes and the throbbing engines to the head of the jam, where policemen, Walls Oil security guards and truck drivers were gathered in a shouting mass.

Sitting silently in the road in front of them, and absolutely blocking their way, were Isaiah the elder and the other venerable Mayan *chacs*, decked out in full ritual regalia. Pachal and more Mayans sat behind them. Volunteers, mostly young American and European students, moved about, providing food and water.

'Ah, Burr,' said Isaiah, as though he had last seen him a few minutes ago.

'Hello, Isaiah,' replied Burr.

'See these people? They want to come and build on Xcalan – build a port for oil ships on our land. They want to build jetties. They want to blow up the reef. We will not allow it. Did you see Tenoch?'

'Yes, I did.'

'Good. You are back. Now that you have brought the eye, I can stop sitting here. I am getting stiff.'

'Well, actually . . .'

'It doesn't matter. It is boring sitting here and my shift is probably over in any case. Help me up.'

Leila and Burr pulled the old man gently to his feet. As he moved away, a substantial Mayan woman came over and sat solidly in his place. She glared at the truck drivers, who quailed visibly.

Isaiah peered at Leila, examining her so fiercely that she almost drew back. 'Who is this?'

'This is Leila,' said Burr.

The old fisherman stared at her a moment longer. His expression changed to one of wonder, then intense happiness. He laughed and smiled broadly. He patted Burr on the back. 'Good, good. Tonight we will replace the eye.'

'But—'

'Shhh, Burr!' said Leila. 'Yes,' she went on gravely. 'Tonight we will replace it.'

Burr asked no more questions. He was eager to show Leila Xcalan. Having her there filled him with an almost childish joy. His excitement was tempered by an underlying anxiety.

Almost shyly, he led her up to his house, where they fell into an exhausted sleep for a few hours.

In the late afternoon he took Leila to his study,

where he placed the specimens he had brought back, including the silky grey cocoons of the tear-sucking moths. He walked her past his collections and through into his butterfly aviary. 'It's like walking in a rainbow,' she murmured amid the creeping, multicoloured caterpillars, fluttering red, black and white *Heliconius*, transparent glasswings and glowing blue morphos.

Then he took her down the dunes and out to the shark cave. But although the cave shimmered as beautifully blue as ever, Leila and Burr did not swim with the sharks as he would have liked. The creatures were not asleep, but wide awake and agitated. Later, as the sun set, Burr and Leila swam out beyond the reef and floated for a while, treading water. And there in the middle of the sea, Burr cupped his hands and drank.

'What!' Leila exclaimed. 'Have you gone crazy?'

'No. Try it,' urged Burr. 'Drink it. It's perfectly fresh.'

Dubiously, Leila tasted her top lip with her tongue. Her eyes widened in surprise and she too cupped her hands and drank clear, sweet water.

'But . . . how?'

'It's magic,' said Burr, pulling her close to him and kissing her, the cool, fresh water welling up from beneath them in the middle of the salt sea.

The moment was broken by a metallic banging. Treading water, Burr and Leila looked round at the silhouetted hulk of the Walls Oil drilling ship. They had tried to ignore it all day, hoping that it would somehow just disappear. But the ship was not going anywhere. It wallowed there on the slight swell, in a widening slick of its own greasy fluids and filth. A little way off from the ship floated a permanent picket of Mayan canoes, carrying protesters with banners. The oilmen jeered at the demonstrators and pelted them with empty beer bottles and left-over food.

That night Leila and Burr sat on the wide deck of the house at the top of the dunes with Pachal. As they gazed out over the dark beach and sea, noise from the drilling ship carried clearly up to them on the night air. The drill derrick was lit up like a Christmas tree. Searchlights played on the sea round the rig and powerful beams lit up the water underneath the ship.

'I'm glad you are back, brother,' said Pachal grimly. 'But I think it is too late. This is the end. They have already sunk two wells. They drilled to the north of Xcalan, then they sailed to the south and drilled again. They say they found no viable reserves. Now they are making a final attempt. They are drilling right here off the beach. They think the oil trap lies right under the beach. It will be the end of Xcalan.'

'Don't get me wrong,' said Leila, 'I know the damage these companies can cause. But couldn't it be limited to spoiling the view? If you can impose strict controls on oil spills, it might not be so bad. Eventually you might stop seeing it.'

The Mayan shook his head sadly. 'No. In the first place, as you know, controls often do not work.

There is always leakage and one major spill will ruin Xcalan. Also, you see, if they find oil, they have the right to build a station onshore. They will put in pipelines, pumping stations, tarmac roads, jetties, supply depots. They will blast the reef. They have already tried to start this project – you saw we had to block the trucks they sent. As soon as the ship strikes oil, the police will have the right to move us out of the way by force.'

He sighed. 'Already we can see the effects. This well is drilled right down into the sea bed. The sharks do not sleep any more. The fish have already gone. Everything is disturbed. Right back in the cave of the serpent we could hear the noise and feel the vibration. The drill missed one of the channels of the cenote by inches.'

'When do they think they will find oil?' asked Burr.

'They boast that they are ready to strike the day after tomorrow. There is just a thin layer of rock to break through. There will be a big ceremony. The Governor will come from Chetumal. Businessmen and politicians will come from Mexico and even from the United States. William Walls will be there.' Pachal shook his head and laughed bitterly. 'They have even invited us. To mock us.'

Burr stood up and leaned on the balcony, looking down at the ship. 'What about sabotage? We could go out tonight in scuba gear and cut the drill pipe.'

Pachal shook his head. 'They would just repair it. Anyway, I have checked. They have armed guards on the ship. Below, they have lit the shaft all the way to the sea bed. They have underwater surveillance cameras and patrols of armed scuba divers to guard the pipe.'

'There's still a chance they won't find any oil,' said Burr, trying to reassure him. 'Then the ship will have to go and they wouldn't have the right to build the supply depot. And if we own Xcalan, we will be able to stop them drilling on the beach itself, right?'

'That would be right,' said Pachal with a pained expression, 'if we owned the land.'

'Pachal, what happened with the onshore purchase? Did we make a bid?'

'We placed a bid at Chetumal. The decision has not been revealed yet, but I do not think we succeeded.'

'And Carlo . . . did Carlo help you?'

Pachal looked at Burr ruefully. 'Your friend Carlo did help us at first. But things changed. I did see him there at the last round of bidding. And he filed a bid, brother. But not with us. We think he filed for Walls Oil.'

Burr could not quite believe it. Throughout the mission he had been worried about who the enemy was. And he had been right. His enemies had been the people who hired him, and his own colleagues. But Carlo Maldini? Burr still did not want to accept that he was a traitor. He realized that the people he could trust without question were dead. He wished Ricardo was with him. He would have been fretting like crazy, sure, but he could have come up with a Bullyism to save the day. Burr missed Daniel too.

His partner would have consulted his cards or his feng shui and Burr would have scoffed, but Dan would have concocted some sort of ruse.

They were silent for a while. The moon was rising. Pachal stood up. 'Come,' he said. 'We must go down to the cenote.'

Burr hesitated. 'Pachal, I think you should know that I do not have a stone for the serpent.'

Leila cleared her throat. 'Actually, Burr, we do.' From her pocket she produced a large marble. 'After Ayala took the emerald, it was the best eye I could find. I bought it from some Jemberí kids at the research centre. Traded a pretty good emerald for it.'

Burr was aghast. 'Leila, it's just a marble.'

Pachal's wide smile was white in the darkness. 'It will do.'

They made their way down through the brush and into the cenote. The *chacs* were gathered expectantly under the statue of the celestial serpent. Lit by the flames of torches, Burr told the story of Tenoch, of his bravery and his death. With difficulty, he explained how he had found the eye of the serpent, but had given it up to save another tribal people. The elders nodded sagely at this, as though it had all been foretold. Then, sheepishly, Burr presented the replacement eye – Leila's large marble – to Isaiah.

The elders began to chant and Isaiah ceremoniously placed the stone into the eye of the sacred statue of Itzamna. A clear glass globe with a swirling green and yellow core, it gave the serpent god a slightly jaunty air. The elders looked satisfied. Still chanting, they invited Leila and Burr to sit with them round the fire.

Burr suffered in acute embarrassment. He had not been there for the Maya when they needed him. Their world was on the verge of destruction. He had found, then given away, their ancient talisman, and now they were honouring him with an intense and moving ritual, though he had replaced their long-lost jewel with a child's plaything. The Mayans seemed very happy with developments, but Burr felt like a fraud.

Leila noticed that, as they chanted, the *chacs* were sneaking glances at her, chattering and giggling. After a while, they stopped avoiding her looks and simply stared at her, with beaming expressions.

'They're all staring at me,' she whispered to Burr.

'Well, they are all men,' whispered Burr in return.

'But they're staring really hard, into my eyes.'

'You're right,' he agreed after a while. The Maya were looking at her almost in awe. 'It's odd. Normally they would be very shy.' He turned to Pachal. 'Why are they all staring at Leila?'

'I don't know.' Pachal shrugged. 'I'll ask them.'

He put the question to an elder, who, without interrupting his chanting, looked meaningfully at Leila, then up at Itzamna.

Pachal thought for a moment then he too looked carefully at her and burst out laughing. 'Oh yes,' he said. 'Now I understand.'

* * *

Burr slept fitfully. He tossed and turned in confused dreams, haunted by the skeletal image of the drilling rig. He woke in the small hours, his mind full of a million questions and worries. He was troubled by many things – the deaths of the Argonauts, the apparent betrayal by Carlo and the looming destruction of Xcalan. His life was riddled with failures and endings. The only bright spot was Leila. She had brought something positive into his life. She had a natural way of healing wounds, open wounds he never even knew he had.

He tried to sleep again, but could not. He was agonizing over what he could do to save Xcalan. He was pondering what the hell Pachal had understood about Leila and what it had to do with the goddamn green eye. It occurred to his restless mind to wonder whether Leila loved him – she had not mentioned it. He looked over at her peacefully sleeping form. He realized again that, yes, he probably did love her.

Burr got out of bed and wandered silently through the house. His bare feet on the wooden floors felt the light dusting of fine beach sand blown in by a freshening breeze. Oddly, with Leila there, the house felt different, more complete somehow – as though he had actually built it for her.

He drank some cool water. The only sounds were the ruffling of the palm trees round the house and the distant rustle of the waves on the reef. Alone in the dark, Burr stood and looked out at the star-filled clear sky.

Underscoring the natural night sounds, a faint scratching distracted him from his reverie.

Listening hard, Burr followed the noise to his study, where he had left his pupae from Madero. Five of the moths were emerging. Entranced, he watched the moon-green imagos slide out of their silken sheaths and preen. He watched their intricate feathered antennae unroll. The moonlight reflected off their myriad compound eyes. Their crumpled wings flexed and straightened. Then Burr watched them fly off into the darkened house.

Following their cryptic, fluttering flightpaths, he saw one flit into the bedroom and land softly on Leila's sleeping cheek. In the silver half-light he saw the moth unwind its long proboscis to feed from the corner of her left eye. It sipped then shied away instantly, wiping its feeding tube in disgust.

Burr smiled to himself. She must have put something in her eyes. Thinking nothing more of it, he climbed into bed beside her and slept.

Hours later, in the deepest sleep, realization came to him. He awoke in a flash of understanding. The regret and fear he had felt since giving up the sacred emerald had vanished. He felt a burgeoning mixture of relief and hope. Without knowing it, he had fulfilled Tenoch's quest and brought back the potential salvation of Xcalan.

The prophecies might be proved right after all – the green eye might indeed save the beach. But the prophecies referred not to a child's marble, nor to a lifeless, green crystal of compressed beryl and its varied inclusions, however rare or beautiful. The elders – and now Burr – had realized that the prophecies referred to the living green eyes of Leila Walcott.

Burr shook the sleeping Leila. 'Leila, tell me, what did you put in your eyes?'

'Optrex,' she murmured drowsily.

'Why?'

'I thought it might discourage your furry little vampiric pets. I knew they would hatch and make a mothline straight for me.'

'You may have given us some hope after all,' said Burr; he kissed her tenderly. Thinking how it was always the small things that mattered, he got up and walked back through the darkened house to his office, where in the first light of dawn he scribbled out a list.

Leila was still asleep at sun-up when he went looking for Pachal. He found the Mayan heading for the lagoon to fish for mullet and crocodile perch.

'What time is the drilling ceremony tomorrow?' asked Burr.

'They invited us for three in the afternoon,' the Mayan replied. 'But we have not decided if we will go or not.'

'Oh, we're going all right. What tide is at three p.m.?'

'The tide will be starting to run out. A high spring tide.'

'Good. Then we have a plan. Now, Pachal, we need all this – fast.' Burr handed him the list. 'We are going shopping down in Chetumal.'

Later that day, Burr and Pachal returned from Chetumal and went down into the cenote. They donned diving gear and swam down into the network of channels under the sea bed.

In the night, under cover of darkness, Isaiah led a flotilla of Mayan fishermen quietly past the drill ship's searchlights. They slipped through the reef and round to the lagoon in dugout canoes full of wide rubber tubes, valves and watertight seals. They pulled the canoes up the beach and carried the equipment down into the cenote, where, under the gaze of the marble-eyed serpent, Burr and Pachal were diving round the clock.

The next day dawned bright and clear. The Mayan canoes were out in force, joined by boats carrying international green activists. On board the Walls Oil ship, the drilling team made final preparations for the strike. Burr's bruises ached. He was tired and on edge. The event had to run as scheduled or everything could go wrong. The Mayan fishermen rowed a Mayan delegation including Burr and Leila out to the drilling boat. A rope ladder was lowered without ceremony down the side of the ship and under the amused gaze of the oil workers they mounted it with as much dignity as they could muster. They then stood stiffly on the deck and waited in the sun.

As time wore on, Burr became concerned that the ceremony would start late. He glanced more frequently at the inexorable movement of his watch hands and the impassive water, shifting imperceptibly with the vast, moon-tugged tide on which everything depended. Man's destiny might unfold in unpredictable ways, but time and tide would progress untroubled, as they had for ever.

Then a streamlined, sixty-metre motor-yacht powered round the point and Burr became nervous that things would happen too quickly. The yacht pushed through the flimsy boats of the protesters and slid alongside the drill ship to disgorge William Walls, the State Governor and numerous other dignitaries. Leila's hand searched for Burr's and squeezed it as Walls strode up the gangplank. He wore a white suit, cowboy boots and wide-brimmed hat, every inch the Texas billionaire.

A sharp-eyed observer might have noticed William Walls give a tiny flicker of surprise and displeasure at Burr's presence. But it was only momentary, and most eyes would have seen only the expectant grin that quickly spread across the Texan's face.

'Well, Mr Whitman, come to see this great day in person? To be honest, we never anticipated having you here for this ceremony, but now that you are here I realize that it gives me great pleasure to welcome you.' He smiled smugly. 'I'm sure you'll be pleased to see your good friend Carlo as well.' Walls glanced backwards, and with a mixture of anger and disappointment Burr noted Carlo in the group behind the oil mogul. It was not a pleasant experience. Carlo was looking nervous and trying to avoid Burr's gaze. The Mayan delegation round Burr muttered angrily.

Three p.m. was still a few minutes away, so Burr preferred to talk a little. 'I wouldn't get too confident, Walls,' he warned. 'Have you forgotten Madero already? You won't be extracting much wealth out of there. What makes you think you'll have better luck here?'

'As a matter of fact,' said the Texan, 'I have forgotten Madero. Truth is, emeralds were always a bit of a hobby for me. Madero? Shucks, I've even forgotten about Colombia. By the way, I hope you realize that what Elizabeth and Lester did out there was not company policy. It was strictly a freelance operation on their part. Me, I honour my contracts. No hard feelings, right?' He flashed a fleeting and quite remarkably phoney smile, then turned briskly away.

He made a short speech for the onlookers, ending with: 'Oil will do so much for the development of Xcalan and its great people.' He threw a disdainful look at the Mayan delegation. Then the drill foreman showed Walls to a console and he pressed a large red button. The machinery clattered into life and the drill shaft whirred. Down below the sea bed, the drill began to bite through the last few inches of rock.

'OK, get ready to open the well,' crowed a gleeful Walls over the shrill spinning of the drill. He waved the dignitaries back histrionically. 'Everybody get under cover in case it's a gusher. We don't want you guys to get covered in oil.'

He started to usher the VIPs back towards the shelter of the bridge. Just then the sound of the drill changed and a new vibration set into the pipe. The foreman quickly turned off the drill and moved to cap the well. In the sudden silence, a dull rumbling and gushing could be heard from below. There was a collective moan from the Mayans and green demonstrators in the protest boats.

'Whoo-hoo!' yelled Walls triumphantly, whirling his hat in the air. 'Here we go!' He leaned over the rail and shouted at the protesters, 'Get ready to be covered in crude, suckers!' Walls stood with his arms outstretched, just waiting to be drenched. The VIPs drew back uncertainly.

The rushing-rumbling sound grew louder, then a massive fountain spurted high into the air. But not a fountain of oil. It was a clear jet, falling in crystal sheets like a waterfall from the blue sky. It poured down on Walls and his guests. It soaked Burr and the ecstatic Mayans.

Walls was incensed. 'It must be sea water,' he yelled at the drill team. 'There's a leak in the pipe. Plug it!'

There was pandemonium on the ship as the fountain cascaded from the sky. The Mayans capered in the torrent and laughed uproariously. Dignitaries were buffeted to the deck by sheets of water as they scurried for cover and the oil workers skidded and fell as they rushed over to the wellhead.

The terrified foreman cupped his hands and tasted the water. 'It . . . it's sweet, sir,' he said. He turned his hard hat upside down and it filled in seconds. He carried it over for a bedraggled Walls to taste. 'It's come up from the well.'

'Fresh, goddammit!' Walls yelled, dashing the helmet to the ground. 'This sonofabitch well is water. It's nothing but water. It's worthless.'

'Well, not quite,' said Burr with a straight face. 'You could still sell the concession to Perrier.'

His plan had worked. Beneath the sea bed, he and Pachal had drilled out from inside the secret cenote tunnel and into the drill pipe. They had then plumbed a fat rubber tube from the cenote channel into the pipe. When the spring tide began to run out at 3.00 p.m., fresh water from the cenote had been forced into the pipe under immense pressure. It appeared that the well was full of water. Like a moth finding Optrex in Leila's eye, the oil men would have to withdraw their feeding tube and move on.

The water continued to gush down on William Walls. It turned his shiny suit transparent and pooled in his hat. The oil man growled at Burr. 'Well, know this, smart guy: your precious beach is still done for. The oil is here, I can feel it. And we can still drill on land, isn't that right, Governor?' Walls turned to speak to his VIP guests, but the governor and his entourage had ducked into the shelter of the drilling ship's cabin. 'Anyway,' Walls went on, 'that onshore concession is well bought by now. And there's no way you're going to take this deal from me like you took Madero.' A smile spread across his face. 'Tell you what, let's ask your good friend Carlo. Am I not right, Carlito?'

Carlo came slowly forward, gaze lowered, wiping water from his eyes. Like everyone else he was soaked, his clothes sopping. Water was raining on his head and running down his face. 'Burr, I'm sorry,' Carlo mumbled. He lifted his eyes to meet Burr's. 'Believe me, I'm sorry. I was stupid.'

'What does Walls have on you?' asked Burr, appalled. He had trusted Carlo with the future of Xcalan, with the lives of its people. He still could not believe that Carlo would betray him. 'This isn't you, Carlo. Tell me. It's not too late.'

'Carlo!' Walls shouted.

'Yes, yes . . . OK, Mr Walls is right. The onshore concession has been bought.'

'Yes indeed!' said Walls smugly. 'By Walls Oil.'

Burr felt his hopes evaporating. The Mayans behind him stopped laughing. Standing next to him in the falling water, Leila gripped his arm tightly.

'Well, actually . . . no,' responded Carlo.

'What did you say?' asked Walls in surprise, spitting water from his mouth and turning slowly to look at him.

Carlo cleared his throat nervously, then steadied himself. 'In fact the concession has been bought by a new, non-profit company called Argonaut Ecology. Its beneficiaries are the inhabitants of Xcalan.' Carlo stepped forward through the downpour and handed Burr and Walls copies of a document covered in clear, laminated plastic.

Walls spluttered with rage and incomprehension. 'But Walls Oil bid ten point five million dollars. Everybody was certain the maximum would be ten.'

'You told me you would bid ten,' said Carlo, 'so I guessed you were probably lying and would bid around ten point five, just in case.'

The cold, clear water continued to rain down as

Burr read the document Carlo had given him. 'And, Mr Walls,' he said, a smile spreading across his face, 'thanks to the very substantial amount Argonaut earned working for you in Madero, and thanks to some no doubt creative accounting by my good friend Carlo, it appears that yesterday we were able to bid ten point five million, eight hundred and eighty-eight.'

Elated, Burr was savouring the moment. He pulled the smiling Carlo to his side.

Walls was red in the face, incandescent with fury. The VIPs were filing away from the deluge and making their way back onto Walls's yacht. The media turned their lenses on the jubilant protest boats, which sailed under the tumbling plume of water. Two of the canoes had already been capsized by over-energetic celebratory dancing.

'So the eights did it,' said Leila with a smile. 'Where did the eight, eight, eight come from? The Xcalan prophecy?'

'No,' replied a happy Carlo. 'We can thank Daniel for that – it's feng shui.'

Burr laughed with the rest of them, his joy tempered only by what it had all cost. There was just one more thing he had to do.

Caribbean Sea, south of Miami

Burr turned off the motor and the day was suddenly silent. The *Guajira* rocked gently on a sea ruffled by a constant warm breeze. Miami lay far behind them to the north. There was no land in sight.

Rosa was standing, tearful but stiffly upright and strong, on the deck below. Her children stood quietly beside her, Ricardito in a miniature suit, Paula in her best dress.

Leila stayed respectfully a little apart under the canopy. She was holding a box of smooth black palm wood.

Burr climbed slowly down to the deck. 'I'm sorry, Rosa,' he said.

Rosa looked at him kindly. 'Stop saying that, Burr. I don't blame you. I am proud of my husband. What he did, what you all did, was an honourable act. You took a stand. It was his choice to take it with you. That was his way. Ricardo was a soldier.'

'These are for you and the kids.' Burr handed her a bag full of emeralds, which Rosa accepted and gave to Ricardito. The boy took it solemnly.

'How did my daddy die, Captain Burr?' he asked.

'Bravely. Your father was the bravest man I ever knew.'

Paula squinted up at Burr. 'But why didn't he say goodbye?'

'He did say goodbye to you. And he was happy. He was singing his favourite song.'

Rosa choked. 'You know why Ricardo always used to sing "Guantanamera"?' she asked, tears filling her eyes.

Burr shook his head.

'I am from that province. I was his "Guantanamera", his Guantánamo girl.'

There was a moment's silence, then Rosa took a deep breath, forcing back her tears. 'OK, Leila,' she said.

Leila stepped forward and gently passed Rosa the palm-wood box. Rosa's hands trembled as she took it. With a prayer she and the children opened the box and scattered its contents into the air. The stiffening breeze seized Ricardo's ashes in a chaotic swirl and blew them away, across the sea, towards Cuba.

THE END

Acknowledgements

Thanks are due to Stephanie Cabot, my mercurial, ever-inspiring agent, and to Simon Taylor, the most charming and understanding publisher one could imagine. Thanks also to Tania and Pablo for patient help with the Spanish, to Hoss and Hass for their invaluable advice, and to Tuzzy, editor and wife, for everything. For their kind permission to quote the lines from 'Epitaph on an Army of Mercenaries', we are grateful to the Society of Authors, the literary representative of the Estate of A. E. Housman. The lyrics from Juan Luis Guerra's 'Bachata Rosa' appear courtesy of BMG Music. 'Guantanamera' was composed (or maybe arranged) by Joseito Fernandez in 1930s Cuba. It became famous only in the '60s, when Pete Seeger sang a protest version using lyrics by the revolutionary poet José Martí.

DOG DAYS
By Jeffrey Lee

In a small West African country civil war is brewing. Thousands have already died but it's the savage killing of young British aid worker Miranda Williams that captures the media's attention.

For disenchanted correspondent-turned-film-maker Peter Lucas, Miranda's death conjures up uneasy ghosts and now the Corporation want him to go back into the war zone to make a documentary about her. It should be straightforward: go in, shoot, and get out. Fast. But Lucas's assistant producer has other ideas. Eager to make her mark amidst the jostling egos of the television world, she wants to answer the questions that still hang over the girl's death.

Suddenly, the conflict intensifies and Lucas and his crew are trapped inside the shell-scarred hotel that's become both sanctuary and ops centre for the world's media. Watching as these psychotics and adrenaline junkies manipulate human suffering into the stories they feel the world wants to see, they realise a new madness is growing in their midst . . .

Explosive, intelligent and utterly compelling, *Dog Days* is a thrilling, disturbing journey into the darkest recesses of the human soul.

'Perhaps the most authentic account of what it is like to be in a war zone that I have ever read . . . chilling, darkly comic and superbly written . . . a brilliant début novel'
Robert Twigger, author of *Angry White Pyjamas*

'Sometimes a fictional work can reveal the truth. *Dog Days* is one such . . . A terrific book that, once read, is not easily forgotten, and shouldn't be'
Independent on Sunday

'A great read – beautifully written, wickedly observed and more true to life than any journalist would like to admit'
Saira Shah, award-winning film-maker

9780553814996

BANTAM BOOKS